# The Madolescents

Chrissie Glazebrook has worked in a zoo, a vegetarian restaurant, and as a radio and television presenter. She was a feature writer for the late *Jackie* magazine, and has been published in a range of magazines and newspapers, including a stint as *Jenny Talia*, a spoof agony aunt. She ran away at seventeen to live in a beatnik colony in St Ives, Cornwall, returning to her Black Country home after being busted for drugs.

She now lives in Newcastle upon Tyne. She has an MA in Creative Writing (with distinction) and has won the Waterstones' Prize for Prose. *The Madolescents* is her first novel and she is currently working on her second, *Blue Spark Sisters*.

## Praise for *The Madolescents*

'It cracks along and to put it mildly, the hot anarchic humour scythes through some weird scenarios. The author is a born writer: blackly hilarious, biting and not nice' *Sunday Times*

'[Rowena] is more than enough to carry this original, moving novel and give it the cult status it deserves . . . It is imossible to read this book without falling in love with her, biker boots and all' *Scotland on Sunday*

'Brutally funny' Kevin Sampson

'The reader becomes addicted to [Rowena's] random acts of rebellion . . . We care about her, which is a feat in the world of popular fiction where so many characters remain robotic. Way to go, Rowena, warrior princess' *Irish Independent*

# The Madolescents

## Chrissie Glazebrook

ARROW

Published in the United Kingdom in 2002 by
Arrow Books

1 3 5 7 9 10 8 6 4 2

First published in the United Kingdom in 2001
by William Heinemann

Words by Mark Roberts, Paul Jones, Cerys Matthews, Aled Richards
and Owen Powell taken from the song 'Strange Glue'. By kind
permission of Sony/ATV Music Publishing

Arrow Books
The Random House Group Limited
20 Vauxhall Bridge Road, London SW1V 2SA

Random House Australia (Pty) Limited
20 Alfred Street, Milsons Point, Sydney
New South Wales 2061, Australia

Random House New Zealand Limited
18 Poland Road, Glenfield
Auckland 10, New Zealand

Random House (Pty) Limited
Endulini, 5a Jubilee Road, Parktown 2193, South Africa

The Random House Group Limited Reg. No. 954009

www.randomhouse.co.uk

A CIP catalogue record for this book
is available from the British Library

Papers used by Random House are natural, recyclable products
made from wood grown in sustainable forests. The manufacturing
processes conform to the environmental regulations
of the country of origin

Printed and bound in Great Britain by
Bookmarque Ltd, Croydon, Surrey

ISBN 0 09 941092 3

*For Denise and Amy-Jo*

## *Acknowledgements*

The author would like to thank the following for their help, support and encouragement: Gail Acaster, Andrea Badenoch, Janice Campbell, Julia Darling, Steve Dearden, Andrew Dixon, Diane Fisher-Naylor, Kitty Fitzgerald, Rita Ann Higgins, Paul Houghton, Claire Malcolm, Northern Arts, Sean O'Brien, Wendy Robertson, Penny Smith, Amanda Stafford, Debbie Taylor, tutors and fellow students at University of Northumbria MA Creative Writing, Erica Wooff. And, most especially, to Margaret Wilkinson.

Huge thanks to Jane Gregory, Lisanne Radice and the team at Gregory & Radice; and to the Random House Massive, in particular Kate Elton, Victoria Hipps and Thomas Wilson, for true faith in The Madolescents.

Don't think about the past; it only fucks you up.
Likewise the future.

Rowena M. Vincent

# 1

## *Stoppy-in Night #1*

'No flaming luck.' Mum flings her lottery ticket into the fireplace. 'I've hardly had a sniff since Anthea Turner left, at least she won me a couple of tenners. I can't stand that other wossname, smarmy get.'

'Hold still or you'll get a lobotomy.' Mum's off out on the razz so I've coloured her hair Rimini Red and I'm teasing it with a tail-comb into a punky topknot like that girl in the Coke commercial. 'It's for losers, the lottery. Maison well chuck your money at beggars.'

Mum squinches up her face as I mist her hair with firm-hold spray.

'Somebody has to win,' she reasons. 'It could be us.' Yeah, right. She unscrews her eyes and stares at herself in the mirror. 'Oh, Rowena, it looks fabulous. I feel ten years younger. Only what if, you know . . . what if people think I'm mutton dressed as lamb?'

I shrug. 'Brush it out then. Go like mutton dressed as mutton, makes no odds to me.' I flop on the couch, grab a packet of Hula Hoops and switch to Channel 3 for the last bit of *Stars in Their Eyes*.

Mum wets her finger with spit and tweaks a spikey fringe-bit.

'No, I like it, as long as it won't flop about when I'm dancing.' Fat chance. It's set like concrete, a force ten wouldn't budge it. 'Right, I'm off upstairs to get dressed,' she says.

This lass on the telly, she's murdering that song by Texas, plus she looks nothing like Sharleen.

*Bing-bong*.

'Get that, Rowena,' calls Mum, like I'm some kind of slave. The Sharleen girl's just missed the high note by about half a mile and

Matthew's telling her, in that really patronising voice, that she was ay-mazing.

*Bing-bong.*

I'll take a mallet to that door-chime, swear down. Can't a person even watch the telly in peace?

*Bing-bong. Bing-bong. Bing-bong.*

'Rowena, get the flaming door!' yells Mum from upstairs. The commercials come on so I haul myself up from the couch with a big dramatic sigh which I realise is totally wasted.

'Hiyaaah.' It's Mandy Sweeney, Mum's dead common mate from the chip factory. She's a right lardarse, makes Roseanne look like a class act.

'What?' I go. I can't look at her.

'Lerrus in, it's blowing a gale out here.' She waddles past reeking of Poison which like *nobody* wears any more. 'Where's Jean?'

'Upstairs, fixing her look.' Mandy flumps down on the couch. I give her the once-over. What a friggin' mess. She sure could use some hot oil treatment, her hair looks like something the baby Jesus slept in, plus she's squeezed into Lycra leggings that tight you could count the blackheads on her bum. Doesn't she look in a mirror? 'Go up,' I say.

'Nah, I'll stay and keep you company,' she says. Oh, triffic. 'Gorra glass? And an ashtray, there's a pet.' She sparks up a Marlboro and pours herself about half a pint of voddy from a bottle out of her bag. 'Get a bit of a glow on before we go out.' She sniggers. 'Them bars don't half rip you off up the town.'

On telly, Matthew's chatting to a baldy old gadge who works in a DIY store. 'So tell us, Clive, who are you going to be?'

'Tonight, Matthew, I'm going to be . . . Phil Collins!' He stands by the door and waves, then the dry ice comes on and he walks out looking like – a baldy old gadge. I zap the Off button.

'Aww, leave it on, Roey,' squawks Mandy. '"Groovy Kind of Love"'s one of my favourites.' Tough. I pick the new Puff Daddy from the CD tower and stick it on. Mandy's slugging away at the vodka. 'I can't abide this rap stuff,' she moans. 'Haven't you got any Bee Gees? *Ah-ah-ah-ah stayin' alive.*' I'm itching to punch her lights out but then Mum appears swishing about in her new slinky red dress from What Shop.

'Does this colour drain me?' she goes. 'Do I need more blusher?'

Only if she wants to look like Barbara Cartland. 'You look the dog's,' I say. 'Where you off, anyway?'

'Down the Bigg Market.' Mum laughs. 'It's Grab-a-Granny night at the Phoenix.'

'Divvent tell her that.' Mandy's eyes are bloodshot from the booze and her face has gone all blotchy. 'It's Divorced and Separated evening for the over-25s,' she explains. I suppose Mandy qualifies as separated; her boyfriend's doing a stretch at the Big Hoose in Durham for aggravated burglary. 'We have a great time, proper cocktails with umbrellas, a disco, and the last half hour's a smooch session, Barry Manilow and stuff. *Oh Mandy, you came and you gave without . . . something.* Howay, Jean, I feel lucky the neet.'

'I'll fetch my coat,' says Mum.

Mandy stuffs the voddy back in her bag. 'Having a stoppy-in night, Roey? Not seeing the boyfriend?' Like it's any of her business. She checks her face in the mirror. It's all red and shiny like a baboon's bum. 'That whojimaflip, Dean?'

I can feel my hands bunching up into fists. 'He's not my boyfriend. We're just work-related acquaintances.'

'And I'm the Queen of Sheba,' snorts Mandy. More like next-door's Alsatian Sheba. 'Eee, Jean,' she goes to Mum. 'You look sensational. C'mon, let's knock em dead. Divvent wait up, Roey.'

I stand by the window and watch them down the road, linking their arms in, laughing. I flick a hundred V-signs at Mandy.

So this is what my life amounts to. *Zero plaisiro.* It's Saturday night, the world's out clubbing, pubbing, tripping, one global dancey, sweaty, laughy party. The whole world, except for Rowena

M. Vincent. M as in Mad. As in Madder Than Logs. Look at me, sprawled on a lumpy couch, stuffing my face with Hula Hoops, while Mum – my *mother!* – hits the bars down Newcastle's Bigg Market, the partiest part of Party City. I sometimes think I've been dropped in a dump bin in the Reject Shop of Life. Plonked in a council house in Fozzy Hall, next-door to the family of Mutants with a barky dog and a clapped-out fridge in the garden. Honest, it's like living in a permanent Jerry Springer show, surrounded by povs and white trash, with my very own caption. *Rowena: Thinks Her Life is Shite.* No wonder I've turned into a desperado. I walk alone, me. Ever since Dad . . .

Ever since Dad, the legendary Lonnie Vincent . . .

It's no good, I can't even think about it, let alone utter the words.

Ever since I've been, let's say, Dadless.

Apart from *Xena: Warrior Princess*, telly is pure guano on a Saturday night. I wish I had some speed but I haven't done drugs since I left school so I dissolve a couple of Solpadeines in Pepsi Max and neck it down while it's still fizzing. The spot on my chin's grown into a huge bubo because I tried to squeeze it before it had a proper head. It's all red and glowing like a clown's light-up nose. I slap on a Fatboy Slim CD and practise my moves. There's a full bottle of Bailey's Irish Cream in the cupboard so I pour myself a glass and flick through the pages on Teletext. The TV poll is Vote for Your Favourite Soap. I dial the 0891 number (calls cost no more than twelve pence) for *Brookside*, then change my mind as there's a dead good storyline in *Coronation Street* at the mo, so I ring *that* number twice to cancel it out. So then I have to dial the *Emmerdale* number five times, don't I, because I really, really rate that sarky lass. Finally I decide on *EastEnders* as my all-time fave so I tap out that number and keep pressing the redial button to infinity.

I pour another glass of Bailey's. It tastes divine, like liquid Mars bars.

It's been ages since I plucked my eyebrows, they're like a forest, so I get the magnifying mirror and tweeze out the stragglers, then decide to reshape them. I overdo it a bit trying to get them equal and they end up looking thin and astonished, like Princess Anne's. All that plucking, it's given me a right headache so I have some more Bailey's. Funny, the bottle feels light when I pick it up. The Hula Hoops have all gone so I microwave some chips which Mum gets on discount from the factory but they're disgusting, full of eyes, so I sling them on the floor and make a stack of brown sauce sarnies. Maybe I'll watch a vid. As I totter to the cabinet my feet skid on the chips and the CD tower tips over. The vids are packed so tight they shoot everywhere when I try to pull one out. The film I pick up at random is *JFK* which I've seen, like, a hundred times but I fast-forward it to *that* bit and play it again and again in freeze-frame. Jesus, the tape must be knackered. The picture looks really, really blurred.

I'm bobbing, floating in a creamy Dead Sea of Bailey's amniotic fluid. It's warm and comfy here, in Anthea Turner's womb. If I reach out, I can touch her liver, kidneys, pancreas, all squeezed together and shaped like Hula Hoops. We'll be on telly, Anthea and Lump, in *Pots Win Praises*. On my forehead, Brooke Shields's eyebrows, thick and glossy, bristle like juicy caterpillars. Then – and I'm not saying she's pushy, right? – Anthea *pushes*, and I plop on to a mound of soft earth. A grassy knoll. Kevin Costner severs the umbilical cord with his expensive teeth. 'Welcome to Deeley Plaza,' he says. 'Just in time for the motorcade.' Tickertape tickers. Texans cheer. Shots (I keep meaning to count them) crack out. Brooke Shields looms over me, a sore-looking patch where her eyebrows used to be, a big gob of brain tissue glistening on her chin. *If I said you had a beautiful body*, she croons . . .

*Would you hold it against me?* A sound like Mum's voice, only giggly and daft. Metallica at full thrash doing a stadium gig inside my head.

'Come on, gimp, you can do it.' An old bloke, about fifty,

stumbles through the doorway with Mum draped round his neck. She's mortal! 'What's been occurring here?' says the bloke. The floor's littered with squashed chips and bits of sarnie and CDs and vids. 'Been having a rave?'

I glare at him. 'No, we're expecting a photographer from *Hello!*' Mum giggles, then groans and collapses on the couch, spark out. She's all floppy like one of those rag-doll cats. Luckily her hair hasn't moved.

The old bloke shakes the Bailey's bottle and tuts. 'There'll be some blinding heads around here in the morning. Come on, let's get her to bed or she'll be as stiff as a board when she wakes up.'

'I can manage,' I snap. I'm not having some nosy minicab driver traipsing through the house clocking what we've got. I shove him out into the hall and open the front door.

'Well, if you're sure,' he says. 'Tell Jean I'll give her a ring tomorrow, see if she's still in the land of the living.'

'Right.' I push him out and slam the door. My head's thudding like a boombox. I feel dead nausy so I crawl upstairs to the bathroom, hold my head over the bog and stick a toothbrush handle down my throat. I retch a bit, then my forehead comes over all cold sweaty and I sick up a bunch of Hula Hoops marinaded in Bailey's.

*Jean*, he said. He knows Mum's name.

## 2

## *Filthy Muscles In*

Vesuvius erupts in the night leaving a massive crater on my chin and bloody pus on the pillow. Hundreds of little white underskin zits have appeared. Jesus, my face is so spotty, Stevie Wonder could *read* it. Mum says it's the badness coming out of me. The Bailey's, more like. I might ring in on a sickie tomorrow on account of stress-related acne.

Mum has two Solpadeines for breakfast. She looks like the undead, last night's make-up all over her mush. Her hair still hasn't moved.

'Look at the state of this place,' she moans. 'It's like McDonald's flaming skip. Those chips are all trodden in, next thing you know, we'll have vermin.'

I remember the minicab driver. 'Who was that old bloke brought you home last night?'

'Old bloke? You are funny, Rowena, he's not much older than me. That was Bernard,' she says coyly. 'Someone I met at the Phoenix. I hope I didn't make a show of myself, I was a bit tiddly.'

'Tiddly? You were *slaughtered*!' Bet she was hitting the Malibu. 'He said to say he'd phone.'

'Did he now?' says Mum. She's got this cheesy grin going on.

I'm monged out on the couch watching a God programme and trying to work out whether Gloria Hunniford's wearing a wig, when the phone rings. Mum's voice sounds weird, sort of girly, and she's laughing. I can only make out bits. 'Straight to my head . . . hope I wasn't too much trouble . . . that would be lovely . . . about five o'clock then. Bye.'

She flutters in with the polish and a duster. 'That was Bernard,' she says, like I might have thought it was the Pope. 'He's coming round for tea so we'd better shape ourselves. You can start on the bathroom and make sure you do round the toilet rim, it's all spattered.'

'Why did you have to ask him round?' I snap. 'We never have Sunday tea.' Not unless you count double egg and chips while we're watching *Coronation Street*.

'It doesn't hurt to be civilised once in a while. You'd better not sulk and ruin things, Rowena. Bernard's a nice man.'

'He's Jurassic. Anyway, I'll be in bed.'

'At five o'clock?'

'I'm knackered.'

Mum sighs. 'Don't be stroppy, Rowena. It wouldn't kill you to be pleasant, just for an hour.'

I shrug.

'It's not a lot to ask,' she says. 'Look at the Queen, she has tea with strangers all the time.'

'Stop going on at me. It'll be cool.'

'It better flaming had be. Now run round the bathroom with the mousse. I'm popping out to Kular's for some proper food.' I head upstairs. 'Rowena,' she yells after me. 'Don't *flounce*!'

The loo's pebble-dashed with Bailey's bile. It smells like old cough mixture gone off and I nearly puke again. I pinch my nose and squirt about half a can of Jif round the bog. While I'm waiting for it to work I slap on a jojoba face pack. What with a white mask and nearly no eyebrows I look like that Queen Elizabeth the Somethingth, except my teeth aren't rotten.

Lordy, Mum's dressed like a waitress in the black frock she bought for Nana Vincent's funeral, and strappy sandals. She says I look like the contents of a hoover bag and sends me upstairs to get changed. I dig out my yellow latex miniskirt from B'Zarr and wear it with a black body and lacy tights and my brilliant biker boots. Mum just stares at me.

'What?' I say.

'Oh, never mind,' she sighs.

Dead on the dot of five a blue Sierra pulls up outside.

*Bing-bong.*

I curl up on the couch with my head stuck in *TV Quick* and try to will myself into a parallel universe. I hear them muttering in the hall for a bit, then Mum wheels him in.

'Rowena, this is Bernard. Bernard, my daughter Rowena.' He grabs my hand and nearly crushes my knuckles. I can't bear to look at his face. Oh Jesus, he's wearing a tie tucked into his trousers!

'On shon tay,' he says. 'And which Spice Girl are you?' I can't bring myself to speak. Mum, how *could* you?

'Oh, Scary Spice, most definitely.' Mum laughs. Too right. Be afraid, old man. Be very afraid.

She's laid the table with things I never knew we had – matching plates, knives and forks with red handles and, Omigawd, place mats with hunting scenes! 'You'll have to take us as you find us,' she says to Bernard, like she hasn't been bottoming the place since dawn. I nearly die when I see the food. Tiny pork pies, frilly ham you could read through, and *salad* – lettuce and cucumber and stuff, which I'd rather swallow slug pellets than eat.

'I'm ready for this,' says Bernard. 'Me stomach thinks me throat's been cut.' He dives on his food like that eagle after a salmon in *Wildlife on One*. 'Tuck in, lass,' he says to me. 'You could do with feeding up. I've seen more meat on Lester Piggott's whip.'

I count to ten – well, four. 'Can I do some chips?' I ask Mum. 'I'll hurl if I eat this green stuff.' She flashes her eyes at me.

'They want chips with everything these days,' says Bernard. 'It's a wonder they haven't got scurvy.'

'Who's "they"?' I say. Mum shoots me a meaning look, meaning, *Don't start.*

'Come on, Rowena. It won't hurt you to go without chips for one meal. Might help to clear your spots up.' I could throttle her. I clap some ham between two slices of bread and smother it with brown sauce. 'Rowena, must you behave like a terrorist?' she hisses. I roll my eyes towards Bernard. He's polished everything off his plate in a nanosecond, quicker even than next-door's dog.

'Dessert, anyone?' says Mum. *Dessert*? She pours a big tin of cling peaches into a glass bowl and shoots me a warning look like she's worried I might let on it's the dish where she usually keeps her Carmen rollers. As if. The peaches are all slimy, like orange slugs, but I manage to swallow some by drowning them in Dream Topping. I can sick them up later.

'That was champion, gimp,' says Bernard, patting his paunch. 'Revived the inner man. Anyone mind if I smoke?' Mum hands him the ashtray that Mandy Sweeney brought back from Prestatyn so she could smoke in our house. I escape into the other room, saying I need to watch *Songs of Praise*.

They stay nattering in the kitchen for a bit, then Mum makes a pot of tea and brings it into the room. Bernard plonks himself opposite me in the big chair with his legs wide open. I can see the outline of his bits. Gross-gross-gross! He's got an ironed-in crease in his trousers plus his hair's cut in a fringe and it looks too brown to be real. Those little piggy eyes and pudgy face remind me of someone off the telly.

'Fancy a swift half in the Scotsman, gimp?'

'That would be very nice, Bernard. I'll just go and freshen up.' Mum pootles upstairs and we both sit there like dummies, listening to her pee.

'What's with this gimp business?' Oh God, did I really say that? I thought I was just thinking.

He lights up another tab without asking, like he owns the place. 'Because of her name. Jean. Jean Vincent, you know.'

I shrug.

'Gene Vincent. He was a rock 'n' roller way back, bust his leg in a motor accident or something, walked with a limp. Ergo, gimp. *Be-*

*bop-a-lula, she's my baby.*' I glare at him. From the corner of my eye I can see his kecks nearly cutting him in two. 'It's a nickname,' he says. 'An endearment, if you like. Everyone has a nickname.'

'No they don't. I don't.' Mr Scudamore calls me Ribena at work sometimes, but I'm not telling *him*.

'Not that you know of, maybe. I had a nickname once, when I was an apprentice, never found out till years after. The lads used to call me Filthy.'

He's a *perv*, I knew it! 'Filthy?'

'Filthy Luker. That's my surname, Luker. Fil-thy Lu-ker. You're not with me, are you?'

Mum comes downstairs all tarted up in her fuchsia microfibre jacket from Principles and a matching lipstick I robbed specially from Fenwicks. 'How do I look, Bernard?'

'Filthy,' I correct her, under my breath.

'You look a real smasher, gimp. Let's make tracks. Be good, young 'un,' he goes to me.

I flash my on/off killer smile. I wish I could remember who he reminds me of, it's driving me mental.

I'm lying in bed updating the music for my funeral when I hear them come back. Filthy trudges up to the bog, makes a racket like Niagara Falls, then goes downstairs without bothering to wash his hands. I creep on to the landing, listening, but they're playing dadrock music and all I can hear is them laughing now and again. I go back to my room and do my nails Patootie Pink and make a right mess of them because I can't concentrate. I'm canny knackered but I still manage to stay awake till he goes. It's turned one o'clock.

Just as I'm drifting off it comes to me. Filthy's the dead spit of Elton John!

# 3

## Grim All Round

Treacle on toast for breakfast. Mondays can be dead busy and I need the sugar rush.

I work at Crowther & Son, Funeral Directors (est. 1971). Some people think it's morbid, but it's just a job, not that much different from working in McDonald's or Kwik Save, and at least I don't have to smile all the time. I used to tell people I worked at the Body Shop, which is true in a way, but now I couldn't give a bugger's arse what they think. Plus I get luncheon vouchers, only a tenner a month, but still. My real ambition was to be a beauty therapist but, surprise surprise, I didn't get any GCSEs so that was out. It doesn't make sense, having to pass exams just to wax bikini lines and pop a few blackheads. I mean, it's not exactly astrophysics.

My first job was in a cinema, flogging ice cream and ripping up tickets. It wasn't a multiplex or owt, just a little fleapit down a side alley, where they showed foreign films no one had heard of. On the plus side, I got to eat all the freebie Rolos and nachos I could stuff in my gullet. *And* I was handling cash. I left after three weeks, told them I was suffering from eye strain through working in the dark. Truth is, I needed to do one before they checked the stock and found out how much I'd fiddled.

It was fate that led me to the job at Crowther's, following a chance encounter with Dean Fairley. I was on a make-up robbing expedition in Superdrug and he tipped me off that I was being clocked by a store dick just as I was about to palm a duotone blusher with sable applicator. After that, we became friends. He always had this weird smell about him. At first I thought he was a glue-head, then he said it was chemicals off his job as a technician.

When he found out I wanted to be a beautician, he said there was a job going at his place, he even fixed up an interview for me. I nearly pooed my pants when I saw it was a funeral parlour but I took the job anyway as it was on the front desk, answering the phone, dealing with personal callers, stuff like that, same as in a normal office. It was then I learned that Dean's clingy smell was the whiff of formaldehyde.

One day, after I'd been there a couple of months, Mr Crowther called me into his office.

'You may have heard,' he said, 'that Cliff is leaving us. To become a carpet fitter.' He explained that everyone would move up a notch, so there'd be an opening for a trainee funeral assistant. It would mean a modest pay increase and a chance to learn more about the technical side of the business, if I was interested.

'Me?' I gasped. *Rowena: Beautician to the Recently Deceased.* I was wearing a new bra at the time and it was digging in, so I just said, 'Cool.'

'I'll take that as a yes,' said Mr Crowther.

Mum was horrified. 'A receptionist's one thing, Rowena, but touching dead bodies . . .'

'It's a promotion,' I pointed out. 'And I'll be wearing rubber gloves. Like a surgeon.'

She shuddered. 'Just as long as you don't bring work home with you, Morticia.'

Part of my job is to wash them and do their hair. I shave the men, also the biddies if they have tufty chins, and I slap a bit of face powder on them if they're going to be viewed in the chapel. I'm not involved in the real technical stuff, embalming and that, but I like to watch if there's not much doing. The men think I'm funny; they reckon girls ought to be squeamish.

Once, right, I was prepping this woman, she was canny old but you could see she'd looked after her complexion. After the powder I dusted on a bit of blusher, vile pink stuff I nicked from Boots, then

13

some Mediterranean Shimmer eyeshadow and Cornflower Blue mascara and, to finish it off, Coral Kiss lip gloss. She looked dead glammy.

Mrs Marr reckoned the husband went ballistic. 'He said she'd never worn make-up in her life and she wasn't going to her grave looking like a tart.' Honestly, there's no pleasing some people.

Mr Scudamore, the embalmer, went totally apeshit. 'Who d'you think you are,' he yelled, 'Helena Bleedin' Rubinstein?' He acted like he was real mad but Dean said they had a right laugh about it in the pub after work.

So anyways, here I am, wearing an all-black denim ensemble and my usual Monday frown.

'Morning, Rowena,' says Mrs Marr, the so-called office manager. Lordy, she's had her hair permed again, it looks like dead men's pubes. 'Good weekend?'

'Yeah, triffic,' I lie. I head for the kitchen to make the coffee which is *still* my first job of a morning, even though I'm a trainee funeral assistant. It's pure exploitation, they treat me like a general fatscrotum. I wish they'd hurry up and get a junior so I could have someone to boss around.

All the staff have their own special mugs and they don't half pull faces if I get them wrong, like they might catch herpes or something. The black mug with purple lettering belongs to the head honcho, Mr Crowther, from an undertakers' convention in 1992. Mrs Marr's is bone china that chinks when you touch it. The Fred Flintstone one the size of a bucket is Mr Scudamore's, and Dean's is a Number 9 Shearer mug from the Toon Army shop. Ray the driver used to have one with a pair of bosoms for a handle but I smashed it, accidentally on purpose, and he went right out and bought a Spice Girls one. Me, I use any old mug from the spares we keep for reps. They're all stained to buggery but I can't be arsed to go and buy one, even though Mrs Marr says I can take it out of petty cash.

There's a weird atmosphere this morning. Mr Scudamore, the embalmer, goes, 'Thanking you,' and twitches his mouth without flashing his joke teeth like he usually does. 'Ta,' is all Ray says, he doesn't even call me sweetheart or crack some sexist gag to try to wind me up. Dean doesn't say much either, but that's nothing new. I wonder if they know something I don't, like I'm getting the sack and they're all embarrassed to look at me. This is the thought in my head when I go into Mr Crowther's office. The tray's shaking like it's got Parkinson's and I slop coffee on the desk, all over a pile of invoices. He wipes the mess up with a hanky, then makes a big deal of standing his mug on a coaster. I'm halfway out the door and he goes, 'Rowena. A word please.'

Jesus, this is it! The big heave-ho. I saw it on telly once that you should always fire people on a Monday morning, never on a Friday afternoon because they might top themselves over the weekend and you'd never forgive yourself. My legs are like jelly but I frown at Mr Crowther like I'm dead hard.

'Well?' he says. 'Don't I get a Gypsy Cream this morning?'

Mrs Marr gives me the crack. 'We've had a wee baby in,' she says. 'SIDS.'

'Who's Sid?'

'Sudden Infant Death Syndrome.' Why is she whispering? 'Cot death. It always affects the men. They see some rare sights in this job but they never quite get used to that.' I'm about to say, 'That's a relief, I thought I was up for the chop,' but I stop myself just in time. 'Parents are in there now, poor things,' says Mrs Marr, disinfecting the phone. 'Not much more than bairns themselves. It makes me wonder if there is a God.'

I stare at her wrinkles. It makes me wonder if she uses a moisturiser.

At lunchtime I walk into town with Dean. He's a funeral technician, which means he can do embalming, glueing eyes, sewing mouths, packing cheeks and stuff. The thing I like about

Dean is his look, which is all skinny arms and legs and specs, sort of nerdy-chic, like Jarvis Cocker. He wants some floppy disks from CompuMart and he says I'm not to rob them.

'Why not?' I say. 'It's a doddle.'

'Just *promise* me,' he goes.

'Suit yourself.'

In Burger King Dean has a barbecue double cheeseburger and I have large fries. We share a banana milkshake.

'Mum met this bloke the other night,' I tell him. 'He's vile. He's called Filthy Luker.'

Dean bursts out laughing and all bits of crumbs fly out of his mouth.

'It's not funny,' I say. 'He's a right dickhead. Plus he looks like Elton John, only ancienter.'

'What a bummer,' goes Dean, frowning and pretending to look dead serious.

I flick a chip at him. 'Don't patronise me, lankyshanks, or I'll flob in your drink.'

'Yes'm,' goes Dean, and does a daft salute. He can be really annoying sometimes. When we get back to work he slaps a Dime bar in my hand so I decide to forgive him.

The baby's family's just leaving. They've been in that chapel for hours. The mother hits the jackpot on Mrs Marr's scale of Upset/Distressed/Distraught/Beside Herself/Absolutely Inconsolable. Her hair's lank, hanging in rats' tails, and a string of snot dribbles down her DKNY jacket.

'Nathan!' she's screaming, in between sobs. 'Nathan, my baby.'

Something goes *clunk* in my stomach. I hide behind the yucca plant on the front desk and peer through the plastic leaves. Mrs Marr yanks a wodge of tissues out of the box and shoves them at the mother. I catch a glimpse of her face, it's red from all that blarting. Then Mr Crowther comes out of his office (he can't stand commotion in reception), sits the mother down and talks to her in his hypnotist's voice. I can't make out what he's saying but whatever it is, it works like magic, like turning a tap off. She looks up, shakes his hand and even tries a weak little smile. Something inside her mouth glints for a nanosecond. A gold tooth. *Clunk* goes the stomach again.

Omigawd, I know her! I know the mother! It's Gemma Probert, this lass who was in my year at school. She got preggers with baby Nathan and left, just before sitting her GCSEs. That's her lowlife boyfriend, Taz Donnelly. He's called that on account of the Tasmanian devil tattooed on his neck. Once, when she was pilled up, Gemma told me he had go-faster stripes on his dick, though I'd rather drink Domestos than check *that* out.

Always immaculo, she was. Coulda been a model, everybody said so. Now she's scruffy, puffy-faced, looks a right mess. I slide down behind the fake greenery and watch, dumbstruck, as Gemma shuffles out, clinging on to Taz's tattooed arm, sobbing fit to bust.

Poor old Gemma Probert, she must be gutted.

Mrs Marr drops the snotty tissues in the bin. 'Rowena, tell Dean the family's away now, if he wants to collect the casket,' she says. 'It's in number one chapel.'

'No sweat, I can do it,' I offer.

There it is, this tiny white coffin, not much bigger than a shoebox. I've never seen a dead baby before. Most people, you know for sure they're dead, the life's drained out of them like liposucked fat, but baby Nathan looks as if he could wake up and start bawling for his dinner any second. I stroke his wispy hair and run my finger round the curly-wurly rim of his ear. His eyelashes are mega-long and curl right up at the ends. I'd die for eyelashes like that. He's got a real cute mouth, it curves up at the corners like he's smiling, or maybe has a spot of wind. There's a geet big lump in my chest like when I eat chips too fast. I feel the dimples on his wee hand, then tease out his fingers and touch his tiny nails. He's perfect. When I roll the shawl down I see he's dressed in a shiny white romper suit with blue ribbons, and lacy socks. There's a Care Bear and a fluffy panda tucked in either side. I've never held a baby. Gemma wouldn't let me hold Nathan that day she brought him into school. She was scared I might drop him. As if. I reach in, wrap my arms round him and lift him out, remembering to support his head because babies' neck muscles are weak and it's dangerous to let them loll about. Baby Nathan weighs nothing, nothing at all. Put him on a string and you could fly him, like a helium balloon. I cuddle him in, rock him right gentle and sing a little kiddy song.

'*Bye, Baby Bunting.*' Big long sleep, baby Nathan.

'*Daddy's gone a-hunting.*' His forehead's cool, but not ice-cold, when I kiss him.

'*Gone to catch a rabbit-skin.*'

'Rowena! What in God's name . . .?' Mrs Marr stands at the door gawping like she's seen a ghost.

'Ssshhh,' I go. She scuttles out. Baby Nathan sleeps on.

'*To wrap my Baby Bunting in.*'

Next thing I know, Mr Scudamore's there. 'Come along, Ribena,' he says, in this really weird voice. 'I'll take him now.' He walks towards me dead slow.

'Watch his head,' I say. 'Don't let it flop.'

'I've got him,' he says. He lays Nathan back in the casket and Dean appears from nowhere and carries it out. He looks at me right funny over the top of his specs.

Mr Scudamore gives me a bit cuddle. 'Come on, Ribena, let it all out,' he says. 'There's no shame in having a good cry, we've all done it.' He looks at me to see if I'm blubbing. Even though I'm well choked, there's no way with this purple mascara on, it smudges like buggery. He leads me out of the chapel. 'I think we'll all feel better after a cup of tea,' he says.

'Right,' I say with a big fat sigh and start mooching off towards the kitchen to brew up. Mr Scudamore says Ray can make it for a change, even though Ray makes a lousy cuppa as he never warms the pot and sometimes doesn't even let the water boil. Mr Scudamore takes me through the front, past Mrs Marr who's got her trout mouth on and doesn't look at me, and into Mr Crowther's office.

'Take a seat, Rowena,' says Mr Crowther. The room smells of breath freshener. 'How are you feeling?'

'Sound,' I say, even though I've got a bit bellyache. Ray comes in with the tea and Omigawd, he's made it in the wrong mugs! I'm waiting for Mr Crowther to go spare but he just picks up the Flintstones mug, takes a few sips and dabs his chops with a hanky.

'Tell me, Rowena, do you enjoy your job here?' Mr Crowther leans his elbows on the desk and makes a steeple with his hands. They're white and wrinkly, like tripe.

'Yeah,' I say. 'It's cool.' Round the walls there's loads of certificates in wooden frames that I've never noticed before, and photos of hearses, some of them with big black horses wearing feather headdresses and blinkers like Ray-Bans.

'Sometimes the pressure gets to us, it's only natural in our line of business.' The secret, says Mr Crowther, is to learn not to become emotionally involved, to show compassion while remaining dis-passionate, if that's not a paradox. 'While our duty is to the bereaved, we need to show respect for the deceased,' he says. 'A *healthy* respect, if you follow me.'

'Right.' I have a slurp of tea. Yuk, no sugar. Ray is totally useless.

'I suggest you take some time off,' Mr Crowther's saying. 'Give yourself a breathing space, a bit of R & R.'

I've been squinting at the Post-it notes on his blotter, trying to read them upside-down, but suddenly my brain clicks into gear. 'You're firing me, right?' My promising career, brutally curtailed. That's it then. I haul my ass to a standing position.

'No, no, goodness me, no.' Mr Crowther walks round the desk and slides his arm round me. I'm a breath of fresh air, a valued member of Crowther's team, he says, and my wellbeing is vital to its performance. I should take tomorrow off as a rest day and come in bright-eyed and bushy-tailed on Wednesday. Oh, right. 'Don't let it blight things, Rowena,' he says. 'There's more to life than work. You have to strike a balance, keep things in perspective. It's been a difficult day for you, but that doesn't mean your life is grim all round.'

I have a wee blub on the bus. I can't stop thinking about baby Nathan and how shit Gemma Probert must be feeling.

When I get home there's a note on the fridge from Mum. Filthy Luker's picking her up from the chip factory at ten o'clock, they're going to catch last orders somewhere and will I see to my own tea.

You were wrong, Mr Crowther. Dead wrong. My life is *totally* grim all round.

# 4

## *Rowena: Warrior Princess*

I'm vegged out on the couch, watching *Corrie*, possessed by the biscuit demon. Half a pack of Jammie Dodgers – gone. I nearly don't answer the phone as I'm too stuffed to move but then I think it might be Mum saying she's changed her mind and she's coming straight home. It's Dean, checking my wellbeing. I tell him no worries, everything's cool and at least I can have a lie-in tomorrow.

'You really don't get it, do you?' says Dean.

'What's to get?'

'Messing with a corpse, is what. You just don't do stuff like that.'

'Stop talking like I'm a grave-robber. Jesus, Dean, I just wanted to hold the baby. It's a girl thing, you wouldn't understand. A nurture thing.'

'There's nothing to nurture,' says Dean. 'The baby's dead.'

'I know that. Look, get off my case, OK? Why's everyone making a big deal of it?'

'People are worried about you,' he says. '*I'm* worried about you. I thought you'd lost it.'

'Thanks a bunch.' Dean asks if he can come round for a bit but I go no because *EastEnders* is about to start, plus my nail polish is peeling so I've got *that* to sort as well. I say I'll see him on Wednesday.

After the programme I go for a long soak in the bath. I shave my legs and pits and smother myself in Mum's Clarins body stuff which is dead expensive in the shops only she buys it cheap from some dodgy bloke at work. He can get anything – Berghaus jackets, mobile phones, Reeboks, you name it. He says it's end-of-line gear but the shops are still selling the Discman Mum bought off him last Christmas so I reckon it's ramraid knock-off. I clean the chipped

Patootie Pink, file the sides of my nails so they look longer, and paint on a couple of coats of Black Tulip which is dark mahogany, next colour up from Ebony which I used to wear a lot in my Goth phase with fingerless black lace gloves. In Mum's room there's a biscuit tin chocker with different perfumes which I bring down for a testing session. After a few squirts the scents get all mingled up so I can't tell which is which. It smells like the Tarts' Department in Boots, Aladdin's Cave of robbable cosmetics, which, by the way, I've decided to boycott until they've fired all those orange-faced slappers and had a complete staff turnround.

At nearly midnight a car pulls up outside. I peek through the curtains. Mum climbs out of the Sierra and, Omigawd, Filthy's getting out too! They're laughing as they come down the path.

'Still up, Rowena?' Mum seems surprised to see me, like I'm a squatter or something.

'Looks like it.' I wonder what they've got in those carrier bags.

*He* pokes his head round the door and sniffs. 'Cor, what a pong. Smells like a brothel after a busy weekend.'

I glower at him. 'I wouldn't know.'

Mum's rattling plates and stuff in the kitchen so I go to see what's what. They've bought an Indian takeaway. 'Care to join us?' says Filthy. 'There's chicken tikka, lamb pasanda, cashew nut pilau—'

'Any chips?' I goes.

Filthy asks if I've got an A-level in chip-eating and Mum says it's the only qualification I'm likely to get, so I say who needs bits of paper, at least I've got a job which is more than a lot of wanky students can say.

'She could have a point there, Jean,' says Filthy, and asks me how I earn my crust. Mum flashes her eyes at me and goes not to talk about it while people are eating. Actually I'm starving but the scran looks like little yellow maggots covered in gloopy stuff and it stinks like the spice aisle in Kular's, so I go in the other room and flick through the One-2-One saddo pages on Teletext. Must find out what Pre-Op T/S means.

After they've finished scoffing, Mum and Filthy come into the room. He plonks himself in the big chair again and sparks up a tab.

Mum glares at me. 'If you don't go to bed soon, you'll meet yourself getting up,' she says. I tell her no sweat, I've been given tomorrow off as a rest day owing to work-related stress. She does that thing with her eyebrows so I say to phone Mr Crowther if she doesn't believe me. She shoots me a look and says she'll have to take my word for it but another late night won't help my complexion. They're guzzling Heineken out of the best glasses. Filthy's telling her about his own business which is called Damascene Conversions, whatever that means. Apparently trade's booming and he's considering taking on a youngster to train up to work with him and Pete. That'll be a fun job, not!

'Loft conversion is the new rock 'n' roll,' he quips, looking at me to see if I think it's funny. It's pathetic. When he gets up to go to the bog I notice his jeans are from *C&A*! I can't handle this.

'Rowena, I can see you're struggling to stay awake,' says Mum. 'Why don't you call it a night?'

My eyes feel gritty and heavy. 'I'm not tired.'

'Look, I know what your game is, young lady, so I'm telling you. Go to bed. No backchat, just do it.'

Filthy potters in, lights a tab and pours himself another lager. I hope he gets done for drunk-driving. Mum pushes me towards the door. 'Rowena's turning in,' she says.

'Good night, young 'un,' he goes. 'Up the wooden hill to Bedfordshire.' I flick him the finger all the way upstairs and collapse on the bed. When I open my eyes, it's daylight.

Jesus, I must have slept all night with my clothes on. My tights feel sticky and dusty, like old J-cloths. I peel off my kit and chuck it in a heap on the floor, pull on an old Manumission T-shirt and pad along to the bog. My bladder's busting. It's sheer bliss, nearly as good as an orgasm, to feel it whoosh out of me and into the North Sea.

'Oops, don't mind me.'

I cut off in mid-pee. It's Filthy, in the doorway, wearing just his trolleys! He potters out again. Oh, gross, he's got a hairy back! And double-double-gross, the bastard clocked me on the bog!

My face is on fire. I race back to my room, slam the door and hurl myself on to the bed chanting, 'Shit-Shit-Shit-Shit-Shit!' My heart's thumping like a lunatic. I clench my hands into tight fists and dig my fingernails in till they really really hurt. When I shut my eyes I can feel my eyeballs darting about like steelies in a pinball machine. *Ping-Ping-Ping!* My whole body's rigid, toes bunched up tight with cramp. I can't get my breath. I'm choking in little gasps like a forty-a-day asthmatic.

This is it, then. I'm going to die. A life of genius tragically cut short. Any second now I'll be whizzing down a long tunnel towards a bright white light. I'll land in a garden full of beautiful thingies, flowers and stuff. My Nana Vincent will be there to show me round, her face surgically reconstructed like before the stroke. And where's Mum while my spirit's departing my earthly body? In the next room satisfying her carnal lust with Filthy Luker. She'll be overcome with remorse when she finds me, the late great Rowena Vincent, my features set in a puzzled frown as if to say, *Mum, how could you?*

Then it dawns on me that my heart's stopped thudding and I'm breathing normally again. The toe-cramp's disappeared and I feel strangely . . . *serene*, is that the word? Something weird's happening. I'm being taken over, possessed by a mystic life-force, an other-worldly power pumping through my earth-body. A divine energy surges through me, transforming me into a mighty butt-kicking superwoman. From now on I shall take no prisoners and no shit.

I am *ROWENA: WARRIOR PRINCESS.*

I am invincible.

Filthy Luker is my mortal enemy.

I think my period's started.

There's some mumbling and shuffling in the hall, then the front door goes and Filthy's car drives off. Mum taps on my door and sidles in, sheepish-like. 'Rowena, we need to talk.'

'Later, I'm off into town.'

I leap off the bed with my new-found energy and dash past her into the bathroom. Yes, my period's come and instantly I get this dragging ache in my guts.

After taking a quick shower, I Oxycute my menstrual spots and apply full slap – Pagan Gold eyeshadow and Red For Danger kiss-proof lipstain, a deadly combination. The black scoop-neck sweater looks totally top over a balcony bra and I slip into a PVC micro-skirt, stripey tights and my biker boots. Then I backcomb my hair, clip it up in a cone slide and, final touch, silver crucifix earrings to ward off evil spirits. Check out the look. Strictly the biz. I grab my leather jacket, hotfoot downstairs and hoy a couple of Solpadeines down my throat to kill the curse-cramps.

Mum's sitting at the table supping coffee. 'Rowena,' she says in a sort of pleading way. 'We have to talk about this.'

'Some other time,' I say. She's got a face like a smacked bum so I peck her on the cheek. 'Ciao, Mommie Dearest.'

I catch a Metro to the Monument. After Top Shop and Warehouse, I go for a mooch round B'Zarr, this little shop round the back of the market, next to the so-called hair extension clinic, brothel more like. They sell rediscovered (i.e. second-hand) and retro gear plus fetish stuff like bondage masks which you'd have to be well weird to buy. They've had some new stock in. Most of it's average but then I clock this totally wicked outfit in black and bronze leather, a bustier and miniskirt that both do up at the front with studs and bootlace things. Pure Warrior Princess. My stomach goes all fizzy with excitement. Some clothes do that to you. I grab it off the rack and head for the changing rooms. The only cubicle's full so I have to use the communal bit where people check you out in the mirrors to see if your bra's clean or if you've got cellulite (yes and no). Wow! It fits like it was designer-made specially for me. I swivel round, suck in my cheeks and pout. This is class kit. I've got to have it. I check out the price tag, like I could afford it in this life.

It shall be mine. Just needs a bit of forward planning.

Mum brings a pizza home for supper, plain cheese and tomato as she knows I hate anything fancy. 'Can we have that talk now?' she says.

'OK, shoot.' *Rowena: Warrior Princess* is armed and ready for battle.

'I know it hasn't been easy for either of us,' she begins. 'Especially since your dad—'

'Don't!' I snap. 'Leave Dad out of this.' My skin comes over all hot and prickly.

'But it's important, Rowena. You can't go on pretending it never happened. We should be able to talk about it without you getting all twisty.'

The pizza tastes like sick in my mouth. 'That's the deal,' I say. 'Otherwise I'm outta here.'

* * *

Lonnie Vincent. It's a way cool name, like a sixties rock star. Lonnie Vincent and the Gonefathers, disappearing from a town near you. Laurence, he was christened, after some old movie star that Nana Vincent had the hots for. Sir Laurence Oblivion.

The day after Dad vanished, it was like he'd never existed. Down came the photographs, the wedding picture that used to sit on the telly, the one of him and our old mutt Georgie on Cullercoats beach, even the one of his graduation with Dad dressed in a black gown and a square hat with a tassel. He was real proud of that one. Mum took the piss, saying if he was a 'mature' student, all the others must be foetuses.

I searched everywhere for the photos, for *anything* that belonged to him. There was nothing. Nothing. It all seemed to disappear over-night, sucked into a black hole, turned into anti-matter. Once I found an odd sock and hid it under my pillow, but it smelled of Lenor, not of Dad. When Mum changed the sheets, the sock vanished too.

26

Since there was nothing to remember him by, I gradually forgot how he looked, the deepdown sound of his voice, the springy thickness of his hair, the man-tang of his breath, the feel of his stubble scratchy against my cheek. The last thing I remembered was his smile. It used to come to me at night, just as I was drifting off to sleep. A lopsided smile, with the crinkly lines it made in his cheeks. I could just about picture it, but the rest of him had faded, like the Cheshire Cat. When I tried to summon it up, the memory evaporated like a fading dream.

Now there's nothing. Less than that, really.

* * *

'All right, all right. I'm sorry.' Mum goes to the cupboard and pours herself a slug of gin and lime. 'Try to see it from my side,' she says. 'Work, home, bed, work . . . that's all my life – my *existence* – amounts to. And I'm not getting any younger.'

'Tell me about it. What's your point?'

'Enough of your lip, Rowena. My point is, I need to dig myself out of this rut before it's too late. One day you'll have a life of your own . . .'

'Oh, cheers, Mum.'

'. . . and I don't want to end up a lonely and disappointed old woman. Don't you think I deserve some enjoyment?'

'Course I do,' I say. 'Only you can do a lot better than Fil— than Bernard.'

'I don't understand what you've got against him,' says Mum. 'OK, maybe he's not Tom Cruise.'

'No shit.'

'But he treats me like a lady. He's fun – God knows I could do with a few laughs – *and* he's got his own business.'

'He's a wuss, Mum,' I point out. 'He wears grandad gear, I bet he dyes his hair, plus he's always coming out with cringey jokes. And, oh God, oh God, he saw me having a wazz. He won't be staying over again, will he?'

She comes and sits next to me and gives me a bit hug. 'He might, now and again.'

'But, Mum, it's damaging to my emotional stability,' I protest. 'It was on *Ricki Lake*. This dating coach said you shouldn't let men stay the night, not if you've got children living at home.'

'You're sixteen, that's hardly a child, Rowena. Anyway, forget *Ricki Lake*. We don't live in America, and even if we did, no dating coach is going to tell me how to run my life. One day you'll understand that a woman has certain . . . Well, let's say I'm not ready to take holy orders just yet.'

'Stop it! Shut up!' I clap my hands over my ears. 'You don't need to draw me a picture.'

'It's the same old story,' Mum continues, ignoring my distress. 'Every time I meet a man, you turn into a monster. You know you'll always come first with me, Rowena, but there's a limit. You have to learn to face up to things, stop thinking of your dad as some kind of superhero. He's not going to swoop down like the Caped Crusader and whisk you off to a better world. This is it, Rowena. This is your life, like it or not, and mine too, so we might as well make the best of it. There's no point going into a strop every time your dad's mentioned.' She grabs my head with her hands, forcing me to look her in the eyes. 'Listen to me, Rowena, I'm going to spell it out. Your Dad's gone, G-O-N-E, and he's not coming back. All the wishing in the world isn't going to change that. Do you understand?'

And something roars up in me, something black and evil and demonic. It starts churning deep in my bowels and claws its way through my stomach, gripping my internal organs, coating my insides with foul-smelling sludge.

'Rowena?'

Now it's clamped on to my heart, squeezing the breath, the life out of me. It sinks its vicious teeth into my veins, releasing a slick of poisonous mucus, whizzing deadly contamination through my body. Festering, colonising, multiplying.

'Rowena, what's wrong with you?'

The demon slithers up my chest and into my throat, clutching my windpipe, choking me, making me gag. I gasp, gulp for air, retch. It locks a strangulation hold on me from inside, stifling my breath.

'Rowena, for God's sake, what is it?'

Now it's in my head, tendrils spreading like poison ivy, suckers pressing, gripping, glueing themselves to my skull, injecting venom into the cells until my brain feels paralysed, rigid, dry and useless as chewed-out gum. It darts behind my eyeballs, scratching, tearing, twanging them for devilment.

'That's it, I'm calling the doctor.'

'No!' My voice comes out as a scream. 'It's cool. I'm OK, really. I just need to lie down.'

When I stand up it feels as if I'm levitating, floating on a cushion of air like a hovercraft. I stumble towards the stairs in a zomboid fashion. Mum follows me into my room, brandishing a facecloth. I collapse on to the bed, knocking a pile of CDs clattering to the floor.

'Let's cool you down,' says Mum, plastering the damp flannel to my forehead.

I shove her away. 'Leave me alone. Please, Mum. Just let me sleep.' I'm so desperate to be on my own, I get a mindflash of how murderers must feel in that split second before they stab or hack or pulp their victims to death. Fortunately for Mum's life expectancy, she doesn't push it.

'All right. I didn't mean to upset you, Rowena, saying that stuff about your Dad. Sometimes you have to be cruel to be kind. But will you at least *try* to get along with Bernard, give him a chance?' she pleads. 'It would make life so much easier all round.'

'Suppose so,' I say. Obviously Filthy's put her under some sort of spell, but he's no match for the supernatural powers of *Rowena: Warrior Princess*.

He will be vanquished!

# 5

## *Releasing the Red*

Mum tippytoes downstairs and turns the telly on. Even though the volume's down low it's still irritating me to death, a maddening unscratchable itch on the inside of my skull. My legs and arms tingle with pins, needles, darts, hatchets, and my head feels stretched tight, as though it's about to explode. What's wrong with me? Maybe I've got an interminable disease, or a brain haemorrhage. Once I read a piece in a magazine about this bloke's head swelling like a massive balloon and bursting right open, splattering brain tissue for miles. I pat my scalp. My head feels bumpy but not noticeably huge. It's throbbing, though, pulsating as if it's revving up for take-off, preparing to sever itself from my body with an almighty *shloop* and launch into the cosmos, where it'll float around for infinity with assorted space junk, mystifying cosmonauts and extraterrestrial aliens. Maybe they'll bounce signals off it, invent a new satellite TV station, *The Rowena Head Channel*, wall-to-wall Jerry Springer, all live, no bleeps or out-takes, just fist fights and foul language, white trash heaven.

Listen to me! I'm Mad-Madder-Maddest!

I haul myself up into a sitting position. The damp flannel peels itself off my face, leaving a film of icy sweat on my forehead. *Bang!* thumps my head. I slide down the duvet like a passenger whooshing from a burning aircraft on one of those inflatable chutes, landing on top of the scattered CDs with a thud followed by the crack of broken perspex.

Opposite me is the long mirror, the one for checking out the total look. I stare into it. A gorilla stares back at me, a gorilla in a foul mood, a gorilla with menstrual tension, excruciating toothache and galloping bellyache. My forehead's set in a deep frown, practically overhanging my nose. Rowena Vincent: Neanderthal Woman, Missing Link, Ugly Daughter of Peatbog Man. My jaws are clenched tight together. Spaghetti veins stand out in my neck and my mouth's pursed up like a camel's anus. A muscle in my thigh keeps twitching. Suddenly my foot kicks out and sends the smashed CD covers shooting over the pink fluffy rug. A shard of perspex lands in my lap, jagged and dangerous. I pick it up and run the sharp edge across my finger. The demon, which is now in control of my entire body and mind, orders me to roll up my sleeve. Powerless to resist, I dig the point into the white skin of my inner arm, puncturing the flesh, freeing the bubbling blood.

It doesn't hurt. That's the first thing I notice. The no-pain factor is a surprise, also a disappointment. I feel elated but slightly cheated, as though it should have been more of a challenge. It's like winning the jackpot on *Who Wants To Be A Millionaire?* by answering hundred-quid questions. No need to phone a friend or ask the audience. Ee-zee.

The second thing is, it's beautiful to watch. It's the colour of Red or Dedd lipstick, a pure, bright, perfect crimson. I'm fascinated, mesmerised, by the sight of it trickling out of my body, inching down the alabaster white of my arm. It's thick too, good, strong, healthy lifeblood, amazing when you consider all the junk I stuff down my gullet. I lift my arm and follow the bright red trail with my eyes. At first it runs straight, then meanders as it flows down towards my elbow, landing in rhythmic splashes on my leg.

The best thing is the relief. The calm. The unbearable tension released, dripping, draining away. I used to sneer at girls who cut up at school, mutilating themselves, scoring tracks on their bodies with compasses, nail scissors, bits of broken mirrors. One or two of them even stuck things inside the wounds – paper clips, earrings, biro refills. That's going too far in my opinion. But I think I understand the point of it now.

31

Aaahhh. I feel so relaxed, this has to be the ultimate chill. My eyelids flicker, my head fills with helium and sails high above the clouds, drifting, floating in endless space.

The next thing I see is a pumpkin topped with candyfloss. As my brain clicks into gear I realise it's Mandy Sweeney, all orangey make-up and frizzy hair. She's waving a wee bottle of something under my nose. Jesus, it stinks worse than putrefying corpses!

'Howay, bonny lass,' she says, slapping me on the cheek and blasting me with her foul faggy breath. 'See, I told you the smelling salts would bring her round, Jean.'

Mum's face comes into focus. Her eyes are red and her hair's all anyhow and scraggy, like tumbleweed. 'Rowena,' she blubs. 'Whatever made you do it?' She breaks down crying, all wet and slobbery. 'I knew you were upset when I said those things about your dad, but to drive you to *this!* Thank God we found you in time, I'd never have forgiven myself.'

That's when I remember about the cutting up. My arm, the one I carved with a sliver of CD cover, feels numb and heavy. I try to lift it to check the damage but nothing happens, it won't budge. Hell, what if I slashed a nerve and the arm's lost all feeling? I'll have to go through life with a useless thing dangling from my shoulder and learn to eat with a fork in one hand, like an American. I try again to move it but it won't work, it feels like a ton weight. Omigawd, what if I sliced right through the bone and amputated my own arm! I'm suffering from phantom limb syndrome!

'My arm,' I murmur. 'Where's my arm?'

Mandy hovers over me, a cigarette clutched between her fat fingers. 'Your arm's all right, pet,' she says. 'It's bandaged up tight. Think yourself lucky your mum phoned me. I'm a trained first-aider, went on a course, only to skive off work, mind. Florence Friggin' Nightingale at your service.' She sucks on her tab, stubs it out on a saucer and blows the smoke into my face.

'What the fuck were you up to, Roey?' she whispers. 'Trying to top yourself like that, you daft bint. Your mum's frantic, she blames herself.'

*Eh?* Omigawd, they must think I tried to end it all by slashing my wrists! I want to explain it wasn't like that, I never meant to kill myself, I was only letting out some of the tension in my head. I'm not suicidal, not even a serial cutter-upper, it was just a little nick to make me feel better. But I truly can't be arsed.

'Open your eyes, Rowena.' Mum's voice echoes inside my head. Somehow I'm lying on the couch, though I can't remember how I got here. 'Look at me. Please.'

I feel dead woozy. It takes a mega-human effort but I manage to lift my head and fix my eyes just past Mum's right ear. I can't seem to look straight at her. She's been blarting, her face is all red and puffed and there's a soggy tissue in her hand.

'What am I going to do with you?' she sighs, rubbing my toes through the stripey lurex socks. 'Come here, give your mum a cuddle.'

She slides over and grabs me real tight. Her eyelashes flicker wetly on my neck and her breath comes hot and damp.

I flinch. 'You're squashing my arm.' I'm not in the mood for a big emotional scene. The inside of my head feels like one of those Rubik's cube things, still in one piece but all jiggled and jumbled up to buggery.

'I'm sorry, love,' she says, pulling away. She stares at my arm, tears welling up in her eyes. 'It's all my fault,' she says. 'God knows what you've been going through. We should have talked about it. I can't bear to think you've been bottling it up all this time. I'm sorry, Rowena, I'm really sorry.'

She collapses on to my shoulder, crying big-time. Good job I'm not wearing anything that shrinks.

I'm in a daze. I try to remember how this whole thing happened but my brain won't work. Lately I can't tell which dimension I'm in,

Earth or Planet Rowena. I seem to be clicking in and out more often. Maybe I'm losing control.

Mum blows her nose on the sodden tissue. 'We'll get through this somehow,' she sniffles. 'I'm going to find you some help, professional help. We'll go and see Dr Pooley tomorrow, he'll know who to contact.'

My stomach gurgles like bathwater going down a plughole. When did I last eat? Apart from a nibble of pizza I haven't swallowed anything since yesterday teatime, that's twenty-four whole hours. No wonder I'm ravenous.

'I could murder some egg and chips,' I mumble. 'With brown sauce and thick-sliced bread.' My fave comfort food.

'Coming right up,' says Mum, pecking me on the cheek. 'You lie there and rest, Rowena, I'll see to it. Want the telly on?' I shake my head in a vacant fashion. I need to think this turn of events through without any distractions.

After the egg and chips Mum puts me to bed, tucking me in and kissing me like when I was little and had measles. 'Try to get some sleep,' she whispers. 'We'll sort this out together, starting tomorrow. Love you lots, Rowena.'

As soon as she's out of the room I examine my arm. It's bandaged real tight but there's no blood seeping through so the gushing must have stopped, and it doesn't hurt, not a bit. I reach for my manicure set and clean off the Black Tulip nail polish. Jeez, I must have been off my head when I robbed it, the colour's shite, it looks like I trapped my fingers in a door. When I tiptoe to the bog I can hear Mum talking on the phone. I creep on to the landing and strain my ears to listen.

'It was terrible, Bernard,' she goes. What's she playing at, spilling her guts to Filthy Luker? She's got no right to tell him our family secrets. 'Rowena was in a really bad way, blood all over. Her arm was completely lacerated. I've been talking it over with Mandy, and we put it down to her losing her dad. She must have been suppressing her feelings all this time, trying to contain her grief. It's like a pressure cooker, all that rage and confusion, it's a miracle she hasn't exploded before now.'

Filthy chips in with something, I'd give anything to know what he's saying.

'That surly attitude, the sullenness, the lying, the swearing,' goes Mum, reciting my rap-sheet. 'They're just symptoms, ways of expressing her anger. A cry for help. But this latest episode, it's serious. Oh Bernard, she must have been so desperate, so unhappy, poor Rowena.'

She pauses for Filthy to get another two-penn'orth in. The interfering sod, it's none of his friggin' business.

'It all falls into place now I think about it,' Mum goes on. 'The way she behaves with *you*, Bernard. Don't you see, she resents you taking her father's place. It's nothing personal against you, she'd be the same if it was – I don't know, Clint Eastwood, whoever.'

Oh really. That's what *she* thinks! I could quite fancy old Clint as a stepdad, he must have piles of dosh, though given a choice I'd prefer John Travolta. Shit, I think I'm going to sneeze. I pinch my nose tight till the feeling goes away. Mum'd go harpic if she caught me earwigging.

'There's no point being cynical, Bernard, you don't know the history,' she's saying. Butt out, Luker, don't ruin it. 'Rowena's been through a lot, all that terrible business with her dad, it's time to get her some professional help. These people know what they're talking about, it's nothing they haven't come across before. I'm taking her to the doctor's first thing tomorrow, see what he suggests. Oh, Bernard, I feel so guilty, I should have spotted the warning signs. What kind of parent am I?'

Try *gullible*, Mother dear.

In the morning, Mum rings the doctor's surgery. She tells the receptionist that it's an emergency, which makes me feel dead important as they usually make you wait a week, or until your leg

35

drops off, before they agree to fit you in. Then she calls Mrs Marr and tells her I'll be late for work as I have a medical appointment. Uh-oh. That means the old bat'll be flicking through her medical dictionary and giving me the third degree when I get in.

I sit there in the quack's office like a lump of lard while Mum bangs on. The room stinks of Dettol and, more faintly, of sick. Dr Pooley unravels the bandage from my arm, assures me I won't have to wear a sling, I won't be scarred for life, and there's no need for plastic surgery quite yet. Pity, I was hoping to get cheekbone implants at the same time. He sends me down the corridor to see the practice nurse who smears some cold gooey stuff on my injury and slaps a dressing on it. The wound's a bit of a disappointment, to be honest, more like a scratch than a life-threatening gash, so I must have miraculous healing capacity. Then I'm sent to perch in the waiting room while Mum and Dr Pooley gab some more. It gives me the creeps, all those pathetic sick people, you never know what they've got, there could be pubic lice crawling about trying to get into your knickers or dickies taking flying leaps into your hair.

Mum insists on taking me to the bus station café for a cheese toastie before I go to Crowther's.

'Dr Pooley's referring you for assessment,' she says. 'He's marking you as a priority so we can expect to hear something soon. It won't be long before you're back on track again.'

'What sort of assessment?' Yuk, this cheese tastes like soap. I bet it's past its sell-by date.

Mum slurps her tea. There's no way I'm drinking mine, it's got globules of grease floating on top. This place is a health hazard, they want reporting.

'Somewhere called Altamont Lodge,' she explains. 'As I understand it, you go and talk to someone about your feelings and they work out the best way to treat you. They call it wossname, psychological evaluation.'

'I'm no psycho!' I yell indignantly. 'I'll murder anyone who says

I am! Look, I refuse to see a shrink and that's final.' A workman at the next table turns round and grins at me. 'What's your friggin' problem?' I snap.

'Calm down, Rowena, there's no need to shout,' goes Mum. 'Nobody's saying you're a . . . a *psycho*. It's just that you might need some help sorting out your emotional problems. There's no shame in that, it's no different to, say, breaking a leg. Some people pay a fortune for therapy, it's supposed to be trendy.'

'It's complete bollocks. Anyway, it's for proper mad people, loonies, schizos, blokes that knife you in the street for no reason. There's nothing wrong with me, you're all making a big fuss just because I accidentally cut my arm.'

Mum smiles in a patronising way. 'There was more to it than that, as we both know. Don't get yourself into a state, Rowena, we'll see what happens when you have your assessment. You might not need counselling, maybe they'll put you on medication for a while.'

My feet start stomping under the table. 'I'm not taking any wanky tablets, they put all sorts into them. I could end up a zomboid and need round-the-clock nursing care. Then what would you do? You'd have to pack in your job, we'd be stony broke, then they'd evict us and we'd have to live in Cardboard City with winos and dossers. Fancy being a bag lady, do you?'

Mum sighs. 'Nobody's going to force you to do anything you don't want to, Rowena. I'm sure people only want to help. Come on, they'll be expecting you at Crowther's.'

As we're leaving, the workman on the next table stares at me again, so I bump my rucksack against his cup and knock his greasy tea down his overalls. Serves him right for being a nosy bastard.

# 6

## Mr Collard's Legacy

They're all sickly nice to me at work after that business with baby Nathan, sort of pussyfooting around, humouring me. It feels like I'm in that movie where Meryl Streep wears a pudding-basin wig, only I'm the dingo that did a runner with the baby. Mr Crowther asks if the day off helped and I go yes, I definitely feel more rested, emotionally speaking. Good, he says, as far as he's concerned the subject's closed, we'll say no more about it.

Mrs Marr examines my arm, sniffing the dressing, trying to guess the brand of antiseptic cream by the smell. 'Your mother never told me how you injured yourself,' she says.

'It was a freak accident,' I tell her. She raises one eyebrow. 'With an electric can-opener.' She frowns. 'Made in Korea.' She smiles, satisfied. Mrs Marr won't have any truck with foreign goods.

Dean's got this old gadgy on the slab. 'Want to give him a wash down?' he says. The bloke stinks to high heaven. He hasn't gone off, it's more your chronic soap-dodger pong. 'Poor old sod,' says Dean. 'When we undressed him, one of his toes fell away with the sock. Gangrene.'

'What did you do with it?' I say. 'The toe?' Dean shoots me a funny look. 'Only asking,' I goes.

'His nails want cutting,' says Dean. 'They look like a Chinese Mandarin's.' No kidding. They're hard as – well, *nails*, geet long and twisty like old elephants' tusks. I'll need a chainsaw.

His name's Kenneth Shrapnel Collard and he's covered in about half an inch of grime. The washing water turns a disgusting colour, like mud. I shave his whiskers and comb his little bitty hair. Now for the nailectomy. I soak the sponge in really hot water, hold it on his toes for ages to soften the nails and keep hacking little bits off them until they're short enough. It's no salon pedicure but it's the best I can do. Mr Collard looks better than he has in years.

When Dean and Mr Scudamore pop out for a tab I gather the nail clippings, wrap them in a paper towel and stuff them in my bag. I want to study them in private.

At break-time, we're in the kitchen supping tea and Ray goes, 'Oh friggin' hell, I just remembered – the cat!' He tells us about when him and Gerry went to collect Mr Collard. The house was a right tip, piles of old newspapers, three inches of dust everywhere, you needed a gas mask, squalid wasn't the word, etc.

'What's this about a cat?' I say.

'Cat? Bleedin' panther more like, the size of it. An evil bastard, it was. Wild, with slitty yellow eyes like that sprog, the devil's spawn in *Rosemary's Baby*. We never seen it at first, just heard this rumbling noise. Thought it was the deceased, emitting stomach gases. Then this – this *thing* flew at Gerry, hissing and spitting, tetanus on legs. It had claws like bleedin' scalpels. Made a right mess of Gerry's hand, ripped it to ribbons. Think I can squeeze another cuppa out of that pot?'

'Come on, Ray. What happened next?' This is good crack, plus it beats working. Ray says the beast was going apeshit, flying at them and wailing like a banshee. Gerry was all for knocking it one on the head but they found a cardboard box, cornered the cat and managed to trap it inside. Then they dumped it in Mr Collard's shed where it was now unless it had clawed its way through the roof, which Ray wouldn't put past it. He'd have to phone the animal shelter to go and collect it.

'I can do that,' I offer.

I write down Kenneth Shrapnel Collard's address out of the receiving room book. It's down the rough end where the crims and druggies live, not far from Mandy Sweeney's. After work I hop on the 38 and get off near the bowling alley, calling into a corner shop to buy a tin of cat food. A little kid of about nine serves me and I tell him it ought to be fresh salmon at that price, they want reporting for extortion. He just smirks and snaps his chuddy at me. I feel like chinning him.

I suss which is Mr Collard's house straight away. There's a blanket up at the window and a pissy mattress in the jungle that passes for a garden. The shed's dropping to bits, like a lean-to with nothing to lean against, and when I open the door the hinge snaps off. Inside there's a rusty old bike, a lawnmower out of the Ark and hundreds of bin bags full of I dread to think what. The cardboard box is on top of the bags. I poke it but there's no sound, nothing moving inside. No wonder – they forgot to make airholes, the cat's probably suffocated! I untuck a corner of the lid and suddenly this paw shoots out, all black and bristly like a bog brush, only with massive claws, and takes a swipe at me. The cat starts yowling and hissing like a thing demented so I force the lid down and haul it to the bus stop.

Total friggin' nightmare! People on the bus keep staring at me as if I'm a fur trapper or a vivisectionist, tutting and saying, 'Poor thing,' meaning the cat. It's howling like a Fed-car siren, thudding and bumping about in the box, it's even scratched a bit hole in the side and keeps jabbing me with its claws. By the time I get home I'm practically in shreds.

After dumping the box on the kitchen floor I decide I need a drink before I tackle the cat so I take a swig of Teachers whisky straight from the bottle. It tastes burny and vile. To avoid lacerations I put on Mum's scuzzy anorak out of the hall and zip it up tight, then go into the kitchen and shut both doors. The thing doesn't move or make a sound so I tippytoe round the box, grab the fish slice and poke the flaps of the lid with it. The cat makes a little mew like a kitten. It probably wants some milk. As I open the fridge door the box lid bursts open and the cat flies out at Mach 1, just like the thing that shot out of that bloke's stomach in *Alien*. It leaps on to the draining board, shoots up the curtains and perches on the pelmet, spitting like a cobra. Lordy, it's a monster, with pointy teeth and cauliflower ears. I open the cat food, spoon it into a saucer and slide it on to the worktop.

'Come on then, you ugly bugger, grub's up,' I say. It bares its fangs and growls. 'Starve then, see if I care. I'm off to watch *Coronation Street*.'

I listen outside the door for a bit. Nothing. Zapping on the telly I sprawl on the couch with a Teachers topped up with Lucozade which isn't quite so foul. Half an hour should be long enough for the cat to chill out. I decide to chance it without the anorak, it makes me look a right divvy.

Omigawd! The stench in the kitchen nearly knocks me out. Obviously *it* is a *he*, and he's sprayed tomcat wazz up the wall. The cat food's disappeared. So has the cat. I take a good skeg round but I can't see him anywhere. Then I hear this sort of muffled bellow, like a cow with its head in a bag. It really spooks me. Sounds like it's coming from the swingbin. The cat must have dived on it and gone through the top. I lift up the lid dead slow and sure enough, there he is, sinking in a quicksand of kitchen waste, snarling. I grab a towel. He jabs me with his claws as I haul him out of the garbage but I wrap the towel round him like a straitjacket and give him a good rub-down. He struggles like a lunatic and eventually wriggles free, takes a flying leap and crouches on top of the microwave, hissing, his ears laid flat. I fill the saucer with milk and go in the other room to watch *Brookside*, leaving the kitchen door open. Half an hour later when the credits roll, I glance down and there's yer man stretched out in front of the Cosiglow, washing his tail. Bless.

Mum gets home on time, minus Filthy Luker.

'My God, Rowena, is there a skunk loose in here? I could niff it all the way down the path.'

The cat's still by the fire, scratching himself to bits like a junkie gone cold turkey. I point at him with the remote.

'Look, we've got a pet,' I say. 'Wicked, innit?'

The beast can sleep in the shed for one night, then he has to go. Those are Mum's orders. We manage to capture him, stuff him in the box with the towel and shut him in the shed. He starts yowling worse than bagpipes which sets next-door's Sheba off barking like mad.

'See?' goes Mum. 'The thing's only been here five minutes and the neighbourhood's in flaming uproar. We'll have the bizzies round next.'

Even though it's nearly midnight, she vacuums all round and makes me Dettox the worktops and scrub the wall with bleach where he's sprayed. My nails are ruined. Half a can of Haze later the kitchen still howls of tomcat pee.

'I shan't sleep,' moans Mum. 'We could be harbouring all sorts of germs. I'll bet the thing's alive with fleas, then there's cat flu, infectious enteritis. Oh God, they carry Aids as well, I read it in *Bella*.'

'Well, it's not as if you'll be having unprotected sex or sharing needles with him,' I say. 'Cat fleas can't live on humans anyway, not unless they get in your pubes.' She says to stop trying to sidetrack her with scientific wossname, the thing's not staying and that's final.

'You're going against an old man's last will and testament, it'll bring bad luck,' I warn her. 'Mr Collard left instructions in a letter, hang on, I'll fetch it.'

Using a page from the pad where I've written my funeral music, I scrawl a note using my left hand to make it look doddery.

*Do not let Council take cat. Please find him a nice home pref with women as he does not take to men. He has been good friend & mouser. This is my dying wish.*
    *Signed*
    *K. S. Collard.*

42

Mum reads it. 'If this is some kind of joke . . .' she goes.

'It's for real, swear down,' I say, making my eyes big and round, and not blinking.

She stares at me for ages. This could go either way.

'You've got a week to get the wretched thing cleaned up,' she says. 'It'll want worming, and you can pay for it to be neutered. Until then it's not allowed in this house, right?'

'Right.'

In the morning I feed him a tin of tuna chunks in brine. While he's wolfing it down I give him the once-over. This is one mean mutha, a street-fighting cat with battle-scarred ears and missing clumps of fur. His balls are the size of conkers.

'We're gonna be partners, you and me,' I tell him. '*Rowena: Warrior Princess* and her Trusty Sidekick.' He scrats and scrawms like a maniac, bits of fur flying everywhere. 'But first, we need to evict those lodgers.' I leave him some water and lock him in the shed. As an afterthought I scribble a note and pin it on the door: *Beware Viscous Cat!*

Pippa's Pet Shop down Percy Street is full of stuff I never knew existed, e.g. a three-storey gerbil tank with loads of little tunnels and a carpeted bedroom. A penthouse pad for rodents, what next? I buy some worming tablets and rob a flea spray with free comb and a cat collar that glows fluorescent in the dark. Fleas, it says in the leaflet, can jump mega-distances to get on cats, and females lay up to 500 eggs that hatch into tiny larvae and move away from light into the depths of carpets, crevices, cracks, bedding or furniture. They also carry tapeworm eggs which the cat swallows when it grooms itself. Ugh, my skin goes itchy just reading it. Death to all fleas! I feel sorry for the cat, it wasn't his fault Mr Collard lived in a bug-hutch, so I buy some fish-flavoured biscuits from Kwik Save and a tin of gourmet food which costs a bomb even though it's only boiled kangaroo lights.

When I get home from work I creep up to the shed and unlock

the door real quiet. The cat's sprawled out on the towel looking geet cool as owt, like he's on the beach in Benidorm or something. He cocks one eye open and miaows, just like a proper pet. 'Yo, cat,' I say. He has a good stretch and yawns, then starts scratting, tearing away at his ear. Fleas must have woken up as well. I rattle the box of biscuits and scatter a few on the floor. He plods over and sniffs at them, crunches one or two and ignores the rest. Then, in a flash, he darts between my legs and scoots up the path like greased lightning.

My Trusty Sidekick has escaped!

To pile on the agony, like I'm not demented enough, Filthy Luker comes home with Mum and settles himself in the big chair.

'It's for the best,' he pronounces. 'Sounds like he was half wild anyway, you'll never domesticate a feral cat. Don't worry about him, he'll be off tomming after some randy female.'

'Well, you're the expert on that,' I say.

'Ouch! Back in the knife drawer, Miss Sharp,' he goes, but I can see I've rattled him. He unzips a Head sports bag and pulls out a pair of fleecy moccasins. 'I might as well be comfortable,' he says with a smirk. 'Since I'm staying.'

I could garrotte him. My scalp goes all prickly and I march into the kitchen where Mum's making corned beef sarnies.

'Nothing on the telly?' she asks.

My neck flares up in a red rash. 'Nah,' I reply. 'Just One Man and His Gob on the couch.'

She shoots me a look and says to remember what we agreed.

'You promised you'd make an effort, Rowena, so put your flaming face straight and let's see how mature you can be. Bernard means well,' she says.

I shrug. 'So did Hitler.'

She flicks me with a tea towel so I go outside the back door for a bit to cool down. It's times like this I wish I'd never packed in smoking. Stop it, Rowena. Get a grip.

There's something on the doorstep. I flick on the outside light and poke it with my foot. It feels squidgy. I bend down for a closer look. It's a mouse, or what's left of it. The head's still there but there's hardly any skin on its body and the giblets are oozing out.

'Mum, come quick!' I yell. She runs to the door, still clutching the bread knife. 'Look, the cat's been back, and he's brought a trophy! That means he knows where he lives!'

'Get rid of it!' hollers Mum. 'The dirty rotten beast won't be living at all if I lay eyes on it.'

I remind her that Mr Collard's note said the cat was a good mouser and at least we'll never have to worry about vermin. She goes she's never seen a mouse in all the time we've lived here until that flaming thing dropped one on the doorstep. I say no need to get hysterical, it's well dead and I'll give it a full Christian burial if that helps. She makes wild stabbing motions with the knife like that mad bloke in *Psycho* and slams the door in my face. I guess she's premenstrual. I scoop the deceased into a dustpan and hoy it over the fence into next door's garden as a treat for Sheba.

That night I hear them having sexual intercourse in bed, making unnatural noises and going, *Ssshhh, ssshhh*. I stick my head under the duvet and pull it tight over my ears. I wish I was dead.

How can Mum act normal, like a proper caring parent, after she's been fornicating like a polecat with that pervert? How can she bear to make breakfast after he's contaminated her with his bodily fluids, without wanting to be scrubbed raw, like Meryl Streep in that film where she goes radioactive. I slouch in the doorway and watch her munching toast, trying not to think of Filthy's sperms wriggling about inside her.

'What's this?' There's some stuff like hamster food in a polythene bag, all different things mixed up together.

'It's muesli,' says Mum. 'Bernard brought it with him for his breakfast, he doesn't care for Frosties. Don't mess with it, Rowena.'

I tip some into my hand. There's some flakey things that look like woodlice, brown rubbery rabbit pellets plus little yellow cubes and white slivers that remind me of something. It looks revolting.

Filthy's just roused himself from his stinking pit. Fancy making Mum get up this early when he knows she works the afternoon shift, selfish sod. I'm fizzing while I'm doing my face. It's only when I poke in my bag for a lipstick that I remember . . .

'You must eat something, Rowena, you'll be fainting by eleven o'clock,' says Mum. Filthy's at the table wearing, Omigawd, a nylon boiler suit! This is the man-with-own-business that Mum's fallen for.

'Have some muesli, young 'un,' he goes, stubbing his tab out in a saucer. 'More fibre, less fat, that's what you need.' Right. And what I don't need is *this* joker advising me on healthy living.

'I'll skip it this time, thanks Bernard,' I say, flashing my sincere smile. 'But I'll get yours if you like, save you getting up.' Mum looks up sharpish, beams at me and winks. I tip some muesli into a bowl on the worktop. Checking that no one's watching, I take the paper towel out of my bag and mix in a few of Mr Collard's toenails, swirling it all up with the top of the milk. 'Enjoy.'

Mum follows me into the hall. 'Thank you, Rowena,' she says, squeezing my hand. 'For being nice to Bernard. I'm so proud of you.'

'Nee bovva,' I go, deadpan.

On the way out I sprinkle some cat biscuits by the door. When I get home they've disappeared and there's two dead mice on the step. They've been skinned, just like the last one. Feline serial killer on the loose!

I've thought of a name for the cat. I shall call him Bundy.

# 7

## *Shrink Rapping*

An envelope plopped through the letter box today, containing a three-page questionnaire from Altamont Lodge, the psycho clinic where I'm to be assessed for insanity.

'Shall I help you fill it in?' offers Mum. 'It seems quite detailed.'

'I'm not answering this,' I say firmly. 'They're probably in cahoots with MI5 or the CIA. They'll stick it on a database and spotty schoolkids will be able to hack into it and read my private and personal secrets.'

'I doubt that very much. You'll have to complete it, Rowena, it'll save time at the assessment interview. Come on, let me help.'

'Omigawd, look what it says here!'

*As this is a teaching department it may be that other professional colleagues are present in Altamont Lodge as part of their training. In some of the clinics there are video facilities to view consultations which, if operating, will be made known to you when you meet with the psychotherapist.*

'They're going to tape me! Next thing you know, I'll pop up on telly in one of those real-life action programmes where they buy old security videos and show them on prime-time TV. No friggin' way, I'm not going and that's that!'

'Let me see.' Mum reads through it. 'It'll only be other doctors, or maybe students, they've got to learn somehow. They can hardly put rats on the couch, can they? You won't be on the telly, Rowena, look, it says everything's kept in the strictest confidence. Now let's fill in the questionnaire.'

'I can do it myself.' I snatch it off her and head for my room.

*What is the nature of your current difficulties?*
My current difficulties are of a Filthy nature.
*Please describe your relationship with:*
*Your father*
Ain't got one.
*Your mother*
Cool.
*Your siblings (please specify)*
What's a sibling?

And so on. Why am I wasting time racking my brain over this? It's all complete bollocks. Mum pootles in and asks to see what I've written but I've already sealed it up in the envelope and she hasn't got another stamp so tough shit. She offers to mail it but I'm not risking that, she'll only steam it open and pry into my innermost thoughts. Before I leave for work, she makes me *promise* to post it and checks to see my fingers aren't crossed behind my back as that means the promise doesn't count. Honestly!

In the end I do drop it in the postbox but only after I've made a lipsticked mouthprint over the sealed bit so they'll be able to tell if the CIA intercept it.

I'll say one thing for these loonbusters, they don't hang about. Barely a week later Mum has a phone call from Altamont Lodge saying they've received my questionnaire and they're fast-tracking me through the system. This could mean one of two things: (a) I gave the right answers and they want to wipe me off the books as soon as; or (b) I gave the wrong answers and they're worried I'm a danger to society. Either way, since they've had a cancellation, they can fit me in tomorrow at two o'clock. Ms P. Herron, that's who I have to see. I wonder what the 'P' stands for? Pandora, Phoebe, Petronella? It's bound to be something poncey. What on earth am I going to wear?

Naturally, I'm late. My hair wouldn't go right, even though I moussed and backcombed it to buggery. Good job I decided on my kit last night, i.e. yellow latex miniskirt, black clingy-rib top, diamond-patterned tights and my biker boots. I go easy on the make-up, only three coats of mascara with lash-thickening fibres, and Terracotta Crème lippy which doubles as eyeshadow. Mum shoots me a pained look. She says first impressions count and we don't want the psychotherapist thinking I'm a slapper before I've even opened my gob. I go Ms Herron won't give a toss about my lipstick, she's only interested in my psychological make-up so it doesn't matter whether I dress like the Queen or that mad Vivienne Westwood, I'd still be the same person inside. Mum says she's been on this earth a lot longer than me so please give her some credit and don't daub the slap on with a trowel as per usual.

Anyway, like I say, I'm late.

Not *very* late, only about ten minutes, and that's because I got lost as I couldn't be arsed to look in the *A to Z*.

Altamont Lodge is round the back of the university. It's a big stone building, the sort of house Father Ted might live in, or a potty old rich woman with twenty cats and a hunky young chauffeur who shags her for cash. The receptionist sits behind toughened glass with holes and a little microphone like in a bank. I suppose it's to protect her from axe-wielding homicidal maniacs whose treatment hasn't kicked in yet.

'I'm Rowena Vincent,' I say. 'Here to see Ms Herron. I'm a bit late, the bus driver had a heart attack at the wheel and they had to send another one from the depot. Otherwise I'd have been early.'

She flicks through a big diary. 'Take a seat in the waiting room,' she goes, without even looking at me. Maybe she's been trained not to make eye contact. I wonder if she does kung fu night classes to cope with violent loonies?

The magazines in the waiting room are pure guano. There's no *Bella* or *Chat*, just ones called *Private Eye* and *New Statesman*, full of poshgit words, hardly any pictures and no horoscopes at all. How do people know how to behave if they can't check their stars? After about ten minutes a tall woman with frizzy red hair comes down the stairs.

'Rowena Vincent? This way please.' She's wearing a long brown skirt made of sacking material and the backs of her shoes are scuffed to buggery. Her ankles are neat though, real skinny, the sort that look good in flat heels. She shows me into a room where everything's beige and tweedy – the carpet, the curtains, the chairs. The window looks out on to the university yard where all these wanky students huddle in groups, plotting demos and scoring drugs.

'Take a seat.' She waves vaguely in the direction of a chair. 'My name's Ms Herron, I'm a consultant psychologist in psychotherapy, and I'll be conducting your assessment. Thank you for returning your questionnaire so promptly.' She looks up at me and I feel myself blushing for some reason. 'We'll be returning to some of those issues in greater depth, though I'm afraid this session will be shorter than usual as we're rather late starting.'

'It wasn't my fault,' I tell her. 'There was a fatal accident on the dual carriageway, jack-knifed lorry, all the traffic had to be diverted.'

She gives me a long hard look.

'What?' I say.

'You weren't late because you felt you didn't want to come?'

'I just told you. It was total thingy, carnage. Mangled wreckage. Cop cars and ambulances everywhere, swear down. You'll see it on the news tonight. Probably.'

'Very well. Now, during this interview I'd like you to speak as freely as you can about your problems. It may be that a further appointment will be arranged. After that, I'll outline possible treatment options for you and if psychotherapy appears to be appropriate, I'll let you know what the future arrangements are likely to be. Would you like to ask me anything at this stage?'

'No. I mean yes. Where's the loo?' My bladder's busting, I should have gone before I left home.

'Do you need it right at this moment?' Her face is canny stern, I feel like I'm back at school.

'Now would be favourite. I only want a pee, I'm not going to shoot up or anything,' I assure her. 'It's probably shock from witnessing that pile-up.'

She leads me into the corridor and points me to a door with a bisexual sign, typical right-on bollocks. It's like a cupboard inside, hardly room to get my pants down, and there's no bog-paper so I have to use a tissue that I've blown my nose on. After washing my hands I see the towel roll's run out, there's just the end bit trailing on the floor, absolutely sopping. It's totally unhygienic, they want reporting to the Health & Safety people. Stuff like this could drive a maddish person over the edge.

I'm lost. Can't remember my way back. I try a door which turns out to be a stationery cupboard. As luck would have it there's some bottles of Tipp-ex staring me in the face so I pocket one as I need to make amendments to my funeral music and I can't be arsed to write it all out again. The next door I try is the right one. Ms Herron's sitting gazing out of the window. I'll bet she gets paid top dollar for this job, you'd think she could be doing something useful, filing or whatever.

Walking over to the chair I spot something I hadn't noticed before. All along the back wall there's a window, tinted dark brown. Why would they put a window in an internal wall, it's not looking out on to anything?

Then it hits me. Omigawd, it's the spying room! It's probably full of video equipment plus doctors, students, police, CIA, all watching ME! Keep calm, Rowena. Think this through. You haven't told her anything about yourself yet, so keep stum and let her do the talking. Jesus, they must have heard what I said about the fatal accident! They'll know it's a lie! I'll just have to pray that a lorry jack-knifes and someone *does* get wasted, then I can say I had a premonition.

My chair's facing the spy window. I try to move it but it won't shift, they must have bolted it to the floor. I grip the sides till my knuckles go white, then twist my head round the other way as far as it'll go, like that spooky lass, Regan, in *The Exorcist*. At least now they won't be able to see my face full-on. I keep absolutely still, listening for the whirr of a camcorder.

'Try to relax,' goes Ms Herron. 'Perhaps you'd like to begin by talking about the problems you're having at the moment.'

I clench my teeth and butt cheeks. This is an excruciating way to sit, I'll probably seize up and have to be winched and driven home on a breakdown truck.

'Rowena?' I keep my head in the sideways position and swivel my eyeballs round towards her. 'Why not get a little more comfortable in the chair.'

'*Ttthhhssssccchhh.*' A weird hissing noise comes out from between my teeth and a gobbet of spit runs down my chin. I'm straining so hard, my neck muscles are busting and my eyes feel about to pop out of my head. This is crazy. Chill out, Rowena. Let yourself go limp, pass out if you must. But I can't. I'm big fat stuck in this position, set like concrete. My heart's pounding like a jackhammer, sweat's trickling down my back and I can't get my breath. My muscles feel gripped, my whole body's locked rigid, like a stone statue. I'm petrified with tension, only trembling at the same time. Omigawd, I'm paralysed!

'Rowena, whatever is the matter?' Ms Herron looks alarmed.

I jerk my head wildly. My eyes roll about in a manic fashion.

'Stay right there,' shrieks Ms Herron, like I'm going to do a runner. She'd be crap in a crisis, she's flapping about like a shot pigeon. 'I'll get some help.'

*

I can see stars floating above me. Am I in heaven?

'Rowena? Rowena, wake up, please.' It's Nana Vincent, leaning over me, looking worried. As my eyes slowly focus I realise I'm gazing at the stick-on fluorescent stars on my ceiling. I'm in my own bed. And it isn't Nana Vincent. It's Mum, looking really, really old, her face lined with creases. We must have a girlie chat about moisturiser.

'Thank God you're all right, Rowena, I've been out of my mind with worry. The doctor's here to see you.'

Dr Pooley's nasal hairs materialise above me, followed by his horse's nostrils and saggy cheeks. He shines a light in my eyes, holds my wrist for a bit, then pats me on the hand. 'You'll live,' he says.

I can't remember how I got here. I can't even remember the last thing I remember. My head feels fuzzy, like it's filled with cotton wool, and my fingers and toes are tingling. I feel as if I'm floating, weightless, like a cosmonaut, or bobbing gently on a giant lilo, warm waves lapping around me. If I'm still alive, this is how I want my life to be.

Calm, safe, no worries. Cocooned from the world.

Mum tries to explain what happened. Her voice sounds watery and strange, like a mermaid's.

'The doctor says it was probably a panic attack. Someone from Altamont Lodge drove you to hospital, they were very concerned, especially Ms Herron. They rang me at work and when I got to the hospital, you were sitting in a day room watching telly. You spoke to me, don't you remember? We came home in a taxi, you told the driver to turn his country music tape off. He wasn't too happy about it, I'm sure he overcharged me. You must remember that, surely?'

I shake my head. At least I try, but it feels like a ball of candyfloss.

'Dr Pooley came out straight away,' continues Mum. 'I was beside myself with worry. He gave you something to calm you down, then you fell asleep. Never mind, you'll probably remember everything in the morning when the effects have worn off.'

Oh, but I won't, Mother dear. Count on it. I've decided not to remember.

This is cool. I'm a *real invalid*. The doctor says I'm to have complete bed rest, which includes the couch so I can watch telly. The floaty sensation's gone off a bit, at least I feel connected to my body now, but my head's still woolly.

Mum's perching on the side of the bed. 'I've brought you some milky coffee, like your Nana Vincent used to make.' She feels my forehead. 'How are you today? Still a bit groggy?'

'Uh-huh. What time is it?'

'Past three. You've had a canny long sleep, it'll do you good.'

'You're late for work.'

'Don't be silly. I'm not leaving you on your own.'

'But—'

'No buts, Rowena. You're not to get anxious. Just relax, there's nothing for you to worry about. Now finish your coffee and I'll run you a nice bath with that White Musk bubble stuff.'

That's the last thing I remember. Now here it is, tomorrow. Mum reckons the hot bath must have tired me out because when she put me back to bed I slept right through.

'Mother Nature's healing you the holistic way.' It sounds dead soppy coming from Mum, I hope she's not going all vegetarian on me. 'I rang the doctor just in case but he says you're to get as much sleep as you like at the moment. Try to sit up now, I've made you some toast. Goodness knows when you ate last, it's no wonder you feel weak.'

But the food won't go down. It's as if there's a tennis ball stuck in my throat. Choked, that's how I feel. Well choked. I manage a couple of spoonfuls of tomato soup but instantly my gut starts churning so I have to stagger to the bog and it runs right through me. I feel naused out and retch over the sink but nothing comes.

When I peep in the mirror my eyelids are half shut and my skin's pale yellow, like watered-down custard. My hair's hanging down in rats' tails. I look a hundred years old. Jesus, what's wrong with me?

I'm limper than an old dishrag. My legs are shaking like bastards and my knees keep buckling under me. Mum insists on washing my bum with a flannel, the shame of it! I haven't got the energy to protest. Then she dresses me in my old jim-jams which I thought she'd chucked out years ago. They're soft and snuggly and remind me of when I used to feel safe and . . . *happy*? Have I ever been happy? Suppose I must have, perhaps it was in another life. She wraps her towelling dressing gown round me, the one I've always loathed because it makes her look like a hippo. It's spotless white and fluffy and smells of talc. I shuffle downstairs like an old biddy, clutching on to the banister, scared of falling arse over tit. Mum lays me on the couch and puts a bucket by the side in case I need to vomit. She turns on the telly with the volume down low.

This ancient couple, as thin as a pair of skellies, have been married for seventy years and they're 'celebrating' the anniversary in an old people's home with loads of other coffin dodgers. A smarmy interviewer asks them the secret of a long and happy relationship. He has to yell because their ears don't work.

'Don't sleep on an argument,' says the gadge. You can hear his dentures clacking around in his gob.

'Aye, he's right, is Bert,' the biddy goes in a little thin voice. 'Never go to bed without making up.'

That's rubbish. Everybody knows you should cleanse, tone and nourish at night otherwise your pores get clogged to buggery and your skin ends up like a lunar landscape. I ought to ring in and tell them, only I can't be arsed. Maybe I'll have a wee kip instead.

'You could sleep for England,' says Mum, running her fingers through my feggy hair. 'Let's freshen you up a bit.' She rubs a damp flannel over my face. Jesus, I hope it's not the cacky one she washed my bum with! 'I'm going to do you some scrambled eggs, get some goodness inside you.' She kisses my forehead and potters into the kitchen.

What does she mean – get some goodness inside me? When my face goes spotty she always says it's the badness coming out of me. Maybe that's it. I'm *rotten* inside. Full of wickedness, festering evil, eating me away, multiplying and spreading like cancer of the – I dunno, the *soul* or something. You can't cure that with scrambled eggs. *Badness.* It's written all through me like lettering on a stick of rock.

Was I born this way? Expelled from the womb with a black heart and a warped mind? Perhaps they couldn't test for stuff like that in those days. But say they *had* known – what then? I'd probably have been left on a hillside to starve, or dismembered and thrown to a pack of starving dogs. I could have ended up in a laboratory, floating in a pickle jar labelled GENETICALLY BAD BABY for wanky students to snigger at.

Or else . . . Or else something happened, some majorly traumatic event too horrible to remember, that made me this way. Perhaps that's what they suspect, which is why they sent me to a shrink, forcing withdrawals from my memory bank, like sticking a bit of plastic into a cash machine. Well, tough shit. Read the flashing message.

*LEAVE MY MIND ALONE!*

Anyways, it doesn't matter whether I was born bad or made bad. Either way it's not my fault, so who cares?

Mum's voice tickles my ears awake.

'Someone from Altamont Lodge rang this morning asking if you're better,' she says. 'They want to wossname, reschedule your appointment.'

'No! I'm never going back there!' I scream. 'They can't make me. I'll top myself first.' Jesus, what's wrong with me? I'm totally freaked.

'All right, calm down.' Mum sits on the bed and holds my hand.

'Of course they can't *make* you, Rowena, not if you really don't want to go. But you'll never get better on your own, they're only trying to help.'

Tears start welling up behind my eyes so I bite my bottom lip until I taste blood, and twiddle with my pyjama collar for comfort like I used to when I was little.

Stop it! Stay hard, Rowena. Rock hard.

'Budge over, let's have a snuggle.' Mum sneaks under the duvet and cuddles me in close. 'Now, what's all this about? You can tell me, Rowena. I'll understand, no matter how daft it sounds. It does me in to see you so miserable.' She kisses the top of my head. 'I do love you, more than you realise. I'm your mum. That's what mums do.'

And I'm thinking, but what about dads?

Guess what happens? I only friggin' crack, don't I? Only sing like the proverbial canary, tell Mum all about the video equipment, police, CIA, etc. So much for being hard. I'm about as hard as a friggin' blancmange, me. I might have known Mum would be on the blower to Altamont Lodge as soon as, grassing me up to the so-called professionals.

'You're not to be cross with me,' she begins. 'I spoke to Ms Herron, explained why you were so upset the other day.'

Betrayed! By my own mother!

'She says to assure you there was no one behind the window, she'd have had to ask your permission first. We've arranged for you to see her next week, and I'm coming with you this time,' she says, like that's a bonus. 'I've cleared it with work, told Mrs Marr you've got a chill in your kidneys. Oh, and Ms Herron says she'll see you in a different room. One without windows.'

But walls have ears, don't they?

Mum takes me to Altamont Lodge in a taxi, as a treat, so my madness won't be seen in public. She stands clutching her handbag in the doorway while Ms Herron lets me look round the new room.

It's geet poky, about the size of our bathroom, with two chairs, a tiny coffee table and a single bed with loads of cushions. There's a box of Kleenex on the table.

'Feel free to inspect it,' Ms Herron goes. Mum nods in encouragement. I thump the cushions and peer under the bed, searching for electronic devices. They conceal wee microphones anywhere these days, in stiletto heels, felt-tip pens, tampons even, plus they make tiny cameras the size of matchboxes. That box on the table could be bugged, but I'll never know without yanking all the tissues out. Suddenly I spot a red light high up in a corner, blinking on and off.

'What's that?' I challenge her.

'I think it's attached to the intruder alarm,' says Ms Herron. 'Nothing to worry about, it's not activated at the moment.'

'So why is it flashing?'

'It's probably on standby. The security person switches it on after the last staff member leaves.'

I cross my arms and stare silently at the floor. I'm not saying another word and that's that. Intruder alarm? She must think I fell off a Christmas tree. For all I know it could be a mini polygraph thingy that lets out a deafening bleep if I tell a lie. Or a machine that sucks thoughts out of my head and turns them into 3-D computer graphics. Well, it *could* be. They put stuff in swimming pools that turns the water blue if you piss in it, so anything's possible.

The upshot is that Ms Herron scuttles out to reception and gets them to turn off the so-called 'intruder alarm' while the interview's in progress, which proves they must have had something dodgy to hide.

Mum says thank you to Ms Herron and tugs my sleeve, meaning I ought to thank her as well, though I don't see why. I'm beginning to get the hang of standing up for my own human rights so I insist on looking in the rooms on either side. One's the cleaner's cupboard where they keep the bin bags and hoover, and the other's an empty office belonging to a bloke who's on extended sick leave. I can't find anything incriminating but that only shows how clever they are.

'Happy now?' says Mum.

'Suppose so.'

'Be a good girl and answer the questions truthfully. I'll be downstairs in the waiting room.' She gives my hand a little squeeze. 'Thank you for being so patient, Ms Herron,' I hear her whisper on the way out.

This is it, then. An hour from now the woman with the frizzy hair will decide whether (a) I'm fit to be released into the community, or (b) I should be certified insane and locked away with terminally mad people. I can see the upside to (b). No worries, doped up on major tranx, I could sit hugging my knees and rocking for the rest of my days. The downside is hospital scran, three starchy meals a day – porridge, mashed spud and rice pudding. Suppose I could always hold the dietician hostage until she agreed to get in a supply of chips and brown sauce specially for me.

'You describe your relationship with your mother as "cool". Would you like to elaborate on that?' God knows how long Ms Herron's been talking, I haven't heard a word she said.

'Shouldn't I be on the couch?' I ask.

Ms Herron stares at me. 'Would you *like* to be on the couch?'

'Is that what other people do when they see shrinks?'

'Do you *want* to be like other people?'

I shrug. 'Don't care. No, not really. Not like any of the people I know, anyway. What are you saying – I should stay on the chair?'

'I think that would be preferable.' Ms Herron crosses her legs with a swish of stockings. 'Now, about your relationship with your mother. You appear to be quite fond of one another.'

'I guess.'

'Yet you said previously that your relationship with her was cool?'

'Yeah. And?'

We go round in circles for ten minutes before I realise the stupid bint doesn't know the meaning of the word 'cool'. And she's supposed to be educated! Hasn't she got a friggin' dictionary?

'Cool, you know. As in Cool as Fuck. Dope. The Business.' She looks blank. '*Great*, comprende?'

'Oh yes, I see. I assumed you meant chilly, frosty,' she goes. 'I understand now that you've explained, but it would help if you could avoid using colloquialisms.'

'I don't use *any* drugs.'

She sighs and checks her watch. 'Perhaps we should move on to your relationship with your father? He's an absent parent, correct?'

'Couldn't be more absent.'

'In what sense?'

'In the sense that he's never coming back.'

'Why do you say that?'

'Because . . . Because he's *dead!*' It sounds brilliant, mega dramatic. I don't flicker a single eyelash, even manage a bit lump in the throat for effect.

Ms Herron looks flustered. 'I'm sorry, I hadn't picked up on that.' She riffles through her notes. 'Would you like to tell me about him?'

'Nope.'

'Do you find it painful to talk about?'

'Dunno.'

'You don't know? Could you explain?'

'I never talk about it. Never.'

'Perhaps now might be a good time to try.'

I bury my head in my hands, feeling suddenly exhausted and overcome. Hot tears appear from nowhere, melting my mascara.

'I'm scared to,' I gulp. 'It was so terrible. The way he died . . . No one should have to suffer like that.'

I can't control the blubbing, the tears are cascading out of me like waterfalls. This time they're for real. Ms Herron shoves the tissues towards me. When the crying finally subsides, I get an attack of hiccups, typical!

'We can talk about this some other time if you'd prefer,' Ms Herron says, her face completely expressionless, like I haven't just had a nervous breakdown right in front of her.

'No. Give me a minute. I know I'll have to – *hic* – deal with it sometime.' I wipe my snotty nose with the tissue and pull another fistful out of the box. 'Maison well be – *hic* – now.'

'When you feel ready,' she says, settling back in her chair and fluffing up her frizzy mop.

I gather my thoughts and take a deep breath.

'It was awful,' I begin. 'Like something out of a – *hic* -horror movie . . .'


Mum's waiting for me downstairs, flicking through one of the poncey magazines. 'How did it go?' she asks. 'Was it very upsetting?'

'No pain, no gain,' I tell her. 'Sure, it was hard work but once I got going it was fine. She's given me another appointment.'

'How do you feel about that?'

'Cool.'

'That's a relief. I'm so proud of you, Rowena. Come on, I'll treat you to a burger.'

'With double fries?'

'Naturally,' she goes. The lines vanish off her face like magic when she smiles.

On the way to Burger King we pass Wyley's cybercaff. Normally I'd jump out of a plane sooner than enter a saddo dive like that but an idea flashes into my head. I need to go over what I told Ms Herron and try to figure out what her reaction will be. Shrinks are supposed to be unshockable but she looked pretty gobsmacked to me. Maybe I went overboard on the details of Dad's untimely demise. I make a mental note to visit the cybercaff and surf the Net for info.

# 8

## Lost in Cyberspace

Filthy sleeps over at our house three or four times a week now. Weird and unspeakable things are going on. Once when I went to the bog in the night I heard this squelchy noise coming from Mum's bedroom, it sounded like baby Maggie from *The Simpsons* sucking her dummy. I earwigged outside the door for a bit until it hit me – it was them, *doing it*!

Another time I heard a power tool buzzing, and figured Filthy must be putting shelves up in Mum's room. I nearly stormed in and read them the riot act about doing DIY in the middle of the night as *some* people have to get up for work. The next day I had a snoop round and instead of shelves, I found, Omigawd, a *sex toy* under Mum's bed! It was a massive rubber penis with veins like lugworms and a switch to make it vibrate. My mum plays sordid sex games with Filthy Luker! I was so naused out I wrapped it up in a tissue and slung it over the fence into next-door's garden where Sheba pounced on it thinking it was a bone and crunched it to bits. Maybe I should have taken the batteries out first. Anyway, I've decided to stick empty eggcartons round my room to soundproof myself from their primitive animal behaviour.

Then, when I was borrowing some money from Mum's purse, I found a box of slimy things in the bedside cabinet. They're called Femidoms. I nearly vomited when I read the instructions – surely you're not meant to shove them *up there*! I hoyed them in the dustbin along with Filthy's skidmarked underpants which he'd chucked in the washing basket right next to our stuff.

I also discovered a packet of condoms, 'ribbed for extra arousal', right there in the bathroom for all to see. I snatched them off the shelf and stuffed them down the bottom of my sports bag underneath all the make-up. It's disgusting. This sort of thing could psychologically scar a sensitive adolescent for life.

Mum corners me in the bathroom. 'Have you been moving any of my things, Rowena?' She's mad but embarrassed at the same time. I decide to front it out.

'Certainly not,' I go, all innocent. 'Why, have you lost something?'

'Aye, the will to live,' she snaps. 'Now what have you done with my stuff?'

'What stuff?'

'Personal objects.'

'Like what?'

'You know exactly like what, young lady. Now what have you done with them? I won't ask you again.' She raises her hand to bop me one on the head.

I stand my ground. 'That's right,' I say 'resort to violence.' She drops her hand. 'Look, don't blame me. I wouldn't touch your wanky personal objects with a bargepole. It sounds more like the sort of stunt an earthbound spirit would pull, like in that film *Poltergeist*.'

She glares murderously at me. 'If I catch a poltergeist or anything else interfering again I'll chop its flaming fingers off.'

I really don't know how long I can cope with this shit, it's making me mentally ill. To keep myself sane I do random acts of rebellion in secret, like shave the mould off the damp bit in the bathroom with Filthy's razor and use his toothbrush to scrub round the rim of the lavvy. In front of Mum I try to keep my lip buttoned and pretend not to loathe and detest him to infinity. It's all part of my game plan to lull them into a false sense of thingy before I make my move and annihilate Filthy for good. I deserve an Oscar, honest I do.

Well, looks like it's backfired on me, big-time.

They've just got back from the stupid line dancing down the Labour Club and they're farting about showing me how to do the Tush Push. It's beyond sad, it's tragic.

'You should come with us next time, young 'un,' says Filthy. His check shirt's stained with sweat under the armpits, total gross-out. 'You don't need a partner – hey, and you never know your luck, you might cop off with somebody.' Right. Some paunchy old tosser in a fake Stetson. I'd rather be in traction.

Mum pootles in with a tray of cheese sarnies. 'Rowena,' she says, shooting a quick grin at Filthy. They're cooking something up, I can tell. 'Bernard has something to ask you.'

Oh, Jesus, he's going to ask for her hand in holy matrimony! My gut does a triple somersault and all my past life flashes in front of me. Filthy Luker as my stepdad – the shame of it! I'll have to kill myself! I curl up like a foetus and brace myself for excruciating news.

Filthy sparks up a tab. Maybe I'll die naturally from passive smoking. 'It's my birthday on Saturday,' he goes. 'I'll be forty. The big four-o. Life begins at, and all that.' He's lying, he's got to be fifty at least! 'I'm taking Jean out for a meal and I'd like you to come too, celebrate our new spirit of détente, as it were.'

(Spirit of day tont? What's that, some sort of cocktail?) Whew, well at least they're not getting engaged. It feels like a last-minute reprieve from Death Row. A bunch of stuff flashes through my brain in a millisecond. How can I get out of it? Should I go, for Mum's sake? Will there be chips? What could I wear?

'Depends,' I say, cagey like. 'Where are you taking her?'

'I thought that Indian restaurant, the New Bengal on Staveley Street. They serve big portions and it's not over the top pricewise.'

Indian! I hate hotbum scran, it stinks like dead dogs. Plus it sounds like a cheapskate joint, typical!

'It'll be my treat,' he smarms. 'And you're welcome to bring a friend.'

64

Oh, triffic. 'Like who?'

'I don't know, you must have friends. Who were you pally with at school?'

'That wanky lot? Puh, I wouldn't piss on them if they were on fire.' Mum taps her finger on her mouth meaning, *Watch your language*.

'What about that girl who had the baby?' she suggests. 'Gemma Probert. You used to be matey with her.'

'No I never, not specially.' Someone walks over my grave, making me shudder. 'Look, there isn't anyone, right? You two go on your own, don't bother about me.'

'Celebrate without you?' says Filthy, like the idea's unthinkable. 'Over my dead body.'

'Whatever,' I goes.

Mum flashes me a look. 'Why not ask Dean, that boy from work?' she says. 'He sounds like a nice young man.'

'He's out clubbing on Saturdays.' She does that eyebrow thing. God, cut me some slack, Ma! 'OK, I'll mention it, but if he says no, I'm not going, that's the deal, right?'

'Agreed, young 'un.' Filthy winks at Mum and she smiles and wiggles her shoulders in a bimboid fashion. Uh-oh. I'll have to put plugs in my ears tonight, that's for sure.

I friggin' dread bedtimes. They're at it like trains. How can they inflict this on me? I ought to report them to the NSPCC or something for emotional abuse. I tried to ring ChildLine a couple of years ago to complain about Mum not letting me have my earlobe tattooed but the number was always engaged and anyway I went off the idea in the end. I listen to a few tracks from *Urban Hymns* turned right up loud on my Discman, praying they'll be quick about it, and maybe there *is* a God because when I take the headphones off, Filthy's snoring like a bull elephant with catarrh. I lie in the dark staring at the stick-on fluorescent stars on my ceiling. I wonder what it feels like to be dead. It couldn't be worse than this.

All of a sudden there's a bloodcurdling yowl from outside. My bowels turn to water and next-door's Sheba goes ballistic, barking her stupid head off. I rush to the window expecting to see a rabid werewolf and there's long-lost Bundy, struggling over the fence into our garden, trailing something between his legs. My Trusty Sidekick has returned!

I hurtle downstairs and unlock the back door. Bundy plods round the corner, dragging a rabbit nearly as big as himself which he drops on the doorstep. Omigawd, it's still alive! Not for long though. When Bundy offs it, it squeals like a stuck pig.

'Drop it! Leave, Bundy!' I shout a bit hysterically, but he's ripping the skin off the poor rabbit in a frenzied attack, disembowelling it and growling like a crazed tiger. I shut the door and leave him to it. My pet's a bloodthirsty psycho! Darren the Mutant from next-door flings the upstairs window open and yells at Sheba to shut the fuck up. He maison well save his boggy breath for all the notice she takes, though of course English isn't Sheba's first language, her being a German Shepherd dog.

After a few minutes I peek outside. There's hardly anything left of the rabbit, just an ear, an eye and the scut. Bundy's scoffed the bones as well as the innards, the poor lad must have been starving. Now he's sprawled out next to the dustbin washing his face all innocent, like he hasn't just committed a brutal homicide. I crouch down and reach my hand out to stroke him, thinking he'll spit or bat me one but he rolls over on his back, cocks his legs up in the air and lets me tickle his big bunnyful tum. I saw it on *Animal Hospital* that cats only do that when they totally trust you as it means they're showing their vulnerability. That's not all he's showing. I'm sure his balls have grown, they're as big as satsumas.

'Come on, son,' I murmur. 'Give us a bit cuddle.' Bundy lets me pick him up and put him on my shoulder. He weighs a ton. When I tickle him behind his ear he starts purring really, really loud, like a cavalcade of Lambrettas. I can't shove him back into the urban wilderness and Mum'll throttle me if I let him indoors so I shut him in the shed and nip back into the house.

I rummage round in the washing basket and pull out Filthy's cowboy shirt. It stinks of rotten armpits but it'll have to do until I can find something more decent. When I lay it in his box, Bundy does that treading thing with his paws, turns a few circles, then flops down and shuts his eyes, still purring.

I have a brilliant night's sleep, the best in ages. Now Bundy's back, at least I've got someone on my side. *Rowena: Warrior Princess* and her Trusty Sidekick can begin their campaign for world domination.

Filthy Luker, prepare to meet thy doom!

It's the day for my appointment with Ms Herron. I nick off work early so I can call at Wyley's cybercaff to do some research on the Internet. The place is full of nerds and wankpots drinking treacly coffee and gassing on about URLs and ISPs. I print off the Web pages I need and leave the SADs to their empty lives.

The receptionist at Altamont Lodge shoos me into the waiting room where I kill time by reading leaflets about mental health services and how to reclaim bus fares if you're on benefit. They're boring as fuck but still more interesting than the stupid magazines. I'm trying to work out how to blag a Kit Kat out of the vending machine without paying when a bloke wanders in. At first I think he might be one of the quacks as he's wearing a suit but then he sits down and starts flicking through *Private Eye*. He keeps giving me shifty glances over the top of the mag and fidgeting about in his chair. There's something dead scary about his eyes, they remind me of that crazy in *One Flew Over the Cuckoo's Nest*. Oh Jesus, I'm alone in a room with a madman! Now he's fiddling in his trouser pocket, I'll bet that's where he keeps his hatchet. Should I chin him one or try to reason with him? I'm working out the odds when Ms Herron appears. My shrink! My saviour!

We're in the room with the bed again. After I do a quick inspection for electronic surveillance equipment, Ms Herron rings reception and asks them to turn off the 'intruder alarm' until further notice.

'That guy in the waiting room,' I say. 'Is he mad?'

'What do you understand by the word "mad"?'

'Oh, never mind,' I go. I'm about to ask if I should lie on the couch, but life's too short. It's pointless asking her anything, she always answers a question with another question. Maybe she doesn't know the answers herself.

We sit there for ages not saying anything. I check out the pictures on the wall, they're just a load of squiggly lines and splodges, a chimp could have painted them. Call that art? Bollocks more like. Her eyes burn into me. This is hopeless, a total waste of money, at least it would be if I was paying.

'What?' I go. 'Why do you keep staring at me?'

'I was wondering what you were thinking.'

'Nothing. I'm thinking nothing.' She cocks her head to one side and raises her eyebrows like a question. '*What?*' I snap. This is starting to piss me right off. 'I dunno what you want me to say.'

Ms Herron does that swishy thing with her stockings. 'Let's pick up on something we talked about last week. You seem to feel responsible for your father's death. Why is that?'

Oh shit. Good job I spent some quality thinking time on this. *And* checked out the details on the Web. I sort the words in my head. Need to get this spot-on.

'I'd been naughty,' I begin. 'They told me never to play with knives and stuff but my fringe was too long and I needed it cut so I nicked Mum's nail scissors. Made a right mess of my hair, hacked it off too short, looked like a Council lawnmower job. Didn't know any better then, I was only a kid.'

'This was how long ago?'

'Erm, eight years. Yes, I'd have been about eight. Course, they could see I'd cut my hair even though I swore black was white I hadn't. I hid the nail scissors in a little plastic purse I used to wear round my neck. I was trying to sneak them back into Mum's bag when Dad walked in the room. I nearly pooed my pants! He asked what I was hiding behind my back. When I wouldn't show him he turned it into a game, a sort of wrestling match, only just teasing. That's when it happened. It was an accident, swear down.'

I pull a tissue from the box and blow my snitch, playing for time. Ms Herron watches me like a hawk. Doesn't she know it's rude to stare?

'Somehow he got jabbed in the leg with the scissors,' I continue. 'Blood started seeping through his trousers, only a few spots but it set me off crying like a loony, dead hysterical I was. Dad showed me his leg to shut me up. You had to look really hard, it was just a tiny wee scratch, and he said it didn't hurt so I calmed down after a bit.'

'But you say it was an accident. No one's fault. Why would you hold yourself responsible?'

'Because that's what set it off. Just that little nick in his leg.' I start blinking like a strobe light to keep back the hot tears welling up. 'Can I have a breather now?'

'Of course, if that helps.' Ms Herron slides the tissues towards me. 'Would you like a drink of water?'

I dab my eyes carefully, trying not to smear my make-up. 'Aye, I'm canny parched.'

She shimmies out of the room, leaving me staring at the floor. Or rather, at her handbag. It's bulging wide open, stuffed with letters and books, that's no way to treat real leather. I crouch down for a quick skeg and my hand finds a little wooden thing, about the size of a packet of tabs. What can it be? It rattles a bit when I shake it. There must be a secret way to open it but I can't suss it out. Then I hear her slingbacks slapping up the stairs so I stuff it in my pocket right down deep so it won't fall out. I'll study it at home.

'In your own time,' says Miss Herron, settling down for the next thrilling instalment. I take a deep breath and begin.

'The cut on his leg turned red in the night. Dad felt like shit, thought he had the flu, so he stayed off work the next day. Anyway, it started spreading and swelling up. After a while it turned purple and blue, then this massive blister appeared, full of bright yellow pus, just like custard.'

Ms Herron plucks a tissue out of the box and holds it to her mouth.

'By that night you could see it spreading, about an inch every hour. The blister was humongous, dark purple, like an aubergine growing out of his leg. Mum called the doctor. They rushed him to hospital and pumped antibiotics into him but it was too late. Gangrene had set in. He died in excruciating agony. His skin was totally eaten away. Devoured by a flesh-eating bug.'

Ms Herron's eyes are like saucers. She shudders slightly and coughs into the tissue. I hope she's not going to spew.

'Necrotising fasciitis, that's its proper name,' I continue. 'Caused by a type of bacteria, Strepto-something "A". You know that bloke who invented the Muppets? Well, he died of the same thing.' It's amazing what you can find out from the Internet.

'Excuse me, I'll be back in a moment.' Ms Herron scuttles out of the room holding a tissue to her mouth. She's gone for ages, I could risk another rummage in her bag but actually I'm too knackered from all this hard brainwork. When she comes back her hair's wet at the front so either she splashed water on her face to cool down, or she's been throwing up in the bog.

'So you see why I feel to blame?' I continue. 'If only I hadn't cut my stupid fringe, none of this would have happened. Plus it took months for it to grow back right.'

She scratches her frizzy head, releasing a shower of scurf. 'We must end there, Rowena. I'd like you to come back at the same time next week and we'll discuss possible treatment options.'

'Cool. I mean, triffic.'

Back in my room, I work out how to open that thing I nicked from Ms Herron's bag. It's made of two pieces of smooth reddish wood that slide apart. There's a little round mirror inside. I hold it above my nose to check for bogeys and a really weird thing happens. *It's not my face!* Well, it is, sort of. It's the face I used to have when I was little, before I started plucking my eyebrows, before I ruined my complexion with chips, a cute, flawless, rosy-cheeked face. How spooky is that? It's wearing a worried expression, like a wee child in a supermarket about to burst out crying any second because she's lost her mum. Or her dad. I stare and stare, then it seems to morph into my *now* face, the one with smudgy mascara and chin spots.

No, it can't have happened. My eyes are canny tired, that's all. I must have imagined it.

At my next appointment I nearly tell Ms Herron about my weird experience with her mirror but manage to stop myself in time. She's chuntering on about my problems, some crack about unresolved conflicts around Dad's death. 'Incomplete mourning', she calls it. She reckons some talking therapy will do the trick. I'm not really listening because I can't keep my eyes off her kit. She's wearing an embroidered turquoise top and Chinese silk trousers, those half-mast ones, with ballet pump things.

'Given that I feel you would benefit from psychotherapy, we appear to have two options.' I wonder if she's off to a fancy-dress party straight from work. 'Option one: I could assign a psychotherapist to work with you on your problems.'

I click back to earth. 'Man or woman?'

'That depends on a number of factors. Availability is one, we'd have to do a caseload audit. Compatibility is another, obviously you and the therapist need to feel you can work together. Do you have a preference as to male or female?'

I shrug. 'Not fussed.'

'You would meet here, probably once a week, for an hour's session, fifty minutes to be exact.'

'Will I get to lie on the couch?'

Ms Herron frowns at me. She frowns a lot. 'That would be for you and your therapist to decide. I have to tell you at this stage that our waiting list is around six months so unfortunately your treatment wouldn't start immediately.'

'I can't be *that* mad, then.'

'I'm sorry?'

'If you thought I was a real basket case, you'd get me in sooner.'

When Ms Herron frowns her eyebrows nearly meet in the middle, like Liam Gallagher's. She doesn't do herself any favours by pulling faces, somebody ought to tell her. I'll bet she doesn't shave her armpits. I wonder if she's got a boyfriend. Shouldn't think so.

'It's not quite as clear-cut as that.'

I start picking the skin round my nails. This whole deal is boring as fuck. 'What's the other option?'

She flicks through her file and pulls out a sheet of paper. I'm supposed to sit here like cheese at ninepence while she reads through it, as if she couldn't have done that earlier. It's a friggin' liberty, my time's valuable, plus I want to get to the Void before it shuts as they've got some leather kecks in.

'Option two,' she goes after aeons, 'is for you to attend group therapy.'

'What, like the AA?' A picture flashes into my mind. Me, in front of a load of alkies. *My name is Rowena Vincent and I sink three bottles of Bailey's before I can drag my ass out of bed.*

'If I may explain,' she says. 'We have a group of younger people who meet here on Wednesdays. They're from varying backgrounds but the common denominator is that they're all experiencing psychological or emotional difficulties.'

'Nutters, you mean?' I say. 'Psychopaths, that sort of thing?'

Ms Herron does the Liam thing with her eyebrows again. If the wind changes, they'll stick like that. 'I don't consider those to be helpful labels. And I can assure you, you won't be in any physical danger. They're young people, such as yourself, working through their problems in a safe, non-threatening environment. It's a recent experiment, but it appears to be working successfully. You might find it more comfortable, more *productive*, to work in a group context than on a one-to-one basis.'

Jesus, it's half past five already. The Void shuts at six.

'Go on then,' I tell her. 'Stick us down for it. Is that all? Can I go now? I've got a salsa class in half an hour.'

She witters on saying someone will contact me blah blah blah, but I've already got my coat on and I'm legging it down the stairs.

It's dead quiet at work next morning so Mrs Marr asks me to file invoices in Mr Crowther's office.

'Put them into alphabetical order,' she goes. '"A" first, then "B",' like I'm an imbecile.

When I get to 'F' I think, fuck this, it's pure braindeath, so I switch on the computer. I bet there's a blackjack game on it somewhere, I just need to work out how to access it. *Click-click-click.* There's no security on this system, a chimp could get in, it's disgraceful. I open Mr Crowther's correspondence files and read a few of his personal letters, mostly boring tax stuff, then into the payroll program to check out how much everybody earns. Jesus, how does Ray feed a family and run that gas-guzzler on his measly salary? He must be on to some scam or other. The only time the computer asks for a password is to get into Mr Crowther's e-mails. I try Death, Funeral and Hearse, but zilch. Corpse, Remains and Stiff, ditto. Then – I don't know why, it just flew psychically into my head – I try Margot, which is Mrs Marr's first name. Bingo! I'm in.

I scroll down the list of messages. Most of them are spam but there's a long boring one from Mr Crowther's daughter in

Germany attaching a picture of her new baby who looks like a Martian. Then I spot one from somebody called Camilla so I open it.

*Hi, I'm a 22-year-old white female, 5'5" tall, weighing 110 lbs. I have long black hair, hazel eyes and am considered attractive. I also have many gifs of myself so you can see exactly who I am. I'm very interested in Phone and Casual Discreet Encounters, seeking to have some fun while still young and wild. Just visit my Web page, see my pics and contact me directly.*

Shit a brick! Old Crowther's a cyberperv! I'm so gobsmacked I nearly jump out of my skin when the phone rings.

'Your mother wants a quick word, Rowena,' squeaks Mrs Marr. 'Oh, and hurry up with that filing, Mr Crowther's on his way back. Putting you through.'

I'm in a right flap, clicking the mouse like buggery to shut the computer down. 'What?' I shriek into the phone.

'Is that you, Rowena? You sound frantic.'

*Click-click-click.* I press the delete key by mistake and Camilla the Hooker hurtles into cyberspace.

'I'm really busy. Quick, what do you want?'

'No need to snap. I just wanted to remind you to ask Dean . . . you know.'

*Click-click-click.* Jesus, I just deleted Crowther's daughter's e-mail – and the baby Martian photo too!

'Ask him what?' Oh shit, the screen's frozen.

'About Saturday. Bernard's birthday meal.'

'Right. Right.' *This program has performed an illegal operation and will be shut down. This may result in loss of data.* Oh fuckshit, it's crashed! I slam the phone down so hard it bounces.

Panic-panic-panic! I'm sweating like a fat lass, you could fry eggs on my face. I yank the computer plug out of the wall socket. Jesus, what if I've wiped all the company records – accounts, payroll, Mr Crowther's e-mails, the lot! A thriving business bankrupted. Now I really *will* have to kill myself.

Dean catches me leaving Mr Crowther's office. 'What's up?' he goes, peering into my wild, stary eyes. My mouth won't work, my legs are wobbly and my hands feel useless, like flippers. 'Come out the back,' he says. 'I know what you need.'

We go behind the joinery shop and Dean fiddles in his pocket and pulls out a baccy tin. 'I usually skin up about now, anyway.'

'I friggin' hate the smell of dope.' My voice sounds weird, like I'm being strangled from the inside.

'It's shitkickin' stuff, this, you'll be buzzing till Christmas. Come on, Rowena, it's only herbs.' Dean rolls a spliff one-handed, his other arm round me. He sparks up and takes a long deep drag. 'Mmm, sweet,' he goes, blowing smoke out of his nostrils. Yuk, dope smells worse than decaying corpses. 'Nought to sixty in one toke. Here, try it. Take it right down.'

When the smoke hits the back of my throat it feels like my internal organs are being cremated. The sicky sweet pong makes me nearly throw up. 'It's foul,' I say. 'My lungs are on fire. Here, take it.'

Dean says the trick with skunk is to persevere, it's always a blinder the first time. He has a few pulls on the joint and offers it to me again. I shake my head. That business with the computer's really got to me, my eyes are hot and stinging and I've got all on not to burst into tears. 'Hey,' says Dean, pulling me in for a cuddle and resting my head on his shoulder. 'What's all this about?'

He kisses my hair and a warm glow spreads through my stomach, like when you wet yourself, only nicer. A switch clicks in my brain. Get a grip, Rowena.

'It's that shit you're smoking, it's stinging my eyes.' I pull away from him. 'Now give over, you're messing my hair up, it took for ever to get it right this morning.'

Jesus, that was close, I was on the verge of confessing all about the computer catastrophe.

Dean laughs. 'You're a spacemonkey, you. I don't know where you're coming from.' He kisses me right gentle on the forehead. My insides go all tickly and I feel like I want to pull him to me and hug him tight but I fight off the urge.

'Back off, pot-head,' I say, sharper than I need to. 'I've got something to ask you.' I tell him about Filthy's birthday meal, how it'll be a total nightmare and I'll fully understand if he says no, in fact he'll be doing me a favour. I daren't look at him so I stare down at my Docs. They could do with a polish.

'Hell, why not,' says Dean. 'Let's go for it. It'll be a laugh.'

'Don't put money on it.'

I'm rigid with shock, but pleased, sort of. He said yes! So what if I *have* wiped the computer? Who cares? I'll just deny it.

When I get home there's a brown envelope with a City Health franking mark. It's a letter from Miss Virginia Prosser at Altamont Lodge, asking me to attend a group therapy session next Wednesday at half past four in meeting room two.

It's official. I'm a teenage loony, a psychobabe.

A Madolescent!

# 9

## The Madolescents

Mrs Marr lets me off at lunchtime on Wednesday as I tell her I've got an appointment with the psychotherapist.

She laughs. 'I think you mean *physio*therapist, pet.'

'If you say so.'

So here I am, at Altamont Lodge, for my first meeting with the Madolescents. I'm a bit late as I spent ages in Heaven Scent deciding which perfume to rob, and in the end I came out with zilch. The door of meeting room two is slightly open. Somebody – a girl – is gabbling away nineteen to the dozen. I poke my head round and this dykey woman with cropped hair gets up and waves me over.

'Come in,' she says. 'You must be Rowena, yes?' It throws me a bit as I was planning to use a false name, something exotic, like Cordelia. That's this girl who was on *Babewatch*, she got to be a catwalk model even though she wore a dental brace. 'Take a seat,' the woman goes, pointing to a black plastic chair, the type I hate as your legs stick to them and they make a farting noise when you stand up. As if life wasn't enough of a minefield!

There's about five, six people there, sitting in a circle round a coffee table with two king-size boxes of tissues on top. I glance at the others, then pretend to look at the floor, only really I'm checking under the chairs for hidden machetes or weapons suitable for a sudden attack of mindless violence. Just to be on the safe side, I stuffed a tail-comb into my pocket. I run my fingers over the metal spike to assess its stabability. Probably OK for eyes but not much cop for heart or lungs.

'I'm Virginia Prosser,' the woman's saying. 'Call me Ginny,

everyone else does.' Too late. She's already fixed in my mind as Prossie. Just look at her clothes – baggy T-shirt, old Kickers, patterned leggings – they went out with the Ninja Turtles. Somebody ought to have a quiet word with her.

'I'll explain briefly how the sessions work and then we'll introduce ourselves,' she says. 'First, the ground rules. We expect everyone to attend each week and to come on time. Any information brought up during a meeting must be kept confidential. There's no pressure on you to talk, or reveal intimate issues when you don't want to. Obviously though, the more you can be open and talk about yourself and your feelings, the more you'll gain from the experience. If you feel distressed during a session, just signal and we'll find a safe space for you to take time out. Or you can use Huggypunch.' She points to a beanbag covered in denim patches. 'Huggypunch is a great stress reliever. Hug it, punch it, whatever feels right, it's indestructible – well, almost. We've had to do a few running repairs as you can see.'

Lordy, what is this place – a playgroup for the criminally insane?

'Are you with me so far, Rowena?'

I nod.

'Good. We start off with Announcements. That's when we report on something positive that we've done in the last week, no matter how big or small. After that we move on to a group discussion, usually on a subject set by one of the members, perhaps to do with problems you're experiencing at the moment. Feel free to suggest a topic of your own, Rowena, all proposals are given equal consideration, you'll find us very democratic. Any questions?' I shrug. 'Fine, let's introduce ourselves to Rowena. Would you like to kick off for us, Coralie?'

This is the fidgety lass sitting opposite me. She's wearing a red leather mini skirt with side zips, a black devoré shirt, and punky ankle boots with loads of straps and buckles, quite smart in a cheapo way.

'I'm Coralie, right,' she goes, squirming about and twisting a piece of hair into a tendril. 'I'm seventeen, I live in Byker, I work as a sales assistant in the Kit Pit and erm . . . what else? I've been coming here since the group started, couple of months ago.' She crosses and uncrosses her legs a few times, and giggles. The Kit Pit, so that's where her clothes are from. Wonder if she gets staff discount.

'Thanks, Coralie,' says Prossie. 'Maybe we should do Announcements as we go round, to save time. All agreed?' Nobody says a word.

'OK, OK, I've got one,' goes Coralie, jigging up and down in her chair. 'Last night, right, I redecorated the kitchen, I've been meaning to do it for ages, I've done the living room and bathroom, I never miss *Changing Rooms* on the telly and I'm always down at Homebase.' She jabbers away, words tumbling into each other, so hyper I want to slap her. 'First I washed everything down, that's all I was going to do but then before I knew it I'd got the paint out so I did the walls Mexican Spice and the woodwork Etruscan Gold.' That explains the coloured bits in her hair, I thought it was a nightmare highlight job. 'Took me till nearly three o'clock, then I got up early this morning and fixed everything back on the walls, it looks fab if I say so myself.' I wish she'd give over jumping around, it's making my head ache.

'Well done,' says Prossie. 'A round of applause for Coralie.' Everyone claps half-heartedly. Apart from me, that is. Well, I'm *new*, I dunno if it's worth putting my hands together just because someone slapped a bit of paint on a wall. 'Please join in, Rowena,' says Prossie. 'Being supportive to our peers and applauding their achievements is part of the group's ethos.' *Eh?* 'Mickey, would you like to go next?'

This is the short guy, dressed in a Guns 'n' Roses T-shirt and ripped jeans, with long crinkly hair that might be a bad acid-perm or a recessive gene. He's got a squashy little face that reminds me of Chucky in *Child's Play*.

'Hi, I'm Mickey, as in Metal Mickey. I'm nineteen, into heavy rock – Anthrax, Iron Maiden, Slayer, all that. I like leather and lager . . . oh, and pulling chicks.' Does he mean what I think he means, or is he a poultry slaughterer? 'Been in therapy off and on since I was ten. This here's a top gig.' He grins at the others. 'My Announcement is that I went all day Monday without having a wank.'

'Well done,' says Prossie, not batting an eyelid. We all clap like idiots.

'Made up for it on Tuesday, though,' adds Mickey, leering hideously.

'Thank you, Mickey. No need for information overload. Reuben?'

I've been watching this one chuntering to himself and playing with his fingers, like he's counting or something. He's not bad looking, in a Christian Slater kind of way, and he's wearing Adidas top to toe. Pukka gear, too, by the looks of it.

'I'm seventeen. Go to sixth-form college. That's about it-it-it-it.'

'Do you have an Announcement for us?' asks Prossie.

Reuben mumbles something under his breath, then goes, 'No-no-no-no.' I get it. It's like he says a word then does an echo three times. How weird is that?

'Not to worry, Reuben. Over to you, Ash.'

This lad is soooo gorgeous. Skin the colour of milky Nescafé, dark brown eyes you could drown in, and black hair slicked back into a ponytail which is usually max naff but on him it looks kinda cool. He doesn't say a word, just stares at the floor and chews his bottom lip. His chin quivers and his eyes start misting up.

'You don't feel up to it, Ash?' Prossie asks. He shakes his head. A tear trickles down his cheek. 'All right, no problem. Gemma?'

This is the fat lass. What a friggin' mess. She looks about eleven months preggers, like she's swallowed a space hopper or something, and she's wearing one of those gospel singer frocks, all shapeless and rent-a-tenty. Her ankles are dripping over her shoes like lardy legwarmers, and a shampoo wouldn't go amiss. I can't bear to look at her. People like that should stay indoors and not inflict themselves on the public.

'I'm nearly seventeen,' she goes. She twists her head and looks me right in the eyeballs. Something goes *clunk* in my gut. I turn away. 'I'm a kitchen assistant in that wholefood café, the Hill o' Beans, in Westgate Road. I live in a flat over the shop, I'm going to do it up ethnic when I get time.' From the corner of my eye I watch her picking the skin round her chewed-off fingernails. I feel someone walk on my grave. 'My Announcement is – I've bought an exercise bike.'

'Excellent, Gemma, that's a positive move.' But it works only with a calorie-controlled diet, or maybe a stomach staple. Pause for applause. 'Now, Rowena. Tell us about yourself.'

I've been dreading this, hoping they'd run out of time or something before it was my turn. Everyone's staring at me expectantly, apart from Ash who's snuffling into a tissue. Maybe I should leg it now, or say I wandered in by mistake, thinking it was Spanish for Beginners. Too late, I'm trapped. Oh well . . . I flip through my mental filing cabinet. Which persona do I use?

*(a) I'm Rowena. I've just bought a luxury warehouse apartment on the Quayside with some money I inherited from my nana. She was a famous movie star, pops up all the time on telly in those black and white films on Sunday afternoons . . .*

*(b) I'm Rowena. Last year I was experimented on by alien gynaecologists who injected me with galactic semen using a turkey baster. I live with my six-month-old twins, Procter and Gamble, who have silver skin and almond-shaped eyes . . .*

*(c) I'm Rowena (not my real name). I can't give out personal information as I've just moved here under the Witness Protection Programme and I'm living in fear of my life. If anything should happen to me, believe the conspiracy theory . . .*

'I'm Rowena,' I begin. 'I'm sixteen, live in Fozzy Hall with my mum. I'm a beautician.' Suddenly it hits me how pointless this whole thing is. My skin comes over all prickly. A fireball burns in my stomach, flaring up, blazing out of control. 'Look, this is *so* beyond stupid!' I yell. 'Youse lot might be mad, but there's nothing wrong with me. I'm outta here!' Jesus, did I say that in real life, or just inside my head?

'That's fascinating, Rowena.' Prossie smiles at me in a strained way. 'Do you have an Announcement for us? Something positive that's happened this week?'

I stare at the ceiling, struggling to get my breath, willing my ticker to stop thudding.

'In your own time,' says Prossie. 'No pressure.'

My mind goes blank. Think think think, Rowena. 'Erm . . .' I mutter after aeons. 'Looks like Ross and Rachel might get back together. I never thought they would after he copped off with that other lass.'

'Ross and Rachel?' Prossie twists her face into a thicko expression. 'Are they friends?'

'*Friends*? Yeah, course.' Doesn't she watch Channel 4?

'Well, I suppose that counts, if it impinges on your life. But try and think of something that *you've* done for the next meeting. Thank you, Rowena.'

I sit there like a loon, blushing scarlet, while they clap. Coralie jumps up and down in her seat, grinning maniacally, and Mickey shoots me a thumbs-up sign.

'Let's move on to our discussion. Any suggestions for topics? Yes, Mickey?'

'I wanna know what lezzies do in bed.'

Coralie groans. 'You say that *every* time, you pervert, it's so boring.' She jiggles about in her chair like she's got ants in her pants. 'Can we talk about dreams, Ginny? I've been having some real scary ones, I'd like to know what they mean.'

'Dreams, yes, that could be useful,' says Prossie, jotting it down in a notepad. 'Reuben, any suggestions?'

He mutters something and counts on his fingers again. 'Not fussed. Dreams will do-do-do-do.'

'That's two for Dreams,' goes Prossie, making a tick with her felt-tip pen. 'What about you, Ash?' He shakes his head without looking up. 'Gemma?'

'I was gonna suggest, erm, body image.' She shoots me a quick glance. I scowl back at her, double hard. A blush spreads over her moony face like a total eclipse. 'But I'll do Dreams if that's what you guys want.'

She flashes me a quick pathetic smile, and I catch the glint of a gold tooth inside her flabby chops. *Clunk.* My stomach does a triple cartwheel.

It can't be.

It is.

Omigawd, it's Gemma Probert!

Prossie scribbles. 'Three for Dreams, then. Rowena?'

'Eh? I dunno, whatever.' I'm gobsmacked. I can't believe Gemma Probert's turned into such a slaggy old bloater. Gemma Probert! Like a stick insect, she was. Coulda been a model. Got her figure back about half an hour after dropping her sprog. Her baby. Baby Nathan. I feel choked. Gutted. Like there's a monster squatting on my chest.

'Dreams it is, then. Still with us, Rowena?' Prossie raises her eyebrows at me. I shrug and stare at my feet. 'Coralie, it's your topic so you can go first.'

My mind separates and floats off. How could Gemma Probert get so fat so quickly? She used to live on rice cakes, lettuce, black coffee and fags, the Supermodel Diet. Went to aerobics, swimming and stuff. Ran a couple of half marathons for charity. Now she's like a suet dumpling. I bet the tops of her legs chafe together when she walks.

'Rowena?' They're all looking at me expectantly.

My brain clicks in.

'What? Time to go?'

'You were telling us, Rowena,' says Prossie. 'About the dream.' I try to look at her but my eyes won't focus. 'The dream where you were inside Anthea Turner's, um . . . womb.'

'Was I?' My mind's a total blank. I must have drifted off. Jesus, what have I been saying? And what if I did something awful like, Omigawd, snoring or blowing off! Aww, so what, I'm never coming here again so who gives a shit.

'Anyone like to hazard a guess about what Rowena's dream meant?'

Coralie sticks her hand up and jiggles about on her seat like she's wet herself. 'It's a regression dream. She wants to go back to childhood – no, further back than that. To the womb. She's looking for security.'

'Bollocks,' chips in Mickey. 'She's denying her sexuality. She's probably a lezzie, wants to know what it feels like to be inside a woman.'

'Huh, like you don't, I suppose,' snaps Coralie. 'Everything comes down to sex with you.'

'Me and Siggy Freud,' he snorts, clutching his lunchbox in a naff imitation of Wacko Jacko.

'Bloody brainiac!' barks Coralie.

Reuben finishes counting. 'But why Anthea Turner-turner-turner-turner?'

Ash clutches Huggypunch, rocking and weeping silently to himself.

Mum comes back from her shift weighed down with carrier bags.

'Fancy some Salmon Mornay?' she says. 'I got it for free from work, only it needs eating straight away.'

'Salmonella Mornay, more like. No way. I'll just have chips, me.' I'm watching this programme on Channel 5 about people having cybersex in Internet chat rooms. It takes me ages to work out what they're on about. I'm picturing some 3-D penis popping out of the screen but it turns out they just send each other dirty messages while they jerk off. How sad is that?

The microwave pings and a smell of gone-off fish floats through from the kitchen. 'You're never going to eat that, it stinks worse than a tart's knicker drawer,' I yell.

'It'll be all right. I think I caught it just before it went on the turn.' Mum plonks the sauce bottle and a bowl of chips on the table, but I can't face them, not with that foul fishy stench everywhere. She prods the poisonous gloop with her fork, holds the plate up to her nose and sniffs it. 'Dear God,' she goes, wrinkling her face in disgust. 'You're right. It's off.'

'Don't scrape it into the bin, it'll rot the metal and stink the kitchen out for weeks. Hoy it over the fence for Sheba.'

So much for frozen *haute cuisine.* Mum makes a stack of marmalade sarnies and I rip open a pack of Hula Hoops only I can't get them down my gullet as the stench of rotten fish is making me gag.

I hate my car crash of a life. Look at the state of me, sprawled out on the couch, hair like a mad bird's nest, a geet big hole in my tights, retching into a packet of crisps. I look worse than Waynetta Slob starring in a fly-on-the-wall docu-soap about the urban underclass. And now, to put a tin lid on it, I'm branded a mental person, lumped in with a bunch of no-hope loonies. Nice one, Big G. Some existence, huh.

'I forgot to ask,' says Mum, wiping a gob of marmalade off her chin, 'how did you get on with those young people at Altamont Lodge? It *was* today, wasn't it?'

'I'm never going there again. They're all mad.'

'That's your professional diagnosis, is it, Dr Vincent?'

'It's true. They're madder than snakes.' I can see she won't give up until I've told her, so I reel them off on my fingers. 'There's this hyper lass who works in the Kit Pit, and a sex maniac, another boy who repeats everything you say, plus a lad who can't stop blubbing

– they're all on Planet Ga-Ga. Oh, and that Gemma Probert from school. The one who left to have a baby.'

'That's nice,' says Mum. 'At least there's someone you know. A girlfriend.'

I go Gemma Probert's never gonna be anyone's girlfriend, not unless she keeps her piggy snout out of the trough and loses half a ton of blubber and anyway, I'll end up as mental as them if I have to go again. Mum says not to expect miracles after one session, my emotional difficulties have been building up for a long time so I'm hardly going to get better overnight, Rome wasn't built in a day and so forth.

'Mum, am I dysfunctional?' God knows where that word came from, it just flew into my head.

'Dys-*what*?'

'Forget it.'

Mum snaps open a can of lager, takes a guzzly swig and lets out a rattling burp. That's what being Filthy Luker's floozy has done to her.

'Touch of dyspepsia,' she explains, patting her chest.

'Dys-*what*?'

'Just go to one more session, Rowena,' she pleads. 'Do that and there'll be a big treat for you.'

'What? What treat?' I need to find out if it's worth my while.

'Something extra special,' she says, shooting me a false smile and tapping the side of her nose with a finger. 'A really big surprise. It's so exciting, you'll be made up when I tell you.'

My heart plummets to my boots. Why do I figure it's bad news?

# 10

## *Going Equipped*

Bundy, my Trusty Sidekick and animal companion (I discovered it's politically incorrect to call him a pet) can get in and out of the shed as he likes since I had the brainwave of wedging the bottom of the door open with a brick. I'd have preferred a proper catflap but he's still a secret from Mum and Filthy for the moment. He's stopped dumping wildlife cadavers on the doorstep and now dismembers them in the shed, judging by the feathers and tiny bones scattered on the floor.

Yesterday I crushed a worming tablet in some tinned salmon which he guzzled down in no time flat so maybe now his bum won't itch and he'll lose that pot belly.

Mum goes supersonic when she finds out the salmon's missing. 'I bought it specially for Bernard's pack-up,' she rants. 'Now he'll have to make do with fish paste.'

'It must be that poltergeist again using its telekinetic powers,' I tell her. 'The salmon'll probably materialise in a log cabin in Memphis, Tennessee.'

She glares at me with homicidal eyes. 'It had better materialise in our food cupboard PDQ otherwise somebody in this house will be in Deep Shit, Arizona.' I buy another tin from Kwik Save, not the same brand but I think it's done the trick. Another domestic crisis averted.

I seem to have established a rapport with Bundy because he lets me groom him with the flea comb, but only in short goes as he has a low boredom threshold. His teeth are canny sharp, I've got puncture marks all over my arms, but it's all in a good cause. Fleas are sneaky bastards and travel at 90 mph, you have to be real smart to catch them. My method is to scrape them off the comb with kitchen paper, screw it up and flush it down the bog to drown the little beasts but some are too quick and leap off the comb. I've been bitten a few times and it doesn't half knack when they sink their fangs in.

I've just had the most brilliant idea! Fleas could be vital allies in the Filthy Offensive. All I need is a jam jar.

Dean saying yes to Filthy's birthday meal creates a major problem. What am I going to wear on Saturday? I yank everything out of my wardrobe but there's nothing, it's all rags, worse than charity shop stuff. I'm desperate for some new kit. Then I remember the Warrior Princess outfit. Perfecto.

I know the routine in B'Zarr, I've checked it out a few times. They've got three assistants plus a skinhead called Spoiler on the door with a walkie-talkie and one of those timeshare dicks who works some other shops as well. All the gear's electronically tagged but that's no problem. Right then. Sorted! Time to tool up.

I fetch the cooking foil from the kitchen and line the inside of my rucksack, then double-line it to be on the safe side. Foil deflects the rays, microwaves, whatever they're called, so you can get past the scanner without setting the alarm off. Some stupid boosters still use those metal-lined ice cooler bags but you maison well walk into a store with SHOPLIFTER tattooed on your forehead, everybody knows your game.

First thing in the morning I ring Mrs Marr. 'I'll be in a bit late, I need to go to the doctor's. I'll make the time up, honest.'

'Don't be soft,' she says. 'You're allowed time off if it's medical. Nothing serious, I hope?'

'Woman's troubles,' I lie.

'It's a cross we have to bear,' she goes. 'Are your monthlies due?' Jesus, she wants to know the far end of a fart and which way the wind blows. I maison well get a menstrual calendar and stick it up in reception.

'It's probably just a mild infection,' I ad-lib. 'Nothing catching. Some cream should clear it up in no time.'

'Describe your symptoms,' she says, like suddenly she's a muff-doctor. 'Does it itch? Is there a discharge like cottage cheese? You want to try live yoghurt, my sister's prone to bouts of thrush and she swears by it.'

I know the nosy old bint means well but I'm not about to get involved in a conversation about vaginal mucus. 'I'll have to rush,' I say. 'That receptionist's a right battleaxe and she'll excommunicate me if I'm late.'

I check my rucksack again because any gaps in the foil could prove fatal, and head for B'Zarr. I've worked it so I get there for nine thirty as that gives them time to open up and get the kettle on for their first fag break. When I go through the door my insides are fizzing with nerves but I control my body language so I look calm. Björk blares out of the speakers, that woman's totally barking, swear down. I stroll round the accessories bit, checking out hair ornaments and S & M masks. This Vampyra wifey with black lipstick comes and stands by me, staring down her pierced conk like I'm a lump of dog shit on her shoes. She pretends to tidy up the earring carousel but she's keeping her eye on me. I wander round the coats, pick out a shiny black monstrosity and hold it up against me. It's cavernous, just the job.

Vampyra sidles up to me. 'Are you buying that?'

Yeah, right, like I'd be seen dead in the thing. 'It's a definite possibility. I'll keep browsing.' I pull out a black velvet cape with satin lining. Who'd wear this – the Phantom of the Friggin' Opera? 'Mmm, that's a maybe too.' All the time I'm scanning the hangers for the Warrior Princess outfit. I'll die if they've sold it. I reach for a leather trenchcoat covered in chains, take it over to a mirror and hold it up. How can they sell this stuff? Everybody knows neo-Nazi gear went out aeons ago.

Then I spot it, the Warrior Princess outfit, tucked on a rack between a Catwoman suit and a clingy latex frock. My ticker starts thudding.

'Found anything yet?' goes Vampyra, checking her watch. Must be nearly time for her fix of virgin's blood.

'Still mulling.'

She sighs and starts fiddling under her fingernails with a flick knife. This is a good sign, it means she's bored. Spoiler swaggers over and they whisper and giggle for a bit, then wander to the front of the shop and stare out the blackened window, slagging off people walking past. The place could be swarming with shoplifters and they'd never notice. They're useless, they want sacking.

I grab the three coats, they're that bulky I can hardly carry them, and head for the changing rooms. This skinny lass with pink hair's lounging against the wall, a mobile phone clamped to her ear. 'Hang on a sec, Claudia,' she goes, glaring at me like I'm interrupting important business when it's obvious she's on a personal call. 'How many?' I hold out my arms and she hands me a tag with a big number three on. 'Go on, Claudia, what happened next?' The staff here are pure crap, somebody should report them to the owner.

In the cubicle I draw the blackout curtains, dump the three disgusting coats on the floor and peel my kit off. Hidden inside the vile velvet cape is the Warrior Princess outfit. It's totally tops, even more wicked than I remember. I really get off on the smell of leather, it's pure raw sex. I rub the bustier against my body. The feel of animal hide rough on my bare stomach shoots a thrill right through me like an electric shock. The touch of skin against skin gets me real horny and my nipples stand to attention as I lace the thongs tight around the metal studs. I squeeze my breasts hard then reach under the skirt and stroke myself down there where I'm moist. It doesn't take long.

After I'm done I fold the outfit into my rucksack, being careful not to rip the foil, then get dressed and hand the coats back to the skinny lass. She's still gassing on the phone.

'Any good?' she goes, like she gives a shit.

'I'll think about it.' Vampyra and Spoiler are nattering by the door. He holds it open for me and I clench my bum cheeks tight as I stroll through, praying the alarm won't go off. It doesn't. Piece of piss, really.

Jesus, I must be off my head. I just shagged my new clothes!

## 11

## Sex, Lies & Car Alarms

I wake up with a banging head and a sense of doom. It's Saturday. Filthy's birthday and the dreaded Indian meal. There's still time to get out of it. This headache might be a brain tumour – I could go up the hospital and demand a CAT scan, they're bound to keep me in overnight for observation. Or I could throw myself downstairs and break a limb or two and people could write witty remarks on my plaster cast. Perhaps if I hold my breath long enough, I'll lapse into a coma from oxygen deprivation and Richard from The Verve will rush to my bedside and sing 'Bitter Sweet Symphony' a cappella to rouse me back into consciousness.

'Any danger of you getting up today, madam?' Mum flaps round the room and throws open the curtains. The sunlight nearly blinds me. 'I don't suppose you got a birthday card for Bernard?' I move my head in a negatory fashion. 'Thought as much. Good job I bought one for you then.' She flings a big yellow envelope on the bed. I squint at the card. It's a cartoon of a bloke with a medallion and chest wig and says *Birthday Greetings to the Oldest Swinger in Town.*

'I'm not giving him this, it's well naff,' I complain.

'Suit yourself,' says Mum. 'You'd better go down Kular's and buy him one then.'

Stuff that. 'It'll do, on second thoughts.'

'Right. Now get your backside out of bed and change those sheets. It smells like rotting meat in here.'

Where's the day gone? It's now turned six and I need to start getting ready. I decide to do the full bit – jojoba face mask, rose-water skin wash, mahogany hair tint – as I want to do justice to the

Warrior Princess outfit. It's taken me hours to get the security tag off, my hands are raw from using the pliers, but at least I managed it without ripping the leather.

My make-up goes on like a dream, Gunmetal eyeliner and Bronze Pearl shadow for that primitive, untamed look plus Aztec Red glossy lipstain. I plaster my hair with wet-look gel, scrape it back so tight it hurts, then fasten it in a cone clip. Pure dominatrix. My bosoms look fantastico pushed up in the bustier, just like I've had a boob job, and I add a studded leather choker, metal amulets and silver skull earrings. Under the thonged skirt I wear a leopardskin G-string, shiny black tights and my brilliant biker boots. I hardly recognise myself in the mirror. The look's fuck you, don't-mess-with-me perfect.

Mum taps on the door and pootles in. She throws her hands up in mock shock – well, I assume it's mock. 'My God, Rowena, you're not leaving the house like that. It isn't the *Rocky Horror Show*, you know.'

I glance at her red silk shirt and black kecks. 'At least I've made an effort. You wore those same clothes last week, I hope you've washed them.'

'That's enough backlip.' Mum runs her hand down my skirt and rubs her snout in the material like a sniffer dog. 'This is new,' she says. 'Real leather as well. I'll bet it cost a tidy penny.'

'It's eco-friendly mock leatherette,' I lie. 'They distress it and spray it with something from cows to make it smell like the real stuff. It was dirt cheap, if you must know, from Mark One's sale, slightly shop-soiled.' Please, *please* don't let her check the label!

'You look like a flaming porno queen. God only knows what Bernard will think. Talk of the devil, that sounds like his car now.' Filthy's Sierra pulls up outside. 'Well, you'll have to do, I suppose, there's no time to get changed again. Only keep a jacket on, or you'll catch your death.'

We take a minicab to the restaurant so Filthy can get bevvied up.

Dean's going to meet us there. Mum and the birthday boy are giggling and carrying on like schoolkids on the back seat. I sit stony-faced in front next to a baldy driver with serious personal hygiene problems who keeps looking at my thighs and wheezing, dirty old lech. I clutch my leather jacket round me, he'd have a heart attack if he saw my bosoms and I don't fancy getting facially disfigured in a multi-vehicle pile-up.

The restaurant's down a side street, it looks right dim and dingy, I knew it would. A pissed-off-looking waiter bloke sits us down and hands us menus the size of Monopoly boards. The place is almost empty, which ought to tell us something, and some bint's wailing her head off to twangy-wangy music. Plus it stinks disgusting in here, like ill mice, I'll go mental if the smell gets into my leather.

'Champagne, gimp?' goes Filthy. 'We might as well push the boat out.' He's done up like a dog's dinner in a black suit and white grandad shirt, you could mistake him for one of the waiters. Well, almost.

'Do they have champagne in India?' Mum whispers, looking worried.

'We're not *in* India. This is England, of course they'll have champagne.' But they don't, ha ha, which shows how much *he* knows. They settle for Cobra beer and I have poor man's Pepsi which tastes disgusting, like watered-down diarrhoea. I can feel my frown lines setting in for the night. I wish Dean would hurry up. 'I think I'll have my usual,' goes Filthy, lighting up a tab. 'Chicken tikka masala, onion pilau and peshwari nan. What do you fancy, gimp?'

Mum looks blank, she never touched Indian food until she met him. 'I'll try the tandoori chicken with plain boiled rice, Bernard.' She beams at him, all vacant and stupid. I could vomit.

'What about you, young 'un?' If he calls me that once more, I'll do time for him, swear down. I check out the menu but it's all in foreign. There's no chips, no burgers, nothing decent at all. Call this a restaurant? 'Try a korma,' he says. 'Start off with something mild, give your tastebuds chance to adapt.'

I plonk the menu down. 'Don't want anything, not hungry.' Mum kicks me under the table but I refuse to look at her. I feel a right sweaty betty with this jacket on, plus the G-string's worked its way up the crack of my bum; I'll be bisected before the night's out. Where's Dean got to? If he lets me down he's dead meat.

The pissed-off waiter's hovering about so Filthy orders for himself and Mum and also a chicken korma for me, we'll all be growing friggin' feathers at this rate. He says I don't have to force it down if I absolutely hate it but he can't let me sit there like cheese at ninepence while they enjoy themselves. I ignore him and poke my finger in a bleb in the wallpaper, it pops like bubble-wrap. You can see where other people have done it, they must have been bored shitless too. Mum kicks me again, warning me to behave, then the door opens and there's Dean *at last* looking really mint in his new Tommy Hilfiger jacket.

'Sorry I'm late,' he goes, giving me a wink and sliding in next to me. There's something funny about his eyes, you can see they're spacey even through his specs. Omigawd, he's off his face!

Mum introduces him to Filthy and Dean gets a card out of his pocket and wishes him happy birthday, the crawler, which makes me feel like shit because I forgot to bring mine. Mum fishes this enormous card out of her bag and tells Filthy she'll give him his present later and they nudge each other and snigger in some obscene private joke. The pissed-off waiter comes up and rolls his eyes to heaven when Dean says he'll just have an onion bhaji and mineral water as he hasn't got much of an appetite. That'll be the whizz.

I've never seen Dean like this, he's usually the moody silent type, but now he's running off at the chops talking about when his dad was forty and he went a bit mental and drove round town honking his horn forty times. Mum and Filthy are laughing like drains, obviously impressed and thinking how lucky I am to have a friend like Dean. I'm rapidly losing the will to live, slunk back in the seat with my leather jacket clutched tight round me. Bet they wouldn't be laughing if they knew Dean was off his tits on speed.

The scran arrives in metal thingies like sputum bowls. 'I thought we ordered chicken,' I say. 'It looks like something the dog threw up.' Mum kicks me again. This is pure physical abuse, my legs'll be black and blue.

'Don't knock it till you've tried it,' goes Filthy, shovelling brown vomit on to his plate. 'You could be opening yourself up to a whole new culinary experience. Come on, fill your boots, young 'un. And relax, take your coat off.'

'Leave it on, Rowena,' says Mum, wiggling her eyebrows at me in some mad coded message. 'It's not that warm in here.'

'If you don't take it off, you won't feel the benefit,' goes Dean, doing Mrs Marr's squeaky voice. He slips the leather jacket off my shoulders.

Suddenly there's a big fat silence round the table. Filthy gulps and his eyes pop out on stalks. Him and Dean stare goggle-eyed at my pushed-up bosoms and Mum peers at her plate, fiddling with her food, her mouth all puckered up like a cat's arse.

'What?' I goes. Nobody says a word. '*What?*'

'Nothing. Just eat,' says Mum. She sounds dead irritable, her period must be due.

Just as I predicted, the evening's a total disaster, thanks to Filthy who gets rat-arsed in no time flat and keeps making suggestive remarks about my tits. He thinks it's hilarious.

'Tasty bit of *breast* there,' he goes, pointing to my dinner. 'I'm glad we didn't go to that *udder* place.' Mum forces a laugh but I can tell she thinks he's a pranny. 'I'll have some great *mammaries* of my fortieth birthday.' I'd punch him out if he wasn't so ancient.

Then, like things aren't dire enough, the waiters gang up in a huddle, gawping at my knockers, sniggering and muttering to each other in foreign. This brings on one of my episodes where my throat seizes up and I can't swallow. I spit the food into my napkin.

'For God's sake, Rowena, what *now*?' snaps Mum.

'This isn't chicken,' I go. 'It's . . . it's Indian python, they've drugged it with horse tranquillisers.'

'Is it really? Well, do your best. Bernard's paying for this, you know.'

'You don't get it. Those waiters, they're plotting to kidnap me and sell me to the international sex trade.'

'Don't be melodramatic, Rowena, I'd say that's a highly unlikely scenario. Now quit being paranoid and finish your meal before it gets cold.' She looks at Filthy and rolls her eyes meaning, *Kids, eh?*

'I'd love to know what goes on in that head of hers,' he says, discussing me as if I'm deaf. 'God knows where she gets these ideas from, it'll be alien abduction next.'

'You can mock,' I tell him. 'It goes on all the time, there was a programme about it on Sky. Plus I'd remind you that chicken and snake taste *exactly the same!* So there.'

Mum flings down her fork and bits of rice fly everywhere. 'Thank you very much, Rowena, you've completely ruined my appetite.'

'*Yours* won't be python,' I assure her. 'There's no market for women your age.'

'Shut it,' she snaps. She's really got a cob on tonight. 'It's no good, I can't stomach another mouthful.' Old Guzzleguts Luker says waste not, want not, and scoffs what's left on her plate plus Dean's onion bhajis.

When the bill comes, Filthy pretends to get a shock. 'I'll be going *bust* at this rate,' he says, ogling my bosoms.

'That's enough, Bernard,' says Mum quietly. 'Give it a rest now.'

'Oops, have I made a *boob*?' he quips. I could really twat him one.

Dean leans over the table and stares Filthy right in the eyeballs. 'Are you always so offensive?' he goes in a real quiet voice. 'Or is this a special birthday performance?' What an excellent put-down. I could snog the chops off him.

Filthy looks amazed, he can't believe his ears. 'Come on, mate—'

'I'm not your mate. And I think you owe these women an apology.' Dean, my hero! Filthy splutters a bit and Mum plays peacemaker, trying to shush everybody and act like nothing's happened.

'Well . . . *ladies*,' goes Filthy, the hopeless old dinosaur. 'I'm sorry if anything I said caused offence, though I can't think what. There, will that do you, son?'

Thank God for Dean, he's saved us from total disaster, chatting to everybody and being funny and witty in a completely non-sexist way. He's been touchy-feely with me all evening, squeezing my legs under the table and resting his arm over the back of the seat. And now he's given Filthy what for. I feel really trippy, which leads me to a momentous decision.

I'm going to lose my virginity. Tonight!

As soon as we reach home, Filthy, smashed out of his chops, gets hauled straight up to bed by Mum like a naughty sprog. Dean comes in for a coffee (that's what *he* thinks!). Goodbye virginity, it's seduction time! I fetch the robbed ribbed condoms from my sports bag and stuff them behind the cushions on the couch. Dean stretches out on the sheepskin rug and rolls a joint.

'I just need to mellow out. OK by you?'

'Cool, as long as the smell's gone by morning.' I slap the Manics in the CD player and drape myself next to him in an erotic pose. He offers me the spliff but I wave it away as coughing my lungs up wouldn't come over too sexy.

'You look wicked in that,' he goes, running his fingers up my leg. 'Totally awesome, in fact. Everybody fancied you tonight.' He flicks the joint into the fireplace, takes off his specs and pulls me to him. 'Me included.' He plants a butterfly kiss on my mouth and soon we're having a full-blown snog, tongues, the lot.

My insides are in meltdown. I unlace the thongs on my bustier and Dean fondles my bosoms, groaning with passion, or possibly cramp. He sucks my nipples, they're standing out like rubber bullets obviously, and slides his hand up my skirt. I'm wriggling and writhing, all wet and juicy, mad for him to touch me down there. He's making a real hash of pulling my tights down so I peel them and my G-string off together and fling them across the room.

'I haven't got anything with me, you know, condoms,' he murmurs damply in my ear. 'Want to risk it without?'

'We're sorted.' My voice sounds weird and husky, like Jessica Rabbit. I stretch up and produce the packet from behind the cushion. 'Voilà!' (Apart from *merde*, that's the only French word I remember.)

When I go to pull off my kit Dean says, 'No, leave it on. I want you wearing it when I fuck you,' and just hearing that word sends me into a frenzy. My legs are majorly akimbo, I'm practically doing the splits and the sheepskin rug feels wet and sticky under my bottom. Dean whips off his T-shirt, unzips his jeans and wriggles out of them. Oh, cool, he's wearing Calvin Klein trolleys, I wonder if he got them from the Void? I ease them down past his bum which is totally lush and one of his best features, squeezing and digging my fingernails into his flesh.

At last! Zig-a-zig-ah!

'It's no good,' mutters Dean. 'Shit, I'm really sorry.' This pathetic little thing, like a baby slug, hangs limply between his legs. 'It must be the speed.'

'Triffic. You might have warned me before we got this far.' Jesus, trust me to offer my virginity to someone who can't even get a stiffy.

'I thought I was OK. My head's up for it but my dick's not in the mood.'

'We'll see about that.' If his head's up for it, so's mine.

I can't believe what I'm about to do. Gemma Probert told me oral sex was a type of punishment invented by French people, like that machine they slice heads off with, but every man that ever existed gets off on it, even Presidents of the United States.

I shove Dean back on to the soggy sheepskin, run my tongue over his six-pack and lick round his belly button, trying to hold my breath in case it smells funny down there. He moans softly and grabs my head, pushing it towards his sleepy willy. I'm scared to touch the thing in case it jumps up and pokes my eye out. What does penis taste like? Is it skin-flavoured, like a big toe – which is about the same size, as it goes – or will it taste really revolting, like pigs' trotter, and make me throw up? Jesus, there's a trickle of wet stuff coming out of the end. Ugh, what if he's got a genito-urinary disorder, I'll get ulcers round my mouth and everyone will know what I've been up (or rather down) to. Maybe he's incontinent! Stop this, Rowena. Close your eyes, hold your breath, and be glad you tied your hair back.

It really, really works! A little flick of the tongue round that end bit makes Dean's cock wake up and jiggle about. It doesn't taste much of anything which means I can breathe again. When I slip it between my lips, his todger goes hard and Dean moans, 'Oh God.' I slide my mouth up and down, licking it at the same time, but not blowing, so OK, maybe it's not a proper blow job but who cares? His willy's gone geet big, like one of those giant Cumberland sausages.

Suddenly Dean goes, 'Stop! Get a condom, quick,' which is canny timing because I was getting a bit fed up anyway plus my jaw's aching. He fiddles with the packet and eventually rips it open with his teeth, then slides the thing on to his dick which is as stiff as a poker, so to speak. Wish he'd hurry up, I'm absolutely sopping down there. I wonder if it hurts, losing your virginity? What if I bleed on the sheepskin rug? I'll have to cut my finger or tell Mum my period came unexpectedly.

Dean heaves my legs up on to his shoulders, I must look like an oven-ready turkey, very dignified, I *don't* think. He teases his cock end against my nubbin, the clitoris thingy. It's driving me wild, as good as when I do it myself. I'm gagging for it, right on the edge, I'll be there any second.

'Fuck's sake, Dean, just *do* it!'

*Nee-naa-nee-naa-nee-naa-nee-naa-nee-naa.*

What the—! Christ, a friggin' car alarm, and it's going off right outside our house! Dean's hard-on shrivels to nothing, like a slug that's had salt chucked on it. Footsteps thunder down the stairs, the door bursts open, and Omigawd, Filthy rushes in, bollock-naked! He dashes over to the window, cursing as he bangs his shin on the video cabinet, and flings open the curtains.

'My Sierra!' he yells. 'Jean, come quick. If somebody's messing with my car, I'll rip their bloody faces off.'

Me and Dean are set rigid in the same position, my feet up on his shoulders, our love-bits touching, not that there's any chance of getting it on now. My juices are going cold, it feels like a sticky bun down there. Dean's stomach starts trembling, it could be nerves or he might be suppressing the giggles, not that I can see anything to laugh at.

Then the light clicks on. I crane my neck and there's Mum in the doorway (at least she's wearing a nightie), and she's gawping right at me with a shock-horror expression.

'Rowena!' Her jaw's dropping off her face. 'For God's sake, make yourself decent!'

Before I can untangle my legs from Dean's neck she spins round and flounces out all huffy. Filthy glances wild-eyed round the room. It's like a jumble sale, clothes flung everywhere, but he's too furious about his car to worry about causing *coitus interruptus*. He yanks off the tablecloth, wraps it round his waist and shoots out the front door like a homicidal maniac.

'Quick, get dressed,' I hiss. Dean's patting the carpet with his hands, feeling for his specs. 'Here.' I ferret them out from under the sheepskin, they look a bit bent, well, we've been doing sexual contortions on them. 'Now move it.'

'What about this?' Dean dangles the ribbed condom in front of my nose.

'Get rid of it!' I shriek. Dean looks round the room. 'Not here – outside! Jesus, I can't believe this is happening. When Mum gets hold of me, I'm toast.'

'I could really fancy some of that.' Dean casually slips into his Stussy T-shirt and sticks the lopsided specs on. 'Toast, I mean, I've got the munchies.'

'Look, get your kit on and vamoose.' I'm frantic. What a disaster, I'll still be a virgin when I'm fifty at this rate. Plus, how am I ever going to face Mum? Or Filthy? Or, Omigawd, Dean? What if he tells the blokes at work, they'll laugh their scrotums off. I'll have to pack in my job, leave home, leave town. I wish I'd been abducted and sold into the sex trade, it couldn't have been worse than this – *and* I'd have popped my cherry without a load of palaver. Just as I'm shoving Dean out of the room, Filthy and Mum come in through the front door. Filthy looks a right prat in that tablecloth. His face is like thunder.

'Bleedin' cat,' he roars, to no one in particular. 'Big black bastard only jumped on the bonnet with a soddin' rabbit, there's blood and guts all over. Wait till I get my hands on it, I'll break its friggin' neck.' He karate-chops the radiator with a geet big thunk to demonstrate the technique. 'Oh, fuckit, my knuckles! I wish I knew whose moggy it was, I'd have them up for criminal damage.'

I can feel Mum's eyes burning into me like lasers but I won't look at her. I push Dean towards the door. 'Well, goodbye all.' He grins, like we've just had a tea party. Mum mutters goodnight through her teeth, Filthy gives Dean an absent-minded pat on the back, and I head for the stairs.

'Not so fast, young lady. I want a word with you,' Mum calls. I run into my room, jam the door shut with a chair and go totally mental, punching the bejazus out of my pillow.

My life's in pieces. I can't settle in bed, I thrash about like a harpooned shark and nearly get strangled by the duvet.

Suicide, that's my only option. I'd nip downstairs and get the headache tablets only paracetamol take weeks to work and I don't fancy a lingering death from liver failure, plus they might make me drool and I want to retain *some* dignity.

There's hanging, I suppose I could sling my tights over the curtain rail, but asphyxiation makes your tongue go blue and loll out the side of your mouth, not a glammy sight.

Opening a vein would be too messy, Mum'd kill me if I ruined the sheets with spurts of arterial blood.

I'd jump out the window but knowing my luck I'd just be badly maimed or knock my shin bones through my knees and spend the rest of my life three feet tall staring into people's belly buttons. This is hopeless. Oh God . . .

*Oh God*, that's it! I could *pray* to be taken in the night, peacefully, in my sleep. It'd confound medical science, they'd call hundreds of expert witnesses but the evidence would be inconclusive and they'd have to record an open verdict. How could a healthy sixteen-year-old virgin just stop breathing and expire in her own bed like . . . like, e.g., a candle in the wind?

'Rowena Vincent was much misunderstood,' the coroner will announce sadly. 'She had nothing to live for, so, quite simply, she died. A promising young life snuffed out, such a tragic waste.'

Oh no, I just remembered, I can't shuffle off this mortal thingy until I've finished planning my funeral music. Scrub that prayer, Big G, I'm not quite ready. Now where did I put my notebook?

\*

Sunday. I figure the best plan is to stay in bed all day and hope Mum'll think she was dreaming. Fat chance. She taps on my door at the crack of dawn, well, ten past eleven, same thing.

'Rowena,' she goes. 'I know you're awake. Let me in.' No way, she sounds crabby, she's obviously still premenstrual. 'Rowena, open this door, I'm staying out here till you do.' She'll have a long wait then.

I pull the duvet over my head and I must have dozed off because when I look at the clock it's turned five. My brain feels fuzzy, I can't remember where I am for a second but I know I'm busting for a pee. I press my hand down there to stop from wetting myself. It's all sweaty and sticky and memories of last night come flooding back. Oh God.

Mum must have been lying in wait for me to go to the bathroom. How sneaky is that? She grabs hold of my arm, for a minute I think she's going to wallop me, and barks, 'Put some clothes on and get downstairs this minute, young lady,' and shoves me dead rough into my room.

'If you slap me I'll definitely report you,' I tell her. 'The bizzies are real hot on domestic violence, zero tolerance and all that.'

'Slap you?' she goes, her eyes rolling like a madwoman. 'I'll flaming *splifflicate* you, you brazen young trollop.' It's a waste of time reasoning with her when her period's due. I'll just have to try to calm her down. If that doesn't work I'll get a restraining order.

I pull on a scuzzy old T-shirt and baggy shorts so at least if she assaults me I won't ruin anything decent. She's sitting at the kitchen table with a mug of coffee, like she needs any stimulants. Pointing at a chair, she snaps, 'Sit.'

'What am I, a dog?'

'You tell me,' she goes. 'You were acting like a bitch on heat last night, I've never been so ashamed in my life. Dean should have shown more respect as well, he's got no room to talk about Bernard. I wasn't far out when I said you looked like a porno queen, draping your legs round his flaming neck like that, performing the Kama Bloody Sutra on my sheepskin rug, I've had to throw it in the bin.'

Make a mental note to retrieve it for Bundy. 'You've got it all wrong,' I tell her. My mind's whirling at 100 mph. 'It wasn't anything like that. We were . . . we were practising an acrobatic routine. Like skaters, you know. Ice dancers. You'd think it was amazing if Torvill and Dean did it.' I'm skating on very thin ice here myself.

'Don't insult me, I know what you were up to. Why can't you ever tell the truth?' She slaps the ribbed condoms on the table. 'And how do you explain these?'

'Dunno, what are they?'

'You know fine well what they are, you stole them off the bathroom shelf. And don't dare give me any of that crap about poltergeists or I'll knock your flaming teeth down your throat.'

Deny, deny, that's the trick. Keep cool and front it out. 'Look, you're totally wrong. I know how it must have looked but . . . but me and Dean could never have sex together, for one very good reason.' I rack my brain trying desperately to think of it.

'This'll be worth hearing,' says Mum, dead sarky like. 'Go on.'

'Because . . . because he's *gay*. He fancies boys.' I daren't breathe. Will she buy it? Apparently not.

'I don't believe a word you say, you're a compulsive liar. You needn't think I'm falling for that tosh, anyone can see Dean thinks the world of you.'

I pile on the grief, wiping a non-existent tear from my eye. 'I know it's hard to believe, I was gutted when I found out. But sadly, Dean and I can never be more than plutonic friends.'

Her eyes don't look so mad but she's still suspicious. 'You're lying.'

I pull out my deeply hurt expression. 'I'm not, swear down. Who'd make up a story like that?'

'I wouldn't put it past you. You couldn't lie straight in your own bed.'

'It's the truth, Mum. I promised him not to say anything but you forced it out of me. He wants to keep his sexual identity secret until he's come out to his parents. You mustn't ever mention it, specially not to Dean, he'd go seismic if he thought anyone knew.'

She picks at her nails thoughtfully. 'Well, I suppose I'll have to take your word for it. I won't deny it's a shock, I had no idea. I must say it puts a different complexion on things. I'd better explain to Bernard, though, he's convinced you were up to shenanigans last night.'

'No, you mustn't! We'll never hear the last of it, he'll be cracking non-stop gags about woofters and arse-bandits. Oh *please*, Mum, don't tell him.'

She thinks about it. 'All right then, point taken. Now, shall we have egg and chips?'

Whew, that was close, but at least mother-daughter relations have been restored. While Mum's doing the tea I nick some honey-roast ham out of the fridge for Bundy. My Trusty Sidekick's snoozing in his box, unaware that a death threat's been imposed on him. He must have been shit-scared when that car alarm went off, poor lad. The smell of food wakes him up and while he's busy gobbling the pigmeat, I groom him with the flea-comb, catching seven huge black buggers. They all go into the jam jar, my secret biological weapon in the war against Filthy.

## 12

# When They Come, They'll Eat the
# Fat Ones First

Last night I dreamt about a horde of fifty foot killer fleas rampaging through Fozzy Hall, squirting red venom on Filthy's Sierra, transforming it into a heap of rust. Although it was a brilliant image, it's left me exhausted, so Mum's rung Mrs Marr to say my kidneys are still a bit chilled, which is a coded message for I can't be arsed to get up.

The radio's on low and I'm just wondering what the fuck boy bands are all about when Mum shuffles in.

'Your friend's been on the phone,' she says. 'Three times. Number's on the pad.' I squint at her and yawn. It's the middle of the night, well, half past ten, same difference.

'What friend?'

'How many have you got?' says Mum, sarky like. 'That wossname, Gemma. She sounds like a nice girl. She's at work in some caff. I said you'd call her when you roused your lazy backside out of bed.'

'You had no right saying that. She could be a stalker for all you know.' Jesus, what's Gemma Probert doing ringing me at home? *Three times.* Just then the phone goes. 'If that's her again, tell her – I dunno, tell her I've been kidnapped or something.'

'Chance would be a fine thing,' Mum smirks, thudding down the stairs. 'Rowena,' she yells. 'It's Gemma for you.' The cow! I heave my arse out of bed, shuffle downstairs and snatch the phone off her.

'Thanks a bunch, Mum. I owe you one,' I hiss. 'What?' I snap into the phone.

'Rowena?' says this pathetic little voice. 'It's me, Gemma.' My heart sinks. I let out a long painful sigh. 'Don't hang up on us, please,' she begs. 'I'll only be a minute.'

'Hurry up then, I've got a bath running,' I lie, nibbling my nail polish.

'Can we meet up?' goes Gemma. 'You could come round to my flat, I'll cook us something. We could have a bottle of wine—'

'I friggin' hate wine.'

'Something else then. Whatever you fancy, I'll pay. I just want to talk. Please, Rowena. I'm desperate,' she pleads, like that's some kind of plus.

'Can't,' I say. 'I'm busy. I mean I'm off sick, got a chin in my kidleys.' I can hear her snivelling. Jesus, I *so* don't need this. Clingy people get right up my nostrils.

'Sorry,' she blubs. 'I didn't mean to hassle you, honest, Rowena. It doesn't matter then. Sorry.'

'I'll mebbe see you Wednesday,' I hear myself mutter. 'At the group thing. We can talk after if you like.' What am I saying!

'That'd be fab,' she goes, brightening up suddenly. 'Cheers, Rowena, you're a real mate. See you Wednesday then.'

'Yeah, right.' I slam down the phone. What's got into me? I must be turning soft, I let her patheticness put me under pressure. I decide to act dead hard when/if I see her, don't want her laying her problems on me, like I haven't got enough of my own. You have to be cruel to be kind with some people.

The day looms in front of me, a vast empty space. I spend some time experimenting with make-up, doing my eyes purple and black, like a fake battered wife I saw on *Casualty*. Even after I've cleaned most of it off, I still look as if I've done ten rounds with Lennox Lewis, who, by the way, is starting to look flabby. I can't remember ever feeling so bored, not even before I was diagnosed as mental. Maison well take a trip into town, rob a few CDs or cosmetics before I lose the knack.

The city centre's heaving, a bobbing sea of people all along

Northumberland Street. I stroll along with my head down in case someone from Crowther's happens to take a late lunch and spots me bunking off. Just outside Dixons, this wifey charges out and scrapes my leg with a baby-buggy so I glare at her and let rip with a string of curses. She stares at me like I'm deranged, and says, 'Sorry, I'm sure.' I can feel her eyes burning into me as I stomp down the street so I spin round to flick her the finger, only she's disappeared. Then it dawns on me. She must be a secret agent, hiding in a shop doorway, calling HQ on her mobile, reporting my movements. I need to get off the main drag pronto, give them the slip.

God knows how I got to this place. I never come up this end of town. My feet must have led me here on their own while my brain was panicked with trying to escape from the CIA.

The Hill o' Beans. I peer through the window but it's dead dark and gothicky inside. A bell tinkles as I open the door. What a dump! It's like a demented biddy's front room, all ancient wooden tables and chairs that don't match, purple cushions with mirrors in, candles with zillions of melts running down the sides, and flowers stuck in little green bottles. It reeks of old hippies, that sick-making sandalwood scent, and those taper things they burn, jock-straps, whatever they're called. And garlic, which I friggin' hate as it stinks like gone-off sweat.

The place is full of wanky students and dolies who ought to be actively seeking work, not spending their handouts on poncey scran and roll-ups. I squeeze between the clumps of the great unwashed and sit at an empty table in the corner, underneath a poster of battery hens with their feathers pecked off. A girl with hennaed hair and a pierced eyebrow slouches up to me. She's all in black, a mini-skirt, tights, DMs, and a T-shirt with *It Don't Amount To . . .* on the front. When she turns round, I see it says . . . *A Hill o'Beans* on the back. She's got a look of Cyndi Lauper only young.

'Hi,' she says in a drawly voice, sliding a piece of card at me.

'Here's the menu. Specials are up on the board but there's not much left now. Anything to drink while you're deciding?'

'Coke,' I say. 'Not that diet stuff neither.' She gazes at me in a vacant-like vegetarian way. I want to slap her, or force-feed her with raw pig's liver. 'Is this where Gemma Probert works?'

'Gemma? Yeah, she's in the kitchen. Want a word?'

I shrug. 'Yes. No. Um, OK then.' She shoots me a pitying look like I'm some kind of retard and slumps off. I check out the menu but I've never heard of any of the food. It all sounds foreign, like Aduki Bean Jalfreizi, or Gado-Gado, just a load of cheapo student scran. A hammy hand plonks a glass of Coke on the table. It's Gemma Probert, all flushed and sweaty, wearing a double-outsize T-shirt with a photo of Robbie Williams on the front. At first I think it must be an old pic from his fatboy period, then I realise it's been stretched to buggery so it'll fit over her spare tyres.

'Rowena! You came! You don't know how much this means to us.' She wipes her glistening forehead with a serviette and beams at me.

'Just happened to be up this way. I was starvingly hungry. Never clocked it was your place till I saw the name on the menu.' I wish she'd stop looking so grateful, it's wearing me out.

'You're here, that's the main thing,' she gushes. 'I'm OK for half an hour, Brighid says I can take my break now. Good job an' all, I'm absolutely ravishing.'

I can't be arsed to work out the menu so I go I'll just have a plate of chips. Gemma says they don't do chips but Bombay Potatoes are nearly the same only spicy, or I could try veggie-bangers and spuds mashed with soya milk. I say I'd rather suck sick through a sock but I could go a peanut butter sarnie. She says nee bovva, they cater for all exotic tastes, and waddles through the back to make me one while I have to sit there listening to these wanky students. They're blathering on about music, like they've got a clue. This ginger-haired lezzie type says, 'I think Fun Lovin' Criminals are rilly gid.'

Her ugly mate says, 'They're *quite* gid, but not as gid as Radiohead.' I've never heard a student say 'good' properly, and they're supposed to be educated!

Gemma wobbles back with a mountain of leftovers for herself and a weird-looking concoction for me. It's a slab of brown bread plastered in peanut butter with comma-shaped things sprinkled on top.

'Sprouted mung beans,' she says, shovelling burnt crusty stuff into her mouth. 'Try them, they're crunchy.'

'So's gravel, but you wouldn't slap it on a sarnie,' I tell her. 'I can't eat these things, they remind me of wee dead foetuses. Oh Jesus, I didn't mean to say that, Gem!'

'It's all right, man,' she says, but her eyes have gone shiny wet-look. 'I'm sick of people watching what they say in front of us. It's something I've got to live with. That don't mean it's easy though, specially now I'm all on my own.' She pushes her plate away, fishes a rollie out of her pocket and sparks up.

'What happened to Taz?'

Gemma sniffs. 'He fucked off with a lass from Dunston, a right woofer she was. But you know Taz, he'd shag a crack in the pavement.'

Her face is dead straight but the way she says it, it sounds right comical. I try to stifle a giggle but it comes out my nose as a piggy snort. Gemma looks at me and sniggers, then we both end up laughing like drains till the tears run down her cheeks and I realise she's not laughing any more.

'What time do you get off?' I hear myself ask. 'I can call back if you like.' I must be out of my head, there's no way I want to get involved in Gemma Probert's problems, but I suppose anything's better than going home. She says to hammer on the door about six o' clock. That gives me a couple of hours to kill. 'Later then, right?'

'Later.' She blows her nose on a serviette and starts picking at her food with her puddingy fingers, gazing into space.

I wander round the shops, such as they are up the naff end. I daren't go back into the city centre in case I bump into the CIA and get taken to a basement dungeon in the Pentagon for questioning. There's hardly anything worth robbing round here, but I rip off a whoopee cushion and plastic dog turd from the joke shop, just to keep my hand in.

It's six o'clock. I *so* don't want to get involved with Gemma Probert's problems. This is the last time, the very last time, I give in to someone's pleading.

I bang on the door of the Hill o' Beans. The foundations shake as Gemma thuds across the bare boards to let me in. She looks a right clip, her hair's lank and there's brown food stains all over Robbie's blow-up face.

'I've just wiped round the wet preparation area,' she says. 'Only one more job to do.'

I follow her through to the kitchen. She's setting little boxes filled with blue stuff on the floor. 'For the mice,' she explains.

'You feed the friggin' mice? Jesus, you vegetarians!'

Gemma grins. 'It's poison, you dozy plum. We'd be overrun with the little sods otherwise.'

She sprinkles something behind the cooker. 'Slug-killer,' she says. 'I'm sick of wiping their slime off everything. It works brilliant, I found three dead this morning.'

I wrinkle my nose. 'And you have to hoy them out? Urghh, it's disgusting. You should get a cat, at least they eat what they kill. Christ, Gemma, how can you work in a place like this?'

She stares at me. 'Think about it. It's not that different from what you do.' I shrug. 'And I get free food thrown in,' she goes, like that's a bonus.

Gemma lives above the caff, up some steep stairs that must be deadly when you're pissed. She's puffing like a pair of old bellows. I can't believe this is the person who won the hundred metres two years running. The flat looks like a warehouse inside, boxes stacked up to the ceiling, bin-bags everywhere, and a fusty smell of rodents and wet cardboard. She opens a door at the far end of the hall.

'It ain't a palace,' she announces unnecessarily. 'Ignore the mess.'

That's easy said. The room's a right tip, even by my slutty standards. There's bott-all in the way of furniture – an old plastic sofa and chair, a glass-top table, a portable telly in the corner. You can hardly move for plates stuck up to buggery with congealed scran, half-finished mugs of coffee with tab ends floating on top, and screwed-up chip wrappers. I decide to act like it's normal.

'Where's your exercise bike?' I ask, for something to say.

'What exercise bike?'

'On Wednesday, you said you'd bought one. It was your Announcement. We clapped you.'

'Oh that,' sniffs Gemma. 'I made that up. I couldn't think of anything to say.'

'Right. What's all the stuff in the hall?' I ask. 'Boxes and that?'

She shoots me a look. 'Promise you won't tell?' I cross my hands over my bosoms. 'It's some of Taz's loot. Videos, microwaves, stereos. Him and a mate jacked a Comet van. Them bags, they're full of sports gear, Berghaus and Nike mainly, off a ram-raid. I'm kind of stashing it for him till the heat's off. As a favour, like.'

'What, after he finished you for another lass? You must be off your head.'

'He gave me that telly,' she says defensively. 'And the answering machine. Not much use since they cut the phone off though, but. It's an extension off the café phone now. I'm on call, like a doctor, in case there's an emergency.'

'What, like if someone runs out of black-eyed beans at midnight?'

Gemma grins. 'Want to hear something?' She presses a button on the answering machine. There's a bit crackle and some phlegm-clearing, then Taz's voice comes on.

*Hiya, it's me. Just ringing to say forget about going to the pub tonight. I won't be coming home. Erm, I mean like, ever. Sorry, babe, shit happens.*

113

*I'll send you some cash, tide you over like. Stay loose, doll. See ya.*

I gulp. 'That's *it*? He dumped you on an answering machine? The rotten scumbag!'

'He's not *all* bad. I know he could be a bastard sometimes, but his heart was in the right place.'

'Pity his brains were in his bollocks,' I quip.

'You had to *be* there. Honest, Rowena, he was dead nice after Nathan was born.' Gemma flaps her hand, clutching at invisible straws. 'Like a proper dad, nearly.'

'Lepers don't change their spots,' I tell her, but she's away with the pixies, lost inside her head. My life ticks away in the silence. I *so* don't want to be here in this crummy dive. I wonder whether to tell her about baby Nathan, how I gave him a cuddle and sang him to the big long sleep, but I decide against it. Life's too short.

Gemma sniffs and shifts her huge bulk. The sofa complains creakily.

'After Nathan died,' she mutters, like there hasn't been a gap in the conversation, 'I totally lost it. It was cot death. Nobody knew for sure why it happened, but I felt it was all down to me, like I hadn't looked after him properly, or it was God's way of punishing me for shagging around. That's when I piled on all this lard.' She clutches a handful of spare tyres and flops them around. 'Taz was a useless fucker, out every night, pubbing, clubbing, on the rob, whatever. He'd come home late, we'd have a barney, then I'd raid the fridge and stuff my face for comfort. It all went, I dunno . . .'

'Pear-shaped?' I offer.

'I was gonna say belly up.' Gemma grins and slaps her gut. Her body wibble-wobbles like a jelly, and Robbie's face bobs up and down with her breasts. 'I shot up to a size twelve after I had Nathan. That was bad enough, but when I started bingeing I could put on half a stone over a weekend, nee bovva. Now I'm size sixteen. Look at the soddin' state of me; I could be a body double for Jabba the Hutt.'

114

My nose does a snorty snigger. 'You used to be so skinny, Gem. I'm not trying to scare you, but it's canny dangerous, all that blubber. I saw it on a web site about UFOs and stuff. It said: *When They Come, They'll Eat the Fat Ones First.*'

Gemma gets her baccy and makes a rollie, like she hasn't heard me. 'Anyway, the more bloated I got, the more depressed I was. Never went out the door, only got out of bed to chuck stodge down my neck. I lived on bacon sarnies. Thick-sliced white bread, acres of butter, rashers like bricks, great dollops of ketchup. It was gross. Sometimes I didn't even wait for the bacon to cook – it was practically *grunting*! I couldn't see the point of anything. That's when I tried to top myself.'

I gasp. 'Eee, Gem, you never! How?'

'Bread knife. That's why I wear these.' She rolls the sweatbands off her wrists. It looks like somebody's been playing noughts and crosses.

'Friggin' hell, what a mess. Did it hurt?'

Gemma shrugs. 'Can't remember. I was well out of it, off my head with tequila. Next thing I know, I'm up the hospital. Our Louise came to see me, but not Mam and Dad. They wouldn't have owt to do with me after I moved in with Taz. I don't exist as far as they're concerned. They never even sent a card when we buried Nathan.' She rubs her eyes and blows her nose with a greasy serviette off one of the dirty plates. 'So,' says Gemma, spreading out her arms. 'This is my life. I live in a shithole, work at a shit job, and look ten times worse than shit.'

I decide not to mention the smell.

'So that's why you go to the Madolescents? You know, Altamont Lodge.'

'Aye,' says Gemma. 'They put me on some tablets and sent me to see a counsellor. I only go there to get out of this dump. I can't see that it's doing me much good otherwise.'

I glance at my Swatch. It's nearly eight o'clock. 'I've gotta go,

Gem.' Her face hits the floor. 'Hadn't realised the time. I need to be somewhere.'

'Sorry, Rowena, I bet I've bored you shitless. See you Wednesday then, eh?'

'Right,' I say, brushing past the mountain of knock-off electrical goods. 'Mebbes.'

# 13

## *Mugged!*

I do a massive poo this morning, a pointy thing like a monster walnut whip peeking above the waterline. It's probably irritable bowel syndrome, as Mum's refused to lie for me again and insists I go back to work before I'm sacked for malingering. I'm dreading seeing Dean after our sexual fiasco on Saturday night. If he's told anyone he'd best get measured up for a long box cos he's Dead with a capital 'D'.

'Ah, Rowena, you're here,' says Mrs Marr, checking her watch. I'm only a *bit* late. 'Kidneys back in working order?'

I nod. 'Almost.'

By the state of the old bat, she's been under the sunbed again, her face looks like something from World of Leather. 'Hold the fort in reception, would you,' she says, her voice clippy. 'Mr Crowther's called me in for a meeting.'

'What about the coffee?' I protest. 'There'll be mutiny if it's late.'

'It'll have to wait, this takes priority.' She scurries into Mr Crowther's office looking vexed. What's going on? I sit behind the desk and check out the drawers for incriminating or personal stuff. There's nothing, unless you count her private stockpile of Post-it notes, enough to wallpaper a room. The phone rings a couple of times but I'm straining my ears to catch what they're saying in Mr Crowther's office so I switch off the buzzer on the switchboard and watch the red lights flash in silence. It's impossible to hear them from behind the desk so I get up and pretend to tidy the soft meeting area but I still can't make out what they're saying. Flicking through the magazines, I come across an article about this wifey who had a vulvectomy and was left with just a hole, nothing round it at all. How gruesome is that? I'm scanning the problem page when Mrs Marr pokes her head round the door, looking dead serious.

'Step into Mr Crowther's office please, Rowena.'

'I can't, I'm relieving on reception.'

'I'll take over now. Come along, Mr Crowther hasn't got all day.'

I haul my ass into his office. He's staring at the computer screen, looking really, really cross. Oh Jesus, I'd forgotten about the catastrophe last week. My heart's thudding like a pair of bongos.

'Rowena, we seem to have a problem with the computer.' He still hasn't looked at me. He *knows*, he must do! 'What can you tell me about it?'

'Er, not a lot. We did a bit at school, word processing and stuff.' Best act dumb. And remember – *deny, deny, even unto death.*

He swivels round in his chair and looks me straight in the eyes. My irritable bowel gurgles. 'Do you know what corrupt data means?'

I gaze at the ceiling, screwing my face up like I'm thinking furiously. 'Is it when you download porn from the Internet?' He winces. 'Not *you*, obviously. I mean other people. Sickos. Perverts.'

Mr Crowther gives a thin smile. 'I don't think it's quite as literal as that. We seem to have a problem on the client database, the postcodes have gone haywire, some sort of virus perhaps. I was hoping you might be able to shed some light on it. Was the computer behaving when you used it last week?'

'Me? I haven't touched it, swear down.' I'll never confess, not even if they yank out my fingernails and torture me with electric nipple clamps.

'It's just that some other files appear to have been deleted as well, fortunately nothing that can't be replaced, but I do need to get to the bottom of it. You won't be in any trouble, Rowena, I assure you. Just tell me, did the computer crash while you were using it?'

'I never touched it, I swear I never. It must have been the cleaner, when she was dusting it. Or a gremlin, a poltergeist, I don't know. It definitely wasn't me, and that's God's honest truth.' My scalp tingles. A bead of sweat trickles down my cleavage. Mr Crowther sighs and shakes his head slowly.

'In that case, perhaps you'd ask Mrs Marr to call out Dark Systems.' He uncaps his fountain pen and starts signing a pile of cheques. I stand rooted to the spot. 'That will be all for now, Rowena,' he goes, not looking at me.

He *knows*! Well, he suspects, but he can't prove it so who cares? I'm trembling like an old biddy when I go into the kitchen to make the coffee. Dean's not around, he's gone out with Gerry to collect a stiff, so that's a relief. Mr Scudamore clacks his dentures and goes, 'About time too, a person could die of thirst round here,' like he hasn't got a pair of hands on the end of his arms. 'How ya doin', sexy,' calls Ray. I'd normally flick him the finger but I truly can't be arsed. I set the tray and spoon coffee into the mugs. My hands are trembling, I can't seem to get a grip on the kettle, the water's slopping all over.

'Steady on, pet, you'll scald yourself,' goes Ray. I grab my mug and take a big slurp of coffee. Oh shit, it's boilingly hot, my tongue's absolutely nuked! Ray just laughs, like third-degree burns are some huge joke. 'Why don't you blow it?'

Jesus, he *knows*! Dean must have told him about the other night, about the blow job, otherwise why would he say that? My fingers go all limp, the drink slips out of my hands and I knock the tray crashing on to the floor. The mugs shatter and boiling coffee spills everywhere. Omigawd, they know, they all know! Mr Scudamore comes rushing over and sticks my hands under the cold tap. My head's buzzing with pins and needles and my legs are numb, I think I'm going to faint. There's a thud as I slump to the floor, then nothing, I'm just sinking deeper and deeper into velvety blackness . . .

'Here she is, back in the land of the living.' Mr Scudamore looms over me, a daft smile on his chops. 'Thought we'd got ourselves another client for a minute. Try to sit up, Ribena, and sip this water.'

'The mugs,' I mutter. 'Did I smash all the mugs?'

'Never mind the mugs, we can get new ones. We can't replace you, though.'

I feel a right fool, I hope my knickers didn't show when I passed out, they're old ones with anchors and *Hello Sailor*, thousand-wash grey and only fit for floorcloths.

'Come along, we're sending you home in a taxi.'

'But the mugs . . .'

'Mugs schmugs,' goes Mr Scudamore, and walks me through to reception.

'The cab's outside,' Mrs Marr slips my jacket over my shoulders. 'Are you sure you'll be all right on your own, Rowena?' I nod weakly. 'Don't come in tomorrow if you're no better, we'll manage somehow.'

Cool, a day off with permission. Maybe I could stretch it to a week.

'Drop me in town,' I tell the cabbie. 'At the Monument.'

*Mugs.*

My head feels ready to explode. I'm in torment, I could spontaneously combust at any second. Firstly that business with the computer. Mr Crowther doesn't buy my story, I know he doesn't. He'll never trust me again. Any chance of career advancement is now – unlike me – well and truly fucked.

*Mugs. Mugs.*

Secondly and worstly, I reckon Dean's spilled the beans about our disastrous sexual encounter. I bet they were sniggering behind my back and discussing every intimate detail, how I gave him a crap blow job and begged him to shag me. Oh God, I'll never be able to face them again.

*Mugs. Mugs. Mugs.*

What's wrong with me? The world's caved in around me, my

brain's wired with Semtex and I'm obsessing about *mugs.*

*Mugs. Mugs. Mugs. Mugs.*

Beware the cyborg, the mighty Rowenacop.

*Surrender your mugs, you have twenty seconds to comply.*

See her stride, an unstoppable mug-seeking missile, past Envy, via the Cookie Stall into the mini-Mall and through the plate-glass portals of Gallimaufry.

*This is a stick-up. Hand over the mugs or the puppy gets it.*

Jesus, what's wrong with me?

*Hello, Earth to Rowena. Anyone home?*

*Only me, Rowena M. Vincent. M as in Mad. As in Madder Than Logs.*

Cool it, Rowena. Get a grip. Breathe slowly, through your nose. OK, OK, I'm back in control.

Gallimaufry (stupid name) is a shop that flogs wanky gear to people with more bread than brains. Designer Giftware, they call it. Tat, more like. Elvis mouse mats, pens that light up in case you have a brainwave in the night, leopardskin lampshades, bath pillows shaped like bosoms, who needs 'em? But they also sell the fabbiest mugs with yellow smiley faces, mugs full of sunshine, joyful, have-a-nice-day, mood-enhancing mugs. A-ha, there they are, the happy, grinning, beaming mugs. Locked up in a friggin' display case wired to the alarm! Waste of time looking here, then.

As I trudge frowning out of the shop, the bimboid on the till glares at me as if I'm a demented bag lady. I feel round my bum to check if my grubby knickers are showing. All in order. What's her friggin' problem?

*Mugs.*

Just round the corner is Halfdays, a geet posh department store. Not a place I normally frequent, the assistants are right snotty cows, but it'll kill some time as I don't want to go home until Mum's gone to work. The prices are outrageous, you'd have to be a Lottery millionaire to shop here, or a mental defective. I wander in through the Food Hall checking out the scran with poncey names –

taramasalata, monkfish brioche, spinach roulade which is like a swiss roll only with disgusting green stuff instead of jam. At the Lunchbox counter there's a queue of office types ordering weird sarnies. Prawn Marie Rose with spicy onions on Mediterranean sun-dried tomato bread? I'd rather eat roadkill between two beer mats, thank you.

*Mugs. Mugs.*

Check out the Cookshop, it's full of strange kitchen thingies that could be instruments of torture. 'What's this?' I ask an oily-looking bloke, pointing at a bright yellow thing that reminds me of school gates.

He twinkles over. 'It's a cookbook stand, cast-iron, we do a range of utensils in all the primary colours. This trivet, for example, or a wooden-spoon rest. Were you seeking anything in particular?'

Yeah. Plastic surgery, fake ID and a fast plane to jet me to a new life.

'A wedding present,' I lie. 'What's that over there?'

'The salt pig? Peruvian earthenware, don't you love that divine glaze?' Puh-leeze. Go get a life, sadboy. He shows me a hen's nest made of sticks, an egg dispenser, he calls it. What's wrong with the top shelf of the fridge? 'How about a cafetière?' he goes. 'Or a toast rack? Novelty egg-cups?'

*Mugs. Mugs. Mugs.*

'Got any mugs?' (Apart from yourself, obviously.) He dances over to a pine stand chock-full of crockery, all arty-farty stuff, no Flintstones or Spice Girls anywhere.

'Special purchase, just in,' he creams. 'Leamington Lustreware, all hand-painted, no transfers. Look at that gilding, such exquisite craftsmanship. It's their latest collection, on the theme of farmyard animals, I'm sure it's going to leap off the shelves.' Yeah, right. Straight into my rucksack. 'Oh, do excuse me,' he flusters. 'My presence is required elsewhere. Just ask at the till if you need any help.' He bounds away, a spaniel in a cheapo suit.

These mugs are the business, a bit on the heavy side but the pictures are cool. The one with the pig will do perfect for Ray but I can't decide on Mrs Marr's. Is she a mother hen or a cow? I take the hen, best not to upset her. Mr Scudamore can have the one with the sheep, he's forever calling me his pet lamb. God, my rucksack weighs a ton, better hurry up before I dislocate my shoulder. There's not much choice left for Dean. I could get him a rooster – oh no, they'll all be cracking cock jokes. Can't get him a donkey either – they'll kid him about being hung like one. Forget it, I'll get him another Magpies mug from the Toon Army shop. Time to ship out.

Just as I reach the door this squaddie type latches on to my arm. There's a woman with him, she's wearing a poncho, how naff is that? Oh, I get it, they must be Christian loonies, they're always hanging round the Monument yelling about eternal damnation and stuff. I'm about to say, Not today thank you, I've made a pact with Lucifer, when he goes, 'Excuse me, I'm a security guard and I have reason to believe that you're in possession of goods which haven't been paid for. I'd like you to accompany me to the security office.'

I gasp. 'You're kidding, right?' That's it, it's a joke. I've been set up for one of those TV humiliation shows, they wind you up and get you crazy, then bleep out the four-letter words. Where've they hidden the cameras?

'Please, come with me to the security office.' Omigawd, this guy's serious! I run through my options. One: I could leg it. Two: well, there isn't a two. The poncho woman takes my other arm and they lead me through the store, past the tutters and rubberneckers, up the escalators to the second floor. So this is the infamous security office. Shithole more like. It's totally bare except for a bench bolted to the floor and a window with wire over it. The room starts to come and go in waves and everything seems blurred. I'm in a daze, sweating cobs, but I keep repeating a mantra inside my head.

*Deny, deny, even unto death.*

'The security manager's on his way,' goes the guard. 'You might as well sit down.' I flop on the bench and stick the rucksack between my feet. My head's swimming, like when you're pissed and get the whirly pits. I think I'm going to throw up. A massive bloke, he must be about seven feet tall, comes into the room. He reminds me of that big guy, wossname, in *Third Rock from the Sun.*

'I'm Mr Maxwell, the security manager,' he says. I sit there melting like a tub of lard, staring blankly at his knees. 'I'm going to ask Mrs Benn, who's one of our store detectives, to relate the facts leading to your detention and I'd like you to listen carefully. Mrs Benn?'

She straightens her stupid poncho. 'I observed this young lady acting suspiciously in the Cookshop. I alerted the security guard who kept her under physical surveillance and also contacted the CCTV monitoring unit.' Jesus, sounds like I got a bigger audience than Channel 5! 'I then witnessed her taking three mugs which she deliberately concealed in her bag and made no attempt to pay for. That bag, there.' She points triumphantly at my rucksack.

'Is that an accurate account of what happened?' the tall bloke asks me. His voice sounds echoey, like it's coming from space, or down a long tunnel. 'Do you agree with Mrs Benn's version of events?' I shrug, well, it's more of a tic, just to show I'm alive. 'Would you please remove from your bag or from your person any property you haven't paid for.'

*Click.* My mind switches off. I'm past fear, beyond panic, they'll never reach me now. I'm home, safe on Planet Rowena. My earth-body's here, perched on the hard bench, but the other me, the *real* me, floats through time and space.

Unreachable, untouchable, unhurtable.

# 14

## Busted!

My brain's clicking in and out, channel-hopping, zapping between their world and mine. Mine, mostly. This police officer, a dumpy bint with greasy hair and tree-trunk legs, takes me into another room and frisks me in a pat-down search. That's practically assault, that is. I'll die if she sees my grubby knickers. Oh why didn't I put some decent ones on this morning? Typical!

'... *you are not obliged to say any*thing ...' I know the spiel by heart, I've heard it a million times on *The Bill*, so I lip-synch along with the words. '... *which you may later rely on in court.*' Apparently she's arresting me for theft. *Arresting* me? Arresting *me*?

Images of life in the chokey flash through my brain. Ping-pong, tin cups, snout barons, lesbo screws and, Omigawd, slopping out! If I have to wear those shapeless denim things like in *Prisoner: Cell Block H* on Channel 5, I'm going on hunger strike, that's for sure. Jesus, what if they make me share a cell with, e.g. Rosemary West? Or worse, force me to resit my GCSEs? This can't happen. Visions drift in and out of my head: Mum and Dean spearheading a campaign for justice, a bunch of protestors parading in front of the nick with banners, chanting 'Free the Fozzy Hall One.'

Next thing I know, I'm being bundled out of a panda car into the cop shop, and 'escorted', i.e. shoved, into a broom cupboard. A sign on the door says 'JUVENILE DETENTION ROOM.'

'We'll need to contact your parent or guardian,' says Dumpy. I check out my fingernails. I wish I'd never nicked this Sassy Sapphire polish, it chips like buggery, I ought to complain to the manufacturers. 'Would you give me a contact number for your parent or guardian, Rowena.' Jesus, she knows my name! I mentally run through the contents of my rucksack. It could only be my bus pass, that's all the ID I carry. 'No point being obstructive, we'll find out sooner or later. It's in your interest to co-operate.'

My head won't stay up on my neck, it feels like it's full of snakes, writhing and tangling in knots, injecting venom into my brain. I flop forward on to the table and bang my forehead. Shit, that really, really hurt!

'Are you all right? Would you like some water?' goes Dumpy. I nod weakly. 'Don't try to build up your part.' She smirks, not a shred of sympathy. 'It's not exactly concussion.'

*Concussion!* Thank you, Big G. Thank you for sending me that thunderbolt of inspiration.

'It could be,' I mutter weakly. 'I collapsed at work this morning. Passed spark out. My mind keeps going blank.'

'Oh, blackouts, is it? Well, makes a change from the menopause, I suppose. We've heard every excuse in the book, dear, and blackouts are about number three in the charts, after amnesia and the change of life. Come on now, if we can't contact a parent or guardian, we'll have to call in a Youth Justice Worker to act as an appropriate adult so we can interview you.'

'I need a doctor. A specialist, a consultant. You'll be in big trouble if I die in custody from a brain haemorrhage, specially on top of wrongful arrest.' Dumpy screws up her chops in a sort of grin. 'It's no joke,' I insist. 'I need to have my head examined.'

'Tell me about it,' she snorts. I thought the bizzies were supposed to be trained in this sort of situation, I could be on the verge of death and she's sitting there with a face like fizz making sarky comments.

'I demand a brief,' I tell her firmly. Dumpy just smirks and says I've been watching too many cop shows on the telly. She's a right hard-faced cow, plus she should do something about that moustache, like take a strimmer to it. She's drumming her fingers on the table, trying to stare me down. My irritable bowel starts churning, that's all I need. Please God, don't let me fill my pants,

I'm in enough shit already. If this was real life like on the telly, they'd send for the duty solicitor, some dodgy bloke on the payroll of the Mob, who can get anybody off no matter what they've done. Why haven't they brought me the phone? Everybody's entitled to one call. I could give Ally McBeal a ring and ask her to get a dream team of superlawyers on the case, that'd teach 'em. Maybe they'll televise my trial on Court TV and it'll get massive viewing figures, bigger than Millennium Eve or Princess Diana's funeral. Whoa, stop this right now, Rowena. Grip, get a.

What's going on? Somehow I'm in a different room, with no idea how I got here. Dumpy and another plod with ginger hair are eyeballing me across a table. A hippy-type woman with a plait sits next to me.

'Go on, Rowena,' she says. 'Answer the question.' She's wearing those stupid round specs like that old Beatle bloke, somebody ought to give her a style makeover. 'Explain to the sergeant how the mugs came to be in your bag.'

*Mugs?* Omigawd, I'd forgotten about the mugs! Looks like they're not buying my line about being concussed, then. I'd better think of something else, some majorly traumatic event that's left me psychologically scarred and suffering deep inner turmoil. Time to squeeze out a few tears. At least then if I get done it'll look like wossname, remorse. It was on telly once that when film stars need to cry, they think of crap things that happened to them, like their dog got squashed by a truck or someone said they looked fat. Concentrate, Rowena. Turn on those waterworks.

I try to picture my Nana Vincent after the stroke, her face all twisted and dragged down on one side like melting candlewax. Her eyes really spooked me, they looked scared to death, like she couldn't work out what had happened, how her hand had turned into a useless claw, why her mouth wouldn't make proper words. Thinking about her makes me canny sad but I can't feel any sign of tears.

Then I remember baby Nathan in his tiny white casket, the feel of his curly-wurly ears and his perfect wee fingers. I hope Nana Vincent meets him in heaven, she'll feed him treacle sarnies and milky coffee and spoil him rotten. But still I can't make myself cry, even when I dig my nails into my wrists till they really, really hurt.

Looks like I'll have to go for the Big One.

* * *

I knew something was wrong as soon as I walked through the door. The air felt heavy, stifling and dangerous, like just before a thunderstorm. I remember thinking how strange it was not to smell gravy. It was a Wednesday, mince and dumplings day. I never dawdled home from school on Wednesdays.

'Mum,' I shouted, an edge of panic in my voice. 'Mum, where are you?'

'Ssshh, she's having a lie down.' Nana Vincent padded downstairs in her fluffy slippers. 'Your mum's not feeling too grand, so be a good girl and see how quiet you can be.'

Nana's face was pinched up. Her eyes looked red and sore. I sensed something big was going on, and it wasn't good. Even before she told me, I knew it was about Dad. I never asked, because I didn't want to hear the answer, but the wondering frightened me nearly to death.

Mum stayed in bed for, I dunno, days, weeks maybe. Nana Vincent took food upstairs on a tray, and brought it down again, untouched. I floated around the house like a wee ghost, treading on silent tippy-toes, holding my breath until silver shapes floated in front of my eyes.

The day Mum came downstairs, she looked like a skelly. Her eyes were sunken, dark-circled, and she shuffled as though her bones hurt. At first I wanted to hug her, but I was scared she'd disintegrate, crumble to dust in front of me, so I kept my distance. Mostly I stayed in my room and chewed my lip until it bled, weeping soundless tears and trying to make my mind a blank.

Nana Vincent cried when she told me.

'It's your dad, Rowena,' she said, in a weird husky voice. 'He's gone.'

'I know. I *know*!' Strangely, my ears went funny after that so I didn't have to hear any more.

*Dad. Da-a-a-a-a-a-d!*

Here they come at last, like geet big melted hailstones, uncontrollable sobs welling up and spilling out. My head slumps down on the table, tears, spit and snot splashing off the naff brown Fablon. Can't breathe, ribs aching, chest bursting, full-blown, whole-body crying. I lift my head and an almighty roar escapes from my mouth, like a cow in labour. No, it sounds more like a damned soul, a helpless spirit flung into the everlasting bonfire. Alone, abandoned, beyond hope.

The bizzies look dead worried and so they should, I'm considering reporting them for police brutality. Hippy-chick's got her arm round me, Ginger Plod's holding a glass of water to my mouth, and even Dumpy's taking me seriously now, chewing the inside of her cheek and praying I won't grass her up to the Police Complaints Authority.

'It's . . . it's been five years today,' I find myself saying. I'm all cried out, perhaps I'll die from dehydration like people who OD on laxatives.

'Take your time, pet,' says Ginger Plod, patting me on the back like he's winding a baby. 'You were saying, five years ago today?' He turns it into a question.

I leave a suitable pause for max dramatic effect. 'It was terrible,' I gulp. 'Horrific. The worst day of my life. I've never talked about it to anyone.' I drop my head into my hands to hide my face.

Hippy-chick hugs me. 'It'll help to share your pain, Rowena,' she goes in a daft voice, as if she's comforting a cat that's going to be put down. 'You don't have to bear the hurt on your own. Maybe now's a good time to disclose.'

I lift up my head and gaze bravely into the space between Ginger Plod and Dumpy. I take a deep breath like I'm about to reveal something momentous. Which I am.

'It's my dad,' I say at last. 'That's when he did it. Five years ago today.'

Silence. They fidget and steal secret glances at each other, like they know what's coming. They don't, of course. Neither do I.

'And you'd be how old then?'

'I'm sixteen now so I'd be, erm . . .'

'Eleven. No age at all.' They shake their heads sadly.

'Well done. You've taken the first step, it's always the most difficult,' says Hippy-chick. She pauses. 'Is he still doing it, Rowena? Your father?' I flinch. 'In your own time. And only if you feel up to it.'

'How d'you mean, still doing it?'

'Doing . . . whatever he did. Or was that the only time?'

I raise my head and look slowly at each of them in turn, savouring the moment.

'You can only do it once,' I say. 'That's if you do it properly.'

'I'm not quite with you,' goes Ginger Plod. Who says policemen are thick?

'He . . . he *committed suicide*.'

A big fat silence hangs in the air while they try to take it in. They lean in closer to me. I take a deep breath.

'It was me who found him,' I confide in a croaky voice. 'In the shed, he was. I'd just got back from school, I was going to chop logs which was always my first job once I got home.' Cool it, Rowena, you'll be saying you worked as a chimney sweep in your lunch hour next. Keep it simple. 'I couldn't open the door, there was a dead weight behind it. I shoved and shoved until it gave way. I couldn't believe what I was seeing.'

I pause for a sip of water. They're willing me to go on.

'It was horrible, grisly. I still have flashbacks and nightmares about it. Oh God . . .' I cover my face with my hands and my shoulders shudder.

'You don't have to continue, Rowena, this is clearly distressing for you.'

Oh, but I do, I do. They'll be sorry they put me through hell and wrongful arrest. I jerk about a bit as if I'm having a mild seizure, then pull myself together with a superhuman effort.

'There was blood everywhere,' I sob. 'It was like an abattoir, all this sticky stuff on the walls. I thought it was marmalade at first, couldn't work it out. Then I realised. It was . . . it was *brains*! Great gobs of it, splattered all over the wall like bright red Artex.' I shudder at the memory. 'That's when I clocked the shotgun.'

They're gobsmacked, can't take their eyes off me. I reckon they're getting off on this, the sickos.

'He'd put it in his mouth, pulled the trigger, blown half his head away. There were bits of him everywhere, it was the most gruesome sight you could imagine. I still can't eat mince to this day.'

I stare blankly at the table with a traumatised expression, totally zomboid, emotionally drained by my disclosure.

Silence.

It worked! They're letting me off with a caution. OK, it goes on my rap-sheet but it's not like a criminal record or anything. Is it?

Somehow they managed to contact Mum, devious bastards. The bus company must have given them my address – I'm sure there's some data protection law against that – and they drove round to our house. Mum was at the chip factory, of course, but I guess the Mutants next-door poked their nosy nebs in and told them where she worked. Anyways, she turns up at the nick and takes me home in a taxi and an ominous silence.

There's gonna be World War Five when that door shuts behind us. Jesus, I am SO in deep shit!

# 15

## Couch Heaven

Mum shoots straight upstairs without a single word. She'll beat me to a pulp, I just know it. That'll be her now, choosing weapons. I picture her clouting me on the head with the frying pan till my skull caves in, shattering my spine with the bathroom scales, maybe puncturing my lungs with a knitting needle. How should I react? If I fight back it'll make her even madder, but I can't just cower in a corner with my intestines spilling over the carpet, it's not my style. We'll probably end up locked in a deadly embrace on the kitchen floor, discovered three days later by Filthy when he comes round for his oats, maggots slithering through our eye sockets, stinking like a pair of old bloaters.

My heart thumps as I hear her footsteps coming down the stairs. I curl up on the couch in a ball, pummelling my stomach to stop my irritable bowel gurgling. I daren't look at her. The couch sighs as she flops next to me. Please, Big G, let me die instantly with my features intact.

'Look at me, Rowena.' She sounds, I dunno, sort of knackered, exhausted, unless this is a con to make me relax so I won't fight back. 'Look at me.'

I squint through my fringe, deciding to go for the sympathy vote.

'Don't hit me, Mum, please. I feel really, really sick, honest I do.' It sounds pathetic, even to me.

She squeezes my wrist. 'I'm not going to hit you, you silly girl. I'm concerned for you.'

The knot in my stomach unwinds with relief and a little *phttt* of wind escapes from my bottom. The sound of it makes me want to giggle and I have to fight to keep my face straight.

'Ms Herron warned me something like this might happen,' says Mum. 'It's a sort of healing crisis, it has to get worse before it can get better.'

I screw my face up. 'What, you mean the farting? Oh, triffic, I've been turned into a walking whoopee cushion.'

She laughs. 'No, you daft ha'porth. Ms Herron said the therapy rakes up a lot of old stuff, things you thought you'd forgotten about, or you'd rather not face. It affects people in different ways. I suppose that explains today's little incident. I mean, you've never stolen anything before, have you?'

My eyelids flicker as I picture the Warrior Princess outfit, the sports bag in my wardrobe, chock-full of ripped-off cosmetics, practically my entire collection of CDs, the musical jewellery box, silk scarf and leather gloves I gave to Mum last Christmas, the turbo hairdryer. I could go on.

'No, never,' I say, mustering indignation. As if! 'It was weird, like a sort of red mist came over me.' I saw that in a telly programme about some serial killer. 'I don't remember anything, not even being in the shop.'

Mum tuts sympathetically. 'I explained all this to the police. They were very understanding, said they had no intention of adding to your problems. That ginger-haired officer said they could tell you weren't a professional shoplifter from the clumsy way you did it.'

Clumsy! The dog-faced liar, I'll have him for defamation!

'Anyway,' continues Mum, 'I'm going to ring Mrs Marr in the morning and tell her you won't be in work for the rest of the week. You need to rest, Rowena, give your head a chance to settle.'

Wow, I've got away with it! With everything! Not just robbing the mugs, sounds like the whole slate's been wiped clean. *And* I've got time off work. Also it means I can skive off the meeting at Altamont Lodge so I won't have Gemma Probert bending my ear with her sob stories. Being a Madolescent sure has its plus points.

It's such a relief to be home after my ordeal down the nick. I have a totally zonko night's sleep. In the morning I spend a half hour revising my funeral music. That time when Mum found my notepad she went harpic, said I was in the grip of a macabre obsession. I persuaded her it was just a harmless hobby by saying I'd keep pet rats or collect plaster casts of rock stars' penises if she preferred. It's important to keep the music updated in case of sudden death, like I get banjoed by a reversing refuse lorry or torched and hoyed into the Tyne like a joyrider's cast-off. I'd just die if my coffin rolled into the burner to the accompaniment of, say, 'Dog on Wheels' by Belle & Sebastian, which was one of my less inspired choices made when I was on a mega-downer. After a bit pen-chewing, I cross out 'Road Rage' and insert 'Dead from the Waist Down'. It's just swapping one Catatonia track for another but at least it's got the word 'dead' in it so no one can complain about it being inappropriate.

Eventually I stagger downstairs, scoff a bunch of Jammie Dodgers, collapse on the couch and switch on the TV. Daytime telly is boring as fuck, all rag-rolling and scumble glaze, and style makeovers for lardy old women. How pointless is that? It's not like they're going to suddenly pull a millionaire because they're wearing diagonal stripes to disguise a bum the size of Sheffield. The only good bit is the phone-in about domestic violence. I never realised, some women get knocked about every night and twice on Saturdays and they still stay with the bloke because they love him. That can't be right, their brains must be battered to bolivian. Even the agony aunt's stuck for words, she just sits there frowning and gawping like a geriatric goldfish. Then this old gadge rings in saying what about husband-beating, his wife's been slapping him around for thirty years, he's been hospitalised stacks of times and he's got a permanently misaligned jaw. I jump up from the couch, clenching my fists in a victory salute, roaring, 'Yessss!' and Mum pootles in with a duster and goes she didn't realise the football was on, who's scored?

'I spoke to Mrs Marr, told her you're suffering from General

Debility,' she says. 'She's worried about you. Asked if your fainting fit was related to the women's troubles you saw the doctor about last week. What does she mean by that?'

I shrug. 'Daft old bint, she's forever getting mixed up. Doesn't know what day it is half the time. It's probably the menopause. Or Alzheimer's. Mr Crowther ought to pension her off only she's got a hold over him, some blackmail scam. I reckon he's the father of her love child and she's threatening to grass him up to the Freemasons and ruin his business.'

Mum frowns at me. 'That's enough, Rowena. Let's just leave it there,' she says. 'God only knows what Mr Crowther would think if he could hear you talking like that.'

'How do you know he can't? He might have hired Dean to bug the room the other night. Or implanted a microchip in my brain when I was unconscious at work. You needn't laugh, these things happen every day. Ask Moulder and Scowly. I'll tape *The X-Files* for you, then you'll see.'

Mum's offered to take the rest of the week off to look after me but I tell her no because I need lots of sleep to recuperate and her being at home vacuuming like a maniac wouldn't help. Also I've got secret plans for Bundy and she'd go apeshit if she knew he'd been in the house.

As soon as she's left for work I nip outside to the shed. My Trusty Sidekick's curled up on the rescued rug which Mum flung into the bin the other day. He reminds me of one of those spivs off the market, they all wear huge sheepskins.

'Oo's my ickle Bundy Boo?' I go. Stop it, Rowena. It's condescending to talk that way to your animal companion. I step gingerly over all the tiny carcasses. It's like a miniature elephants' graveyard, whole dynasties of rodents have come here to die, gripped in Bundy's vice-like jaws. What will archaeologists make of it when they dig it up a thousand years from now? Who cares anyway?

Bundy weighs a sack of spuds. I haul him into the kitchen and he jumps straight up on to the worktop. How does he do that? It defies gravity, like Concorde taking off or a cruise liner floating in the sea. He rubs himself up against the toaster, purring like a vibrator, black hairs drifting on to the Marrakesh vinoleum.

I rummage in the freezer and dig out a packet of cod in butter sauce, a fancy new line Mum brought home from the factory. It says to boil in the bag but I can't be arsed so I stick it in the microwave and cook it for ten minutes on full power, only I forget to make holes in the plastic and it explodes. The inside of the microwave's a right mess, bits of fish guts and gloopy yellow stuff everywhere. But intrepid Bundy saves the day. He climbs inside and licks the oven walls till they're spotless, I think he gets off on spinning round on the plate. Saves me cleaning the thing, anyway.

I flop on the couch with a packet of Hula Hoops and gaze in fascination as Bundy washes himself, one leg cocked up behind his ear, little pink tongue rasping away at his satsumas. I'll need to get those sorted before Mum allows him in the house. Vets probably charge a fortune, they all drive round in Volvo estates with Labradors behind bars in the back. Or is that farmers? Maybe I could do a DIY job on him, tie a rubber band round his testicles to cut off the blood supply until they die and drop off. The problem would be getting him to lie still while I do it, he'd jab me to death. The main priority is to get rid of his visitors. I gather the equipment – flea comb, kitchen towel, spray and jam jar. Just as I'm plucking up courage to start on him, the phone rings.

'Hi, babes, wossup?' Omigawd, it's *Dean*! My scalp fizzes and my face goes hot and prickly. I'm not ready to talk to him, not until I've decided what line to take. Do I act like our sexual fiasco never happened, or should I cut him dead and slam down the phone right now? Help!

'You there, Rowena? Speak to me. What's going on?'

'I can't talk right now, doctor's orders. I'm really, really sick . . . swollen glands . . . laryngitis . . . inflamed vocal cords. If I strain my throat I could lose my voice for ever, then I'd have to get one of those computer thingies to speak with and they cost millions. Bye.'

'Hang on a sec. You sound in a bad way. Can I come round and see you?'

'No!' I yell a bit hysterically. 'You might catch it. Anyway I'm covered in huge purple swellings, I look a right divvy.'

He laughs. I'm glad somebody thinks it's funny. 'I'll risk it,' he says. 'I just want to see you.'

'You can't, I'm in that thing, what's it called – sounds like Quentin Tarantino.'

'What, quarantine?' says Dean.

'That's the one. They say it could be Lassa fever, rabies even, we're waiting for the test results coming back from Switzerland. Look, I've got to go, the nurse is here to change my dressing. Bye.'

'OK, OK,' he goes. 'Promise you'll give me a bell if there's anything I can do. We're all thinking about you.'

'Wait, there *is* something. You know fleas . . .?'

'Fleas?'

'Yeah, like e.g. cat fleas. Just imagine a bunch of them in, say, a jam jar. How long could they live without food?'

'Are you for real?' says Dean. 'What's this about?'

'It was a question on *Fifteen-to-One*. Can't you find out off the Internet? It's really important,' I plead.

'Well,' he says thoughtfully. 'They'd eat each *other*, I suppose. Fleas aren't fussy as long as they get blood from somewhere. It's like in that rhyme.'

'What rhyme?' Jesus, how did we get on to friggin' poetry?

Dean thinks for a bit, then says:

> '*Big fleas have little fleas*
> *Upon their backs to bite 'em.*
> *Little fleas have smaller fleas*
> *And so ad infinitum.*'

'Yeah,' he says. 'I guess they could survive by cannibalism.'

'Cheers.' I slam down the phone. Brilliant!

I give Bundy a right going-over with the flea comb. He struggles like a lunatic but I manage to capture eleven of the sneaky little sods and seal them in the jam jar. That should be enough. I squirt him with the flea spray to kill off any remaining ones. This sends him mental and he hurtles round the room with strings of froth hanging out of his mouth. Omigawd, I've poisoned my Trusty Sidekick! I'm just about to dial 999, then I read on the can that sometimes cats do that because the stuff tastes shite so I open a tin of salmon which he wolfs down in one so he can't be at death's door, obviously. While he's washing himself I go over him with Mum's hairbrush to undo the tangles. Underneath all the muck and dust his coat's quite glossy. Then I fasten the fluorescent cat collar round his neck, remembering to leave a gap big enough for two fingers so he can wriggle out of it if he gets trapped.

'You're such a handsome cat. Old Mr Collard wouldn't recognise you,' I tell him, planting a kiss on top of his head. He hisses and lashes out at me with his pointy claws. Obviously he's still in mourning for his deceased owner and my throwaway remark has reopened an emotional wound.

'I forgive you, Bundy,' I say. 'Because I love you.' It's true. He's my best and only friend, and I'll let him sleep with me as soon as he's had his whosits off.

# 16

## *Bundy 1–Filthy 0*

I'm lying on the couch sucking my hair when the doorbell goes. It's a wifey in a white van delivering, Omigawd, a big bunch of flowers! They're for me, from work. The card says, 'Wishing you a speedy recovery. From your friends at Crowther & Son.' Trust them to lay a guilt trip on me!

Mum rings me from the chip factory. 'Bernard's coming round on Saturday, Rowena. I thought we might have a cosy night in together, ring for a pizza and watch a video, the three of us. How does that sound?'

It sounds like shit. 'Sounds fun,' I say. If everything goes to plan, this could be the Last Supper. Filthy Luker will no longer hang his scuzzy boiler suit on Mum's bedpost or shave his disgusting facial hair over the sink. *Rowena: Warrior Princess* and her Trusty Sidekick are going to kick ass big-time.

Filthy, your days are numbered!

Guess what vid he's picked? *The Full Monty*! Bet he thinks it'll get Mum going and he won't have to waste time on foreplay.

'I'd have preferred something more of a family nature,' says Mum, slicing up the pizza and loading Filthy's plate with a mountain of chips. 'Something less excitable, and without all that bad language. It's not an eighteen certificate, is it?'

'Nah, it's a fifteen. Anyway, it's nothing Rowena hasn't already seen, eh, young 'un?'

'Bernard!' snaps Mum, flashing him a look. 'Watch what you're saying.'

I can't see what the fuss is about, I've already seen the film about fifty-three times because I really rate Bobby Carlyle, he's cool as fuck and his nose is dead cute.

The pizza's foul, all congealed on the top with a base like concrete, so I just nibble at a few chips. Filthy wolfs his down like a starving mongrel and lets rip with a real loud rattling belch. Mum jabs him in the ribs and says, 'Manners, Bernard, please.' His feet stink like dead dogs, plus he's got an enormous gut, it's nearly splitting his fake Boss T-shirt. There ought to be a law against people like him eating chips. He guzzles his Heineken and fiddles around under the cushions.

'Bugger,' goes Stilton-socks. 'I must have left my tabs in the Sierra. Just when I'd got comfy as well.'

'I'll get them,' I offer. Thank you, Big G, for providing me with the perfect opportunity. Filthy throws me the car keys and I hotfoot out the back door, stopping off at the shed to arm myself with the ultimate biological weapon. I pick up his cigs from the dashboard and run my hand over the driver's seat-cover. It's lambskin – well, simulated, just as good. Time to put my ingenious plan into operation.

I unscrew the lid and shake the jam jar over the seat, thumping it with the base of my thumb to liberate the contents. Welcome to your new home, fleas! Lurk in those cosy crannies, lay loads of eggs, hide your larvae. Soon the biggest asshole in town will snuggle into that seat and you can bite, nip, suck and feed to your wee hearts' content. *Bon appetit!*

They're going to do Big Sex tonight, no thanks to *The Full Monty*. Mum's obviously forgotten it was a bad choice of vid, she's really getting into it, whooping and yelling, 'Off-Off-Off!' and then, Omigawd, Filthy rolls up his T-shirt and starts gyrating in front of the telly! His big white beer belly looks revolting, like half a ton of condemned veal. I want to stick a knife in him, rip through the layers of blubber and spill his lardy guts all over the floor. So much for a cosy family evening – it's practically turned into a live sex show. Don't they realise how damaging this is to a sensitive adolescent such as me? Mental note to mention this to the shrink, maybe they'll get an injunction banning Filthy from coming within a ten-mile radius of our house. I can't bear to look at him so I pretend to read the paper but the words are swimming all over the page. The only thing that's keeping me sane is the thought of those sneaky bugs in the Sierra, shagging their brains out and laying millions of eggs in the simulated lambskin.

'We're off to bed,' says Mum, the second the vid's over. My, there's a surprise. 'Don't bother with the washing-up,' she goes, like the thought had crossed my mind. 'I'll see to it later.' Filthy's getting antsy for a legover, grabbing Mum's arm and dragging her towards the stairs. 'See you in the morning, Rowena.'

Wearing my sincere daughterly smile, I go, 'Night night. Sleep tight.' They giggle their way up to bed. 'Mind the bugs don't bite.'

There's no way I'm going upstairs till they've finished their disgusting sexual capers so I pull out the vid of *Silence of the Lambs* and watch that bit where Hannibal Lecter bites the guard's face off and slaps the chewed-up skin on himself. I know it's only special effects but it's dead realistic. They sell those masks with the bars over the mouth in the joke shop on Percy Street. Maybe I should get one for Filthy, then he wouldn't be able to bolt his food, plus he'd be better looking by a million per cent.

When I turn off the video I can hear his stupid voice coming through the ceiling. He's singing 'You Sexy Thing'.

Make the most of it, Filthy. You'll be starring in the Itchy and Scratchy Show tomorrow!

Sunday morning ought to be pure paradise. Filthy goes home early to do his accounts, Mum brings me a bacon sarnie in bed, and I can laze about doing bott-all till *Coronation Street* comes on if I like. So how come my stomach's alive with slithery serpents? Why this doomed-out feeling, like there's a maniac with an Uzi lurking round the corner, ready to blast me into the hereafter?

Work, that's why. I'm scared to go back tomorrow. I can't face Dean and the others, not since he told them I'm a nympho and shit at going down.

Then there's the computer business. What if the system's blown and all the company records have been deleted? I could be sent to prison, solitary confinement probably, or locked in a wing with nutters and nonces.

And Mrs Bloody Marr. She'll want a full sickness report, symptoms, bowel movements, white blood-cell count, the whole nine yards.

I can't bear the thought of it. My head's in turmoil, ready to explode, worries racing around like go-karts, colliding, banging and crashing about in my brain. What a mess!

'There's no earthly reason for you to worry,' says Mum. She's sussed there's something wrong as I can't touch the egg and chips, my favouritest meal of the week. 'I'll ring Dr Pooley in the morning, get your sick note extended, then I'll call Crowther's and let them know what's what. There's no pressure on you to do anything, Rowena. You're ill, all you have to do is relax, take things easy.'

Another week off work, brilliant!

Next day Mum has two phone calls. Good news and bad news. One from Filthy, telling her he's covered in mysterious bites (that's the good news, obviously), and one from Altamont Lodge, a reminder about my appointment on Wednesday, like I could forget.

'Bernard's coming over this evening,' announces Mum. 'He's not very well. His body's covered in itchy sores for some reason, he's scratched himself red raw.'

'What a bummer.' I pull out my sympathetic face.

'Him and Pete have been working on a loft in the old town, he reckons it must have been heaving with fleas or dust mites, some sort of insect. Whatever it is, Pete must be immune, he hasn't been bitten once.'

'Poor Bernard, how awful.' I flip to my crumpled expression.

'There's no need to be sarcastic, Rowena. I'm only telling you so you don't make any hurtful remarks, he can't help being itchy.'

'What if he brings disease into the house? We might catch something incurable, bubonic plague, whatever.'

'Don't start fretting about that. I expect I'll know more when I've seen him. There's a tube of Savlon in the bathroom, I'll dab some of that on him. Most of the bites are on his back and he can't reach them by himself.'

'Mum. Puh-leeze, I'm eating.'

I'm also working on a plan involving the combination of noxious chemical substances.

It takes me ages and even then I only manage about an inch. I squeeze half the Savlon down the bog where it floats like a long white tapeworm. Then, using a cotton bud, I ram some gunk that looks identical into the tube. It's cream bleach, the stuff Mum uses to hide her tache, mixed with Immac depilatory cream.

It ought to work a treat on Filthy's hairy back. Blond or bald, I'll settle for either.

'Bloody Nora!' goes Filthy. 'That stuff stings worse than the bites. Sure it's not past its use-by date?' Mum slaps the dangerous concoction on his back and says not to be such a baby. He sure looks a mess, bright red puncture marks all over. Those fleas must have been starving, they've really gone to town on him.

After checking out his injuries I go to my room as I've got some serious thinking to do. About midnight I hear Filthy's Sierra drive off. Mum tippytoes up the stairs but I leap out of bed and accost her.

'What's happening? Have you and Fil . . . you and Bernard had a barney?'

'I persuaded him to sleep in his own bed tonight. He's scratching himself to ribbons, says the bites feel as if they're on fire. I've told him he must see the doctor, and not to risk coming round here till we find out what's wrong with him. Wipe that silly grin off your face, Rowena. Poor Bernard, it's driving him mad, you wouldn't believe.'

Oh, but I do. I do believe. Big G exists, and S/He's banned Filthy from our house.

# 17

## *The Fourth Horseman*

Wednesday, I manage to peel myself off the couch and haul my ass to Altamont Lodge for half past four. It's not fair, having to go for a psycho session when I'm a physical invalid, but still. In the end I figure I maison well go because afternoon telly is pure guano; the contestants on *Fifteen-to-One* look shifty, like a bunch of child molesters, and I can't stand that bint who does the sums on *Countdown*.

Hallelujah! Gemma Probert's washed her hair. It still looks crap, mind, but at least she's made an effort. She moons up at me like a daft puppy and pats the seat next to her but I pretend not to notice and park my butt in another chair, don't want people thinking we're special friends. Mickey says yo, leering at my bosoms, and Coralie, looking fabby in hipster flares and a crochet top, dead sixties, grins and bounces up and down.

Prossie opens her notepad and uncaps her pen. She's wearing those same scuzzy leggings, scruffy tart. 'We're a bit thin on the ground today, but let's make a start,' she says. Then Reuben walks in, doesn't say a word, just plonks himself in a chair and starts counting on his fingers. 'Who'd like to make an Announcement?'

'Me-me-me-me!' Coralie waves her hand in the air. 'I went to Manchester on the train this week to see my mate Toyah. She's got this weird boyfriend, his name's Spider and he's, like, an eco-warrior.' She winks at me, and Mickey nudges her in the ribs and sniggers. Prossie says that's a remarkable achievement deserving a big round of applause, particularly since Coralie couldn't even cross the Tyne Bridge at one time as she believed the world ended at Gateshead. We clap like fools and I'm thinking that's a coincidence, as there was this lass called Toyah off *Coronation Street* who went out with a tree-hugger called Spider.

Mickey says his Announcement is that he met this chick called Daria who he respects as a person even though she's a right plain brain and his mates all fancy her kid sister Quinn. He goes it's the first time he hasn't sized up a bird as a potential shag plus he hasn't even jacked off about her yet. Prossie says that's very encouraging and however hard it gets, Mickey should do his best to keep it up, which is a bit ironic in the circumstances only she's too dim to see it, even though we're all snickering like monkeys when we applaud. Then a bell goes off in my head as I remember this cartoon programme on MTV about a brainy lass who goes to Lawndale High and has a bimboid sister called Quinn. The girl's name is *Daria*! Now I get what they're playing at – it's wind-up time, with Prossie as the dupe! Bet she's never watched a soap in her sad old life. I give the thumbs-up to Coralie and Mickey to let them know I've caught on. Then I see Gemma and Reuben grinning, so obviously they're clued in as well. This could be a right laugh.

Just then the door opens and in shuffles Ash, looking well zonked. He slumps into a chair opposite me. I notice he's wearing blue eyeshadow, black eyeliner and bright pink lipstick. Gemma shoots me a look, shrugs her shoulders and flashes her palms in a don't-ask-me gesture.

We carry on with Announcements. Reuben does one about how he stood up to a foul-mouthed farty fatboy called Cartman, and Gemma spins a story about how she's learning to play saxophone to annoy her slobby dad who works in a nuclear power plant. When it gets round to me, I tell them how I went to visit my Aunt Peggy, Cousin Bobby and Uncle Hank who sells propane and propane accessories. Prossie soaks it all up like a sponge, she hasn't got a clue that we're doing a massive piss-take on her. She goes it's very gratifying to see we're all taking ownership of our problems and working through them in a positive way and who knows, once the pilot results have been monitored and evaluated, this group could serve as a model of good practice and suchlike crap.

We carry on radging her right through to group discussion when Prossie asks us to propose topics.

Coralie shoots her hand up. 'Regrets,' she says. 'I have a few.' Prossie jots it down in her pad. 'But then again, too few to mention.' Prossie scribbles it out.

'Life,' suggests Mickey. 'It's a Bitter Sweet Symphony.' Prossie says it's a profound statement worthy of further exploration and perhaps we'd like to form a debating group, fors and againsts.

To my surprise (as she always reckoned Oasis were a bunch of yobby tosspots) Gemma suggests Don't Look Back in Anger. Prossie agrees it's an admirable concept as although anger has its place in the emotional spectrum it can also, when taken to extremes, be counter-productive if not ultimately destructive.

Even Reuben's getting into it, though he's still counting on his fingers and muttering to himself. He goes for another one by The Verve, the ratbag, as I was thinking of using it. 'The Drugs Don't Work-Work-Work-Work,' he says, doing that weird echo thing. This gets Prossie dead excited. She says it's a controversial topic which she'd like to explore in depth so she'll schedule it in for a later date, perhaps inviting a pharmacological expert to ensure a balanced discussion.

'Rowena?' She raises her eyebrows at me, felt-tip pen poised.

'Monsters,' I say. 'Personal demons, like. How to deal with them.'

She plunges arse over tit into the trap. 'Could you elaborate?'

I recite the lyrics of 'Strange Glue' by Catatonia. 'Well . . . *when faced with my demons I clothe them and feed them. And I smile.*' (I flash a quick one to illustrate the point.) *'Yes, I smile as they're taking me over.'*

She stares at me long and hard. From the corner of my eyes I can see the others spluttering and giggling. For a second I think this is it, game over, then Prossie's face relaxes and she says Demons can go on the B-list of topics, in case we ever run short of ideas. She turns to Ash. His eyeliner's smudged in the corners where he's been blubbing. 'Any suggestions, Ash?'

He glances up, fiddling with his ponytail, and his mouth takes on a wee smiley shape.

'It's a nice day,' he mumbles, 'for a White Wedding.'

Yessss! Even Ash has sussed what's going down, even if he hasn't got the total hang of it.

'Anybody for the pub?' says Mickey, as we pile out of Altamont Lodge. Coralie goes it's easy for him, he's the only one old enough to booze, legally anyway. He replies all the pubs round here serve under-age drinkers, they'd soon go out of business otherwise. We all hum and hah a bit, then Reuben says, 'I'm up for it if you lot are-are-are-are,' which coming from him is like a major surprise so we all troop down to the Fourth Horseman and sit in the gloomy back room while Mickey fetches the drinks. I have a double Bailey's shandy, Coralie and Gemma have blood-orange flavour alcopop, Reuben has a bottle of Bud and Mickey gets a pint of lager for himself. Ash mumbles that he's not allowed alcohol as it reacts with his medication so Mickey gets him a Coke which I happen to notice he's spiked with Bacardi.

We have a right laugh, running the session in action replay, doing impressions of Prossie's bewildered facial expressions, plotting ingenious ways to wind her up.

'Why didn't we think of this before?' says Coralie. 'I've been bored shitless for the last couple of months but now I can't wait for next time.' She claps her hands and jumps up and down on the seat.

'It's all down to her over there,' says Mickey, pointing at me with his ciggie. 'She's a subversive influence.' And they raise their glasses, bottles, whatever, and drink a toast to me.

'Fuck off, you loonies,' I snap, embarrassed, only I feel sort of happyish underneath. Must check out what subversive means.

After a couple of drinks, Ash lightens up. We're squeezed up together in the corner seat, his black 501s rubbing against my yellow latex miniskirt and lacy tights. His fingers are long and brown – artistic fingers – and he's wearing pearly pink nail polish. I rest my hand on my leg and compare his goldy-brown skin against my white. His thigh feels warm where it's squashed up against mine. For some weird reason I get a mild electric thrill in my knickies. The others are having a top time, gabbing on about medications and comparing scams for getting extra drugs. Even Gemma's having fun, her face redder than the blood-orange alcopop. When she laughs, the gold tooth flashes and her eyes nearly disappear in cheek fat.

'So,' I say to Ash. 'What's with the war paint?'

His face crumples. 'Do I look a mess?'

'No,' I lie. 'Course not. It's cool for boys to wear make-up. Only . . .' I'm about to tell him his eyeliner's smudged to buggery but I don't want to set him off blubbing again.

'Only what?'

'Only that pink lippy clashes with your skin colouring. You should go for a more orangey or browny tone.' I ferret in my rucksack and dig out a Ripe Tangerine lipgloss. 'You can keep this, I don't wear it any more.'

He twists the tube and smears some colour on his wrist. 'It's a bit tarty. For a lad, I mean,' he says hurriedly.

'S'OK, you're right. Terracotta Crème would go best, you can use it as eyeshadow as well.' I exhume it from my bag, take hold of his hand and daub a bit on his wrist.

'That's well classy.' He gazes at me with his coal-black eyes and flashes a deadly smile. A fire burns inside me. I drop his hand like a hot brick, scared in case he can read my mind.

We loaf in the pub till chucky-out time. By then everyone's more or less pissed, especially Gemma, who lollops down the hill, arms outstretched, tent dress billowing, going, *Wheeeee*, and singing about the hills being alive with the sound of music, which cracks us all up, even Ash. He chuckles and squeezes my fingers, sending a warm thrill that fizzes like liver salts in my stomach. When we reach the bus station, Reuben and Coralie go all gymnastic on the barriers, swinging upside-down and whooping like gibbons. Mickey leaps on to a bench and plays air guitar, screeching 'Bring Your Daughter to the Slaughter', and Gemma's so way gone she does a couple of cartwheels in a bus lane and her frock rides up showing her bouncy bum cheeks. A couple of old wifies with permed hair and matching raincoats start tutting and complaining about the state of youngsters today so Gemma waddles right up to them and gurns, stretching her mouth with her fingers into a Cherie Blair grin, making a pug nose and going cross-eyed. The biddies back off, muttering and sucking their dentures. Me and Ash, we're having a bit smooch next to the timetables, no tongues or stuff, but still juicy. Suddenly Mickey jumps off the bench, trashes his invisible guitar, then charges up to the biddies, clutching his lunchbox. 'C'mon girls, tits oot for the lads. Play your cards right, you could have me,' he says, leering horribly and doing that snake thing with his tongue. One wifey squeals, the other one goes for Mickey with her handbag, calling him a dirty little sod, then they link arms and scuttle off to the taxi queue, grumbling like empty bellies.

'Well, that's a threesome out of the question. Who's up for a loonfest?' yells Mickey. 'Tell you what, why don't we meet up one day and have a works outing. We could go to, I dunno, a zoo or something.'

'Yeah! Or the seaside,' shouts Gemma. 'I could wear my new bikini – hey, just kidding!' She yanks up the back of her dress and flashes her twin moons again. Mickey makes a lunge but she's too quick for him.

Coralie untangles her legs from the barriers and hitches up her flares. 'Let's go to a theme park,' she goes. 'Somewhere with white-knuckle rides. What do you say, Reuben?'

Reuben fiddles with the laces on his hi-tops. 'Cool-cool-cool-cool,' he goes.

'Rowena? Ash?' says Coralie.

'Well . . .' I say, checking out Ash's face for clues. I'm thinking it'll be his idea of total Hades, but he twitches his mouth in a sort of grin, mumbling, 'Yeah, whatever,' and squeezes my hand, setting off a trickle of molten lava in my internal volcano.

Mickey clasps his hands above his head in a victory salute. 'Right, let's make it Friday then, meet here at noon sharp, and try to think of somewhere good for our works outing. Psychos on Tour!'

Just then, the 64 bus draws up, brakes hissing.

'Shit, gotta go,' I say. Ash pulls me to him and kisses me gently on the mouth. My insides nearly explode! I pay the driver and squelch down the aisle to the back seat but the window's so grimy I can hardly see out. As the bus pulls away, the Madolescents start chanting 'Psy-cho! Psy-cho! Psy-cho!' I slide down into the seat, smiling to myself.

See that cloud? I'm on it. It's ay-mazing. The lushest lad I've seen in ages *likes* me! The Madolescents like me! OK, so they're all one track short of an album but who cares. Someone *likes* me!

## 18

## Psychos on Tour

What oh what shall I wear for a day out with the Madolescents? After exhuming zillions of outfits from the wardrobe, the floor and the dirty-washing basket, I decide on the rockin' black denim jacket and skirt, purple T-shirt and tights, and my old monkey boots. I backcomb my hair and fix it in a cone slide, then do my eyes and lips with Plum Loco topped off with fifty-three coats of Endless Lash. The effect's a bit more Gothic than usual so I hope Ash can handle it. On the way out I sneak Filthy's bottle of Jack Daniel's from the cupboard and stuff it in my rucksack.

Mickey's at the bus station when I arrive, flicking through a copy of *Colossal Cahunas*. The cover pic is this wifey with bosoms the size of beach balls and Day-Glo lips pumped up with fat from pigs' bottoms.

'Yo, Ro,' says Mickey, flashing the mag for all to see. 'Classy, eh? You could get lost in them bazoomas.' Right. Or you could just get lost. He'd better not be slavering and walking around with a stiffy like a pole-vaulter all day, otherwise I'm outta here. I'm wondering how to escape if the others don't show, when Reuben and Coralie stroll round the corner, then I spot Gemma mooching out of the newsagent's, cramming a Mars bar down her gullet. But what's happened to Ash? Why isn't he here? A frown etches itself into my forehead and a sicky feeling hovers in my throat. Just as the pins and needles start pricking my scalp, I feel a tug on my rucksack and wheel round, instinctively ready to punch out. It's Ash, his hair loose and floppy over his gorgeous black eyes, looking a total babe. Thank you, Big G!

We cross over Percy Street and bowl into Bar Oz so we can have a swiftie while we're deciding where to go. Mickey's still gassing on about a zoo but the nearest one's two hours away, plus Reuben says he couldn't enjoy it on principle and Gemma says oh well, if he's gonna get all vegan about it, we won't bother, so we have another round of drinks. Coralie jots down the list of suggestions: Spanish City, Marsden Grotto, Metro Centre, Manors multiplex, and the Drive-Thru McDonald's. Three more drinks later, we're still arguing up hill and down dale and Gemma moans she'll die if we don't eat soon. Mickey goes if a camel can cross the Sahara on just a hump full of fat stuff, Gemma can live off her reserves for a wee while longer, so then *she* gets the hump and calls him a sizeist pig and he winds her up even more by grunting and going, *Oink oink*.

'Stop!' I hear myself yelling. 'Stop it now! Let's grab some scran and catch a bus somewhere – anywhere – otherwise it'll be too late to do owt.' Rowena: the voice of reason. Not hard, in this company.

So we roll mob-handed into Bimbi's and order six plates of chips and gravy. While we're waiting, Ash starts fiddling with the salt, pouring it into his hand and letting it trickle out into little white mountains. For me this is like a big turn-on, gazing at his long goldy fingers and fantasising about what else they could be doing. Suddenly Reuben leans over the table and grabs Ash's wrist.

'Don't do that, Ash, please-please-please-please. It's doing my head in.' It's true, Reuben's eyes are big with tears and he looks real sweaty and agitated. Jesus, I hope he's not about to go off on one, or whatever he does. He slumps back and rests his chin on his chest, counting on his fingers and chuntering to himself. Gemma flashes me a look and we all sit there like one o'clock half-struck until the skivvy brings the scran.

Reuben counts his chips, dividing them with the plastic stabber into groups of four, plus an odd one. He slides the plate away and sits clutching his head.

'Sorry,' he says. 'I can't eat them, there's one too many-many-many-many.'

Gemma reaches over and shovels Reuben's chips on to her plate. I glare at her. 'What?' she says. 'They'll only go to waste.'

Coralie drapes her arm round Reuben's shoulder. 'Wanna talk about it?' Kamikaze flies pop and fizz on the Insect-o-cutor. Static crackles in the vinegary air as we will Reuben not to lose it. 'We're your mates,' says Coralie. 'We're all in this together, remember?'

He glances up. 'You'll think I'm mad-mad-mad-mad.'

'So?' says Coralie. 'You're in good company.'

Fifteen pained expressions float across Reuben's face, ending in a twisty grin. 'OK then, I'll tell you,' he says. 'I've got this thing. Obsession, I suppose you'd call it. About the number four-four-four-four.' He sniggers. 'See what I mean? It's like a ritual. Everything has to add up to four, or be done in sets of four. Otherwise something terrible will happen-happen-happen-happen.'

I lean closer. 'Like what? Are we talking Armageddon stuff here, or getting squished by a juggernaut, or what?'

'Who knows?' says Reuben. 'Just something terrible. I daren't risk it, that's why I have to do this-this-this-this. I even wake up counting, so I must be doing it in my sleep-sleep-sleep-sleep.'

No one says a word. Reuben counts on his fingers. It's Coralie who breaks the silence.

'You must waste a lot of time, doing everything in fours.'

Reuben nods. Four times, naturally. 'Years, I suppose,' he admits, 'if you added it all up-up-up-up. I've always done it, even before I knew how to count, I was always getting duffed up at school. I know it's a totally mental thing to do, but I can't stop. I daren't risk it.' He stares up at the ceiling. 'Anyway,' he smiles, 'this is my truth, tell me yours-yours-yours-yours.'

'Let's move on somewhere else,' Mickey suggests. We're getting black looks from the women behind the counter, like we're a cluster of feeding vampires or something. Fast food means eat up and get out. 'We could go down the Bitter End.'

'Where's that?' asks Coralie. 'Sounds like a grot-box.'

'It is,' agrees Mickey. 'A right armpit. It's in Low Fell, out near my gaff, but we'll get served, no probs. Come on, we can catch a bus round the corner.'

The Bitter End isn't the pub's real name, but you can see why people call it that, like calling Bridlington the Last Resort. As Mickey struts his pimp roll through the door, the stink of stale booze and baccy hits like a smack in the face with an old dishrag. Inside, it's all blokes except for a wifey sitting on a stool by the bar. Probably a prostitute, I reckon, the sort with the going rate stuck on the soles of her stilettos. There's no jukebox that I can see, no bandits either, just fed-up looking gadges puffing tabs, swilling pints of Dog and gazing at a telly with the sound turned down. The only noise is a chorus of smokers' coughs and the clack of snooker balls from the back room. A spooky feeling comes over me, like we've wandered into a parallel universe, or a money-laundering front for the Mob, or a den of paedophiles. We plonk ourselves round a table in the corner while Mickey gets the first round in.

'What a cockin' dump,' moans Gemma. 'I wouldn't fancy the pub grub here, and I'll eat anything, me.' Ash nudges my leg under the table and squeezes my knee with his artistic fingers. My insides turn hot and snuggly until I'm so gone, a little whimper escapes out of my mouth and I have to convert it into a cough.

When the drinks arrive and the smokes are handed out, Reuben says, 'Whose go is it then?' We stare at him. 'I told you my shit, come on, fair's fair-fair-fair-fair.'

Everyone fidgets and looks at the floor, then Coralie takes a fierce puff of her ciggy. 'OK then, but it's not to go outside these four walls, right?'

We all nod.

'I'm bipolar,' she announces.

For some reason, maybe because I haven't a clue what she's on about, I start to laugh. 'Whew, that's a relief,' I go. 'I thought you were gonna say bisexual.'

Coralie scowls. 'And that's a sin, is it?'

A blush creeps up my neck. 'Sorry, I didn't mean . . .' I say. The Madolescents are all gawping at me. 'Shit, I'm sorry, guys. It's just I don't know what bi-thingy means.' Please, God, let the floor open up and swallow me.

'Bipolar Disorder, if you want its proper name,' explains Coralie. 'I'm manic-depressive. It means my moods swing up and down, only I don't stop till I hit the jackpot, the very top or the very bottom, *capisce*?'

Mickey takes a swallow of lager. 'You don't seem that bad. I've met worse – a lot worse. My auld fella, for one, he'd jump off a roof yelling "Geronimo" when he was up, then he'd be laid out in bed catatonic for a week.'

'I'm OK at the moment,' says Coralie. 'Now I'm on the right dose of medication. Still get ups and downs but nothing too extreme. Like when I spent all night painting the kitchen, that was a manic trip, but at least I can hold down a job, if you call working at the poxy Kit Pit a job.' Coralie sparks up another tab and rests her head on the back of the seat, gazing at the nicotine-brown ceiling. Her chin starts to wobble. Reuben squeezes her hand and Coralie blinks her eyes fast. 'Don't mind me,' she says. 'I'm a bit pissed, that's all. Sorry.'

'Don't apologise,' says Mickey. 'I've been in therapy for years and I still tell my shrink a pack of lies.'

'Why?' says Gemma. 'What's the point of that?'

Mickey shrugs. 'It's easier than facing the truth, I suppose. Plus I like seeing his face when I tell him some wild story, like Ozzy Osbourne popped round for a bat casserole, or I've shagged Pamela Anderson's brains out.'

A piggy noise comes down Gemma's nose. 'That wouldn't take too long,' she snorts. 'Anyway, Tommy Lee beat you to it.'

Mickey ignores her. 'It beats the crap out of saying what really happened. Woke up, scratched balls, stared at ceiling, and so on.' He necks his lager and bangs his glass on the table. The ashtray bounces, scattering fag ends. 'Friggin' shrink, he said I had a rich inner life. Twat.'

Coralie giggles. 'I like that. A rich inner life. Hey, come on, Mickey, chill. This is supposed to be our works outing, right? Who's for another bevvy?'

I dig in my rucksack and pull a tenner out of my purse. It's only then that I remember the bottle of Jack Daniel's. 'Just get Cokes,' I tell Reuben. 'I brought some firewater.'

'Get some crisps as well,' orders Gemma. Her cheeks are fiery red where the wine's made her capillaries pop. 'Cheese and onion ones, and Worcester sauce. Oh, and prawn cocktail, if they do them in this crummy dump.'

Ash drapes his arm around the seat and gives my shoulder a wee squeeze, then he slides his hand across and starts playing with my wispy hair bits and stroking the back of my neck with his fingers. His nails are a bit scratchy. Ten zillion volts of pure sex shoot down my spine and fizz like radioactive Solpadeines in my stomach. I press my thighs together and feel myself go squishy. It takes a mega-human effort not to squirm on the torn leatherette. I turn my head and gaze into Ash's dark chocolate eyes, almost hidden beneath the floppy fringe.

'Sorry,' he says. 'Didn't mean to mess up your hair,' and pulls away his hand. I fight off the urge to grab it and press it between my legs, guiding his goldy fingers inside me where I'm hot and wet. What's happening here? Stop it, Rowena. Get a grip!

Reuben brings a tray of Cokes and doles them out. I sneak Filthy's booze out of my rucksack and top up Ash's glass with JD's, then do the same with mine. We pass it round under the table so everyone can pour a shot into their drinks, and by the time it gets back to me, the bottle's half empty. My head's a bit spinny, and there's music whirling round inside. It sounds like Shania Twain, 'Man! I Feel Like a Woman', which Mum's always singing, just to drive me mad as a bus. I figure it must be happening in the real world, as Gemma joins in the words, then Coralie, both giggling and clarting on. The Replicant behind the bar twiddles a knob on a CD player and Shania sings louder. Then the hooker wifey, who's been eyeballing us for a while, shuffles her bum off the bar stool and Omigawd, starts dancing towards our table! She's doing that hippy thing with her hands, snaking them around in front of her face, pouting her thin red lips and heading straight for Mickey. The gadges at the bar are glued to the boxing on the telly, watching two meat-heads punching seven shades of shit out of each other. Now and again they take a slurp of Dog or suck on a ciggy, but they might as well be watching Teletubbies, for all the interest they show. Now the wifey's wiggling her belly in front of Mickey, mouthing the words to the song, flashing her scrawny tits and giving him the come-on. Omigawd, it's obscene!

'Yay, Mickey, go for it,' squeals Gemma, digging him in the ribs. Mickey's eyes are spacey and unfocused, like a newborn baby's. The woman reaches out and grabs his hands, grinning horribly through the gash in her face, and pulls him towards her. Mickey stumbles to his feet and the woman wraps his arms round her middle. She's a good bit taller than him and she grasps his head and rests his acid perm on her shoulder. Gemma and Coralie join hands and sway to the music. Mickey and the old slapper shuffle round the floor for a bit in a grotesque smooch and the woman plants him a kiss, leaving a greasy red smear on his forehead. Suddenly she pulls away and stares into Mickey's face.

'I know you,' she says in a smoky voice. 'You're that lad of Tom Leathley's.' The gadges at the bar unglue their eyes from the telly and twist round on their stools to look Mickey up and down. One mutters something to the other. 'Don't deny it, you're the dead spit of him,' she hisses. Mickey's face turns the colour of lard.

Reuben and Ash exchange glances. Gemma and Coralie sit still as statues. I want to die.

The wifey thumps Mickey hard in the chest. 'You've got some nerve, coming in here, after what your father did, the murdering bastard. Get out! Go on, piss off!' She gives Mickey an almighty shove, knocking him flying into the table. 'And take the rest of the toerags with you!'

She teeters back to the bar, climbs on to the stool, lights a tab and knocks back her gin. The gadges turn back to the silent boxing again, like they haven't just witnessed a case of grievous bodily harm right in front of them.

'I thought I was *in* there,' says Mickey, scrambling on to a chair. His face is red now, flushed as a trumpeter's. He's canny upset, you can see that, but he's still playing the joker. I glance over at the wifey; she's glugging her drink, back in her own alkie world. Shania's singing 'That Don't Impress Me Much'. Mickey shakes out his sweaty curls. 'I had a funny feeling I'd pull tonight.'

Gemma mutters something about he couldn't pull a lavatory chain but Coralie gives her a sharp nudge and frowns, meaning, *Shut it*. Ash fidgets and stares at the floor and Reuben tears bits off a beer mat and arranges them into four piles. My toes curl and uncurl inside the monkey boots. The air's thick with smoke and awkwardness. Someone needs to *do* something.

'Come on,' I say, 'we're outta here.'

# 19

## The Angel's Frozen Ones

It's chucky-out time anyway and bunches of people are spilling out of the pubs and into curry houses and chippies. A gang of girls in skimpy tops and skirts the size of belts totter past, singing 'Livin' La Vida Loca'. This lass with purple hair stops suddenly, clutches her belly, and pukes up in the gutter right outside a kebab shop. The sick steams and splashes her shoes. She's making a proper racket of it, roaring like a rutting stag I saw in a nature programme, and the smell turns my stomach over. Just then a seven-seater taxi pulls up and a bunch of office types pile out, squawking and squealing like they do after a couple of shandies, while a greasy-haired bloke pays off the driver with a twenty. An idea hits me. I poke my head through the driver's window.

'Can you take us somewhere?' I say.

'Is it far?' says the driver. 'I've got another party to pick up.'

'Just down the road. To – I dunno – to the Angel.' It's the first thing that pops into my head.

The driver nods. 'Hop in then.'

The Madolescents are standing round on the kerbside, looking like spare dicks at a knock-shop wedding. 'Get in the cab,' I tell them. 'Come on, shake your friggin' tail feathers.'

'Where are we going?' asks Mickey as the taxi heads down the A167. His voice is dull and flat. He's still brooding on the bad scene in the pub, still embarrassed, still wondering what the rest of us make of it.

'On an adventure,' I say. 'Sort of.' No one says a word. We're all sober, even after the gallons of booze we've packed away, just because of that stupid old tart who radged Mickey up in the Bitter End.

At the end of the dual carriageway, the driver hangs a right and doubles back, pulling to a stop at the roadside parking spot near the Angel. I slap him my last tenner and we bundle out into the night.

'Fuck's sake, Rowena, why have you brought us out here? It's freezing,' complains Gemma.

'Don't fret,' I tell her. 'You'll soon warm up.' I'm talking bollocks, there's no way we can warm up unless we do aerobics or have wild group sex or something, but I'm teetering on the edge, and if Gemma carries on moaning I might just tip over. Truth is, I've no idea why we're here, except we needed to get away from the negative vibey situation at the Bitter End. 'Come on, youse lot, let's go see the Angel.'

The Angel of the North is this geet big statue on Eighton Banks. It looms up at you suddenly, like that helicopter near the end of *Thelma and Louise*. It's made out of rusty metal, with a body like a giant Oscar and massive sort of airplane wings spread out either side. It looks right awesome and spooky silhouetted against the night sky, like a man-shaped spacecraft, or a stern god figure sent to teach earthlings what's what. The locals call it the Gateshead Flasher because it looks like a bloke holding his raincoat open, except it hasn't got a raincoat or a dick to flash. Once, somebody climbed up and draped a black and white stripey Magpies shirt on it with the magic Number 9, i.e. Shearer, on the back, which was such a cool stunt it got on the telly and in all the newspapers.

Ash is standing with his hands stuffed into his pockets, looking lost and confused, so I link my arm into his and lead him up the path towards the Angel. Coralie and Reuben follow, then Gemma grumbling about the cold, as per, and Mickey in a sort of silent stupor. So much for the Madolescents' works outing. We'd have had more laughs viewing stiffs in Crowther's chapel.

'What are we doing here?' Gemma bleats. 'Let's go home, I'm starving hungry.' If she doesn't stop bitching I'll deck her, swear down.

'Look at the Angel,' I say. We're up on the hillock right next to the statue. The moon's out and the wind sends the clouds scudding across the night sky. 'Its wings are moving.'

It's only an optical wossname, illusion, but if you stand still and stare upwards, it looks as if the Angel's preparing for take-off.

'Wow, that is so spook-ee,' whispers Coralie.

'It feels kind of mystical,' says Reuben. 'Like something cataclysmic's happened and we're the last people left in the world-world-world-world.'

'The Angel's chosen ones.' Ash clutches my cold hand with his warm one and sticks them both in his pocket.

'Frozen ones, more like,' sniffs Gemma. 'Anyone got a hanky? My nose is running a friggin' marathon here.' I unearth a wodge of Crowther's tissues from my pocket and shove them at her.

My stomach feels queasy. Lord knows why I brought us here, it's only made everyone cold and wretched. Then I remember the Jack Daniel's in my rucksack.

'Here,' I say. 'Pass this round, it'll warm us up.'

Gemma takes a massive slug of JD's and has a chokey coughing fit so Coralie thumps her on the back until the attack wears off. The wind whistles around us, biting into our bones, and the Angel's wings seem to creak eerily, though it could be my imagination on overtime. Then another noise, faint at first then distinct, a sound we all recognise. The sound of someone crying. It's Mickey, crouching between the metal struts that would be the Angel's toes, if the Angel had toes. He's rocking, hands over his eyes, drop-curls cascading down his face, shoulders heaving. Now he's sobbing, gulping, choking, trying to stifle the tears. Moaning, wailing, the sound of utter despair and misery. My heart leaps mouthwards.

'Mickey, what is it? What's wrong?' Coralie kneels beside his shivering body and lays his head on her bosoms. Mickey looks even more like a Chucky doll with his face wet and crumpled. The sobbing gradually subsides into weeping, then tails off into snuffles. I dig in my pocket for more tissues and offer them to Mickey.

'Cheers.' He sniffs, lifting his head off Coralie's chest, which must be soppy with tears and snot. His voice sounds sore and husky. 'Sorry.'

Coralie's eyes are wet and shiny in the moonlight. 'You don't have to apologise, not to us. We've all been there, right?'

'Right-right-right-right,' says Reuben. He holds out his hand and helps Coralie up from where she's been kneeling at the Angel's feet.

'Here, try some snake oil medicine.' I offer the bottle of Jack Daniel's to Mickey. He pulls a twisty smile and takes a couple of glugs, gulping loudly as if he's swallowing a ping-pong ball. Ash moves right up close behind me and circles my waist with his arms.

Gemma runs her puddingy fingers through Mickey's hair. 'You OK now, Mickey man?'

He nods. 'I feel such a twat, breaking down like that. Fuck knows what came over me. A ghost from the past, I guess. I wasn't expecting it.'

'You mean that woman in the pub?' goes Gemma.

Mickey blows his nose again. 'Yeah. We should never have gone there, too close to home. People know me, know my auld fella, know what he did to my mam.' He pauses, sniffs a few times, and wipes his nose on the sleeve of his leather jacket. 'He knifed her, see. He was fucking raving at the time, we should have seen it coming. This was years ago, but folks round there, they'll never forget. We're marked, our family. Loonies, madmen, murderers. All tarred with the same brush. The neighbours moved out, Council couldn't get anyone to live next door. Kids shout abuse in the street, hoy bricks, spray filth on the walls. Bastards even poisoned our dog. Do you know how it feels?' A great heaving sob shudders through Mickey's body. 'It's shite,' he gulps. 'It's fucking shite.'

As one, we all gather round him in a communal hug. My eyes are

163

stinging with hot tears. Gemma's blubbing noiselessly too. Ash squeezes me really, really tight so I know he must be feeling the same way. We stay like that for ages, locked in the Madolescent hug. Safe. Six people, one emotion. My brain's going, like, this feels so special, I don't ever want to forget the moment.

It's Reuben who breaks away first. 'Blood brothers,' he says. 'Blood brothers and sisters, that's what we are. We look out for each other. I wish we could always stay this close-close-close-close.'

We stand in silence, listening to the faint creaking of the Angel's wings.

'Reuben's right,' says Mickey. 'We should do something magical, some sort of ceremony, to seal the deal.'

Coralie jigs up and down on the spot. 'Let's mingle our blood like proper blood brothers. We could cut our wrists and—'

'No way,' barks Gemma. 'I've done enough wrist-slashing, thank you. It'd only remind me.'

Ash peers through his floppy fringe. 'We could mingle other stuff. Body fluids of some sort.' I can tell by the shy way he says it that he's blushing.

'What sort of body fluids?' says Gemma, a trace of panic in her voice. 'You mean like in an orgy?'

'Wow!' Mickey surfaces from his downer.

'Don't even *go* there,' I warn him. Time for Rowena to take control. 'It's a cool idea, Ash. I think we should do it, only each of us in private. We'll polish off the Jack Daniel's and use the bottle to mix our, y'know, *stuff*. We can take it in turns to go behind the Angel and drop some bodily fluid in the bottle. I don't care what you decide to use, it's the principle that counts, the fact that bits of us will be swirling round together.'

'And we could bury the bottle,' suggests Coralie. 'Like a time capsule, here, next to the Angel.'

'Wicked,' agrees Mickey. 'Can I go first?'

We each take a biggish swig of JD's and hand the empty bottle to

Mickey. I'd prefer he went last as I've got a shrewd idea which bodily fluid he'll go for, but as the whole caper's really down to him I decide to let it pass. He disappears round the back of the Angel and stumbles down the hillock to the trees. Coralie, Gemma, Reuben, Ash and I snuggle in together next to the Angel's feet, trying to shield each other from the wind.

'What's the deal with you, Ash?' says Gemma. 'How come you got mixed up with a bunch of weirdos like us?'

Ash fidgets beside me.

'You don't have to say if you don't want to,' I tell him.

'It's OK,' he says. 'I'm cool about it now. It's just there's not much to tell, not really. Can someone lend me a ciggy?'

Coralie takes for ever lighting a couple of tabs as the wind's quite wild now. The Angel's wings seem to be shifting more than ever, though it could be the optical thingummy against the drifting clouds.

Ash tells us how he used to live in Hexham, in the wilds of Northumberland, with his folks. There was some sort of mega family bust-up so he split. He doesn't go into detail. He reckons his dad's a consultant up the hospital, and his mum's a solicitor. To look at Ash, you'd never guess he's from a poshgit family, so maybe that's a lie.

His crack-up happened one Saturday in Eldon Square, just outside that poncey French shoe shop. He totally lost it, trashed the racks and hoyed boots at shoppers. Then the Feds turned up, Ash got sectioned and nutted up in a psychi unit for a month.

'That's it, more or less,' he says. 'They put me on happy pills, but they didn't seem to make much difference. Anyway, I decided in the pub last night to stop taking them so at least I can drink now. I can't remember what it's like, not to feel depressed. End of.' He sniffs a couple of times and stares up at the Angel.

Mickey reappears, bottle in hand, grin on face.

'All done,' he says. 'Still warm. Who's next?'

No one seems in a rush to answer, so I volunteer, as it was my stupid idea. I dig a few tissues out of my pocket and wrap them round the neck of the bottle in case of stray Mickeygerms. Holding the bottle at arm's length, I shuffle down the bank towards the trees. I've decided to donate some spit as it seems the quickest and most hygienic. The thought of what's already in the bottle makes me want to heave, and for a minute I wonder if I can go through with it but I manage to do it by holding my nose and kind of dribbling into the neck of the bottle. Yuk-yuk-yuk to infinity!

By the time I get back to the Angel, Gemma's halfway through the story about baby Nathan and the shit she put up with from her pondlife boyfriend and how she turned into a lardarse. Her voice is breaking up, like when a mobile phone loses its signal.

'I'm gonna lose some weight,' she's saying. 'I'm sick of being me, wobbling around like a pin-toed sloth. Honest, I really mean it.' The others clap like at the group meetings when we do Announcements, and Coralie gives Gemma a bit hug.

'Go, girl, you can do it,' she says, and plants a kiss on Gemma's mouth. 'Give us the bottle, Rowena, I'll go next.'

By the time everyone's done the business, I've discovered loads more stuff about Ash. He's into Catatonia (yessss!), TLC, Skunk Anansie, the Manics. And – gulp – Dolly Parton.

Tonight's the first time he's worn slap on the street.

He's *not gay*!

And he proves it by kissing me full on the mouth. Pure bliss! No tongues, but still horny enough to set my ticker racing.

'Right then,' says Mickey, brandishing the Jack Daniel's bottle. 'We've taken DNA samples. Now what?'

'We plant it, of course,' says Coralie. 'Down there, by the trees. Stop swinging it about, Mickey. We put blood, sweat and tears into that.'

'And a few other things besides.' Mickey grins. 'Potent brew, this.'

'Hang on,' I remind them. 'We said we'd have a ceremony, a sort of burial rite, something mystical to imprint it in our minds. Any ideas?'

Silence. Exchange of vacant glances. We traipse down towards the trees and Mickey digs a bit hole – well, it's more a dent, really, because the ground's geet hard – with the heel of his boot.

'We ought to swear an oath of allegiance, like the Three Musketeers,' says Reuben. 'To make it official.' The only Musketeer I know is the pub on Great Lime Road, so I keep my lip buttoned.

Coralie lays the bottle in its shallow grave, then Reuben joins our hands, clasps them over the time capsule and says solemnly, 'We swear by the cryogenically preserved head of Walt Disney that we, the Madolescents, will be everlasting friends. Amen-men-men-men.'

'Amen,' we echo, then we observe a minute's silence before trudging back to the statue.

The Angel's body seems to be humming in the wind, a low droning sound, like an alien spacecraft. Clouds chase each other across the moon, and we gaze open-mouthed as the rusty brown wings creak and shudder against the silvery sky. For a few magical seconds it appears as though the Angel's coming to life, flexing its giant calves, straining for freedom, preparing to ascend. It's a sign.

Without a word, the Madolescents join hands and form a ring around the Angel. We circle it on tippytoes, anti-clockwise.

I think it's Gemma who starts singing, but the words are already there in my head, waiting.

*I believe I can fly . . .*

When I get home, Mum's in the kitchen supping a Heineken and flicking through *Take A Break*.

'Fancy spaghetti hoops with your chips?' she says. I nod. She carries on yattering but I'm not really listening. I'm dreaming about Ash, touching my lips and remembering the way he kissed me. The thought of his body next to mine makes me burn, melt, turn totally soppo down there.

'So,' Mum's saying, 'that's the surprise. I wanted to tell you last weekend, only Bernard said to wait until you were in a good mood.' She does a sarky laugh. 'I said he wouldn't live that long.'

I click back to the world of now. My hunch was right. They're engaged to be married.

'Fffffark, fuck-fuck-fuck,' I hear myself stutter, like a hen with a speech impediment. Mum glares at me. 'Fork,' I explain with a smile. 'I've dropped my fork.'

Naturally I'm mortified. Like it's not degrading enough that Pukey-Luker's taken up shagger's rights in our house, now I'll have to suffer the humiliation of everyone knowing that Mum's plighting her troth, linking her loins, surrendering her minge to the vile Filthy – officially! My skin crawls at the thought. Some deal, huh? This time last week I'd have gone apeshit but now – well, who am I to deny true lust? If Mum wants to shack up with a flea-bitten Yeti, that's down to her, but I'm having nothing to do with it. A nervous rash flares up on my neck. I twitch my mouth in an inane grin but can't quite bring myself to speak.

'I'd like you to be happy for us.' Mum doesn't sound too hopeful. 'It's not a lot to ask.'

I force the words out through a mouthful of spaghetti hoops. 'I'm delirious.'

'I thought you were looking on the pale side,' she goes, touching my forehead for signs of fever.

'No, I mean I *am* happy for you, swear down, Mum.' It only sounds a *bit* false. 'Show us your ring.' She flashes her left hand. The tiniest diamond in the history of the world glimmers dimly on her third finger. I manage a whistle. 'Cool, must have cost him a bomb.'

She does that irritating coy smile thing. 'Well, he couldn't have afforded it without the lottery win.'

'The *whattery* win?' This is news to me. I push the plate of spaghetti hoops away and dab my chops with kitchen towel.

'That was the other surprise I was telling you about. Keep it under your hat though, we don't want begging letters.'

'How much did he win then, a tenner?' I smirk, eyeing the engagement ring. It's a cheap shot but I can't resist it.

Mum does a husky giggle. 'It was a darn sight more than a tenner. He got five numbers plus the bonus ball. Shame it wasn't the jackpot, but it'll see us right for a few years, if we take it steady. And it means we can get out of this godforsaken place. I've got my eye on a three-bedroomed semi on the new Barratt's estate. Things'll work out, you'll see. We're moving up in the world, Rowena.'

I stifle a snort.

'And Bernard says to tell you he's going to treat you out of it.'

My voice comes out all smirky. 'What, another Indian meal?'

'No, you daft madam. He wants to give you some money, you can spend it how you like.'

'Hey, wicked. How much?'

'You'll have to wait and see.' She grabs me and gives me a bear hug. 'I'm so pleased you've come round to Bernard,' she says. 'We'll be like a proper family.'

'Yeah, right,' I go. Fat chance. The day my ma moves in with Filthy Luker, Rowena Vincent moves out – for good! If they're getting married, I'm getting gone. But at least if he sticks me enough mazuma, I'll be able to afford a decent pad. Wriggling away, I peck her on the cheek and head for my room. The situation with Filthy is a right bummer but I'll just have to be wossname, philosophical and not think about it. Besides which, I'm desperate to be alone, to spend some serious wideawake dreaming time about Ash. I think I've fallen in love!

## 20

## *Down the Elbow*

Today's the day I return to Crowther's Body Shop. It's been so long since I was at work, I can't remember what to do. It takes for ever to get ready, mainly because I can't decide what colour rings to paint under my eyes. I need to look *ill*, don't I? In the end I go for blue to match my (counterfeit) Lacoste shirt, as I get brown circles when my period's due and I fancy a change.

My nerve-ends are jangling as I walk through the door but I needn't have worried, they're all over me like a cheap suit.

'Row-*eee*-na,' squeaks Mrs Marr, all excited like she's having a multiple-O. 'It's good to have you back.' She leans close and whispers confidentially in my ear. 'How are you? Sorted your little problem?'

What? Jesus, I bet she thinks I've had an abortion! Aw, who cares what she thinks? She's only the office gopher, after all.

'Yes, I'm on the mend. My General Debility seems to have cleared up nicely, thank you.'

Mr Crowther pops his head round the door. 'Welcome back, Rowena. Glad you're feeling better. You're not the only one who's been suffering, we've had to put up with Ray's muddy coffee for the last fortnight. At least we can look forward to a decent cuppa now, eh? Bit tied up at the moment, talk to you later.' He shuts his office door, then opens it again. 'Rowena, any chance of a Butter Crunch this morning? I've gone off Gypsy Creams, they must have changed the recipe.'

I'm still nervous about going into the back in case they wind me up about the Great Sexual Disaster. Just let Ray crack one gag, that's all, and I'll scoop his stupid brains out with a spoon and take them home for Bundy's tea. Anyway, I could always threaten to report him for sexual harassment in the workplace if he starts anything, then he'd be sacked and never work again because who wants to employ a nonce?

'Ribena, my little wounded soldier.' Mr Scudamore gives me a bit hug but I wriggle away as he stinks of baccy. 'Eee, pet, I'm glad to see you back. This place has been like a morgue without you. Time for a brew yet?'

Huh, so it's not *me* they've missed, it's my coffee-making skills. I slouch off to the kitchen. Omigawd, the cupboard's full of new mugs! They're all gaudy and disgusting, orange, purple, lime green, must have been a job lot from a shop for the colour-blind.

Next to the kettle there's a parcel in silver wrapping paper with a matching tag that says WELCOME BACK, ROWENA. I rip off the paper to find a little box with fancy writing on it. LEAMINGTON LUSTREWARE. MADE IN ENGLAND. Oh no! A big fat blush spreads hotly over my face and neck. When I undo the flap, I find a mug, just like one of the mugs I got busted for, only with a fluffy yellow chick painted on the side. What is this, some kind of sick joke? How did they find out about my brush with the Feds? Maybe the cops came round to check out my fainting alibi and gave them the full SP. Well, I'll just deny it. There was a warning the other night on telly about bogus policemen in the local area. I'll say it must have been them, spreading malicious lies.

When I turn round they're all standing grinning in the doorway, Mr Scudamore, Ray, Gerry, a couple of the drivers and, Omigawd, Dean! I'm so gobsmacked I nearly drop the mug.

'Hope you like it,' says Mr Scudamore. 'We couldn't think what else to get. Sort of friendly gesture, to show we care about you. Mrs Marr picked it out, it's from Halfdays.'

'I know. I mean, cheers. I'll try not to smash it.'

'You'd better bleedin' not, we had to take out a second mortgage to buy that,' says Ray. 'Has the kettle boiled yet?'

'Bog off and do some work,' I snap.

'Glad to see your temper's improved,' he goes. I flick him the finger but he just laughs.

Dean comes over and stands behind me, so close I can feel his breath on my neck. I push him off with my elbow.

'Leave it out. Can't you see I'm busy?'

He spins me round to face him and gazes into my eyes. 'Too busy for a cuddle?'

Jesus, if he thinks he can paw me just because we nearly had sexual congress, he's in for a letdown. 'Forget it, right? There's nothing going on between us so stop acting as if we're an item.'

'Gimme a break, Rowena. How can you say that after . . . you know.' He tries to put his arms round me but I shove him away.

'It was a mistake. I wasn't thinking straight. You took advantage of me, whatever. Now let it lie, I don't want to discuss it.' The kettle takes for ever to fill. My arm trembles as I hold it under the tap, I'd forgotten how heavy it is. Dean grabs it from me and plonks it on the draining board.

'Let me take you to Pizza Hut after work. Talk this through.'

'No,' I say firmly. 'There's nothing to talk about and anyway, tonight's impossible. I'm off to a limbo-dancing class straight from work.'

Ray pops his head round the door. 'So here you are,' he goes to Dean. 'Give us a hand with this stiff, would you, he weighs a friggin' ton. We'll be burying bleedin' mammoths next.'

I'm on light duties this morning as Mrs Marr says I'm to ease myself in gradually and not to strain any muscles. Suits me. After I've done the washing-up I plonk myself behind the front desk and flick through the magazines, only she makes me hide them when customers walk in as we don't want to give the impression of being slack. She scans through the obituaries in the paper and highlights the ones who came to Crowther's. She won't be happy till we get a hundred per cent, it's a wonder she doesn't send me out chasing ambulances. When I look at the clock it's lunchtime already.

'Get yourself off to the park,' says Mrs Marr. 'You could do with a bit of gentle exercise, blow those cobwebs away.'

No chance. I'm off down the Jolly Fryer to see if they've changed the fat. I fancy a tray of chips with loads of salt and vinny plus maybe a frankfurter in batter. I'm just out the door when someone grabs my arm. It's Dean, loitering with intent!

'Come on, we're going to the Elbow,' he announces. 'I'll buy you a bar meal.'

'I can't, I'm under-age.'

'We'll sit in the children's garden then, you can play in the Wendy House or have a go on the bouncy castle.'

He practically frog-marches me down the road. Loads of people walk past but nobody bats an eyelid. He could be a pimp forcing an innocent virgin into a life of sleaze, or a gangland killer about to execute me down an alley, they wouldn't lift a finger to save me.

The Elbow's heaving with bimboids and geeks who work in banks and stuff. It's always full at lunchtime as the food's cheap and they sell real ale with names like Old Hoagy's Heavy and Sheep Dip. Rat-piss, more like. Dean plonks me at a table in a dingy corner near the bog door and sticks a menu in front of me.

'Baked spud with melty cheese for me,' he says. 'How about you?'

'I'll have a chip butty, and don't forget the brown sauce. And a double Bailey's with ice.'

He wiggles his eyebrows at me and heads off to the bar. There's a constant stream of blokes pootling in and out of the bog, all giving me the eye. Every time the door opens I get a waft of stale piddle mixed with disinfectant, *very* appetising, I don't think! It's totally unhygienic, I'll bet there's all sorts of bacteria floating about on the scran, E-coli, salmonella and suchforth. They want reporting to the Environmental Health.

'One chip butty and brown sauce.' Dean slides a plate across the table. 'And one large Bailey's frappé.'

173

'That's not what I asked for. I said with *ice*, dumbo. Oh, never mind, I'll drink it.' I tip back my head and drain it in one. It tastes divine, slithering creamily down my throat. The bottom of the glass is full of little-bitty pieces of ice, like frozen gravel, which I spit on to the carpet.

Dean stares at me all googly-eyed. 'What?' I go.

'Nothing. Something wrong with the chip butty?'

'It's disgusting.' I push my plate away. 'The chips are frozen in the middle and it's that cheap watery brown sauce, tastes like bile. Pigs wouldn't eat this rubbish. Where's my drink gone? I'm thirsty.'

Dean says he doesn't fancy his potato since I pointed out some green poisonous bits on the skin. He goes up to the bar and comes back with half a lager for himself and a Coke with lemon pips floating on top for me, like I'm five years old or something.

'Come on then,' he says, lighting up a tab. 'Tell me what's going on. I don't see you for two weeks and then you give me the cold shoulder. I thought we were mates.' He peers at me over the top of his specs, it's quite fetching in a Jarvis Cocker kind of way.

'We *are* mates. It's just that . . . Well, you know.' I rip up a beer mat for something to do.

'You're embarrassed about the other night, is that it?'

I shrug. 'No. Yes. I dunno. OK then, I feel shit about it. I wish we'd never done it.'

'Well, we didn't exactly *do* it, did we?' Dean laughs and puts his face close to mine but I refuse to look at him. 'Talk about a farce. That Filthy, what a headcase, bombing around in his loincloth, threatening to murder the cat. Come on, Rowena, you must see the funny side. I couldn't stop sniggering all the way home.'

'Suppose so.' I glance up at him and twitch my mouth in a lightning grin. 'You should have seen Mum's face when she turned the light on and saw us,' I tell him. 'It was a picture, her eyes popped out on springs like Jim Carrey in that film, *The Mask*.'

Dean pulls a bug-eyed face, he can be quite amusing sometimes. 'Remember when Filthy karate-chopped the radiator?' he goes. 'Ouch, I felt it myself. It's a wonder he didn't bust his fingers.' He swishes his hand on to the table. 'Kerrr-unch!' We giggle like daft schoolkids for a bit, then I remember.

'Have you told anyone at work? Tell me the truth, Dean, it's important.'

He rolls his eyes to heaven. 'What d'you think I am? Course not. Honest, Rowena, I'd never discuss stuff like that, specially not with Ray, he'd only scribble it on the bog wall.'

'OK, OK. But if you're lying you're dead. Jesus, look at the time. I told Mrs Marr I'd only be half an hour.'

'Stuff her. That clock's probably fast anyway. Just tell me, we *are* still mates, aren't we?'

'Course we are. It's just . . . it's just that I want to keep it that way. Plutonic like. Don't get the wrong idea, you're dead canny. It's just that I've thought about it a bit and I'd rather we didn't, you know – *shag*.'

'Never say never,' goes Dean, and winks at me.

## 21

## *Stoppy-in Night #2*

As soon as I'm fit and back at work, Mum abandons the caring act and resumes her nymphomaniac lifestyle.

'I'll be staying at Bernard's tonight,' she announces. 'He's asked me round to check his bites. They don't seem to be clearing up at all, in fact he says they're getting worse, he's in agony, poor thing. It doesn't make sense.'

I splutter into my Irn Bru. 'Well, you can't refuse an invitation like that. Spending all night staring at a spotty back? Nothing wrong with *your* social life.' Who does she think she's kidding? It's disgusting, she's *so* gagging for it she's even willing to shag a leper.

'You won't do anything silly, I hope?' she goes, stuffing her nightie and clean panties into a Netto bag. She's never left me on my own for a whole night before and she's getting twitchy about it.

'Like what? Spray graffiti on the walls? Invite the Mutants round for cocktails? I'll just be glued to the telly, as per usual. Look, Mum, I'm not a kid, I can take care of myself for a few hours.'

She shoots me a sideways look. 'I'll give you a ring later on, just to be on the safe side. You've got Bernard's number in case of an emergency. Now, have I remembered everything? Toothbrush, deodorant . . .'

*. . . brains, Mother?*

*In my knickers, dear.*

*Self-respect?*

*Oh, I binned that old thing when I met Filthy.*

'That'll be Bernard now. I told him to wait outside the house.' She scoops up her stuff and kisses me goodbye. 'You're sure you'll be all right on your own?'

'Just go.' Filthy honks his horn. 'Romeo's getting impatient.'

Yesssss! A whole night on my own. I can do anything I want to, anything in the world. I'm FREE! I'll start off with a brown-sauce sarnie. And a celebratory glass of Bailey's.

Telly's crap tonight, typical. I can't be arsed to go round the video shop so I dig out a couple of old faves to watch the good bits, like in *Thelma and Louise*, where that creepy bloke says, 'Suck my dick,' and Susan Sarandon blasts him to Kingdom Come. I fast-forward it to the part where Brad Pitt gets it on with Geena Davis only I'm not really in the mood for sexual stuff so I watch the end where Thelma and Louise hold hands, step on the gas and fly over the cliff to escape the Feds. It reminds me of when I was arrested and the thing I told the bizzies about my dad. A hot flush creeps over my body just thinking about it. Why did they have to be *real* cops? Why couldn't it have been like in *The Blues Brothers*, where the wifey goes, 'Are you the police?' and Ellwood says, 'No, ma'am, we're musicians.'

Stop wasting time, Rowena! You're meant to be having FUN!

More Bailey's, glug-glug-glug.

What a fool I am! Why am I sitting bored out of my skull when my Trusty Sidekick's only feet away in the shed? He ought to be here with me, sharing my freedom in front of the Cosiglow, two independent creatures spending quality time together. I nip outside in my Toastie socks. Disaster! The shed is bare!

'Bundy, here, Bundy, come on, boy,' I go. 'Nice salmon for tea, Bundy.' Silence. Apart from next door's Sheba going seismic, obviously.

Maison well have some more Bailey's.

I dunno why people go on about freedom, it's boring as fuck. In the end I decide on a bath and an early night. *So*? There's no law against it, I can do anything I like. To make it special, I tip in loads of Mum's aromatherapy stuff and crank TLC up loud on the CD player.

This is the life. Stretched out, soaking in a warm sea of bubbles, scented candles flickering gently, supping the last of the Bailey's straight from the bottle. Mmm, bliss.

*Crackle-crackle-crackle.*

What's that noise? Omigawd, the shower curtain's on fire! Flames licking up to the ceiling , a horrible stench of melted plastic, thick black smoke everywhere. Quick, Rowena, *do* something! I thought shock was supposed to sober people up but my brain's totally befuddled with the Bailey's. Help me out of this pickle, Big G, and I promise I'll never touch alcohol again. Not till I'm old enough, anyway.

I clamber out of the bath in a blind panic, banging my knee on the side. Christ, it really knacks, whoever called it a funny bone needs shooting. I hoy all the candles into the water, then climb on to the lavvy seat and yank the blazing shower curtain off the hooks. It lands in the bathwater, sizzles a bit, then phutters out in a cloud of smoke. I feel sick with shock. I lift up the bog lid and hurl up ten quids-worth of liquid stomach contents. Why me, God? Why *me*?

I can just about manage to stagger to bed, then I start feeling queasy again. Lie still, that's the trick, even though the room's spinning round at 100 mph. Wait for the feeling to pass.

Uh-oh. Too late . . .

Voices swirl round in my head. That shrink was hopeless, I'm going completely mental.

*'What's that smell? . . . It's coming from upstairs . . . Something's burning . . . Oh dear God, look at the bathroom . . . Where's Rowena? . . .'*

I'm in the doghouse again. Just because I never heard the stupid phone. Dunno why Mum had to check up on me anyway, I was doing fine. I'd have had the place well sorted by the time she came home. But oh no, Mrs Neurotic Mum has to shoot round in a taxi with half-pissed Filthy Luker to make sure I'm not lying unconscious in a pool of blood.

For 'blood', read 'vomit'.

'You stupid, *stupid* girl,' she rants, stripping the sheets off my bed as I lie in a crumpled heap on the floor, cords of sicky spittle drooling from my mouth. 'I can't trust you on your own for a second, you're a flaming liability.'

'Don't go on at me,' I croak tearfully. 'Can't you see I'm gutted?'

'It's a miracle the whole flaming house wasn't gutted,' she yells. 'What in God's name were you playing at? Have you gone completely mad?'

'You tell me, you're the one who sent me to a shrink.' Where's her sympathy? What happened to the caring, doting mother who couldn't do enough for me? Too much sex must have addled her brain, she's forgotten I'm deeply traumatised and suffering from painful recovered memories. All she's bothered about is getting the house shipshape.

*He* pokes his nose in. 'Seen the bathroom ceiling? It's covered in thick black grease, that'll never come off in a month of Sundays.' Thank you, Filthy, for that gesture of support, for taking Mum's mind off our fire-ravaged home, for dropping me even deeper in the shit, if that's possible. 'It's like downtown Sarajevo in there, you were lucky the whole house didn't go up. Could have taken next-door as well.'

That *would*'ve been a tragedy, specially if the Council had to rehouse the Mutants. They're such brilliant neighbours, how would we live without their cursing and banging, using knackered fridges as garden ornaments, and Sheba barking her tits off at all hours? *Naaaaaay-bours. Pick your nose and taste the flaaaaay-vours.*

'Mum, I'm starvingly hungry. You couldn't rustle us up a sarnie, I suppose, just to put a lining on my stomach?' My guts feel raw after puking up a whole bottle of Bailey's. I've got a right headache as well, it's like somebody tightening a leather strap round my brain. 'And a couple of Solpadeines? *Please?*'

She glares at me with homicidal eyes. 'Don't speak to me. Don't even *look* at me. Get out of my sight this minute or I won't be responsible for my actions.'

She's down on her knees, scrubbing the sick off the carpet with bleach. I hope she's not expecting me to sleep in this room, the ammonia fumes'll choke me to death. Filthy plonks his spotty arse on the bed and sparks up a tab.

'That goes for you too,' she yells at him like a deranged psycho. 'If you can't turn your hand to anything, you might as well sod off home. And put that bleeding cigarette out, we've had one inferno already.'

Filthy nips the end of his fag and pulls a daft face at me, meaning, *What's eating her?*

'I can see you're a bit wound up,' he goes, the master of understatement. 'I'd better let you get on, don't want to be in the way. Give me a ring tomorrow.'

'Piss off!' shrieks Mum, scrubbing like fury. Filthy just grins and heads downstairs. 'Bloody men!' she goes. 'About as much flaming use as an ashtray on a motorbike.'

This is a good sign, it means she's not totally blind to his faults. Could it mark the Beginning of the End?

Rigor mortis has set in! I'm stiff all over from sleeping on the couch. The whole house stinks of burnt plastic, like barbecued Barbie dolls. When I crawl upstairs to the bogatory and see the full horror in broad daylight, I'm paralysed with shock. The ceiling's covered in tarmac, and in the bath there's a layer of shiny sludge that used to be the shower curtain. Even the mirror and walls are coated in black powdery stuff. Jesus, what a mess! Plus I can't have a shower! I consider ringing in on a sickie until I realise there's no way I want to spend time with my maniac mum. Better spruce myself up at work.

Mum's tacked a note to her bedroom door.

*KEEP OUT! THIS MEANS YOU!*

Still a bit grouchy then, obviously.

I creep back into the bathroom and scrawl a message with my finger on the soot-covered tiles.

*V. sorry for the ~~incovience~~ mess. Later,*
   *Rowena.*
   *XXX*

I'm late for work again. Mrs Marr gawps at me like I'm a vagrant crawled in off the street.

'I don't wish to be personal, Rowena,' she whispers. 'But to be brutally frank, you look like the wreck of the Hesperus this morning.' Her nostrils twitch. 'And there's a faintly unpleasant whiff about you, reminds me of burning car-tyres. You know I'm the last person to pry, so you don't *have* to explain . . .'

Oh, but I do, I do. *Burning car tyres, eh?* She sits me down in the soft meeting area and pats my hand. I take in a huge breath and let it out slowly through my nose.

'It was horrific,' I begin. 'The scariest experience of my life . . .'

'Hold that thought,' she says. 'I'll get Ray to bring you some hot sweet tea, it works wonders for shock.' She phones through to the back, then sits beside me and holds my hand.

'There was a terrible accident,' I say. 'A head-on collision. A car and a minibus. On the central motorway, it was, near the Jesmond turn-off. I'd just got off the Metro, I was heading for the road bridge when it happened.' I clap my hand to my forehead. 'Oh God, I think I'm going to flake out.'

'Head between your knees, come along,' she goes briskly, forcing me into a gymnastic contortion. 'Let the blood run into your brain. Thank you, Ray, just put the tea on the table.'

'What's occurring here?' he goes. 'Smells like a bleedin' crematorium.'

'That'll do, Ray. Rowena's been involved in an incident, but I'm dealing with it, I'm sure you've got work to be getting on with.' I wait till he shuffles off then slowly lift up my head. 'Better, dear?' I nod in a pathetic fashion. 'Good. Now you were saying . . . ? About the accident?'

'It was an awful prang,' I say. 'Brakes screeching, one hell of a crash, it's a miracle there were no fatalities, although I'd have made sure we got the business, seeing as I was there at the scene.'

Mrs Marr tuts sadly, she hates to think of Crowther's losing trade.

'All the traffic had stopped, it must have been backed up for miles. The people from the minibus were OK, a few cuts and bruises, a bit dazed, wandering about like zomboids. Then suddenly there was an almighty roar. I thought it was thunder at first, then I realised it was . . . it was the car! The petrol tank must have ignited, the whole thing went up like a bonfire – *Whoosh!*'

'Oh, dear God,' squeaks Mrs Marr. 'Thank goodness you weren't any nearer.'

'But I *was*. By that time I'd scrambled down the embankment. I was so close I could feel the flames singeing my eyelashes. Then this woman crawls out of the driver's door, her hair on fire. People dash over to help her get out before the car completely explodes.'

'Mother of God,' goes Mrs Marr, crossing herself. 'Was her face blackened?'

'No. Dunno. Erm, bits of it, yes. So they're trying to drag her away but she's yelling something and pointing at the car. Well, I couldn't just stand there, could I? I run to the car and there, in the back, strapped into a child-seat, there's a little boy, bawling his head off.' I pause and take a sip of tea. It's like treacle, yuk.

'Yes?' pants Mrs Marr. She's enjoying this a bit too much for my liking. I guess it goes with the job. 'And . . .?'

'The car's well alight by this time, the metal's red hot on my arms, it's a miracle I wasn't frazzled to death. Anyway, I manage to yank the kid out of the seat even though he's struggling like a maniac.

His clothes are on fire so I roll him over and lie on top of him to kill the oxygen, right there in the middle of the road. Next thing I know, the paramedics arrive, slap a mask on him and rush him away, flashing lights, sirens, the lot.'

'Thank God you were there, Rowena. Just think, you risked your life to save a little boy.' Mrs Marr gulps down the rest of my tea, she's welcome to it.

'Wait, you haven't heard the best bit. Everybody's clapping and cheering, someone even comes up and asks for my autograph. Anyways, I slip off through the crowd because I didn't want to let you down by being late for work.'

'You're a real heroine. You deserve a medal,' she goes. 'I've a good mind to ring the local paper, they love human-interest stories like that. And you could tell them you work at Crowther's, it might bring in a bit of business.'

'*No!*' I yell in a demented fashion. 'No, no publicity. It's my Mum, see. She blows things up in her mind, in fact she's seeing a shrink at the moment. She'd only have nightmares about it and . . . and funny turns, then they'd have to hospitalise her again. It was six months before they let her out last time.'

Mrs Marr tuts in sympathy. 'Dearie, dearie me,' she says. 'I had no idea. Well, of course I'll respect your wishes.'

'And you mustn't breathe a word to anyone here, just in case it gets back to Mum, you know how these things travel. Please, Mrs Marr, promise me. *Please.*'

'All right, I promise, Rowena. Now, if you're feeling better, why don't you try to clean yourself up, you'll be more refreshed – and smell a bit sweeter. I think you'd better work in the back today, we don't want to alarm the customers.'

I wash myself down with a sponge we use on the corpses, pinching my nose to stop myself from gagging. My hair still stinks of smoke but so what, Mr Scudamore always smells like that.

## 22

# The Séance

When I get home, the house windows are flung wide open. Mum must have taken the day off, I guess she couldn't face coming back from work to a burnt-out shell. Even with all that fresh air, the pong of scorched plastic mixed with ammonia nearly knocks me out, she must be using tankerloads of bleach. Wonder what her mood's like? I pad warily up the stairs, ready to do a runner if she starts hurling missiles or threatening to flay me alive with a scrubbing-brush.

There's a strange noise coming from Mum's room. Sounds like two people – two wifies – bawling with hysterical laughter. She must have the radio on loud. I stick my head round the bedroom door. What a sight! It's Mum and Mandy Sweeney, curled up on the floor, clutching their bellies and roaring their heads off, not that there's anything to laugh at.

'What's so funny?' I demand. Perhaps the fumes have spongified their brains.

'Howay, it's the pyromaniac!' squawks Mandy. 'Quick, Jean, extinguish all naked flames.'

Mum appears to find this hilarious. 'Aaargh – my daughter the arsonist!' she shrieks. 'Get a bucket of water.' They collapse in hysterics, rolling round the carpet like two daft dogs.

Then I spot the empty vodka bottle on the dressing table. 'You're *pissed*!' I yell accusingly.

'Completely bladdy bloodered.' Mum giggles.

'Utterly fit-shaced,' squeals Mandy.

'You're a disgrace, the pair of you. You're supposed to set me an example. Some role models, I *don't* think!' I stamp off to the bathroom. This'll be fun, sitting on a lavvy in the middle of a bomb site.

But, Omigawd, it looks like new! The black grease on the ceiling's vanished, they've even slapped on a coat of Barley White. All that sludge has been scraped off the bath, the mirror and tiles sparkle, and the bottles of bubble stuff have been washed clean. If it wasn't for the missing shower curtain, I'd think I'd dreamt the whole thing. Then I spot the poster tacked on the back of the door. It's my old one of Keith from the Prodigy, that picture from the *Firestarter* video. Oh, very droll, I *don't* think.

Still, it's an ace job. Mum should set up in business as a cleaner. It was on telly once about a wifey in America who goes in after messy suicides or murders to scrape the brains off the ceiling and give the place a good bottoming so the families needn't be arsed. I might even be able to put some business her way. VINCENT & DAUGHTER: SPECIALISTS IN TRAUMA-SCENE HYGIENE. We could employ Mandy Sweeney. She moonlights as a part-time cleaner and it always helps to have a scrubber on the team.

'Bathroom looks mint, Mum,' I say, but she's spark out on the bed, with Mandy Sweeney crashed next to her doing her world-famous impression of a beached whale. I wish I had a camera, this is blackmail material.

It's teatime when they eventually surface. Mum microwaves some lasagne, plus a ton of chips for Mandy.

'Don't know if I'll be any good tonight, Jean,' the lardarse goes, between gobfuls. 'My aura's a bit flattened. I'll give it my best shot, though.'

'Mandy's going to tell my fortune,' says Mum. 'She was spot on last time, told me there was a new relationship round the corner, then – lo and behold – I met Bernard.' She mops round her plate with a slice of bread. 'Good job you never said he'd be tall, dark and handsome, otherwise I'd have done you for trades description!'

'You're not wrong there,' snorts Mandy. 'What about you, Roey?

I haven't got my tarot cards but I could read your palm, or do a psychic forecast, whatever.'

'I don't believe in it. It's a load of pants,' I tell her. 'Anyway, you shouldn't dabble in the occult, it rips the curtain between worlds, like hairspray making holes in the ozone layer. Then demons sneak in and possess you, drive you totally mental.'

'That could explain a lot,' goes Mum, winking slyly at Mandy. 'Maybe we should send you to an exorcist instead of a shrink. Honestly, Rowena, I've never heard such tosh in my life. Demons, indeed. It'll be little green men next.'

'She's not far off, Jean,' says Mandy. 'These things happen. I could tell you stories about the supernatural, make your hair stand on end. You've no need to worry about me, I've got Romany blood in my veins, I treat the spirit world with respect. This shrink business, though – now that's what I call *dangerous*.'

After they've sided the pots, Mum and Mandy park their butts round the kitchen table. I switch on the Xpelair to let the stink out but Mandy goes to turn it off as it disturbs the negative ions, like her chain-smoking doesn't, I suppose.

'It might confuse my spirit guide,' she says between puffs. 'He won't be up to speed on technology, him being a Red Indian chief.'

'Native American,' I correct her. 'You have to say Native American.'

'If you don't stop chiming in, you'll have to go in the other room,' says Mum. 'Mandy needs to concentrate her psychic energies.'

After stubbing out her tab, Mandy shuts her eyes and grabs hold of Mum's hand. 'Oh dear, you've had a rough ride lately, I can feel a lot of suffering inside.' Mum smiles pathetically. 'You've been bitten by the love bug . . . but things haven't worked out as planned. Someone's let you down, you feel betrayed.' She reaches for another fag and lights up without opening her eyes, fumbling round the table for the Prestatyn ashtray.

'*Yes, yes, I can hear you*,' she goes over her shoulder. 'There's a crowd of them here, Jean, all talking at once. *Pipe down, one at a time!'* she snaps. *'What?* Trouble with authority, they're saying. Somebody in uniform, a copper, maybe. Hold on, there's a man coming into your life, a man with pots of money. Maybe you haven't met him yet. And a child. I can see a baby, a boy, I think. He's wearing one of those blue disposable nappies. It's clouding over now, I'm losing the connection . . .'

Mandy takes a deep drag on her ciggie and opens her eyes.

'I'm not sure what to make of that.' Mum frowns. 'It seemed a bit jumbled up, maybe you got a crossed line and the spirits were talking about somebody else.'

'No, it was definitely you, Jean,' goes Mandy. 'You'll have to remind me what I said, I was in an altered state of consciousness, see.'

'She said you'd been bitten by the love bug,' I offer helpfully. 'That'll be Bernard's back bites. And someone letting you down – the selfish sod wouldn't help you clean the bathroom, he just bogged off home. There, see, it's true!'

'Was there something about trouble with authority?' says Mandy, sparking up *again*, filling the kitchen with 200 known carcinogens. 'I got a picture of a man in uniform, could have been a bizzy. What's that about?'

'I'd rather not go into that. It's in the past – or it had flaming well better be.' Mum glares at me, recalling the night she was summoned to the nick, obviously. I turn away and study Mandy's nicotiney fingers, they look like overcooked chipolatas.

'You said there was a new man coming into my life. A man with money. Any idea when?' Mum picks at the skin round her thumb, it's what she does when she's worried. Dunno why, she ought to be over the moon.

'In a three,' says Mandy. 'I definitely got a three. Could be three days, weeks, months . . .'

'Not *years*, I hope?' Mum's voice sounds panicky, imagining a three-stretch with zero rumpy-pumpy.

'I doubt that. It seemed quite near. Could be three hours for all we know.'

Mum nibbles a sliver of thumb skin. 'And where's Bernard in all this?'

'Out of the picture.' Mandy smirks. 'Not that I see actual *faces*, but this man was definitely well endowed, financially speaking. Surrounded by gold, he was, and drawing you into it. That doesn't sound like Bernard.'

Mum looks disgruntled. 'You're enjoying this, Mandy.'

'*Que sera sera*, Jean,' says Mandy smugly. 'You might have to let him go, clear the way for this other bloke.'

It's on the tip of my tongue to blab about Filthy's lottery win but Mum frowns and puts her finger to her lips, meaning *Keep it buttoned*. No point in letting Mandy Sweeney in on the secret of our new-found fortune – she'd only be after a slice to spend on shell-suits and zillions of cancer sticks.

'What about the baby?' I go. 'You saw a sprog in blue nappies. Oh Mum, it's disgusting. At *your* age! I'll die of shame if you're up the duff.'

'You and me both,' says Mum. 'I've got enough on my hands with you.'

'It might not be yours, Jean.' Mandy reassures her. 'It could be someone close to you.' They both turn their heads and stare at me.

'In a pig's bum!' I snap. 'There's no way!'

'Well, why don't we find out,' says Mandy. 'I'll do you a reading, that way we'll know for sure. Shall we have a little nip, Jean, keep our spirits up? Go easy on the lime.'

How can they even *think* about a drink when they've seen off one bottle of vodka already? It's a wonder they're not dead from alcohol poisoning. Mental note to check out where the nearest AA branch meets.

Mandy clasps my hand in her big fat puddingy one, takes a slug of voddy and closes her eyes. I shift the tabs out of her way so she won't find them till she comes out of her trance.

'I'm getting some powerful signals here,' she goes. 'The energy's shooting through me like a flash of lightning, good job I'm wearing rubber soles.'

Suddenly she grips my hand like a vice, nearly busting my knuckles. I try to wriggle away but it feels as if we're welded together.

'It's *you*!' she says. 'Buzzing with it, like a psychic pylon, you are. You've got some high-up friends on the next plane, they're protecting you. I can see you dressed in barbed wire, metaphysically speaking of course. And . . . *what*?' She flips her head round to hear my invisible friends. 'They've sent a spirit to guide you. He's here already, helping you.'

'What, you mean a dead person?'

'Not as such. Could be what we call a familiar. A bird, an animal.'

'Like that dog, the Rottie who minded Damien in *The Omen*?'

'Summat like that.'

Bundy! She's talking about Bundy! My guardian angel in cat form, whizzed down from the spirit world to help me get rid of Filthy. I should have realised he was no earthly mog.

'*Don't all chatter at once*,' she snaps over her shoulder. '*You'll get your say.* Sweet Jesus, look who's here. It's that baby, I can see him clear as day. A little bairn with a fluffy toy. Oh, it's not in the future, he's in spirit. He wants to thank you for helping him with the transition. *What's your name, sunshine? Baby Bunting? God bless you, sweetheart.*'

It's baby Nathan! She's talking about baby Nathan! This is SO beyond spooky.

Mandy unscrews her eyes and fumbles for her cigs. I'm completely gobstruck.

'Eee, I feel wrung out, Jean. I wouldn't say no to a wee tipple, make it neat this time. Well, Roey, did I make any sense?'

'Like hell you did,' I lie. 'Told you, it's bollocks.'

Truth is, I'm totally spooked out.

My head's still swimming with it next day at work.

'Do you believe in ghosts? Spirits, like?' Dean's prepping this lad who copped it in a motorbike accident, a real bad case. It'll take for ever to build up his face.

'Haunted houses, you mean? Things that go bump in the night? Grey ladies, blokes running around with heads under their arms, that sort of thing?' Dean grins, I wish he'd take me seriously.

'No, *ordinary* people. Like him.' I point to the deceased. 'What happens to him when he dies?'

'We pump him full of embalming fluid, make him look nice for the rellies, and stick him in a long box. Why are you asking? You know all this.'

'Is that it?'

'Then he ends up as toast, or worm fodder.'

He can be so crass sometimes. 'This is important, Dean. Did he have a soul, a spirit, whatever?'

'Fuck knows. Ask me one on football.'

I spin round and there's Mr Scudamore, snapping on his rubber gloves, preparing to drain the cavities.

'We only know one thing for certain,' Mr Scudamore says. 'And that's that we know nothing, not till our number's called. What we *believe*, though, that's a different matter. I happen to think that what we call death is the start of a new life somewhere else. I've seen a spirit leave a body. Well, not *seen* exactly, more *sensed*.' He gives me a bit squeeze. 'There are more things in heaven and earth, Horatio . . .'

'Rowena,' I correct him. 'My name's Rowena.'

## 23

## *Gemma Gets a Life*

'A call for you, Rowena,' says Mrs Marr. 'It's personal, by the sound of it.' She hands me the phone with a look that means, *Hurry up about it, there's work to be done.*

'Crowther's Body Shop, Rowena speaking,' I say in a daft poshgit voice. Mrs Marr's eyebrows nearly fly off the top of her head. She pretends to polish the yucca plant only really her ears are flapping like an elephant's in a gale.

'Rowena? It's me, Gemma.'

Amazingly, I don't squirm, sigh, or pretend to drop the phone when I hear her voice. The Madolescents bonding sesh at the Angel must have really, really worked.

'Hey, Gem, what's up?'

'Are you doing anything tonight?' Her voice sounds strange, sort of choked up.

'What, you mean after the gig at Altamont Lodge?'

Gemma clears her throat. 'I won't be going. I'm giving it a miss.'

I fake a coughing fit to give me time to think. What is this, a trick question? A wind-up? Some kind of trap? Omigawd, maybe the CIA are holding Gemma hostage and using her as a decoy to smoke me out! That's why her voice sounds strangulated – they've probably slipped a noose round her neck. Think-think-think, Rowena!

'Erm, not sure,' I say, cagey-like. 'I might have a small window. Why?'

Gemma clears her throat. That'll be them, tightening the noose. 'It's just that me and Coralie are meeting for cocktails and we wondered if you'd like to come along.'

Gemma Probert? Cocktails? If she'd said cock*roaches* I wouldn't have batted an eyelid. Gemma is to cocktails what kippers are to custard. Now I know for deffo it's a set-up.

'Sure,' I reply, cool as a Slushpuppy. 'Where?'

A piece of paper rustles. Gemma says, 'The Cluny, that place under Byker Bridge, next to the Ship Inn, six o'clock.' Obviously the CIA are now holding a Kalashnikov to her temple, forcing her to read their note.

'Ten-four,' I say, whatever the fuck that means.

'Later then, Rowena.'

'Yeah, later.' I slam down the receiver, ignoring Mrs Marr's tutting noises, and head for the receiving room where I can make a phone call away from her earwigging. Flicking through the *Yellow Pages*, I find the number for the Kit Pit and tap it in.

'Is Coralie Henderson there?' I blurt out, before anyone has a chance to answer.

'Yeah, this is Coralie. Who's that?'

'It's Rowena. I've just had Gemma on the phone. What's going on?' Best not to give her too much time to think, in case she's in on the conspiracy. I know, I know, it's unlikely, but CIA agents infiltrate all sorts of organisations, so they might have planted someone in the Madolescents to try to access my innermost thoughts.

Coralie hesitates. 'It's hard to talk right now, we're in the middle of stocktaking. Are you on for that drink tonight?'

My head's in a spin, trying to figure out whether Coralie's on the level. 'Maybe,' I say.

'Try, Rowena,' pleads Coralie. 'Gemma's got a problem, we need to help her sort it out. I've asked the others to come too. We're all bunking off the Altamont Lodge meeting.'

I cave in. 'OK then.' If Ash is going to be there, I'll risk being arrested and transported to Alcatraz by the MIBs.

At five o'clock I take a taxi and charge it to Crowther's account as

I can't be arsed to work out which bus to catch. The Cluny's this old warehouse building near the river, right next to the City Farm where they take schoolkids to see real-live sheep and stuff. Oddly enough, it's just up the road from Dallas Carpets where they sell a range of sheepskin rugs at knockdown prices.

I deliberately got here early to check the place out before the others arrive. A few arty-farty types are perching on bar stools drinking beer or fancy coffee and three of the silvery tables have people sitting round them, chatting, smoking and reading newspapers. No one takes a blind bit of notice of me. They don't look like CIA spooks, but then they wouldn't, would they?

'Hi, what can I get you?' A bloke with dreads and a pierced eyebrow leans across the bar, grinning. I sort of recognise him, he used to work at the Riverside, the kickingest club in Newcastle, until they closed it down.

'Erm, I dunno, nothing,' I mutter, like a mentally-defective person. He carries on grinning, which puts me under pressure and makes me blurt out, 'OK then, give us a bottle of Hooch.' I carry the drink to a table on a raised bit of floor and sit facing the door so I can see who's coming in and out. The Cluny's a geet cool place, tarted up with regeneration money but not in a neo-naff way. There's a pipe like a giant silvery caterpillar running round the walls and down the far end there's some sort of art gallery thing. Behind the arched wooden doors is a longish room with another bar where they put bands on, according to the posters. The dreadlocked barman slaps on a Stereophonics CD, looks over at me, grins again and winks. He must be on something. I pretend to smile back, then check out the clock projected on a wall. Ten to six. At that instant Coralie appears wearing her purple furry coat, spots me at the high table and clomps over in her platty boots.

'It's friggin' arctic out there,' she says, by way of greeting. 'Fancy a hot toddy?'

'Hot totty? Get us a couple while you're at it,' says a familiar voice. It's Mickey, looking even more fetching than usual with a red nose and watery eyes, like a flu-ridden Rudolph.

'Get lost, Mickey man.' Coralie drapes the fake fur on a chair back, revealing a velvety black skintight top that I'd donate a kidney for. 'Since you're here, you can spring for the first round. Two toddies,' she orders. 'Make sure they use Jamesons.' Mickey adjusts his veg and struts to the bar.

'What's the story, morning glory?' I ask, fingering Coralie's sleeve to see whether it's that cheapo velvet. It is, but the top still looks good and that's what counts.

She sparks up one of Mickey's tabs from the packet he left on the table. 'Gemma's having a crisis. A real one, not just up here.' Coralie taps her head. 'I thought we'd get the Madolescents together, see if we can come up with a brainwave.'

'I'm on beta blockers, do my brainwaves count?' chuckles Mickey, plonking three drinks on the table. The glasses are caged in metal holders and there's steam rising from the goldy liquid. It looks like fresh pee. The smell reminds me of the seaside. I haven't a clue what a hot toddy is but I refuse to show my ignorance by asking.

Just then Reuben appears through the door, looking geet cool as owt in a puffa jacket, Cat boots and beanie hat. Right behind him is Ash, in baggy jeans and a parka. My womb flutters. He's wearing slap again, but fortunately not that tarty blue eyeshadow. Reuben glances around, spots us and gives a thumbs-up sign, then digs in his pocket and buys a couple of Cokes for him and Ash. They climb the steps towards our table. When Ash pulls out a chair and sits next to me I get an attack of palpitations.

'What's the crack-crack-crack-crack?' says Reuben.

Coralie crosses her legs. Her skirt's nearly short enough to show her cervix. 'It's Gemma,' she says. 'She's being kicked out of her flat.'

Just as she says it, Gemma plods in through the door. Omigawd, she's wearing a long shaggy coat, black and silver, like something made from Don King's hair. Pure Bigfoot! Mickey leans back and nicks a chair from the next table for her. Gemma plonks herself down and blows her nose real loud, like a trumpeting elephant. Her face is a right mess, tear stains running down her make-up where she's been crying, or her eyes have been streaming in the wind. Coralie brings another hot toddy from the bar and Gemma cups her hands round the glass and inhales the steam. As if in sync with her misery, a Radiohead track drones away in the background.

I take a sip of hot – well, hottish – toddy. It's sweet and a bit sickly but it feels warm and tickly in my stomach, like the first sign of horniness.

Mickey drums his fingers on the table. 'When you're ready, Gemma,' he says, then winces as Coralie kicks him with her heavy orthopaedic-type boot.

A big fat sigh escapes out of Gemma's mouth. 'I've got to get out of the flat,' she says. 'Brighid's split up with her girlfriend and she wants it back.'

'Who's Brighid?' says Mickey.

Gemma knocks back her drink and has a bit cough. 'My boss,' she replies. 'She runs the Hill o' Beans. The lease is in her name, so there's nothing I can do. I'm homeless, or I will be, in a month.' Her chin starts to wobble and a big cartoon tear runs down her cheek fat and splashes on the table.

Coralie squeezes Gemma's leathery hand. 'But that's not the only problem, is it?' Gemma shakes her head, no. 'There's a load of booty stashed there, it belongs to Gemma's boyfriend.'

'Ex-boyfriend,' I correct her.

'Right,' says Coralie. 'A stack of it, still in the makers' boxes, enough to fill a bus. Knock-off,' she whispers, in case anyone was in doubt. 'Microwaves, videos, TVs, sackfuls of Nike and Berghaus gear.'

'And hi-fi systems,' adds Gemma. 'Plus digital cameras, sandwich toasters, kettles. Oh, and a couple of foot-spas, only I wouldn't mind one of those myself.'

Mickey does a low whistle. 'And this boyfriend – *ex*-boyfriend. Where does he fit into the picture?'

Gemma sniffs. 'I'm looking after it for him. He said he'd hire a truck to collect it. That was ages ago. I haven't heard a word from him since and I don't know how to get in touch. Oh God, it's such a mess.'

'You're having a larf,' says Mickey. 'I've got contacts in the business, I can get you top dollar for that lot.'

'No!' shrieks Gemma. 'I can't. Taz would do my legs if anything happened to that gear.'

'Taz?' says Mickey. 'Not Taz Donnelly from Benwell?'

Gemma looks up sharpish. 'Yeah, that's him. Do you know him?'

A wide grin spreads over Mickey's face. 'I know him. And I know why he hasn't been to see you. He's doing a two-stretch for that post-office job in Killingworth.'

Gemma's jaw bounces off her knees. 'Taz, in prison? Are you sure?'

'Sure as eggs come out of chickens' twats,' says Mickey, rubbing his hands together. 'You know what this means? You'll have to get rid of the stuff now, otherwise it'll be obsolete, worthless. I can flog it through a mate of mine, you'll be quids in, then you'll be able to afford a place of your own.'

'But what if—' stammers Gemma.

'If the slimeball comes looking for you, you'll be long gone,' says Mickey. 'Or you could say the cops turned up with a search warrant and confiscated the gear. He's hardly going to ask them for it back, is he?'

Coralie jiggles about on her chair, clapping her hands. 'Oh, Gemma, it's a brilliant idea. You'll be able to start over, with money in the bank.'

Gemma holds her head. 'I dunno. It's too scary. Moving out of the flat's one thing, but what if Taz turned up at the Hill o' Beans and I couldn't front him out?'

'Get another job. Disappear from that part of town. It's a shit place anyway, they treat you like a skivvy. You're worth more than that.' Coralie takes Gemma's hand between both of hers and strokes it. 'Look, if it helps, you can move in with me, just until you sort yourself out. I don't want any rent, you can help with the housework, that sort of thing.'

I stifle a snort. Gemma Probert and housework, in the same breath!

Gemma starts blubbing. 'I couldn't,' she begins.

'Yes you could. Gemma, you must!' orders Coralie.

'Look, Gemma man, someone's offering you a life,' I chip in. 'Take it.'

Gemma sniffles. 'But—'

'No arguments, you're coming to stay with me.' Coralie kisses Gemma's forehead. 'Cool, that's you sorted then. Who's buying the drinks?'

Crisis averted. Or postponed at least, until Coralie finds out what a slut Gemma is around the house.

Mickey's sharp off the mark. He makes a quick phone call and a while later a clapped-out old Transit van pulls up outside the Cluny. This dodgy-looking bloke in a Def Leppard T-shirt honks the horn.

'Give us your keys, Gemma man,' says Mickey. 'Hadaway, youse two, you can give us a hand.' Reuben and Ash stare blankly at each other, then at him. 'Come on, we haven't got all night, that van's hot.' They shuffle to their feet like demented old gadges and trail after Mickey.

'What will you do with the stuff?' says Gemma.

Mickey grins. 'Do you believe in alchemy?' He flicks a thumb across his fingers. 'I'll be turning cardboard boxes into gold.'

'Remember to keep us one of those foot-spas,' yells Gemma, but

Mickey's already disappeared and the Transit's speeding off in a cloud of black smoke.

What started out as a Madolescent crisis summit turns into a boozy girlie hooley as Coralie recites the cocktail menu and says we have to try them all. She starts off with a Long Slow Screw Against the Wall, Gemma has a Screaming Orgasm Between the Sheets, and I go a Sex on the Beach. Next I try Monkey Brains which is red curaçao with Bailey's poured in over the back of a spoon so it curdles and looks like a wee brain suspended in a jar of red blood. Gemma has a vile green thing called Toxic Waste, and Coralie knocks back a Brazen Hussy. After forcing a Fuzzy Navel down my neck I'm starting to feel a bit queasy and I just manage to swallow the cherry from my Fallen Angel before I have to rush off to the bog, stick a biro down my throat and upchuck the lot. By the time I get back to the table Gemma and Coralie are well ratted and having a right giggle making up dirty cocktail names. When the waiter trolls over for the order, Gemma pretends to study the menu and with a dead straight face, announces she'd like Two Fingers in the Minge. The waiter flicks his ponytail and smiles. After he's gone Coralie tells her she'll be lucky, his boyfriend's a bodybuilder, so Gemma will have to make do with a Kit-Kat Shuffle, which makes us all roar until we nearly wet ourselves. As it's nearly chucky-out time, we finish off with Hot White Russians, vodka, Kahlúa and cream, heated up and served with a massive blob of whipped cream on top. Mmm, truly triple divine.

My ears start to jangle. Then I realise it's Mickey waving Gemma's keys. 'Mission accomplished,' he says, red-faced and grinning like an eejit. Behind him slouch Ash and Reuben, shoulders sagging, looking totally knackered. 'Howay then,' says Mickey. 'Pints for the workers, we're spitting feathers here.'

Ash flops into the seat next to mine. Jesus, all the alcohol must have gone to my crotch. I have this unbearable urge to snog his face off, straddle him and give him a good seeing-to, right here, in a crowded bar. I don't, of course, but when he reaches for my hand, I have to practically strap myself down. My heart throbs inside my head and my insides turn to mush. I'm salivating like a bitch on heat, fantasising about giving him a bj under the table. I'd swallow, too. Well, maybe.

'So, that's your electrical problem sorted,' Mickey's saying to Gemma. 'Lock, stock and two Clairol foot-spas. Disposed of, just like they never existed.' He swallows his lager in one go, then fossicks in his pocket and produces a roll of banknotes. 'Here, tuck these in your bloomers. Not a bad profit for a couple of hours' work.'

'But how . . . ? Where . . . ?' splutters Gemma.

Mickey taps the side of his nose. 'The less you know, the better. Let's just say I know the right faces. There'll be brand-new microwaves pinging and VCRs rolling all over the East End tonight.'

'You're brilliant, Mickey man,' says Gemma, smacking him a kiss on the cheek. 'Come on, they're waiting to lock up, I'll treat us all to some scran.'

'Watch what you're doing, Gem,' I warn her. 'You don't want to go flashing that money about, the Feds could be watching. Remember in *Goodfellas*, where those Mobsters went out and bought fur coats and pink Cadillacs and stuff, and ended up as stalactites in frozen-meat lorries.'

'Fuck's sake, Rowena, I only meant fish and chips,' she goes, and everybody laughs. Everybody but Ash, that is. He's looking geet pale and spacey, like he's about to pass out. I link my arm in his and we follow the others outside into the freezing fog.

'You OK, Ash?' He slumps against the wall, clutching his forehead. 'Ash, what's wrong?'

He runs his tongue over his lips. 'I feel weird,' he replies. 'My head's buzzing. It's like electric shocks coming and going in waves. Shit, here comes another one.' His eyebrows meet in a frown and he sucks air through his teeth.

Mickey drapes his arm round Ash's shoulder. 'Does your head keep tightening up?' he says. 'Do you feel giddy?'

'Yeah,' replies Ash. 'And it's getting worse all the time.'

'Are you on Prozac?' Mickey says.

'Not actual Prozac,' replies Ash. 'Similar. Same family.' He winces as another load of volts shoots through his brain. 'I'm not taking them any more, though. Flushed them down the loo a couple of days ago.'

Mickey shakes his head slowly. 'That explains it. You've got withdrawal symptoms. Jesus, Ash, you shouldn't just go cold turkey like that, you need to come off them gradually. No wonder you're having brainshocks, your serotonin levels must be up and down like a bride's nightie.'

I pitch in. 'How come you know so much about it?'

'Because I did the same thing with my medication and it left me feeling a hundred times worse than before I started. Couldn't leave the house, shit-scared of my own shadow, I was. Totally zonked, sweating like a pig, living on another planet.'

'Nothing new there then,' quips Gemma. I glare at her. 'Oops,' she says.

I take Mickey to one side. 'What'll happen to him?' I ask. 'Will this thing in his head go away?'

Mickey blows a puff of air through his mouth. 'It's like a preggy woman having contractions,' he explains. 'The buzzes get closer and closer together, then he'll hit the comedown, that's the real shitty bit. If he can get through that, he's probably cracked it. Tranx might help, braincosh pills. Fuck, I dunno, Rowena, I ain't a doctor.'

I tug at his leather jacket. 'But he won't die, will he?'

Mickey snorts. 'No, you divvy, he won't die. Now come on, let's find some scran, my stomach's starting to eat itself.'

The nearest chippy's at the top of Shields Road which isn't that far away but Gemma goes her boots are crippling her, so Coralie says we maison well get a cab to her place and stop off for chips on the way. Ash is looking, well – *ashen*, and says he'll take a rain check and a bus home. This really pisses me off as I was hoping he'd stage a miraculous recovery and we might be in line for some physical action, but the way things are going, I feel more like a nurse than a love interest so I give in and try not to look like a martyr as he stumbles off to the bus stop.

The taxi drops the five of us and our fish suppers outside Coralie's gaff. She lives in an old terraced house made out of redbrick, not far from the Byker Wall. The place looks dead ordinary from the outside, the front door opens onto the street, no path or garden or anything. But when Coralie turns on the inside light – wow! The colours leap off the walls and shriek. It's so blaringly, blazingly, blindingly bright, I actually flinch as if some-one's chucking acid in my eyes. Straight away you're into a knock-through living/dining room with wooden beams on the ceiling. It could be like a country cottage or something from the olden days, except the walls are canary yellow and the beams are painted scarlet. At the window there's glittery orange curtains tied on to poles, a massive sofa covered with a purple cloth, and loads of cushions in velvet and satin and animal-print. The floorboards sort of match the ceiling, they're painted in alternate red and yellow stripes, and the walls are hung with swirly black and white pictures. I feel woozy looking at them. Pure psychotic nightmare!

'Friggin' hell, Coralie, it's like something out of *Hello!* magazine,' says Gemma, unfazed by the riot of clashing patterns and colours. 'You'd think Posh and Becks lived here, if it wasn't in Byker.'

'Thanks,' goes Coralie. 'Bring your chips through to the back, I don't want grease marks on the furniture.' We trail behind her into a foreign-looking kitchen ablaze with yellow, mustard, orange, pink and red, like a sunset gone mental. The table and chairs are blue, to go with the cupboards and the louvred window shutters. 'It's supposed to look Mexican,' explains Coralie, straightening a string of plastic red chilli peppers. 'According to that flash bint on *Changing Rooms.*' She spreads cork mats on the table and hands out giant yellow plates decorated with blue flowers. 'Eat up then,' she says.

We scoff our chips in silence. I fancy some vinegar on mine but I don't want to stink the place out. Gemma's spearing hers on to her fork one at a time, not cramming gobfuls into her cakehole as per usual. You'd think she was having tea with the Queen. When I catch her eye she beams at me, meaning, *This is my new home, lucky, lucky me!* Mickey polishes off his chips and washes his plate at the sink. Omigawd, he's evolving!

'Where's the bog, I'm busting for a slash,' he says to Coralie. I might have guessed the New Man thing wouldn't last.

'Top of the stairs, the door facing you. Don't go into any of the other rooms,' says Coralie. 'Anyone fancy a cuppa?'

'I'll just have some milk-milk-milk-milk,' says Reuben, handing his plate to Coralie. He's eaten all his chips, so they must have added up to fours.

Gemma defies convention and starts on the washing-up to show Coralie what a brilliant housemate she'll be, obviously. This'll be a new experience for her, not having to scrape mould off the plates.

'It's totally fab, this house. How come you can afford it?' Gemma's never been one to keep her nose out of people's business.

Coralie hands a glass of milk to Reuben. 'It's complicated. I don't actually pay any rent.' She sparks up a ciggy. 'The bloke who owns it, he was a friend of my dad's, he let it to us. Then about a year ago he disappeared. I think he's been murdered.'

'Murdered!' Gemma splutters into her tea.

'He was way dodgy,' Coralie says calmly. 'A nightclub bouncer, smack dealer, into all sorts. I liked him, he helped me out a few times when I was in a bad way. Money and that. He got too powerful though, plenty of people wanted him off the scene. He'll be sleeping with the fishes under the Tyne Bridge, I shouldn't wonder.'

'So this place is rent-free? Fantastic!' Gemma should get a job in the diplomatic service. 'What about your dad? Where's he?'

'London, last time I heard.' Coralie sniffs, stubbing out her tab fiercely. 'Working as a so-called steel erector. The less said about him, the better. He's no angel.'

'And your mum?' says Gemma. I kick her shin under the table, but when she's on a roll there's no stopping her.

Coralie pretends to spit on the floor. 'That evil witch? I don't talk about her.' She finishes her tea and lights another tab. Her hands are trembling.

The air feels thick with things unsaid. 'Mickey's taking for ever up there,' I remark, to diffuse the awkwardness.

'Oh, God!' Coralie jumps up from the table and bounds upstairs. Reuben, Gemma and I look helplessly at each other as we listen to doors opening and banging shut, followed by piercing screams.

'I told you! I told you not to go in there!' Coralie's yelling hysterically at Mickey.

'Hey, chill, Coralie. Just chill out. What's your problem?' Footsteps thud down the stairs, then Mickey stumbles into the kitchen, pushed and thumped by Coralie. Her eyes are wild and glaring. This is one totally freaked woman.

Reuben curls up on the chair and shrinks into his body as Coralie beats Mickey with her fists, screaming, 'You bastard! You bastard! You bastard!' Mickey shields his head with his arms as she pummels him, knocking him round the table.

'Do something, Rowena,' pleads Gemma, panic reducing her voice to a whisper.

Oh right, seems it's down to me again. As Coralie's madwoman performance arrives at my chair, I leap up and grab her arms, yanking them up behind her back and forcing her face down onto the table. I kick her legs apart with my foot.

'Assume the position, bitch!' I bark. Jesus, I've been watching too many American cop shows.

Coralie struggles to get away, but Gemma and Mickey help me hold her down. Fuck knows what Reuben's doing, probably counting bruises. It seems to take an age but finally Coralie runs out of stamina and seems to calm down. I'm still wary. In *Fatal Attraction*, just as everyone thinks the bunny-boiler's drowned in the bathtub, a wee air bubble floats to the surface and – *Aaarrgh!* – she shoots upright brandishing a knife. Madness gives you a second wind, superhuman strength, deadly cunning, all that stuff.

'Sit her down and hold on to her,' I say coldly, like a terrorist leader. Rowena M. Vincent shows no mercy.

Coralie's all cried out and exhausted, but my trusty lieutenants obey my orders. Reuben lights a cigarette and holds it to Coralie's lips as if she's about to be executed, but she hasn't got the energy to puff on it.

'OK, let her go.' Mickey and Gemma stand back. Coralie's forehead slumps on the table with a dull thud. 'What's going on, Mickey man?' I ask.

He shakes his head. 'I dunno, honest. She went demented just because I peeped in the bedrooms while I was upstairs.'

'What's up there? A dismembered torso or something?' Gemma says eagerly.

'Nothing,' says Mickey. 'Just a couple of rooms with beds in, as far as I could see.'

Coralie makes a croaky noise and raises her head. There's a red swelling materialising on her forehead where she banged it on the table. Reuben turns on the tap and pours a glass of water. Coralie takes a sip, screwing up her face as if it's poison.

'Feeling better?' Gemma gives Coralie a bit squeeze.

Coralie sniffles, then nods. 'Sorry. I don't know what got into me, haven't had a do like that for ages. I'll have that fag now, Reuben.' He lights up and passes a cigarette to her.

'Do you want to talk about it?' I say, my voice gentle-like. 'You don't have to.'

Stubbing out her tab after one drag, Coralie nods. 'It's just that I wanted you to like the house,' she says. 'With Gemma coming to live here and all.'

'We do,' I lie, doing my nodding-dog act. 'We love the house. It's brilliant, really warm and cheerful. It's got great vibes.'

Coralie covers her eyes with her hands. 'But I wanted it to be perfect. It's not finished yet, there's still the bedrooms to decorate. They look terrible, all insipid pink and lemon, not bright sunny colours like down here. I didn't want anyone to see them like that, I feel so ashamed of them. That's why I said to Mickey . . .'

'It's cool, Coralie man,' says Mickey. 'I never turned the lights on, they could have been plastered in green slime for all I could see.'

Coralie sniffs. 'Still, I overreacted. I shouldn't have freaked like that. You must think I'm mad.'

There's a big fat silence round the table. Then Gemma does a piggy snort down her nose, and we all burst out laughing to beat the band, even Coralie. Especially Coralie.

'C'm 'ere,' she gasps between giggles. And we gather round, Mickey, Gemma, Reuben, Coralie and me, holding tight to each other, cuddling and squeezing, our molecules jiggling like microwaved love, in a magical Madolescent hug.

# 24

## *Avoiding the Ring*

'Hadaway then,' says Dean, handing me my leather jacket. 'I'm taking you down the Fiddler's Elbow. It's Poets' Day.'

'Get lost. I friggin' hate poetry,' I snap.

'Nah, Poets' Day. You know – Piss Off Early, Tomorrow's Saturday.'

'I wanna get home to watch *TFI Friday*,' I insist. 'You know – Thank Fuck It's Friday.'

Dean grabs my hand and yanks me through the door. 'You can catch the repeat,' he says. 'I've got something to ask you.'

'What?' I frown suspiciously. 'Ask me now.'

'It's a surprise.' He grins.

Huh, my life's full of 'em.

The Elbow's packed with office types chilling after a hard week at the keyboard, snorting at corny jokes and necking overpriced foreign lager. Dean sits me down next to a pair of middle-aged saddos. They're acting on, can't keep their mucky hands off each other. They must be adulterers; married couples don't behave like that. Dean buys a double Bailey's shandy for me and a pint of Guinness for himself.

I dig him in the ribs. 'Look at those two, they're practically *doing* it. It's disgusting. Can't we sit somewhere else?'

Dean glances round. 'There isn't anywhere. Just ignore them, right? They're not hurting anyone.'

The woman's feeding crisps into the guy's mouth and licking round his lips with her tongue. It's obvious he's getting off on it from the way he keeps squirming and slobbering. I've had enough. I reach over and prod him in the back.

'Oi, do you mind? People are trying to talk here.' The bloke ignores me and carries on snogging the woman. I give him a good thump on the shoulder with my fist. 'Are you friggin' deaf . . . er, hearing-impaired? I said people are trying to have a conversation.'

He stops groping for a second and turns round. '*Have* a bloody conversation then, nobody's stopping you.' Then he clocks my double-hard glare and susses that I mean business. His face takes on an alarmed expression. 'I don't want any trouble . . .' he begins. The woman grabs her coat and pulls him to his feet.

'Let's go, Steve,' she hisses. 'In case she's got a knife.' They squeeze past Dean muttering something about care in the community.

'You want to watch yourself, mate,' the bloke goes to Dean. 'She's a bloody psychopath, her.' I'm about to stick one on him but Dean pushes me back on the seat and pins me down.

'Fuck's sake, Rowena. What was all that about?'

I shrug my shoulders. 'It was indecent, what they were doing. At their age, especially. They needed telling.'

'It's not like they're coffin dodgers,' reasons Dean. 'They're no older than your mum and Fil— Oh, so that's it. I know what the problem is now.'

'Shut it!' I snap. 'You know nothing. Get me some peanuts, I'm famished.'

Dean's 'surprise' is that his folks have gone on hols and left him in charge of the house for a fortnight.

'So I thought you might like to come round.' He peers at me Jarvisly over the top of his specs.

'What, to tidy up your mess? I don't think so.'

'No, you divvy. The cleaner does that,' he says. The *cleaner*! Cool, I've never met a private person with a servant before. 'We could listen to some music, phone for a pizza. I dunno . . . just *hang*.'

'As long as you don't try to get me into bed.'

Dean drops his jaw and throws his hands up in a daft shock-horror thing. 'What, after your performance with Romeo and Juliet just now? I think I'd rather live.'

'Just checking.'

Whoever invented vacuum cleaners needs crucifying. That, or the government should pass a law banning housework on weekends. What's the point of a Saturday lie-in if someone's banging about outside the bedroom door sucking the life out of the carpet? The woolly thickness of total silence is what I need right now so I can concentrate on thinking about Ash. I'm so worried about the buzzing in his head and what the electric brainshocks might do to him. I wish I could speak to him but I don't know his address or phone number, plus the drone of that hoover is driving me mentally ill. Just as I'm on the point of screaming to Mum to shut the fuck up and let me be, she switches the thing off, but only to go downstairs and answer the phone which is chirping its head off like a demented budgie. The sound pierces my skull and sets my teeth on edge. If this carries on I'm reporting her to the Environmental Health for noise pollution.

'Rowena,' she yells up the stairs. 'Phone for you. It's Dean.'

Even though I'm half unconscious I scramble out of bed, hotfoot down the stairs and grab the phone from her before she has a chance to start chatting to him.

'Dean, wossup?'

'Yay, wossup, babe,' he replies. 'Are you on for tonight?'

'Maybe.'

'What's that supposed to mean?'

'Maybe I am, maybe I amn't.'

'Come on, don't fuck about. Yes or no?'

'Dunno. Look, I can't think straight. I'll get back to you, right?'

'Don't bust a gut.' He sounds pissed off with me. 'I'm off to the match this aft, I'll go for a few bevvies with the lads tonight if you're not coming.'

'Suit yourself.' I slam down the receiver, wishing I could cut my tongue out. I wouldn't mind seeing Dean tonight, so why did I give him a hard time?

I nip to the bathroom for a wazz, then crawl back into bed, snuggling under the duvet, trying to catch some zees. That thing with Dean's spinning round in my head. Seeing him tonight might take my mind off worrying about Ash. It would sure beat another Saturday night home alone, so why did I get all twisty with him? Mum's vacuuming must have disturbed me during a period of deep REM sleep – the startlement could have killed me. Seeing as my day's been totally ruined by her carpet-fluff phobia, I maison well ring Dean and fix up to meet him. When I dial the number a machine answers. A woman's voice asks me to leave a message but I bottle and slam the phone down. If my calls are being diverted to the CIA I don't want Dean involved as well. I'll call him later from a payphone.

'Any danger of you getting dressed today?' asks Mum, squeezing past me on the stairs.

I give her the once-over. 'Bloody hell, where you off to – Buckingham Palace?' She's all gussied up in her grey pants suit and pink shirt she got out of Mandy Sweeney's catalogue.

'I'm meeting Bernard. We're going shopping in the town.' She's got a cheesy grin going on. A doomy black cloud settles on my shoulders, forcing me down to the centre of the earth. 'We're going to the jeweller's to choose a wed—' she begins.

'Don't!' I clap my hands over my ears. 'Don't tell me! I don't wanna know!'

'All right,' she says. 'We'll show you tonight.'

*We!* She said *we!* It's one thing for Filthy to think he's sweet-talked her – *brainwashed* her – into marrying him, but once they buy a wedding ring it means there's no going back. The whole world will know. Jesus, the shame of it!

I elbow my way past her, dash up the stairs and lock myself in the bathroom, turning the shower full on so I won't hear if she starts bleating outside the door. My gut starts gurgling. At first I think it's my irritable bowel acting up again, then I realise it's more likely starvation as I've only had Pepsi Max, peanuts and Bailey's in the last twenty-four hours, so I sneak downstairs for a brown-sauce sarnie. I needn't have bothered creeping over the creaky steps – Mum's gone out, she hasn't even left a note. What kind of mother pulls a stunt like that?

My stomach's in a knot. My head feels ready to explode. I have to get out of the house. I can't bear to be here when Mum and Filthy get back – I'll just *die* when she shows me the wedding ring. Dean. I need to talk to Dean. But when I ring it's the CIA answering machine again which makes me so mad I bark, 'Fuck off, spooks!' down the phone. Jesus, what have I done? They'll be sending a SWAT team round, SAS men abseiling down the walls with grenades in their teeth, armed response units, snipers, helicopters, dogs, the full monty. I throw on the nearest rags, hotfoot out the back door, skidding on a deceased rat deposited by my Trusty Sidekick Bundy, and jump on a Metro into town.

Northumberland Street looks like a giant mint humbug, swarming with the Toon Army lads and lasses dressed in black-and-white stripey tops for the Newcastle game. Dean told me it was a Derby match but he must have got it wrong as the red and white scarves mean the Magpies are playing at home to Sunderland, the mad Maccems. I wander round the shops in Eldon Square, keeping my eyes peeled for Mum and Filthy strolling out of a jeweller's shop, gazing lustfully into each other's eyes, clutching a little gift-wrapped box containing the end of my life.

In Havoc I spot a fab black shrug with punched leather trim only it's geet expensive and there's no point trying to rob it as the assistants have eyes in the backs of their heads. Then in Shuh I try on a couple of pairs of fuck'em boots with massive ridged soles which are way cool and clumpy but out of my league pricewise. I have a mooch round Miss Selfridge and T K Maxx but apart from a plastic snakeskin jacket there's nothing that takes my fancy. There's a crusty selling the *Big Issue* outside the Monument Mall. He stares at me and grins and I nearly give him the finger until I remember the CIA are watching me and they'll tick the 'Anti-social Behaviour' box on my file. I wander back up the street to Superdrug for some body glitter. Just as I'm about to palm it, I spot a mumsy woman down the feminine hygiene aisle clocking my moves. She looks away dead quick and pops a box of tampons into her basket, so I plonk the tube back on the shelf and wander out of the shop dead casual. Round the corner down an alley is Hitz, the shop where I liberated most of my CD collection. I pick up the new Charlatans from a rack and turn my back to the CCTV camera, covering myself, ready to pocket it. Then I remember what the police told Mum – that I acted like an amateur. Hairy-arsed cheek! But it's too late, I can't keep my mind on the job. Beads of sweat leak out of my forehead so I take the CD up to the till and pay for it. Cash! Jesus, I must be losing my touch.

Dean. I need to speak to Dean to fix up about tonight. The callboxes outside Haymarket Metro are busy so I kill some time by cruising the Index Shop and BHS, praying no one I know bumps into me, then I buy a can of Fanta and a packet of Hula Hoops from the newsagent's. At ten to six I ring Dean's house but the bloody machine's still on, he mustn't be home from the match yet. 'It's me,' I say, not wanting to leave my name on account of the CIA. 'Catch you later.' I blow a stupid kiss down the phone to let him know there's no hard feelings.

Post-match footie fans roam the streets like packs of council-estate dogs. They pile into pubs, chanting and yelling. Gangs of lasses, already half-cut, in skimpy frocks and goosepimples, totter out of the Metro station for a heavy night of circuit drinking on the toon. Even with my warmish clothes on, I feel cold and miserable and tragic, a real Billy No-Mates, but I daren't go home in case Mum and Filthy are there, gagging to show off Mum's wedding ring to me. No contest then. Maison well jump on a Metro to South Gosforth and turn up at Dean's, and he'd just better be home, or he's D-E-double-D.

# 25

## *Gosforth 90210*

Dean's house is a canny walk from the station, and the backs of my legs are pulling from schlepping up the hill. I know Capes Terrace is round here somewhere, I checked it out in the *A to Z*. Even so, I nearly miss it, walking past the street twice as the sign's rusty and plastered in graffiti. The houses are way ancient and joined together in a line, with big bay windows and little bitty gardens out front. Number fifteen, where Dean lives, has a blue door with a pane of bubble glass and a bell at the side saying PUSH, like it's some hi-tech invention no one's ever seen before. I press my finger on the button for ages and listen to it ringing like a lunatic. Zilch.

Stepping over a teensy wall, I peer through the front window. They've got a dried flower display just like at Crowther's (maybe Dean nicked it!), some of those hippy wind-chime things, and a Neighbourhood Watch sticker. It's hard to see inside as it's getting dark but I can make out some furniture shapes and a digital clock flickering away on the video. I step back to the door and bray on it with my fist. A woman walking past with two spotty dogs gives me a good long eyeball, like she's memorising my details for the cops. Nosy cow, I'd flick her the finger only she's too stuck up to know what it means. Standing on tippytoe, I peer through the bubble window in the door. There's a pinkish light on in the hall, but it could be to fool burglars, right, like they're gonna fall for that old stunt. I press the doorbell again. Nothing. Where the fuck has Dean got to?

I'm in a frenzy of frustration. Bile rises, hot and sour, in my throat. My head's thrumming. I rummage in my rucksack, dig out the robbed plastic dog turd and plonk it slam dunk in the middle of

Dean's doorstep. I hope those spotty friggin' dogs get the blame. Stomping down the path, I kick out at a tub of purple plants and knack my toe, which gets me even more in a rage.

I can't think what to do. There's no way I want to go back to my so-called home to watch the Mum & Filthy Show, co-starring the band of gold, plus the backs of my legs are burning and I'm gagging for a drink. Trouble is, Gosforth isn't the sort of place people hang out, it's mostly Jurassic houses and fancy eating gaffs and pubs with no-smoking areas and no jukeboxes. Then I remember that Mr Crowther lives round here somewhere. I read it on a card when I was going through his wallet one day: twelve Prior's Court, Connaught Park. It's up near the loony bin, only I don't suppose he mentions that when he's giving directions to his poshgit mates. Maybe I'll check out his exclusive residence, the one bought with my toil and sweat.

I trudge up Salters Road and hang a right at the roundabout, towards the headcase hospital. The sweat's dribbling out of every pore, my head's banging, and my feet feel like blocks of molten steel. Maybe I'm having an attack of malaria or I caught the Ebola virus at Gemma Probert's germy flat. I must look a right scary freak. It'd be just my luck if some mad person's escaped from the bin and the men in white coats capture me, strap me to a bed and shoot a squillion volts through my brain. Will my head smoke and burst into flames like that bloke who got fried on Old Sparky? Are lobotomised people happy? Am I only thinking this, or muttering out loud? Jesus, maybe I *am* a psycho case.

Suddenly here I am, at Connaught Park. The name's on a little goldy-coloured plate set in a wall next to three curly iron gates, a double one for cars and a little one for private persons. It's like a zillionaire's prison. As I walk through the archway, I'm half expecting an alarm to go off and some monkey-suited geek to grab me and escort me off the premises. I bet it'll be one of those noises that only dogs can hear, and a pack of starving Rotties will come bounding up and tear me limb from limb. But nothing happens.

I can't believe Crowther lives on this posh estate next to professional footballers. It's like Beverly Hills, where the movie stars live. Gosforth 90210. The houses are all shapes and sizes, and made out of different stuff. Some are brick, some are yellowish stone, others are painted white with criss-cross beams of wood stuck on the front like the cottage where Shakespeare's girlfriend lived. It's nothing like our estate, where the houses are slummy clones full of white trash. There's no dog shit underfoot here, no chucked-out fridges or plastic flamingos in the gardens, just flowers, bushes and stuff, and those trees with long things hanging down like green dreadlocks. I bet they've all got swimming pools round the back. I bet they've all got patio furniture, barbecues, swings for the kids.

I bet they've all got dads.

* * *

It was open house round our place. Dad's biker mates were always there, in their leathers and bandannas, smoking dope and playing rock music really, really loud. They all looked up to Dad, you could see that. He was the King. Leader of the Pack. Big up, nuff respect and that.

There'd be mean machines parked halfway down the street – Harleys, some old British bikes that weighed a ton, maybe the odd Japanese monster. The neighbours were twitchy as owt, muttering stupid stuff about Hell's Angels conventions. They'd cross over the road rather than walk past the gate, daft beggars. As if the bikers were just tooled up dope-heads. Yeah, they looked well hard, but the women were harder.

Mum was way different back then, a cool biker chick, and because she was Dad's Ole Lady, she got respect as well. They had some real laughs, Mum and Dad, horsing around, he'd chase her, she'd scream like a wild kid, then he'd catch her and swing her round. Always touching and kissing, they were. They didn't care, they were mad for each other.

At least that's how I remembered it, until I saw an old movie on the telly. *Mask*, it was called. Cher played this leather chick who was crazy about a biker, and all his hairy mates used to hang out at the house. She had a son, Rocky, who was so disfigured people couldn't bear to look at him.

Had I already seen the film, but forgotten it? Am I Rocky/Rowena, the deformed kid who scares people off? Or did it happen like that in real life?

Am I totally off my tree?

* * *

Suddenly a scary feeling comes over me, turning my sweat to condensed chip fat and my scalp to ice. Why oh why did I have to come to Connaught Park? What if Crowther and his trophy wife cruise past in the Merc and catch me acting like a fugitive? They'll think I'm casing their joint, then they'll call the Feds and I'll be arrested on suspicion of going equipped just because there's a tail-comb in my rucksack. It takes a superhuman effort to lug my leaden feet towards the road. My bones ache and my head's whizzing. Little coloured spots float in front of my eyes and I have to blink like fury to make them disappear.

I *so* don't want to go home.

On the way back to the Metro, I call at an off-licence and buy two packets of Hula Hoops and a can of Dr Pepper's, hurling them all down my throat until I feel sick and bloated. I hate my life. It's total shite. Not as shite as Gemma Probert's, though that's no consolation.

I turn the front door key dead quiet. Mum and Filthy are in the living room, watching the telly, so I figure they won't hear me sneak upstairs, but Mum must have X-ray ears or eyes in the back of her skull.

'Rowena, come and sit in here with us, pet. We're watching a movie on the telly – *Sleepless in Seattle*. It's only just started.'

'It sucks. I've seen better film on teeth. I'm off to bed.'

'Hang on.' She pads out, dressed in a jogging suit and fleecy socks. *Très* elegant. Bet she thinks now she's landed a bloke she can stop making an effort. 'Just come through for a minute or two. I want you to see my wedding ring, it's white gold, real classy. And you can have a glass of Asti with me and Bernard, help us celebrate.'

My scalp tightens. My heart lurches. Hula Hoops and Dr Pepper's churn angrily in my gut. 'I feel sick,' I stutter. 'My head's banging. I need to lie down in the quiet.'

She feels my forehead. 'You are a bit hot. I hope you're not coming down with something. Take a couple of headache pills and have a rest, you can always get up later if you feel better. Try, Rowena. You'll love my wedding ring, honestly.'

'Right.' While I'm in the kitchen dissolving the Solpadeines I spot Filthy's mobile phone on the worktop. I slip it into my rucksack and head upstairs. I'm desperate to talk to Dean. On the way to my room I nip into Mum's boudoir and nick two tranquillisers from her emergency supply which she thinks I don't know about. They stick to the back of my tongue until I wash them down with the Solps. I lie back and wait for the spacey feeling to flow through me.

Dialling Dean's number on the mobile makes me feel dead important, like a supermodel or a crack dealer. I press Send. It's the bloody machine again! Still, if the CIA put a trace on the call, it'll lead them back to Filthy, not to me. Better assume a false accent though, in case they've got my voice-print data on a computer program.

'Eello,' I begin, my voice lowdown and gruffy. 'I eem wanting Meester Dean Fairrrrrrlee. Ees abouta loft convairrrrrsion. Ees airrrrrgent.'

There's a click on the line. 'Rowena? Is that you playing silly buggers?'

'You're there! About friggin' time.' Dean, my saviour! 'Can I come round?' I ask in my own voice, forgetting about the CIA.

'Was that you earlier? I was upstairs, downloading some stuff from the Net. I heard the door, but by the time I got down there you'd gone.'

It's on the tip of my tongue to deny it, in case someone saw me kick the tub of flowers. Then I realise they probably caught me on the security video anyway. I bet all the Neighbourhood Watch narks were nebbing at me on CCTV.

'What makes you think it was me?' I ask cagily.

'You left your calling card. On the doorstep. Who else could it have been?'

Jesus, I'd forgotten about the plastic dog turd. 'So can I come round or what?'

'Sure, I'll go and defrost the fatted calf.'

'I've eaten already,' I assure him.

'You're priceless, you.' He laughs. 'Get your sexy ass round here pronto.'

After phoning a taxi to meet me at the bottom of the road, I swish soap and water round my bits and pull on clean knickies and tights, then a black lacy shirt, leather mini, and my biker boots. My hair looks a right mess, like a madwoman's knitting, so I decide to go for a designer tousled look, backcombing it and clipping it into a banana slide. I sort my bloodshot eyes with blue Eye Dew drops, then outline them with black kohl, slap on two coats of mascara and paint my mouth with Red Or Dedd lipgloss. I've looked better, but it'll have to do.

I creep downstairs, avoiding the creaky steps. They must have turned the video off, Celine Dion's belting out stupid love songs on the stereo, it sounds like a cat being ironed. Brilliant – they'll never hear me sneak out above that racket.

As I walk down the street to the taxi, I feel a foggy calm descend over me. The tranx are kicking in . . .

*

'Morning, sleepyhead. Ready for a cuppa?'

As my eyes focus and the mist slowly clears from my brain, I realise I'm in a strange bed. The sheets are navy blue and the pillows are soft and squashy, not like the lumpy boulders I sleep on at home. Dean's standing over me, wearing just a pair of Calvins, holding out a steaming mug. He's grinning, and squinting slightly as he's not wearing his specs.

'What . . . ? Where . . . ?' My mouth's too dry to work. It tastes like a ferret's crawled in there and died. I try to lift my head, but it flops back on the pillow. Across the room I spot my leather mini on the back of a chair. I grope about under the duvet. I'm completely naked. My eyes feel heavy.

'Do you want this tea or what? I'm not standing here like a friggin' dummy.' Dean plonks the steaming mug on the bedside table and slouches off, scratching his backside through his Calvins.

'Can I stay here today?' We're crashed out on the carpet, Catatonia cranked up on the stereo. Dean's tucking into a bowl of Crunchy Nut Cornflakes and I'm nibbling a triangle of Dairylea cheese. Sunday lunch for slackers.

He zaps the remote and flicks through the footie pages on Teletext. 'Stay as long as you like. Till the cows come home.'

'That's no way to talk about your mam and dad.' He snorts and flings a cushion at me. 'I can't bear to go back to ours, not with Filthy Luker around.' I want to tell Dean about the wedding ring but the words stick in my craw.

'That asshole. Don't blame you. God knows what your mum sees in him. He must be good in other departments.' Dean winks at me. I feel myself blush.

'You know last night, Dean? Did I . . .? I mean, did we . . .? Did you . . .?'

'Fuck's sake, Rowena, spit it out, the suspense is killing me.'

'You know what I mean.' I turn away and pluck some non-existent bits off the carpet. It's dark red, hoovered to within an inch of its life. 'Sex and that. Did we do anything?'

Dean sniggers. 'The state you were in? No way. There'd have been more life in a blow-up doll. Anyway, if you'd had sex with me you wouldn't forget it in a hurry, count on it.'

'You could've drugged me,' I argue. 'Slipped me a Roofie.'

'Look, I never slipped you anything, right? You were bombed out when you got here, like an extra out of a zombie movie.'

'So how did I get to bed? Who undressed me? Where did *you* sleep?'

Dean sighs and counts out on his fingers. 'One: I gave you a fireman's lift to the spare bedroom. Two: I took your clothes off. Three: slept in my own bed, where else? Happy now?'

'You un*dressed* me?' Thank God I was wearing clean knickies.

'Come on, Rowena. I never touched you, not in *that* way. I'd have had to be a friggin' necrophiliac, the state you were in. Forget it now. Fancy a beer?'

'Any Bailey's?' I go.

It's nearly midnight when I get home after a lazy day of dozing, boozing, watching MTV, and rummaging through Dean's mother's wardrobe. My heart plummets as I turn into the street and see Filthy's Sierra parked outside the house. It's all in darkness but I can see the telly flickering in Mum's bedroom, which means they're probably watching porno vids and jumping on each other's bones.

Mum's left a note for me on the kitchen table.

*Rowena – have you seen Bernard's mobile? (Not accusing!) Needed for work Mon a.m. PS. Pls leave note next time you go out for day. Was worried.*

*Love Mum*

*xxx*

I unearth the phone from my rucksack and pop it in the bread bin behind a Warburton's Toastie loaf, then scribble a message under Mum's.

*Not seen mobile. Left u note this a.m. so u not worry. Prob both down 2 poltergeist.*
*R*
*xx*

I'm avoiding Mum as I can't bear to see the wedding ring or hear her banging on about her impending nuptials. Monday after work I go round to Dean's house to watch *The Exorcist* which I've seen before but it still makes me shudder even though it's a snowy picture and sounds hissy as it's a bootleg video. I'm dead standy-up hair scared that time when Regan goes, 'Your mother sucks cocks in hell,' in the raspy voice. It's a top line though, I must remember to practise it to use on Ray at work. My favourite is the projectile vomiting bit when she hurls pea soup, and when her body swells up into a big balloon like Gemma Probert's. Dean thinks it's *so* hilarious to spook me by creeping up behind me and squirting pretend holy water in my hair, then he only gets two wooden spoons out of the kitchen, makes them into a crucifix and rubs them against his crotch, going, 'Fuck me! Fuck me!' in the gravelly voice. I tell him he'll burn for eternity if there *is* a God but he laughs and says religion's just an adult belief in an imaginary friend which is a bit deep for me so I make him call me a taxi and pay the driver upfront.

As I'm walking down our path, a dark shape suddenly leaps out from nowhere. My nerves are so jangly I nearly wet my pants. The fluorescent collar gives the game away. It's my Trusty Sidekick, heading for the shed with a squeaking rodent clamped in his jaws. Even though he's reduced me to a quivering wreck, I forgive him as it's the first sighting I've had in a week. Bundy lives!

In the morning there's a note on the kitchen table.

*Rowena,*

*B's mobile materialised in bread bin – you were right about p/geist!*
*Love*
*Mum*
*xxx*

Lordy, all this marriage shit must have turned her soft in the head.

Before I leave for work, I stop off at the shed. Bundy's spark out in his box, snoring. He squints through one eye, then makes a grumbling noise, turns his back on me and rolls into a big sulky ball, his tail end flicking. Maybe he's suffering from indigestion. Judging from the spare ribs, king prawns in sweet and sour sauce, and egg-fried rice splattered on the floor, he must have been looting the bins at the Chinese down the road, the one the *Chronicle* called 'the toxic takeaway'.

# 26

## Strange Glue

Two utterly butterly blindingly brilliant things happened today. It must be the Angel's doing. My luck's in!

First, Ash phoned me at work. We only spoke for a few nanoseconds, but still. He rang me to say his head's stopped pinging and he wants to see me on Saturday! Ash, my dream lover!

Second off, Filthy's given me two-and-a-half grand! Two thousand five hundred pounds! OK, I had to let my soon-to-be-step-asshole kiss me, smudging my make-up and scratching my cheek with his disgusting stubble, but here it is – a cheque for £2.5k, made out to me. Miss Rowena Vincent. I'm rich! I'd rather have had it in cash but Mum said it'd be squandered within a week so I've got to stick it in the bank. Never mind. I'm an heiress. A multi-thousandaire! I can spend it on – what? A month in Torremolinos, a stretch limo to drive me to work every day, a zillion CDs, a Harley chop, all the kit I ever want from the Void or B'Zarr.

The world is my wossname!

Ash said he'd meet me at the Monument at twelve. It's hell in town on a Saturday, what with thousands of shoppers plus all the animal rights crusties shoving leaflets in your face. Then there's the Christian loonies bellowing about salvation, and old biddies with clipboards signing you up for catalogues. As if that wasn't enough, there's a stupid street-theatre thingy, half a dozen wackos on stilts, dressed in black costumes with big yellow insecty eyes like those shades Bono used to wear, or that Jeff Goldblum in *The Fly*. I park my butt on the Monument steps next to a Chinese-type girl reading *Viz*. Her rucksack's wide open and I spy a big fat wallet sitting on top. Ee-zee. I'm just about to dip 

Anyway, I bet it's full of foreign mo

Just then I spot Ash wandering o

looking lost and a bit anxious. He's 

which is *so* way beyond cool. My sto

pancake.

'Ash!' I yell, waving like a Mexican. H

Street. 'Ash! Wait on!' I run as fast as I ca

him up and tug on his hood. 'Ash, hold u

He shoots me a scaredy-cat look and say ...e on, quick. Hop on that bus.'

We ride for two stops, then get off. His face is shiny with sweat and his eyes are big and staring. He keeps glancing over his shoulder.

'What's going on?' I shake his sleeve. 'Ash, what's up, man?'

'Have they gone?' he hisses. 'Is anyone following us?'

I take a good skeg round. No CIA in sight. 'It's cool. We've lost them.'

'Christ, that was close.' His face relaxes.

'So,' I say. 'Back to your place?'

Ash lives in Fenham, Land of Lentils, in a first-floor room in a terraced house. It's got the feel and dossy smell of a hostel but I decide not to ask. Everything looks worn; the stair carpet's threadbare, the wallpaper's scuffed to buggery, and the paint on the banister's peeling off. The card on his door says ASHLEY MALLISON. He unlocks it and shows me in.

Omigawd, it's like stepping into a brothel! Red-painted walls with gold cherubs, huge sequinned cushions, vases full of ostrich feathers, and floaty pink drapes round the bed. The maroon velvet curtains are shut tight, and a Tiffany lamp glows orange in the corner.

'Welcome to my world,' says Ash.

He unzips his parka and yanks half a dozen shiny new books out

pockets. 'Science fantasy, mainly,' he
of Waterstone's.' He's robbed them! I thump
and giggle. It's fate. We were made for each other.
e closest to paradise I'll ever get. I'm glowing all over
ing next to him. We share a bottle of Lambrusco and Ash
es daft drunk on one glass because he's not used to alcohol as he
never used to drink it when he was on medication. Then he gets
the giggles and digs out his make-up collection which he keeps in
a biscuit tin covered with pink velvet and seashells. There's some
canny good stuff, plus false eyelashes and long fingernails and
glittery eyeshadow like lap dancers wear. And he said my Ripe
Tangerine lipgloss was tarty! I teach him how to blend the
Terracotta Crème on his eyes and draw a pencil line inside the top
and bottom lids before rolling on two coats of mascara and
separating the lashes with a tiny comb. He shows me how he
makes the most of his mouth by tracing over the lipline with a
tawny pencil before filling in the colour with a fine brush. His
complexion's golden brown, totally flawless, no need for
foundation, but I highlight his cheekbones with a light dusting of
bronze blusher. The look's subtle, understated, shitloads better
than that tarty slap he wore. Next I slide the band off his ponytail,
backcomb his hair and shush it up, wetting my fingers with spit
and teasing it into a spiky bouffant shape.

'Eat your heart out, Mossy,' I say. 'You look a real stunnah, Ash.
Here, check it out.' I open the curtains a chink to let some daylight
in, and hand him the mirror. There's a little gasp, followed by a
long drawn-in sucking sound. He spends ages gazing at his
reflection, pouting his terracotta lips, running his tongue over his
perfect white teeth and fluttering his eyelashes at himself.

'Rowena, you total makeover mistress,' he says, hugging me but
not too tight as I haven't sprayed his hair yet. 'I love these colours,
they're so cool.'

'You've got the skin tone and bone structure, you don't need to go over the top with heavy make-up,' I advise him. 'Just remember, less is more. Well, no, actually less is less, but you know what I mean.'

'I've got something else to show you.' Ash tears himself away from the mirror, crouches down and reaches under the bed. He slides out a suitcase and snaps it open. It's chock-full of women's undies, lacy teddies, silky French knickers and camisoles, Wonderbras, thongs and stuff. Jesus!

'Would you think I was mad,' he asks shyly, 'if I wore some of these?'

I gulp, but recover myself. 'Hey, I *know* you're mad. We're *both* mad. That's how we met, right?' I riffle through the undies. 'You can't wear burgundy, not with that make-up. You might get away with peach – hey, this is way fab.' I hold up a lacy teddy in purple. Wouldn't mind that myself.'

'What about white?' says Ash. 'I've got loads of white.'

'Too stark,' I insist. His face falls in disappointment. 'Ooh, but this ivory's triffic. Come here, try it on.'

Ash unbuttons his shirt and slips it off, revealing a goldy brown body, totally smooth and hairless, with copper-coloured nipples like rivets on 501s. I'm itching to touch him, but force myself to act real professional, like a doctor or something. Trying not to disturb his hairdo, I slide the camisole over his head. The cami's a bit baggy round the bosoms but a few tacking stitches could sort that.

'There's matching knickers somewhere. And a suspender belt.' While I rummage through the suitcase, Ash unzips his jeans and steps out of them. He's wearing snowy-white boxers.

'Get your trolleys off, then,' I say in a brisk voice, like I'm not dying to see what's inside them. He tucks his thumbs in the waistband and slides them off to reveal, Omigawd, a *massive hard-on*! I make a superhuman effort and pretend not to notice as he steps into the French knickies and pulls them up to his waist. His whole body's quivering. I hand him the suspender belt. 'Put this on.' It sounds like an order. Ash obeys in silence, sliding the satiny material round his middle, fastening the hooks and eyes, easing the ruched suspenders through the knicker legs.

'There's some stockings,' he mutters, pointing to a wee chest of drawers. 'In there.' His voice sounds hoarse and strange, as if he's coming down with laryngitis. Inside the drawer it's like the undies department at Marks & Sparks. I flip through dozens of packs of stockings, all colours, all patterns, all brand spanking new, until I come across a pair of creamy-coloured ones, 15 denier, sheer and shiny, with seams up the back. Ash steadies himself on the dressing table, lifts his foot on to a chair and points his long toes like a ballerina. His toenails are painted coral. 'You do it,' he pleads.

When I kneel down, I'm right on eye-level with the bulge in his satin knickies. If I stuck out my tongue, I could lick him. Molten lava starts to trickle through me.

His legs are paler than the rest of him, and waxed smooth. I roll the stocking slowly over his ankle, up his calf, along his thigh, running my palms over the sheer material, smoothing it, straightening the seam. Ash seems to be having trouble breathing. My fingers feel under the knickie legs for the suspenders, sliding the hooks round the little rubber buttons and fastening them in place. Ash strokes my hair and makes a whimpering sound. I spend for ever pulling the other stocking on him, teasing him, tantalising him, making his cock twitch inside the knickies. A tiny wet stain appears through the satin. He scrunches my hair tight and pushes my head into his crotch, moaning softly.

I'm sopping down there, gagging for it. There's no time to hang about. I untangle his fingers from my hair and stand up, pushing him towards the bed. Ash falls back on to the pillows, groaning. He's clutching himself through the shiny wet knickers, and I'm tearing off my clothes, desperate to get some action before it's all over.

But I'm too friggin' late! He arches his back and squeezes his cock, moaning *Yesssssss! Oh God, yesssssss!* The stain spreads on the satin knickies, and he slumps down, his eyes closed. I'm standing there like a lemon, half undressed, left high and dry. Well, high anyway.

Slowly I peel off the rest of my kit and climb on to the bed. Ash's eyes flicker and he pulls me towards him.

'Thank you,' he murmurs, like I had anything to do with it. 'I needed that. It was soooo good, I can't tell you.'

It feels weird lying next to a boy dressed in girlie undies. I want him to touch me there but I sense now's not a good time as he's canny knackered, so we cuddle up like spoons and I listen to his breathing get deeper and deeper until I realise he's fallen asleep.

I must have nodded off as well because when my eyes open, there's Ash, leaning over me, gazing into my face, tracing his artistic finger down my cheek. He smiles and turns me over to face him, wrapping his arms round me and snuggling my head against his chest. Then I feel a hairless leg slide over mine, pulling me towards him. He's completely naked. Our bodies are hot, touching each other all the way down. He strokes my mussy hair and kisses the top of my head. I run my hands over his goldy smoothness, feeling him grow hard and twitch against my stomach. My insides turn to liquid.

And it's like he's sliding into me, gently, slowly, and I'm so wet for him, arching my body towards him, wanting him inside me, all the way home. And we move together, the rhythm building deeper, faster, harder until my whole body's melting, sucking him into me. And he draws it slowly all the way out and then drives it into me *bang-bang-bang* into the juicy *squish-squish-squish* of my wetness and the *slap-slap-slap* of his balls against my ass. I wind my legs tightly around him, squeezing, pushing, forcing him deeper, deeper, deeper inside and that's when I know it's going to happen for me. I slow the frenzied grinding and give myself up to him. *Go for it*, he whispers hotly in my ear. *Come on, baby, come on over*. And it overpowers me, this red-hot rush of ecstasy, flooding through my body, ripples of pleasure building into huge waves exploding and crashing till I feel I'm drowning.

And he stays big and hard and motionless inside me while my muscles contract, gripping and loosening and gripping him again. He kisses my eyelashes and we lie very still until my breathing subsides. And then he begins to move inside me, slow, tiny movements at first, then faster, deeper, wilder, only this time it's different, the edges of me feel hazy and blurred. And he drives himself into me, squeezing my ass, digging his fingers into the flesh, thrusting urgently, hard, harder, harder, right up to my womb, and I hear myself saying, *Give it to me. Just let go . . .* Then he moans quietly, and I hold him tight while the length of him twitches in me, and gradually softens. I feel his heartbeat slow down as his body relaxes.

'I love you, Ash,' I whisper, kissing his throat. 'I really truly love you. More than anything in the world in space.'

He nuzzles my neck. His lashes are wet. 'Don't,' he murmurs, and I realise he's weeping. 'Don't say that.'

'But I do,' I insist. 'I love you to pieces.'

'Don't,' he says again. 'It's too late now.'

It strikes me as a canny weird thing to say, as it's only teatime. But what do I know about sex? This is my first proper time. Maybe I should be crying too.

When we wake up it's dark outside. Ash heats some curried beans on a teensy electric ring and we eat them out of one dish, a spoon each, to save on washing-up. His make-up isn't a bit smudged, even after all that lurve action. It sounds right soppy, but I can't bear to take my eyes off him. He's the lushest, the tastiest – the most *beautiful* – boy I've ever been with. I'm in heaven, even when he slaps on a Dolly Parton CD.

'Tell me your deepest secret,' he says, massaging my shoulders. 'Tell me something you've never told anyone else.' I try to think but

I'm laid way too far back, chilled to the max, my body gently buzzing with electricity from his long goldy fingers.

'Mmmm, that is *so* divine.' I feel squirmy all over. He brushes his lips against my neck, making me shudder. 'It's no good, Ash, I can't concentrate on secrets and stuff. You go first.' We swap positions and he lays his head in my lap while I brush the tangles out of his bouffant hairdo.

He starts to tell me about when his mum and dad chucked him out. It was the day before his sister got married. His dad found him in her bedroom, dressed in the wedding gown, veil, everything. Caught him jacking off. He'd been doing it for weeks, at least twice a day, ever since the wedding dress was delivered.

'I lived for it,' he says. 'My life revolved around finding ways to get into Astrid's room, just to look at the gown at first, then to touch it and imagine how it felt to wear it. The thought of it hanging in the next room kept me awake all night. And once I'd tried it on, there was no going back. It was like a drug, I needed more and more fixes. You should have seen it, Rowena. The bodice was covered in tiny seed pearls and bugle beads. It had a heart-shaped neckline and the sleeves tapered into a point. So elegant, so feminine. Pure white Thai silk, with a scalloped hemline and six-foot train. And the veil was gossamer fine, like a butterfly's wings. I adored that dress. It made me feel like a princess.'

'Sounds fab,' I agree, trying to imagine myself wearing it. I'd have to get my split ends seen to first, no point getting toffed up in a posh frock with hair like a knackered old mop.

'You know what my dream is?' says Ash. 'The thing I'd like more than anything? To wear a white wedding dress, veil, flowers, all the trimmings, just like a real bride – *in public*. I want people to think I'm beautiful.'

'You are, you're canny beautiful.'

'No I'm not. You don't know what goes on here.' He taps his head. 'I'm weird.'

'Oh yeah, sure – but *cool* weird, not kinky weird.' He squeezes my hand and kisses my fingers one by one. 'Go on with the story then,' I say.

Ash reckons his folks went mega-ballistic. There was no time to get the gown cleaned before the wedding. His dad came the old 'never-darken-my-door' routine while his mum was shrieking and wailing, going hysterical. Astrid went for his eyes with an ornamental dagger.

He tells me how he slept in the boneyard the first night, curled up on a tombstone, freezing his tits off. Next day – his sister Astrid's wedding day – he traipsed round the shops like a zomboid and ended up in an amusement arcade. A baldy bloke got talking to him and treated him to a fish supper at Bimbi's. He seemed an OK type, Ash thought, especially when he offered to put him up for the night.

'You can guess the rest,' sighs Ash wearily. 'When he said he'd put me up, I never thought he meant literally! I was desperate, yeah, but not *that* desperate. Didn't fancy ending up flogging my ass for the price of a burger down the Pink Triangle, just another scummy rentboy.' His eyelashes flicker wetly on my bare thigh. Suddenly he slaps my knee. 'Anyway, enough of my boring life story. Tell me about you.'

'I can't top that,' I reply. 'Maybe next time.' Suddenly I feel nervous. 'Will I see you again soon?'

Ash reaches up and kisses me deep on the mouth. 'Soon, yes.' His eyes tell me he's far away, in some private place I can't reach.

'Tomorrow?' I say.

He shakes his head, not looking at me. 'Not tomorrow, no.'

'Don't say I have to wait until Wednesday, at the group meeting. Aww, that's ages away.'

'I wish I'd met you sooner,' he murmurs. 'It's too late now. Too late.' His eyes start misting up, and he squeezes me so tight I can hardly breathe. Then I realise he's crying again.

My body feels ready to spontaneously combust. 'Come on, babe, let's go back to bed,' I say.

I whip Dolly Parton out of the CD player, riffle through Ash's collection and slap in the Manics. No wonder he was blubbing. It's enough to do anyone's head in listening to Dolly's bimboid whining. By the time I slip back into bed he's asleep, his face turned to the wall. Mmm, I'm *so*, so happy.

The room glows reddish. I open the curtains a chink and realise it's Sunday morning. Ash dozes next to me, his legs knotted in mine. I run my fingers over his goldy shoulder and practise some mental arithmetic.

A month ago I loathed everybody in the world. Now I've found my soul-mate and I'm heartburstingly breathstoppingly bodymeltingly in love. And the coolest thing is – I think he loves me back!

One week ago my life was total shite. Now it's like a fireworks display, lit up and sparkling with brilliant crazy colours, zooming skywards, exploding with possibilities. I feel – I dunno, like everything's *opening up* for me.

Fifteen and a half hours ago I was a virgin. Now I've done it loads, and OK, it wasn't safe sex, but so what? Nothing, not even a condom, should ever come between us. I can't keep my hands off Ash, or my mouth. Like sex-mad Siamese twins, we are, bodies joined all the way down. Touching his smooth tawny skin, the feeling roars up like a wild animal in my stomach and I want him there, inside me again.

I squint at my Swatch. Whoa, *ten past eight*! Jesus, I need to make tracks, get home before Mum susses I've been out all night. I untangle my legs and slide out of bed, trying not to disturb Ash. He's purring gently through his nose like a sleepy kitten. He must be canny knackered after all that action – I'm so whacked I could sleep for a fortnight.

I drape his parka round my shoulders and tippytoe to the

bathroom that he shares with the three Replicants who live on this floor. The lavvy could use some bleach but I try to ignore the gravy stains as I hover over the seat and pee. A quick rub round my teeth with a finger and a splash of cold water on my face will have to do me. I'd give a month's luncheon vouchers for a hot scented bath and fluffy clean towels right now.

I throw on my kit. Ash is still fast on. Then I spot an envelope with my name written on it, propped against a Maverick carrier bag. Inside the envelope is a wee note.

*Rowena – thanx for everything. I want you to have this.*
   *Love,*
   *Ash*

It's the purple lacy teddy! A gift from Ash, an intimately personal gift from my first and only lover.

I stuff it in my bag and scribble a note on a bit of card from the stocking pack.

*Ash – had 2 split, sorry didnt say bye but u were coma toes (dreaming about me? ha ha). Teddy is BRILLIANT! Will wear it in bed & think of u. Luv ya 2 bits.\**
   *Rowena*
   *xxxxxxxxxxxx*
*PS. Can't wait 2 see ya Weds if not b4.*
*\*Really truly*

Downstairs in the hall I bump into a bloke in a waxy jacket, he's struggling with a bunch of fishing rods and trying to wheel a mountain bike out of the front room.

'Morning,' I say brightly. 'Want a hand?' This is me, the new Rowena, good Samaritan, Princess Diana of Tyneside, friend of povs and saviour of the cack-handed.

He glares at me suspiciously. 'Piss off,' he mutters under his breath, scraping paint off the skirting board with a pedal.

'Just trying to help,' I smile. Normally I'd have dropped him the nut or trashed his fishing tackle but Ash has brought out a whole 'nother caring side I never knew was in me.

I am loved, therefore I love.

Back home, Mum's shuffling around the kitchen like someone with Oldtimer's Disease. She plinks a couple of Resolve tabs into a glass and slumps down in a chair, clutching her head.

'You get wrecked last night?' Like I need to ask.

'Ssshhh,' she hisses, like a deflating balloon. 'Sorry . . . celbratin' . . . hope dint wake yup.' Cool, so she was in no state to worry about the small matter of my empty bed.

'Nee bovva,' I assure her. 'I managed to get back to sleep eventually.'

'Urghh . . . gobi sick.' My maternal role model skitters out, grasping her stomach and retching. Thank you, Big G, for covering my back. This calls for treacle on toast followed by a marathon kip-out. The bath can wait. The thought of Ash's smell and micro skinflakes and body fluids disappearing down a plughole is unbearable. I want to keep him on/in me for as long as I can, even though I'm canny ripe and sticky. My insides feel bruised and fragile like raw steak that's been pounded with a hammer. I hold the purple teddy next to my cheek and collapse on to the bed.

I'm sitting in the school hall, eating a fish supper out of a newspaper. There's hundreds of plastic chairs set out in rows, like in a multiplex, but I'm the only person in the audience. My eyes are glued to the red velvet curtains as they slide apart with a slurping noise. Dolly Parton wiggles on to the stage, wearing sugar-pink lipgloss, cowboy boots and a parka which she slides off to reveal French knickers and cami top. *Here you come again,* she warbles, flashing a saucy smile and winking at me. I notice a shiny patch of rhinestones spreading across the knickies. Dolly finishes the song, there's a drum roll, a puff of smoke, then a sinister-looking black box appears on the stage. It reminds me of a casket.

'Tonight's masheeyun is Layncelot,' squawks Dolly. 'With set of balls number fahve. And don't forget y'all, it's a durble rollover jackpot.' I fling the chip wrappers on the floor and lick my fingers. They're sticky and smell of fish. 'Raht here's our star guest to set those balls rolling,' yells Dolly excitedly, waving a fishing rod like a magic wand. An organ plays the Wedding March and a cloud of pink smoke clears to reveal Ash, wearing Princess Diana's wedding gown, all creased to buggery. I want to rush up on stage and smooth it out for him, but I'm stuck to my seat. He tosses his bouquet behind him. Gemma Probert, thin as a rake, catches it and cradles it like a baby. Ash lifts the front of his gown. Underneath he's holding an ornamental dagger. Confetti shoots out of the end. He looks pale and ill.

'Thank y'all for comin',' gushes Dolly, doing a neat segueway into 'Love is Like a Butterfly'.

# 27

## A Bad Brain Day

Time passes in a blur. Wednesday can't come soon enough. I dream about Ash all the time – even when I'm filing invoices or washing smelly corpses. I'm lightheadedly, stupidgrinningly, heartlurchingly happy. Naturally, people notice.

'It's gratifying to see such job satisfaction,' says Mr Crowther.

'Whatever you're drinking, pet, I'll have a pint,' quips Mr Scudamore.

'You're getting it, aren't you?' says Ray accusingly. 'Getting my bleedin' share as well, by the looks of it,' he moans. Trust him to lower the tone.

'Are you taking nerve tablets, dear?' noses Mrs Marr.

I smile at them enigmatically. 'Maybe I am, maybe I amn't.'

Dean's the only one who doesn't ask. And he's the only one I tell.

'I'm in love,' I confide over a cappuccino in Jaconelli's. His face twitches slightly, which is as close as it gets to registering surprise.

'A bit sudden,' he says, slurping froth off the spoon, not looking at me. 'Who's the lucky guy, or shouldn't I ask?'

I hear myself gushing, babbling, running off at the chops about Ash. Course, I only give him edited highlights as the sex 'n' undies stuff is our private business.

'This is it, Dean. A true love job,' I assure him. 'Wicked, innit?'

'If you say so.' Dean lights up a tab. As far as I can tell, he looks put out.

'Don't go sulky on me, you lanky lummox. You're still my best mate.'

'Oh, sure,' he goes, sarky-like. 'When it suits you.'

'I thought you'd be chuffed for me.'

He puffs on his tab, staring out the window. 'I am,' he says. 'It's just . . .'

'What?' I tug his skinny wrist, forcing him to look at me. 'What?'

He does that Jarvis thing over his specs. 'It's just . . . well, I suppose a shag's out of the question now.'

I stare at him, gobsmacked. Then his mouth twitches and I realise he's winding me up. 'You're worse than Ray, you.' I splutter out laughing. 'Sorry, man, it's deffo out.'

'Never say never.' He grins at me, and winks.

Mum notices my transformation also, but she thinks it's down to the handout from Filthy. Huh, no chance. I checked the lottery page on Teletext, and the week they won, it was £113,070 for five numbers plus the bonus ball. The lousy cheapskate only gave me two and a half thousand quid. He could easy have made it ten grand, the friggin' tightass. The pre-Ash Rowena would have exacted a terrible revenge, possibly on the physical maiming scale. The New Me decides to rise above it, knowing that I'll be outta here soon and I'll never have to see the Scroogey asshole again, ever!

'We're having a bit of a do next week,' announces Mum. 'In the concert room at the Labour Club, on Tuesday night. We want to celebrate our engagement while we can, seeing as we've decided to get married next month.'

My jaw hits my knees. 'What?'

Mum beams at me. 'The house on the Barratt's estate will be ready by then, so we didn't see any point in waiting. It's not as though we have to worry about money any more, so we thought we'd throw a party for our friends. There'll be lots of people there, work mates and suchlike. I hope you'll grace us with your presence, Rowena. Bring a friend, of course.'

I try to picture me and Ash (my boyfriend!) mingling socially with the lowlifes from the chip factory. The thought of Mandy Sweeney, off her saggy tits on vodka, dragging him on to the dancefloor for the Macarena makes me shudder. I don't want my lover thinking I mix with povs and white trash.

'There'll be karaoke,' Mum continues. 'Me and Bernard have been practising "Summer Nights", that song from *Grease*.' She stands on tippytoe, scrunches up her hair and wiggles her shoulders obscenely. 'I'm not Olivia Newton-John,' she goes, like I might have missed that fact. 'But Bernard's a dead ringer for that bloke, John wossname.'

'Revolta,' I offer. This gets sicker by the minute.

'We're having a country music disco as well. They're all into line dancing down the club, it'll be a canny hoot. And there'll be a buffet,' she adds, like I'm gonna leap at the chance of sausages on sticks. 'You must at least show your face, Rowena. You, me and Bernard – we're a proper family now.'

That clinches it. No friggin' way!

'Wouldn't miss it, Mum.'


Wednesday morning, commence countdown. Only eight and a half hours until I see my lover. I stuff my rucksack with a stack of make-up as a surprise gift for Ash, plus a change of kit and some toiletry things, toothbrush and suchlike, as I'm bound to be staying the night with him, and screw the consequences. My body tingles at the thought.

Time drags. There's not much doing so Mrs Marr asks me to tidy Mr Crowther's office, like I'm a skivvy or something. I spend ages swivelling round on his chair, dreaming of Ash's beautiful eyes and goldy skin, trying not to touch myself. Using Mr Crowther's italic fountain pen, I practise writing Ash's name in different styles on a pad of Post-it notes till they're all used up. The best one I stick inside my bra, next to my heart, to give to Ash as a keepsake.

*Ash Mallison + Rowena Vincent*
*= True Luv 4 Evva!!*

I spend ages in the bogatory doing my make-up and straightening my fringe with spit as for some reason it's decided to act curly just when I don't need the hassle. Quarter to four. Time to leave for my appointment with love, destiny, and the Madolescents.

'I'm off then,' I call to Mrs Marr. 'For my medical thing, you know.' She's on the phone, waving a mad signal at me, meaning she wants me to hang on. I let out a huge dramatic sigh, heave my rucksack on to the floor and stare at the ceiling. If she's expecting me to run to the shop for some biscuits, she can friggin' whistle.

She puts down the phone. 'Someone rang for you earlier, Rowena. Now where's the name, I'm sure I wrote it down.' She fiddles with a pile of Post-it notes. 'A young man, anyway.'

My heart flips. 'Ash?' I go. 'Was it Ash?'

'Might have been. It'll come back to me in a minute.' She flicks through the yellow stickers. 'Here it is, the system never fails. That's right. Ash.'

'What did he say?' My voice sounds a bit frantic. 'Why didn't you fetch me to the phone?'

'You were in the toilet, dear, sprucing yourself up. I think he was ringing from a callbox, he didn't leave a message.'

Brilliant. Just brilliant. She can't even handle a phone call. I should report the senile old biddy to Mr Crowther, she's way past her sell-by date.

I wonder what Ash wanted.

I float all the way to Altamont Lodge, a bunch of butterflies flitting around inside my stomach. But, Omigawd, Ash isn't here! My gut's in a knot, wondering whether he copped a strop because I didn't come to the phone. The rest of the Madolescents are rabbiting on, sniggering amongst themselves, winding up Prossie. She's quizzing them about why no one showed for last week's meeting, bleating on about disruption to the schedule and the importance of continuity in therapy. Coralie lies that she couldn't leave the house as she was convinced she only had one nostril.

Micky says he caught a stomach bug and nauses everyone out with a description of his squits. Gemma reckons she got her leg-hairs caught in the exercise bike, and Reuben gets a fit of the giggles and panics because he forgot to count them. I can't get into it. My ears are straining, listening for the clunk of the outside door, the sound of Ash's Timberlands squeaking along the wooden corridor, willing him to walk in the room and park his sexy ass next to me.

Nothing.

'Rowena, are you with us?' They're all staring at me.

'I feel sick.' My stomach heaves. A ball of acid forms in my throat, choking me. 'Really, really sick.' Gemma Probert waddles over, puts her arms round me and goes she'll take me outside for some fresh air. Tears stream down my face. Melted mascara stings my eyes. I cling on to Gemma's spare tyres and we stagger through the door.

'Christ, Rowena, what's brought this on?' Gemma digs in her pocket and hands me a serviette. 'Here, blow your nose. If you're going to spew, do it in that flower-bed, and mind my shoes.' She props me up against a wall. I retch a bit but nothing comes. I'm gulping like a landed mackerel.

Gradually the sick feeling starts to wear off, then I burst out blubbing like a baby. In between sobs I tell Gemma how me and Ash were getting it together, how he phoned me at work but I found out too late, and now it looks like he's finished me.

'I bet he was just ringing to let you know he couldn't come to the meeting, you soft plum,' says Gemma. 'Or he's having a bad brain day. Everyone gets downers, specially us mad bastards. You're crying over nowt.' She grabs my fingers and rubs them in her fat chapped hands, like she's sandpapering me. 'Get yourself round there. I'll come with you if you want.'

'Would you, Gem?'

'Sure, nee bovva.'

## 28

## Into the Void

Ash's doorbell thing's been vandalised, ripped off the wall, wires sticking out like old spaghetti. I hammer on the door till my fist's on fire. Eventually I see a shape through the frosted door panes. It's the grumpy bloke, the cycling fisherman from downstairs, in a disgusting pair of stained trousers and a grimy vest. He looks like he's just rolled out of his pit.

'Hey up, it's Rab C. Nesbitt's ugly mate,' snorts Gemma.

The bloke makes that catarrhy *mnngghhh* sound with his nose, and glares at me. 'Not you again.'

'Sorry to bother you—' I begin.

'If you're from the Jehovah's Witnesses you can piss right off,' he growls, and goes to shut the door. Fortunately, it sticks.

'No, wait! We've come to see somebody. Ash Mallison. He lives upstairs.'

'Him. Piggin' weirdo.' That's rich coming from Uncle Fester.

Suddenly Gemma gutbarges through the door, flattening the bloke against the wall. 'Come on, Rowena, or we'll be arguing the toss all bleedin' night.'

We're both panting like old dogs as we reach Ash's door, Gemma because the stairs have done her in, and me because I'm geet nervous as owt. My heart's racing like a whippet on speed. I feel paralysed.

Gemma bangs on the door. 'Ash? Ash, it's Gemma and Rowena. Open up.' She peers through the keyhole. 'There's a light on, I think. Here, you have a go.'

I rap a few times with my knuckle. 'Ash?' I say quietly. 'Are you in there?'

'Give it some welly, man,' goes Gemma, landing a flying dropkick on the door. She stands back, puffing and blowing, then glues her ear against the keyhole. 'I can hear music,' she says. 'He must have fallen asleep with the stereo on. You hang on here, I'll go and see if Lurch downstairs has got a key. If this dump's a hostel, chances are he's the warden.'

I'm left standing there like a lemon, rooted to the spot, wishing Ash would appear at the door, scoop me up in his coffee-coloured arms, lay me gently on the bed and kiss me all over. The bloke trudges up the stairs, scratching and grumbling, jangling a bunch of keys. Gemma shoves him in the back, telling him to get a bloody move on.

'I'm not supposed to do this,' he grunts. 'He could report me, invasion of privacy and that. Whatever he gets up to in there, it's his business.'

'Just do it, softlad,' orders Gemma, thumping him in the shoulder blades. She could make a fortune as a dominatrix.

He slides the key into the lock. As it clicks, my head buzzes with pins and needles and silver lights float in front of my eyes. He pushes.

'Piggin' doors, they're always sticking. Bleedin' damp makes the wood swell.'

The bloke pushes again, this time with his hairy shoulder. The door gives a few inches. He peers up and down through the chink, frowning.

'Fuckin' hell!' He jumps away and the door slams shut on its own. His face is the colour of suet. 'Get downstairs, you two. Call an ambulance, double quick!' He bundles me and Gemma down the stairs into his room. 'Go *on*!'

'What's up!' I yell hysterically. 'What's happening? Where's Ash?'

Sweet Jesus. Like I need to ask.

Gemma slams her cellulite against Ugly Bloke's door, blocking my exit while she dials 999. I'm demented, frantic, pounding on the walls, clawing at her like a wildcat gone mental.

'Let me out!' I scream. 'I want to see Ash!'

'You don't, believe me. You're not going up there.' She slaps my face. I slap her right back, only harder. 'Ambulance, quick as you can,' she yells into the phone. 'And police.'

'Move, you bitch! Gemma, let me out! I've got to see him.'

The next thing I remember is a bunch of fat fingers screwed up into a fist, heading for my jaw, like in slow motion. Then, *boff*! Cuckoo. Floating stars. Lights out. My brain explodes. I sink, suffocating in inky blackness.

'Here, sip this.' Gemma's holding a glass to my lips. My head wobbles about on my neck. The smell of whisky makes me want to retch. 'It's for the shock,' she says.

I stare at her numbly. She's blubbing. My scalp tightens. Reality bites.

'Tell me this isn't happening, Gemma. Tell me it's not true.'

'It's true,' she nods grimly. 'Jesus H. Christ. Poor Ash. What a friggin' waste. He must have been totally desperado, I mean, to *hang* himself like that. It's so grisly, so . . . *planned*.' My body goes rigid. 'God, I'm sorry, Rowena, I didn't mean . . .' Tears run down her cheek fat and disappear into her chins.

'Did you see him? Is he . . . you know? For sure?'

'Oh aye, for deffo. The police surgeon's on his way, but there's nowt we can do for Ash, not now. Come on, drink this.'

I gulp the Scotch in one. My throat burns, and my body feels electric, like someone's throwing sand at me. I'm breathing in little gasps; there's a monster sitting on my chest. Blood pounds in my head, sending a whooshing noise through my ears. The light from the table lamp hurts my eyes. Everything hurts.

'Turn the light off.' My voice comes from outer space. We sit there on Ugly Bloke's smelly settee. The darkness weighs a ton. My body feels as if it's shrinking, being sucked into a sea of gone-off molasses. It's like being buried alive, my organs shutting down one by one, shrivelling, decomposing, putrefying. 'I'm scared, Gem.'

'I know, pet. Jeez, you're shivering.' She switches on both bars of the electric fire and straight away trickles of sweat run down my forehead, even though I'm freezing cold. 'This is spooking me, sitting in the dark,' she goes. 'Can we have a bit of light? I'll turn the telly on. Just say if it's too bright.' She clicks the remote, muting the sound and zapping to Teletext. I sit there paralysed. The menu pages flicker on the screen.

A motor – ambulance? Fed car? – pulls up outside. The monster bears down on my chest, squeezing my ribcage like a boa constrictor, gripping me by the throat. I can't swallow, can't breathe. Gemma wraps her chubby arms round me.

*Dad, where are you?*

My eyes sting with scaldy tears. The words on Teletext blur and slide crazily across the screen. Letters jumble up, fade and float, disappearing into the corners. Then suddenly I see, clear as anything, the words *ASH TAPE*, in bright yellow. As soon as I blink, they're gone, and it's flicked over to the next page. *ASH TAPE*. Fifty zillion volts shoot through my body. *ASH TAPE*. We'd heard music playing in Ash's room. It's a sign, a message. My brain clicks in.

'Gem, go see if there's a tape in Ash's stereo. It's just inside the door, to the right. Go on, fetch it down. Quick, before they get in!' Gemma scrambles out. She sure can motor for a fat lass.

Car doors slam. Feet run up the path. Someone brays on the knocker. Someone else – Ugly Bloke? – lets them in. Muffled muttering. Footsteps go up the stairs, not slowly, but not in a hurry either.

My stomach heaves. Hot acid rises in my throat and trickles down my mouth. Cold sweat breaks out on my forehead. I think I can smell my feet.

Gemma wobbles in, clicking the lock behind her. She's wheezing. Her eyes are like saucers.

'Here.' She slaps a tape into my hand and clamps her paw round mine. One of us is boiling hot, the other freezing cold, but I can't tell which is which.

'Did you . . . did you see him? Ash?' My voice comes out in a croaky whisper. 'Is he still . . . like he was?'

Gemma stares wildly at me and nods. Her tears splash on to my hand.

'Tell me, Gem. *Tell* me how he did it. I need to know.'

She starts sobbing and trembling like a giant pinky blancmange. I slide my arm round her and stare blankly at the TV, patting her beefy shoulder, waiting for her to get it together. Then the telly screen clouds over and I gawp, mesmerised, as a picture of Ash's face slowly materialises. He's in full make-up, his hair bouffed up, looking gorgeous. And he's wearing a wedding veil. His mouth widens in a wicked smile. He seems happy. Really, really happy. Then he winks at me. I shoot bolt upright, but the picture fades back into the Teletext menu.

I sit there stunned. Did I imagine it? Maybe it's shock, or aftershock. Or I've finally hurtled into the abyss, the void, the World of Mad.

No. It was real, I know it was. A real supernatural experience. Ash came back through the telly to send me a message. To give me a mission. I understand. Suddenly I feel dead calm, in control. An other-worldly force takes me over. My head fizzes with psychic energy and waves of power pulse through my body. I am transformed into my alter ego, the mighty butt-kicking superwoman.

I am *Rowena: Warrior Princess.*

Ash has chosen me as his Avenging Angel.

His final wish shall be fulfilled.

I could murder a bag of chips.

*

'Get your skates on, Gem. We're outta here.' I slip the tape inside my bra, next to the Post-it note where I'd written our *True Luv 4 Evva* promise. I won't let you down, Ash. Count on it.

'We can't go yet,' complains Gemma. 'The bizzies want to interview us, take statements. They said we had to wait.'

'Fuck 'em. Just keep stum. We know nothing, right? Now come on, shake your ass.'

I'm about to bundle her through the door when the polis come out of Ash's room. We crouch down at the bottom of the stairs and I strain my ears to listen.

'Can't you shift him?' says Ugly Bloke. 'It's piggin' creepy having him hanging there. I was just about to have a serious fry-up when all this happened.'

'Sorry,' goes the Bill. 'We can't cut him down until the SOCOs get here. They need to photograph the body *in situ*. Shouldn't be too long. We'll have him off your hands and down the hospital morgue before you can slice your black pudding.'

Ugly Bloke grunts, like the piggin' pig he is.

'We'll need to contact the family to ID the body before the post-mortem,' the polis goes. 'Any ideas?'

'Nah. Piggin' weirdo, he was. I know bugger-all about him. Ask them slappers downstairs.'

I pinch Gemma's arm fat. 'Quick,' I hiss. 'Get out before they come downstairs. Don't make a sound.' We creep along, hugging the wall and make a dive for the door. It's stuck halfway open with the damp. I squeeze through no probs, but Gemma's lardy bum gets wedged tight in the gap, so I have to kick and bray on the door till it moves. So much for a silent exit!

'Oi!' yells Ugly Bloke down the stairs. 'That's my piggin' door.'

'Hold it right there,' shouts the bizzy. 'I want a word with you.'

'Ouch! I've done my soddin' back in,' squeals Gemma, her face puffed up like a big red beach ball.

I shove her down the stone steps. 'Move!' *Rowena: Warrior*

*Princess* shows no mercy. 'Hide in those bushes. And stop that squawking or they'll hear us.'

Gemma limps into next-door's garden. It's knee-high with weeds and old Christmas-tree things. She collapses, panting, into a witch's forest of overgrown bushes with lethal scratchy bits. I clamp my hand over her mouth to stop her complaining. My ticker's thudding like a time bomb.

Ugly Bloke and the polis appear at the door. 'Where the hell have they got to?' says the bizzy, skegging up and down the street. 'They've disappeared.'

'Must have jumped on a bus,' goes Ugly Bloke. He sounds bored now, probably itching to stuff his gut with cholesterol. 'Could be anywhere by now.'

'Shit,' curses the plod.

We crouch there until we hear Ugly Bloke kick the door shut. My hands are torn and bleeding from the thorns. It looks like I've been cutting up.

'Can we go?' pleads Gemma. 'My back's killing us, I think it's seizing up.'

'Hold on, one more thing to do.' I scrabble in my bag for the pad of Post-it notes and felt-tip pen I nicked from work.

*Ash's fam live Hexham*, I write. *Mr Mallison (dad) works up hospital, Dr or s/thing.*

I fold the note and push it through Ash's letter box, then me and Gemma steal down the road and hide behind the bus shelter until the 46 comes.

Gemma blubs her eyes out all the way to town, halfly because of Ash and halfly because her back's gone.

'I can't work you out, Rowena,' she sobs snottily. 'Sitting there cool as fuck. Aren't you upset?'

'No time. Things to sort, stuff to organise. I'm on a mission.'

'From *God*?' Gemma gazes puppily into my eyes. 'You can get medication . . .'

'From *Ash*. You wouldn't understand. I don't understand myself, I'm still working it out in my head, but I'll need you to help me, Gem. First off, phone round the Madolescents and let them know what's gone down. Put them on standby.'

'Standby,' repeats Gemma. 'Standby, right.' She snuffles noisily into a serviette. 'What do you mean?'

'Jeez, I dunno, Gem. Just do it.' I'm so dazed by all that's happened, my head feels as if it's swirling through the cosmos, out of orbit, bombarded by meteorites of pure pain. Shockblasted.

## 29

# *The Mission*

Somehow, I'm home. Bundy's on the back step, ripping the skin off a young rabbit. There's just enough fur left to see it was black and white, probably dragged squealing from some kid's hutch in the 'Hood.

'Friggin' hell, Bundy, it's a *pet*,' I hiss. My Trusty Sidekick snarls like a feline pit bull and drags his kill behind the dustbin to disembowel in peace.

Mum's left a note on the fridge door.

*Staying at Bernard's tonight to watch boxing on Sky. BEHAVE!!*
   *Love,*
   *Mum*
   *xxx*

This at least is a relief. I need time to think, to rescue my spinning head from the stratosphere, to reel it in by the silver cord from its astral whirlings. To concentrate on planning my mission. I take a few swallows of Bailey's straight from the bottle, *gluggety-gluggety-glug*. Lordy, I smell as bad as a butcher's shop in a heatwave. This calls for a soakathon in the tub where I can wallow in my own effluent and misery.

Meditation, Reflection, Contemplation. These are the bath oils I drizzle into the bathwater. Safeways' ought to sell Depression, Despair, Desolation, they'd go down a bomb with Madolescents like me. I lower myself into the soft scalding water, burning my bum and the backs of my legs. Needing the breathtaking, bodyshocking, skinblistering pain of it. Pain is good. It's what I deserve. Resting my head on a rolled-up towel, I surrender myself to the smarting, stinging, scalding heat, the bathroom so full of suffocating steam, I can barely breathe.

Is this how it was for Ash? Was this what he felt, as the thing – the *noose* – first tightened around his beautiful silky throat? Did he gasp for breath, realise he'd made a mistake, struggle to free himself? Was he overcome by panic as his long goldy fingers tussled hopelessly with the choking knot?

Was it quick, or did he . . . oh, Jesus. Did he die in lingering agony?

Did he think about me?

Stop it, Rowena. Stop torturing yourself. It's too late.

Too late. That's what Ash said to me after we slept together. *I wish I'd met you sooner. It's too late now.* Those were his words. *Too late.*

Then it hits me. Omigawd, he had it all planned! It must have been there in his head while we made love, our first and only night together. That's why he was crying, and why he left me the purple teddy! *Thanx for everything. I want you to have this.* He *bequeathed* it to me! Ash, how could you do this? It's so final. So futile.

How could I have missed the signs?

\* \* \*

On the Saturday Dad took me on the Metro to Cullercoats. We walked along the front, the wind gusting so much it lifted my woolly hat off and Dad had to chase across the beach to catch it.

'Look how white the sand is,' he said. 'Just like the Caribbean. Jamaica, Barbados – they have hurricanes there too.'

We shared a tray of chips, huddling together against the wind on a seafront bench. A scruffy long-whiskered dog, the type that people call Rags, came pootling along, sniffing, wagging its tail, licking its rubbery chops. Dad fed it a few chips from the bottom of the tray where they wouldn't be drowned in vinegar. The dog scoffed them, then rested its nose on Dad's knee and gazed up at him.

'Look, Dad. Georgie used to do that,' I said. Georgie was the

Vincent family mutt, named by Dad after some singer from the sixties. The way that dog died was horrific. It was me who'd found him frothing and fitting in the shed, the fourth victim of the infamous Fozzy Hall Pet-Poisoner. Tears sprang to my eyes at the memory. 'Poor Georgie,' I snivelled. 'I really miss him, don't you?' Dad hugged me and squeezed my fingers too hard.

'Don't cry, princess,' he murmured. 'That's the way it is. Nothing lasts for ever. We all have to say goodbye some time, even if it means leaving the ones we love. It doesn't mean we stop loving them, though.'

His voice was hoarse and chokey. Tears brimmed up in his eyes and trickled down his cheeks.

'You're crying, Dad.' I have this talent for stating the obvious.

Dad sniffed. 'That's because we're sitting in a gale-force wind,' he said, attempting a laugh. 'Who'd be a sailor on a day like this, eh? Come on, sweetheart, your mum'll think we've run away to sea.'

He scratched the waggy-tail dog between the ears. We rode the Metro back in silence, snuggled up on the seat like orphans in a storm. Even though he'd denied it, I knew Dad was upset. I thought it was my fault because I'd reminded him about Georgie.

That was the last Saturday I spent with Dad. The following week he'd gone. Run away to sea, or something.

I missed the signs that time too.

* * *

Ash looked so happy when his face appeared to me on the telly. Undepressed. Glowing and radiant in his bridal finery. That was his dream, to wear a white wedding dress and veil, in public, so that people would think he was beautiful. He came back to visit me for a reason, sending a pure, clear message.

This time I understand the signs. This is my mission. Ash shall have his dream.

A thrill races through me, setting my body tingling with

excitement. My teeth chatter, my knees knock together, I start to shiver. Lordy, this bathwater's freezing!

Slipping into Mum's fluffy white robe, I search for Ash's tape and the Post-it note amongst the heap of flung-off stinky clothes. It's so gutting that Ash never got to see my artwork. I clutch the purple teddy to me and stroke the cassette, feeling for Ash's fingerprints, hot tears welling up in my eyes. It feels scary, not knowing what's on the tape, and my heart's on fast-forward as it rewinds. I dim the lights and stretch out on the couch, zapping the remote on to *Play*.

As soon as I hear the moody string intro, my stomach tightens into a knot and a tingly fizz runs through me. My body buzzes all the way through the tracks:

| | |
|---|---|
| 'Bitter Sweet Symphony' | The Verve |
| 'Suicide is Painless' | Manic Street Preachers |
| 'Strange Glue' | Catatonia |
| 'White Wedding' | Billy Idol |
| 'I Will Always Love You' | Dolly Parton |

I curl up into a tight foetal ball, so choked I can hardly breathe. *Choked!* Oh, Ash, my sweet Ash.

As the tape reaches the Catatonia track, the tears well up and splash over on to my cheeks in an orgy of projectile weeping. '*It was strange glue that held us together,*' sings Cerys in that husky voice, '*while we both came apart at the seams.*' I sob helplessly, hopelessly, it seems never-endingly, until all the crying parts of me ache. Eyes, jaws, cheeks, chest, ribs, belly, head – even my gums come out in sympathy.

Jesus, I'm such a wreck. OK, enough blubbing already. I need to gather my wits. *Rowena: Warrior Princess* has a mission to fulfil.

Naturally, by morning my face is fresh and blooming.

'Rowena, you look terrible.' That's rich coming from Mrs ChammyLeatherFace Marr. 'Your eyes are all puffed and bloodshot. I hope you're not turning into one of those teenage alcoholics I read about in *Take A Break*.'

'Never touch booze,' I lie. 'Poked my eyeball with the mascara wand, that's all. I'll be fine.'

'Well, stay in the back today, we don't want to upset the customers.' Right, like our customers aren't *already* upset. 'And remember to wash your hands before you make the coffee, in case it's conjunctivitis. We don't want an outbreak among the staff.' Me-Me-Me, that's all she thinks of.

It's quiet in the back. The men are having a hand of rummy in the rest room.

'Bloody hell, it's the Night of the Living Dead,' says Ray, clocking my face and grinning. 'Have a session with Frosty Jack, did you?'

'Shut it, you. I wouldn't drink that shite. It's a touch of pink-eye, that's all. Off the cat,' I explain.

'Since when have you had a cat?' goes Dean. I glare – well, more *squint* – at him. He catches my drift and turns back to the cards. I fill the kettle and clatter the mugs about to sound busy.

'The inquest opens on Monday,' Mr Scudamore's saying. 'I shouldn't think there's any suspicious circumstances. A-ha! Rummy!' He splays his cards out on the table.

'You jammy beggar,' moans Ray, chucking his hand in. 'That's the third game you've won on the trot.'

Mr Scudamore scoops up the cards and shuffles the pack. 'Asphyxiation by hanging,' he says. 'Poor kid. I can think of easier ways to top yourself.'

Pins and needles buzz in my head. My legs turn to sponge cakes, and I flop into the empty chair next to Ray.

'I suspect someone's deeply hung over,' says Mr Scudamore, dealing the next hand without looking up. 'There's some Resolve in the cupboard, pet.'

'Friggin' hell, Edgar,' groans Ray, staring at his cards. 'You've dealt me a hand like a bleedin' foot here. Oh well, here goes nothing.' He tosses fifty pence on the table and sparks up a tab. 'They say he was dressed up in girl's clothes. Even used a pair of stockings for the dirty deed. I wouldn't use owt stretchy, me. Too iffy. Give me a leather belt any day. Now that *would* make your eyes bloodshot.' He digs me in the ribs, like he's cracked some sort of joke.

The knot in my stomach unravels and heads up my windpipe.

'Mebbes a kinky sex game gone wrong,' says Gerry. 'Did he have a satsuma in his mouth by any chance?'

'It mightn't have been a perv thing,' says Dean. 'Perhaps he was depressed.'

'Depressed, my arse,' chips in Ray helpfully.

'One thing's for sure,' says Mr Scudamore. '*De Press*'ll have a field day with this, it'll be splashed all over the front page. It's the family I feel sorry for. Gregory Mallison's a Big Tortilla.'

'Enchillada,' Dean corrects him.

'One of the funny-handshake, rolled-up-trouser brigade.' Mr Scudamore studies his cards and grins to himself, flashing his joke teeth.

'Eh?' goes Ray.

'A Freemason. He's in the same lodge as Crowther. They all scratch each other's backs, that's how we got forewarning. Still, it'll be a decent bit of business for us, we might have to hire in an extra car. Rummy!'

'Bollocks!' Ray flings his cards on the table in disgust, knocking the ashtray flying. At the same time, a jet of hot sick shoots out of my throat and splashes over his shoes. 'Fuck's sake, Rowena!' he yells.

'It isn't your day, Ray.' Mr Scudamore laughs, shovelling fifty pences into his pocket.

Ray flicks him a sly V-sign.

'Come on, lads, back to work. Things to do, remains to be seen to,' says Mr Scudamore. 'Ray, clean that mess off your shoes. Dean, looks like you're coffee-wallah this morning. Rowena, get yourself home and sleep it off – and for God's sake put a lining on your stomach next time.'

I splash tap water on my face to get rid of the sicky smell. I feel limp and lifeless, like a punctured inflatable doll. Get a grip, Rowena. Be strong, for Ash.

'You OK, babes?' Dean pushes the side-wisps out of my face.

'Yeah. No. Dean, I need your help.'

We sit at the table and I explain my plan.

'You . . . are . . . joking,' goes Dean. His face is a picture. 'I mean, you can't be serious, Rowena. *Rowena*?'

I look him full-on in the eyeballs. 'I'm deadly serious. You've got to help me, Dean, otherwise the whole thing falls apart.'

He does that whistling thing under his breath. Cogs turn in his brain. 'You know my motto?' he says. 'Never say never?'

I nod eagerly.

'Well – never!'

'Dean, *please*. I'm begging you.' And if begging doesn't work, I'm not averse to physical violence.

'No way, it's too risky.' He shakes his head violently, like a rocknik in a mosh pit. 'If anyone found out – jeez, it doesn't bear thinking about. We'd be out on our ears for starters – probably never work again – and Crowther's would get booted out of the Association. Plus we could get arrested.'

'For what? Fulfilling someone's last wish? Stop looking on the black side, Dean. No one's going to find out, I promise. They'll all be sworn to secrecy. It'll be cool.'

He slouches down in the chair, holding his head. 'Why do I know this'll end in tears?'

'So you'll do it! Oh Dean, that's so totally wicked! I'd give you a bj right now only I still feel a bit spewy.'

'I'll take a rain check,' he says.

Brilliant! I can tick an item off my list.

| 1 | *Sort Dean!!!!* | ☑ |
| 2 | *Get cash from bank* | ☐ |
| 3 | *Frock* | ☐ |
| 4 | *Ring Mads* | ☐ |
| 5 | *Scran* | ☐ |
| 6 | *Booze* | ☐ |
| 7 | *Music* | ☐ |
| 8 | *Vid* | ☐ |

Mrs Marr borrows a pair of rubber gloves out the back and shines the Anglepoise into my eyes.

'Mmm, still very bloodshot.' She wrinkles her face up. 'Heavens, Rowena, your breath's not very sweet. There's some Clorets in the top drawer.'

'I've just puked my guts up,' I explain. 'All over Ray's shoes.' She jumps back, pasting a tissue to her mouth. 'Mr Scudamore says I'm to go home, but I'll stay if we're busy.'

'No, no, we'll manage,' she says sharply. 'People don't want to view their loved ones in chapels redolent of vomit.'

'If you insist.'

Grabbing my coat, I check out the list and head for the bank to withdraw fifteen hundred pounds from my lottery windfall. The snotty bint at the counter gives me a pile of grief as I don't have any ID, just the account number scribbled on a Post-it note. She makes me write my name twice on a form so they can check it against the signature card I filled in when I opened the account. This is a bit problem as I'm always trying out fancy new signatures to keep one step ahead of the CIA and I can't remember which one I used. She stands there frowning a bit, then takes the form to two other wussy bank types. They keep looking at the paper, then at me, then back at the paper. I'm wondering whether to do a runner, then I remember that hey, I'm not on the rob or anything, the money really *is* mine. The snotty bird asks me to write my name again so I try the signature with curly capital letters and a double stroke over the 'T' which obviously works as she hands over the moolah in fifties and twenties. They all stand watching me as I head for the door, like I've just duped them with some really smart con trick only they can't prove it. I wish.

I tick off number 2 on the list.

As I'm walking through Eldon Square on the way to sort number 3, I catch sight of a familiar big fat arse in a shellsuit waddling out of Mothercare. It's Mandy Sweeney, with her youngest bairn Britney, or Snotty Spice as she's called because her nose is always running. Normally I'd crawl a mile over broken glass to avoid her, but I get a weird feeling that fate's sent her galumphing across my path.

'Mandy!' I yell. She wheels round, looking startled. 'Mandy, over here.' Her face unravels with relief.

'Howay, Roey, divvent scare us like that, I thought it was the fuzz.' She eyes her shopping bag meaningfully. Free Mothercare kit for Snotty Spice, at a guess.

'Fancy a cuppa somewhere?' I can't believe I'm risking being seen in public with this common lardski. She'd better be worth it.

'Why aye, pet, I'm canny parched. Not one of they no-smoking gaffs though, I'm gagging for a tab. Britney could do with changing as well.' Right. A skunk would be a fair exchange. 'There's a caff behind the market does mugs of milky coffee, we'll gan there.'

After Mandy's sorted Snotty Spice's nappy in the loo and stuck a dummy in her gob, she lights up a tab and leans over the table.

'It was nae accident, us bumping into each other,' she says, blowing smoke down her nostrils. 'You understand, don't you? It was *meant*.'

'I know.'

'They're always around when you need them most. The angels I'm talking about, pet. There's one at your shoulder right now.' A shiver runs through me. Mandy takes a fierce drag of her ciggie.

'Nothing to be frightened of, Roey, they come through the torn veil to help you. It's someone you've lost, someone close. *All right, I'm coming to you*,' she hisses over my shoulder. 'Somebody here's dying to talk to you.'

My legs start trembling under the table. 'What's he saying?'

'Not *he*, pet. It's a woman, an older lady, says she's looking after you from the spirit world. I feel a lot of love flowing towards you.'

I try not to look gutted. Maybe Ash is busy getting a guided tour of heaven, or stuck in some sort of queuing system.

Mandy's elbow flops off the table. 'Eee, pet, my arm's a ton weight. Why am I tingling down my left-hand side?'

I come over all goosebumps. Omigawd, what if it's Nana Vincent! The stroke paralysed her down that side.

'This lady understands what you've been going through. She says to be strong, it'll come clear in the end, once you find . . . *Say again, hinny?* . . . Once you fit it all together. She's showing me a shiny crown with lots of jewels. Does that mean anything? She's skipping and dancing about, doing the hokey-cokey, nowt wrong with her leg now. Oh sods, the line's breaking up. Sorry, I can't get any more.'

She takes a mega-slurp of coffee and sparks up another tab. Snotty Spice snorts like a wee piglet.

'Was that any help, Roey? Did it mean owt to you?'

I shrug. 'It could have been Nana Vincent, but I didn't understand the crown thing, or the dancing. I was hoping somebody else might be there.'

'I just work on the celestial switchboard, pet. You canna be sure who's on the line, but they're calling for a reason. This lady was very keen to get through to you, so even if it sounded like bollocks, there's a message in there for you.'

'Cheers.' I feel disappointed, desperate to get away before the lung cancer gets me. 'Should I cross your palm with silver?'

Mandy splutters on her tab. 'Why no, pet. I never take money, me. It's a gift I have, see, and what's been given can be taken away just as easy.'

'Oh, right.' I grab my rucksack and scrape the chair away from the table.

'They do a nice all-day breakfast here, though. And alphabetti spaghetti on toast for kids. It's Britney's favourite, that.'

'My treat,' I say, slapping a fiver on the table. Snotty Spice jerks awake and starts bawling. 'See ya.' Wouldn't wanna *be* ya.

*Focus.*

Back on track, heading for Eldon Square. Number 3 on the list: Frock. I toss a pound coin at a crusty beggar with scuzzy dreadlocks and a shivering dog. 'Don't waste it on baccy neither, buy some food for the mutt,' I tell him. 'Or a bar of soap.'

*Focus. Focus.*

Let me through. I'm a woman with a mission, Ash's representative here on earth. Crowds part like the Red-or-Dead Sea in front of me. Window-shoppers dart into doorways to let me pass. Dawdlers stand aside.

*Focus. Focus. Hocus-pocus.*

Eyes front, single-minded, blind to bargains and shoplifting opportunities, I march towards Mecca. Pensioners hobble out of my path. Buggies scatter. Toddlers turn their heads and stare at me in wonderment.

*Mummy, Mummy, look at that lady.*

*Ssshhh, don't point. It's Rowena: Warrior Princess.*

*The Avenging Kickass Angel.*

*The Chosen One.*

*She brakes for no one.*

It's midseason sale time in Perfect Day. Just walking into the shop is canny weird, like stepping into another dimension. The carpet feels springy even through my biker boots, and they're playing music from the olden days, violins, pipes and stuff. I'm surrounded by white and cream and ivory dresses made of material that whispers and rustles and shushes. Everything's pale and luminous, except – I realise from the suspicious looks I'm getting off the biddy salespersons – for me. In my black leather outfit, I must stand out like a beetle in a tub of Häagen-Dazs.

'Do you need any assistance?' A woman with frosted hair and immaculo make-up, tall and slim like a glamorous granny-model, hovers discreetly.

'I'm, er . . . I'm looking for a wedding dress.' Right, like I'd be looking for a bog brush in a bridalwear shop. How dumb is that?

'For yourself?' She smiles thinly.

'Yes. I mean, no. Well, not me as *such*. It's for a friend.' Gibbering idiot or what? Get a grip, Rowena. 'How much is that frock there?' I point wildly. 'The one on the dummy?'

'The gown on the *mannequin*,' she says, meaning I*'m* the only dummy here, 'is from Freya d'Angelo's Young Sophisticates Collection. It's in natural white silk matelassé, with a halter top and empire waist. The train comes as optional. Ninety-five inches of figured organza, with three matelassé rosettes attachés in the back.' I stare at her dumbly. 'Altogether that would retail at around, let's see, eight hundred pounds, although our hire section do a similar style for much less.' She cranes her neck to look at me, weighing up a reaction, but I'm sticking with my expressionless expression. 'Did you have a particular price range in mind?'

'I can go a grand, maybe more.' Her face is like *Yeah, right*, or whatever poshgit people say, but give her credit, she pastes a smile back on double quick.

'This is a very special gown,' she goes, moving to the next one along. 'Embroidered silk dupione bodice, crêpe and chiffon A-line skirt, cut on the bias. Inverted-V empire waistline, ever so flattering. Optional chiffon tails specially designed to bustle up without bulk after the ceremony. Just under a thousand pounds.' I stand there lamely. 'No?'

'Not for me. Sorry, him. I mean *her*!' Her smile slips again, so I pull out the detailed memory file. 'I'm looking for something in pure white Thai silk, with a scalloped hemline and six-foot train. One with a heart-shaped neckline, and seed pearls and bugle beads on the bodice. Oh, and the sleeves have to taper into a point. And a veil like a butterfly's wings.'

This seems to satisfy her. She jots notes in a little pad. 'Do you have a picture of the gown?'

'Only in my head,' I answer. 'Somebody described it to me once.'

'I believe we have a very similar design,' she beams. 'It's in the sale too,' she adds in a whisper.

'Triff. How much can you knock off for notes? Cash, like?'

Her smile only falters for a nanosecond. 'We may be able to negotiate some form of, erm . . . discount. If you'd care to come this way.'

Another tick on my checklist. The wedding gown's perfecto! I decide against the six-foot train as it would only get in the way, so with discount for cash off the sale price, it's a mega-bargain. Looks like shoes are out, they don't do satin pumps in bigboy sizes. Still, it's not as if Ash'll be walking anywhere. The woman looks canny gobsmacked when I ask for the dress to be delivered to Crowther's. For a minute I think she's going to call Security but the sight of crisp readies does the trick. I have to wait ages while she UV-scans the notes to make sure they're not fakes (as if!), then it's all smiles and hope the sun shines on the bride and stuff. I'm so chuffed to have the dress, I nearly invite her to the wedding!

Mum's at work when I get home. I pour myself a Bailey's shandy, kick off my biker boots and sprawl on the couch, listening to Ash's tape. He feels so close to me, I want to sob my heart out but I know I'd never stop so I bite my top lip until I taste blood. There's shitloads to do, and no time to lose. It's important I hold it together. Crying can wait. Ash will understand.

After a quick shower, I take the phone into my room and ring round the Madolescents. They already know the score from

Gemma so I don't have to waste time filling them in on the background. Say what you like about nutters, they pull out the stops for one of their own. Gemma offers to bring the scran. OK, it'll be vile veggie leftovers from the Hill o' Beans but we can hardly book outside caterers! Mickey's sorting the booze as he's in on some scam running cheap beer from Calais, Reuben's bringing his tape decks, and Coralie's borrowing her dad's camcorder.

'It'll be short notice,' I warn them. 'I can't say a date or time yet. Just be ready to rock!'

## 30

## *Puzzling it Out*

Sunday morning I have a long lie-in, clutching the purple teddy and playing Ash's tape over and over on my Walkman till the batteries go flat. I curl up on one side with a pillow behind my back and try to imagine it's Ash snuggling up to me in the foetal position. The fatal position. Hot tears well up and sting my eyes. Don't start, Rowena. Get a grip.

Mum's vacuuming outside my room, bumping against the door with the hoover. The noise slices through my brain like the maniac's power tool in *Driller Killer*. Jesus, can't I even grieve in peace! Pressure builds up inside my head, threatening to explode. I want to scream, smash something, trash the room, burn down the house – *anything* to release the tension. This is how axe-murderers must feel just before they chop into someone's skull. I scramble out of bed and then – don't ask me why, it just happens – I'm down on the fluffy pink rug, crouching on my haunches like an animal, my head thrown back, my throat stretched tight. Suddenly this weird ear-splitting noise, like something from a splatter flick, escapes from my mouth and fills the room.

*Aaoooowwuuuuuuuuuuuuugh!*

'Rowena! Rowena, for God's sake, what's wrong?' Mum bursts into the room and kneels beside me, trying to clutch me to her, quieten me down, but I can't stop the unholy noise coming out of me.

*Aaoooowwuuuuuuuuuuuuugh!*

'Rowena, stop that racket, you're scaring me to death. Control yourself.' I wriggle free with the strength of ten wild animals, pushing, pounding, knocking her flying across the room until she collapses next to the bed.

*Control yourself.* Oh no, no way. That's where I've been going wrong. It feels so good, so powerful, so liberating, to howl like an injured she-wolf. I'm demonically possessed, half me, half that lass in *The Exorcist*. I am *Row-egan* (minus the suppurating boils, obviously!). All the rage, the pain, the frustration, yonks and yonks of it knotted in my gut, hurtle like a thunderbolt through my body and escape from my mouth in a blood-curdling wail fit to wake the dead. If only.

*Aaoooowwuuuuuuuuuuuugh!*

*Rrrrruff. Rrrrruff. Rrrrruff. Uff.*

I follow the final howl with a few gruff barks, finishing off with a sort of yip as a full stop. My head feels empty, but clear. I'm exhausted, but totally calm.

Mum looks terrified. She's cowering like a kicked whippet next to the bed where I shoved her with my superhuman strength.

'You can come out now, I'm done freaking.' I say it sweetly, offering a hand to help her up. My mouth curls in a daughterly smile. Mum glares suspiciously, like she's expecting me to produce a chainsaw from behind my back. 'It's cool, Mum,' I assure her. 'Honest.' Which is the wrong word to use as she knows I always say it when I'm telling porkies.

She won't budge. In the end I have to go downstairs on my own and leave her to recover while I microwave some chips. She's quaking when she comes into the kitchen, eyeing me warily, skirting round the table. I pretend not to notice when she pops a trank from her emergency supply.

'Care to tell me what that was all about?' she says eventually, when the shakes have worn off.

'It was on *Trust Me, I'm a Doctor*,' I lie. 'Or was it Richard and Judy? Call of the Wild therapy, or something. Stop worrying, Mum, I feel tons better now. It's great for curing tension headaches.'

'What's wrong with Solpadeine all of a sudden?'

'I don't want to be dependent on farmer's cuticles,' I tell her.

'Yelling works quicker anyway. You should give it a go. Bernard would be dead impressed.'

She frowns at me like I'm mentally deranged. 'I'll bear that in mind.'

I decide to take an early night as I'm canny knackered, plus I need to rewind the day's events in my head. Even though the howling was a demented thing to do, I feel like my mind's been spring-cleaned (sprung clean?), the cobwebby corners blasted with a high-pressure hose, crystal clear and sparkling.

At 02.17 by the digital clock radio, I'm wide awake, bolt upright in bed. No brainfuzz, no disturbing dream fragments, only a pure, clear sense of what needs to be done. I can't remember ever feeling so lucid, so focused, so definite. Reaching for the pad where I've written my funeral music, I plan the running order for Ash's Big Event. I daren't leave anything to chance; it has to run like a Rolex. I owe it to him.

I feel zapped with power, my brain synapses crackling like fireworks. Nervous energy fizzes through me, making me feel hyper. To calm myself down I root around for the box of nail extensions I nicked from Boots yonks ago. Usually manicures are relaxing but I'm so buzzing I can't be arsed to do all the finger-soaky, cuticle-trimming, buffing and priming stuff so I just glue the extensions direct on to my grimy nails. It warns on the box that results cannot be guaranteed unless extensions are affixed to a clean, dry surface. Well, they would say that, wouldn't they? I'll bet Cher doesn't go through that rigmarole every time. They look OK-ish, but when I try to file them down the nails go all bendy and threaten to peel off, so I leave them as they are, unnaturally long and talon-like, and give them two coats of Purple Rain glitter polish.

Now what? I survey the room with critical eyes. It looks worse than a charity shop, clothes flung everywhere, make-up on every surface, shoes in a tottering pile. How long have I been living in this cesspit? Time to get my shit together.

As the red digital numbers blink to 04.32, my boudoir looks almost fit for human habitation, if you ignore the black bin liners stuffed with chucky-out clothes. The only thing left to sort is the hellhole known as Under the Bed.

This is no job for a human being. They should clone mass-murderers or breed genetically modified terrorists for such a grisly chore. At the very least, I should have a protective suit and helmet like they wear in nuclear plants. I lie flat next to the bed, take a deep breath and reach my hand into the Land That Time Forgot.

Uurgh! Balls of fluff like tumbleweed, dirty knickers flung drunkenly into the Void, and, Omigawd, a sicked-up, decomposing starling! Cheers, Bundy! My gag reflex kicks in. Not that I'm squeamish, but this makes Jeffrey Dahmer's gaff seem like Sunnybrook Friggin' Farm. It's a manky elephants' graveyard of stained undies and regurgitated wildlife. So that's where my stinky sweaty trainers disappeared to. Mental note to hoy them into next-door's garden for Sheba. That'll shut her up for a bit.

My arm won't reach any further under the bed and I don't want to ruin my nail extensions so I straighten a wire coat hanger and poke about with the hook. It catches on the strap of a long-forgotten bra, a lacy black number I vomited over and meant to wash. Something's tangled up in it. A cardboard box. I yank and yank until it's near enough to grab. It's covered in dust and fluff and stains (maybe Bailey's vomit), and it takes me ages to work out what it is.

It's Nana Vincent's legacy.

The Abba jigsaw puzzle.

* * *

She could hardly speak after the first stroke. Mum took me to visit her in hospital. It was scary seeing her lying helpless, her face twisted and pulled down one side, a string of drool trickling from her mouth. I noticed how papery her skin was, almost thin enough to read through, and how her left hand curled up like a claw.

265

'Don't try to talk, Dorothy,' said Mum. 'It's tiring you out. Your speech will come back soon enough.'

But it never did. And I believe Nana Vincent knew it wouldn't.

It was her eyes that spooked me. She looked bewildered and frightened. When they let her go back home, Mum and I moved in with her, just temporary like, until she could see to herself. A nurse came twice a day to wash her and make her comfortable.

'Your grandma's a tough old bird,' she said to me, as if Nana Vincent was the last Christmas turkey in the shop.

One day, when the nurse had got her up to sit in the chair next to the window, I read to Nana from a book she'd given me as a birthday present. It was *Alice in Wonderland*. Up till then I'd only looked at the pictures. I didn't know whether she could understand, or even hear me, but when I got to the bit about the Dodo and the Caucus Race, she started to get agitated.

'What's up, Nana? Do you need the toilet?'

Her head seemed to shake no, but her good arm was waving about.

'A drink? Some Ribena?' I reached for the Tommy Tippee beaker with the dribbleproof spout.

'Gaaaah,' she went. She frowned and closed her eye, which I took to mean no.

She seemed to be pointing towards the bookcase behind her.

'Fed up with Alice? Don't blame you, Nana, she's a right wuss. Shall I read you something else?'

'Gaaah.' She sounded dead irritated.

I went to the bookcase and pulled out a couple of paperbacks that looked well thumbed.

'*The Thornbirds*, Nana? *Tilly Trotter*?'

'Gaaah, gaaah.' Obviously not. She lifted up the claw with her good hand and pointed to the floor. I knelt on the carpet and looked under the bookcase where she kept the games we used to play on rainy days.

'You mean the Monopoly? You want to play Monopoly?'

'Gaaah.'

'Scrabble? Happy Families?'

'Gaaah! Gaaah!'

Right at the bottom was a jigsaw puzzle. The picture on the front was an album cover: *Arrival* by Abba. I held it in front of her face.

'Heh.' She looked relieved. So was I.

'You want to do the jigsaw puzzle?'

'Gaaah.'

Jesus H. I was out of options.

'Goooh.' She aimed her claw at the jigsaw, then at me. 'Goooh.' Her eyes were desperately trying to tell me something. 'Goooh!'

'Me?'

'Heh.'

'You want me to do the jigsaw puzzle?'

'Heh.' But the effort had knocked her out and next thing, she was fast on, snoring like a piggy.

Every day after that, she made me get the jigsaw box out, but I couldn't understand what she wanted me to do. There was a lot of pointing and Gooohing and Gaaahing, then Mum said, 'I think she's giving it to you, Rowena.'

'You want me to keep the jigsaw, Nana?'

'Heh.' She smiled twistily and nodded her head. 'Heh.'

Those were the last words she spoke to me. In the middle of the night she had a mega-stroke. I never saw her again.

All I had to remember her by was the Abba jigsaw puzzle. Even the thought of it made me majorly upset so I stuffed it out of sight, out of mind, under the bed.

\* \* \*

There's a picture of this old pop group on the front, two blokes like garden gnomes and two bimboids, one with reddish hair and one blonde. They're sitting in a helicopter inside a big glass bubble. ABBA/ARRIVAL, it says. One of the 'B's in ABBA is the wrong way round, I suppose they thought it was clever in those days. The box lid's stuck on with Sellotape, all fuzzy and filthy from being under the bed. I shake it. The jigsaw pieces rattle around. It feels as if there's something bigger inside too. I peel the strips of ancient sticky tape off the lid and open the box.

As well as the jigsaw pieces there's a record, a small black vinyl one like on old-fashioned jukeboxes. I wipe it on my sleeve and slap it on the never-used turntable that came with my stack hi-fi rig. It's an Abba song. I seem to have heard Abba before, but maybe I'm getting them mixed up with Steps. The song's called 'Dancing Queen', the sort that gets all the gadges and biddies creaking at discos or grabbing the mic in karaoke bars. *Kerrrr-inge!*

I'm sorting out the jigsaw pieces, looking for the four corners and edges, when something weird comes over me. A scalp-tightening, gutlurching, heartstopping sensation that I can't put a name to, a memory trapped just beyond reach.

*She's showing me a shiny crown with lots of jewels . . . She's skipping and dancing about, doing the hokey-cokey, nowt wrong with her leg now.*

Nana Vincent's message from the Other Side! It's just like Mandy Sweeney told me in the caff.

*. . . a shiny crown with lots of jewels . . . She's skipping and dancing about . . .*

Dancing Queen! Omigawd!

I rack my brain trying to remember what else the lardarse said. Suddenly the words flash like a neon sign in front of my mind's eye.

*She says to be strong, it'll come clear in the end, once you find . . . Say again, hinny? . . . Once you fit it all together.*

Fit it all together! The jigsaw puzzle! Nana Vincent's telling me to do the jigsaw puzzle!

My fingers morph into bananas as I scrabble to put the pieces in the right order. The false nail on my right index finger gets snagged as I jam the puzzle to make the pieces fit. It bends right back and hangs by a thin string of adhesive but I can't be arsed to stick it on again so I try to reconstitute the gum with spit and hope for the best. I'm useless at fiddly, finicky things anyway, thanks to my world-famous zero patience.

'You'll never be a nurse, you don't have the patience.' One of Dad's corny jokes. Patience/Patients, see. I only got it recently. *Stop it, Rowena. Don't think about Dad. You know it does your head in.*

I'm sweating like a fat lass as the last jigsaw piece slots into the box. Abba sit smirking in the helicopter, four scuzzy Swedes primed for lift-off to Where-Are-They-Nowland.

'OK, Nana Vincent. I've fitted it all together like you said. Now what?' Maybe I say it out loud, maybe I just think it, it's hard to tell. Doesn't matter, spirits can read thoughts in pictures, saves them having to learn zillions of languages. Concentrate, Rowena. Focus on contacting Nana Vincent in the hereafter. I squinch my eyes and try to visualise her in my mind, but the image that keeps coming back is the one of Nana after the stroke, when she had the twisty-up face and dangly arm. No wonder she's not answering. She won't recognise the mental picture I'm sending; everyone gets treated by psychic healers Over There and made perfect again.

I peek at the clock radio. 05.42. Stupid me! She won't be awake, maybe not for hours yet. People can lie in bed as long as they like in spirit – that's why it's called heaven, obviously. I'll try again later.

I set the jigsaw box carefully on the dressing table, far back where it won't get knocked. I'd go completely postal if I had to do it all over again. I pull a piece of hanging Sellotape from the lid, so old there's hardly any stickywicky left on it. Something falls out. It's an envelope that was taped to the inside. A big pink one, like a birthday card envelope. The flap's sealed down with an ancient stamp. It's addressed to *Mrs Dorothy Vincent*, aka Nana, in black felt-tip.

I flop on to the bed and tease the envelope open with a tail-comb. Inside, there's a flowery greetings card.

A chill runs through me. Icy fingers clutch my head, stab needles deep into my brain. My bowels churn ominously.

*Happy Mother's Day*, it says. *Much love, Lonnie.*

It's from Dad!

My ticker's pounding like the clappers, threatening to burst through my ribcage. In my hand I hold a clue to the Vincent family history. My heritage, my roots, my very DNA signature.

A key to the identity of Real Rowena.

A link to the mysterious Missing Dad.

\* \* \*

The day after the episode with the dog in Cullercoats, Dad took us out for a picnic. It was Mother's Day. We went to Whitley Bay, Dad, Mum, Nana Vincent and me. First we had a game of pitch 'n' putt but it was so windy the balls skittered all over. Then we wandered up to Spanish City. Dad was ace at pinball, he let the steely ball roll right down before he slammed the flippers. *Ping! Ping! Ping!* We could have played all day with the free games he won.

Nana Vincent gambled on the one-armed bandits, ramming coins in the slot like they were about to be taken out of circulation. 'Ask me, they're fixed, these machines,' she huffed, then the very next go she pulled three bells without nudging or holding. The bandit puked up a pile of silver. *Chunka! Chunka! Chunka!* 'Must be my lucky day.' She laughed, handing me a quid's worth of coins.

That was the day Mum won a bread bin on the prize bingo, only none of us wanted to carry it around so she gave it to the girl in the change kiosk. Nana Vincent told her she shouldn't throw her luck away. Mum said nee bovva, the bread bin was a cheap tinny thing, she wouldn't give it house room and anyway it wouldn't go with the new pine kitchen she was angling for. She grinned and nudged Dad in the ribs, but he looked away.

We sat on rustic benches at a wooden table outside a pub while Dad went inside to fetch the drinks. When he came out his eyes looked sore. Mum unpacked the picnic which was mainly sausage rolls, crisps and wee tubs of chocolate mousse. Nana Vincent asked if they were shop-bought and Mum replied you bet, she wasn't allowed to lift a finger in the kitchen, not on Mother's Day. That's when Dad left the table, crossed the road and stood looking out to sea. He was gone ages.

The wind blew the chocolate mousse pots into the car park and I was sent to collect them and pop them in the litter bin. 'It's like being on *Dallas*,' remarked Nana Vincent. 'It was forever blowing a gale at Southfork, but the Ewings still ate their breakfast outside. What's Lonnie doing over there? Go and tell him to be sociable, Jean.'

Mum crossed over the road and leaned on the railings next to Dad. I watched them for a while. Something went *clunk* in my stomach. Nana Vincent fussed round me, wiping the chocolate off my chops and frogmarching me to the smelly pub lavatory. When we came out, Mum had packed the Tupperware away. She said she had a headache and wanted to go straight home. Her eyes looked red and itchy too. Dad would follow on, she said, though by the time he got home I was in bed.

So that was Mother's Day. My last Sunday with Dad. Whatever it was, it was no picnic.

* * *

It's too scary to think about. Quickly I tuck the card back inside the pink envelope, drop it into the jigsaw puzzle box and snap the lid back on. Then I shove it under the bed as far as it'll go. Why now, Big G? Why *now*? Aren't I already out of my tree trying to organise Ash's Big Event?

My stomach's spinning with whirly pits. Acid rises in my gorge. An attack of spastic legshakes hits me. I feel as cold and lifeless as a two-day-old stiff. Everything's drained out of me – blood, sanity, control of limbly functions. Mind and body perfectly aligned in total collapse, not a zilligram of energy or rational thought left.

*Dad! Daaaaaaaaaaad!*

I haul my ass into bed. Even with the duvet snuggled tight around me, I can't stop the shivers. My kneebones clack rhythmically against each other like castanets. A bolt of agonising pain shoots through my right eye and squats there pulsating, like a malevolent alien, biding its time before colonising my entire body and destroying me cell by cell from within.

*Aaaaaaaaarrrrghhh!*

An inhuman scream rips into my consciousness and ricochets inside my head, stab-stab-stabbing my bruised eyeball with laser-sharp pain signals.

*Aaaaaaaaarrrrghhh!*

Omigawd, it's Bundy!

I stagger out of bed and peer through the curtains. Bundy's perched on the fence between our yard and the Mutants' jungle next-door. He's yowling, a weird piercing noise like the shriek of an unquiet soul. For once, Sheba's not barking her stupid head off. Instead, she's cowering next to a pile of rotting wood (Darren Mutant's DIY travesty of a kennel) and whimpering. It hits me from the furtive way she's looking at Bundy that she's scared shitless of him. Sheba has a sixth sense (that's about four ahead of the rest of the Mutants). And, recalling what Mandy Sweeney told me, I realise why she's spooked.

*They're always around when you need them most. The angels I'm talking about, pet.*

Bundy: my Guardian Angel in cat form! My Spirit Guide, my Familiar, my Saviour from the Further Dimension. Just when I really, really need him.

I tippytoe barefoot down the stairs, opening the back door quietly. 'Psss-psss-psss. Bundy, here, Bundy,' I hiss, trying to ignore the eviscerated vole on the doorstep. Bundy takes a death-defying leap off the fence, lands with a thud in the yard, and darts into the kitchen like a furry cannonball, leaving a trail of muddy pawprints on the Marrakesh vinoleum.

'Bundy-babes, come to Momma,' I say, with relief and out-stretched arms. My Trusty Sidekick springs on to the worktop, fluffs up his tail and pads towards the sink, rubbing his olfactory glands against the cupboard doors as he goes. He's purring. Bundy's *purring*!

While I'm tickling his ears, I check out his condition. Yer man's gained weight. He's humongous, but not flabby massive, more bulked-up muscle. I guess he's been doing some kind of feline bodybuilding, lunging after wildlife, press-ups on horny she-cats, all that tommy stuff. Rent the video. *Workouts for Wildcats,* starring Bundy Collard-Vincent. *Build Biceps Like Bastards.* And, Omigawd, balls like bombs! His testicles have grown from conkers to satsumas to . . . I dunno, pink grapefruits. How can he *walk* with those things between his legs? It reminds me of something I saw on telly once, about this pervy bloke who paid a woman to inject his scrotum with water till it swelled up to the size of a rugby ball. Gerrrr-oss!

Bundy's purr-box is working overtime, like a Harley on full throttle, and he's letting me stroke him and run my hands up his bog brush of a tail. This is a majorly major breakthrough as he's always snarled or batted me before, which confirms (not that I doubt it) that he's been sent from the World Beyond to guide me in my hour of need. I heave his huge black bulk on to my shoulder and haul him upstairs to my room before his good mood wears off and he reverts to psychopathic violence.

As soon as the bedroom door shuts, Bundy goes totally apeshit, hurtling round at the speed of light, digging into the bin liners with his razor-sharp claws, scratching at the carpet in a demented fashion, shooting up the curtains. Maybe he's having an attack of clausters, or an epileptic seizure. Whatever, his grand finale consists of crapping on the bed, then tearing at the duvet to hide the evidence.

'Fuck's sake, Bundy, chill out,' I reprimand him. The poo stinks disgusting, worse than a maggot farm, and I'm gagging as I scrape it up in a thousand tissues and stuff it deep down inside a bag of chucky-out clothes. The sheets and duvet cover will have to be hoyed out as well, but for now they can stay in a bin liner. I'd flush the cat poo down the lavvy and shove the sheets into the washing machine, only my Trusty Sidekick would be sure to abscond if the door were open for a millisecond, and I need him here for his professional spirit expertise.

He seems loads calmer now his bowel's free of putrefying rodents, so I heave him on to the sheetless bed and scrape my false fingernails lightly along his back, which he seems to enjoy. It's a well-known fact that cats are fizzing with ESP, but I decide on verbal communication to back up the thought-transference process, a kind of psychic floppy disk.

'Guide me, O Bundy, Great Cat-God of the Cosmos. Lead me to my original origins, show me the way to my true self.'

Bundy coughs up a hairball.

## 31

# Mr Crowther's Carpet

08.35. Friggin' hell, I should be halfway to work by now! Trust me to oversleep, today of all days, when there's shitloads of stuff to organise for Ash's Big Event. I try to stir my bones out of bed but there's no feeling in my legs, they're completely numb. Omigawd, what if all this overthinking about Nana Vincent has tempted fate and made me have a stroke! I knuckle my eyes and squint down the bed. Bundy, the Arnold Schwarzenegger of Catdom, is phlumped like a ton weight on my feet, stopping whatever it is that circulates from circulating. He opens one eye and glares evilly, defying me to disturb him. It's a canny struggle but eventually I manage to manoeuvre my paralysed limbs from under him and hobble along to the bathroom.

My hair looks like a fright wig, all tangled and cockling up in shagger's tufts. I decide to transform it into a style statement by backcombing it and screwing it up in a banana clip. The false nails are definitely dodgy, but there's no time to re-stick them so I just press hard on them till my finger ends turn white. I run a black pencil inside my top and bottom eyelids and add a quick daub of Rococo Red lippy. My mouth looks like a slit-open wound, I could star in a slasher flick, no probs. What a bleedin' mess.

After chucking on my rockin' black denim ensemble, I ponder the Bundy problem. Somehow he'll have to be smuggled past Mum, who's brandishing the hoover downstairs. Bet he's never seen a vacuum cleaner before, not if the state of Mr Collard's house was anything to go by. I decide against liberating him via the bedroom window. Cats can do somersaults in mid-air so they always land on their feet, but the newly-massive Bundy, anabolic-steroid abuser, would more likely crash through the yard straight into the earth's core, leaving behind a cat-shaped hole, like in cartoons. Too risky. There's nothing else for it; I'll have to stuff him in my shoplifter's bag and make a dash for the back door.

That's easy said. Squeezing a camel through the eye of a needle would be a doddle by comparison. I tip my worldly goods out of the rucksack and creep on tippytoes towards the slumbering Bundy. His ear swivels, which means he's just catnapping, the sly beast.

'Come on, Bundy. Don't give me any trouble,' I warn him. He does that hissing thing, displaying his pointy teeth on which countless rodents have come to grief. With the rucksack gaping open like a giant leather maw, I inch towards him. His body tenses, quadriceps quivering as he prepares to leap to safety. I make a grab for him. He springs into mid-air, using the mattress as a launch pad, and lands on the curtains, sinking his claws into the dralon, swinging dangerously. Like an obese trapeze artist, he stretches out his front leg and heaves himself on to the window frame, paws scrabbling madly on the glass. The top bit of the window's ajar, but surely he can't . . . Omigawd, he can! Bundy manages to squinch his body halfway through the little bitty window, where he wobbles before finding his balance. My heart lurches mouthwards. Bundy lets himself down inch by inch, using his front paws as brakes on the big pane, and hurls himself to the ground.

*Thud!*

I reach the window just in time to see him lick one of his pads, shake the dust off his coat and tootle off, not so much as a limp or a feline 'Fuck, that hurt!' yowl. If ever I needed proof that he's an other-worldly being, this is it. Bundy the Brave triumphs over fear and earthly gravity. My Trusty Sidekick lives!

I'm canny nervous as owt on the bus to work. So much has happened in the last couple of weeks, it feels as if I'm living twenty people's lives. Prioritise, that's what Mrs Marr's always telling me to do. Top of the in-tray is Ash's Big Event, which means putting

Dad in the pending tray. It's not as simple as it sounds, this prioritising lark.

'You're late,' squeaks Mrs Marr. Tell me something I don't know. 'I can't go on covering for you, Rowena. Your appraisal's coming up soon, I'll have to mention your timekeeping to Mr Crowther.'

'Snitch,' I mutter under my breath.

'What was that?' she snaps.

'Stitch.' I clutch my side and writhe in mock agony. 'I got my purse robbed last night with my bus pass in it so I had to run all the way to work. I've got stitch.'

'You poor thing, why didn't you say?' Because I've only just thought of it, Mrs M. 'Peppermint water, that's what you need.' No, what I *need* is for you to get off my friggin' case, woman. She fusses around in her handbag. 'No luck. But I've got some Polo mints, oh, and Rescue Remedy.' Pills and potions rattle around inside the bag. A jar of homeopathic tablets for sciatica and a tube of psoriasis cream roll on to the desk. Jesus, she's one step away from a crack dealer, and she's got the nerve to nag me about timekeeping!

'It's worn off now,' I assure her. 'I'd better go and brew up before the blokes stage a walkout.'

'Just a mo,' she flaps. 'You'll need some money.'

I swivel round. 'Eh?'

'Since your purse was, er, robbed. For bus fares, lunch and suchlike.'

'Oh, right.' Never look a gift horse in the mouth, even if it's got a sunbed tan the colour of nicotine.

'Five pounds?' she offers. I shrug. 'Ten? If you need more I'll have to borrow it out of petty cash.'

'I'll go a tenner. Cheers.' Some people just beg to be taken advantage of.

Dean's in the staff room making the coffees, like the men might shrivel up with dehydration if it's a measly half hour late.

'Any news?' I whisper. 'Have you heard any more about Ash?'

'The opener's on at ten,' he says, meaning the inquest. 'It'll be adjourned, but if there's no suspicious circumstances they'll release his body to the family today.'

My legs start to shake. 'Are you sure he's coming to Crowther's?'

'Yeah, for deffo. The old boys' network crap. Crowther told Ray to give the stiffmobile an extra coat of turtle-wax.' I glower at him. 'Sorry, I didn't mean—'

'Show some respect, you sicko.' A golf ball lodges in my throat. My eyes blink like a strobe light to keep the tears back.

'Sorry, Rowena. I wasn't thinking. Look, that crazy scheme you told me about the other day – tell me you weren't serious.'

I put on my rock-hard face. 'Deadly serious. You can't bottle it now, Dean. You *promised*. As good as. Everything's arranged.'

'But—'

I do my industrial-strength frown. 'We've done all the "buts". There's no going back, it's planned down to the minutest detail. We just want to pay our last respects to Ash.'

'Yes, but—'

'If you say that word once more, you'll get a smack in the mouth. I don't need this grief, Dean. Just do what we agreed, right? It'll be cool.'

He stares at me for a long time. I'm having a tough job holding it together.

'Oh, go on then,' he agrees reluctantly. 'It's your funeral.'

Whatever tenterhooks are, I'm on them, big-time. My nerves are pinging with anticipation. No matter how convinced Dean is (and I'm not convinced that he's convinced), there's still shitloads of things that could go wrong, particularly when you're dealing with emotional disturbos. They're a top bunch, the Madolescents, but they're only reliable up to a point. All it needs is for one of them to be in a hyper phase – or a depressive or paranoid or irrational one, it makes no odds – and the whole fragile edifice of Ash's Big Event could come toppling down. I'll just have to keep my fingers crossed that they've taken their medication.

It's canny busy at work today. All four chapels are on the go non-stop so I'm running around like an eejit with the air freshener and providing drinks of water for the bereaved, as well as making sure the tissues don't run out. That's in addition to my usual duties of prepping remains for viewing and being what Mr Scudamore calls Staff Catering Supervisor, i.e. tea person. It's all 'Rowena, can you do this?' or 'Rowena, leave that for now, this is more important,' until I want to scream, 'Fuck's sake, I've only got *two* pairs of hands!' But I don't, obviously.

It's the waiting that's driving me mad. The not knowing. What if the coroner decides Ash's death was suspicious and won't release him to the Mallisons? It could take a month for the bizzies to complete their inquiries, by which time my nerves will have frazzled totally and they'll have to scrape me in splats off the ceiling.

By lunchtime I'm in ruins, barely able to speak.

'You look like shit,' says Dean, bucking me up no end. 'What's it to be – a spliff or a Bailey's?'

'B-b-both,' I stutter. 'And make 'em b-b-big ones.'

No sooner have I floated back to the office than Mrs Marr's at me. Someone should tell her not to squeak until she's squoken to.

'Thank heavens you're back, Rowena. We're completely out of water.' She makes it sound like a global drought, or at least a hosepipe-ban situation. Talk about turning a drama into a crisis.

'And?'

'And? *And?*' she blusters. 'And we need some more, of course. We're stowed out this afternoon with families coming to view. Run down to Kwik Save and get six bottles – the still ones, not that sparkling stuff.'

'What's up with tap water? It won't poison anybody.'

'Cus-to-mer care, Rowena,' she says, emphasising each syllable as if she's explaining astrophysics to a cretin. 'Other firms may provide tap water if they choose, but mineral water is what gives us our competitive edge, sets Crowther's apart from the common herd. Now come along, look lively.'

She slips me a tenner out of petty cash and practically shoos me out of the door. I truly can't be arsed to schlep down the shop and back, not with this incipient cannabis/Bailey's headache. What's so great about spring water anyway? It's polluted with countryside rubbish – rabbit pellets, cuckoo spit, ramblers' urine. Why bother shelling out for bottles, when we have genuine Northumbrian water specially piped in? As soon as I'm out of Mrs Marr's eyeshot, I nip round the back and exhume some plastic bottles out of the garbage, then fill them up from the receiving room tap and stick them in the fridge. If it's good enough for washing their loved ones, the families can't object to drinking it. All water tastes the same when it's chilled, anyway.

'That was quick,' beams Mrs Marr. 'I'm sorry if I snapped at you earlier, Rowena. I've just changed my HRT tablets and I'm not sure they suit,' she confides, like I give a shit. 'I might have to go back to the ones made with pregnant mares' urine.'

'Yeah, right.' Disgusting old witch.

'My goodness,' she goes, spotting my Purple Rain glitter nail extensions. 'They're bobby-dazzlers. I don't know how you can work with nails that long. Better not let Mr Crowther see them. By the way, where's the change from the water? Did you remember the receipt? I like to keep a running tally of the petty cash.'

'I gave them to you in your hand,' I go, all innocent-like. 'Your left hand, I think it was. Yes, definitely the left one.'

Her face turns the colour of haemorrhoids. She flusters round the desk, picking things up and putting them down again. 'My memory – it's like a colander,' she groans, fanning herself with the *Funeral Service Journal*.

'You want to see your GP,' I advise. 'Score some of that horse-piss gear.'

I know the dozy old bint isn't listening. She's too busy perfecting her headless chicken routine. Dean strolls into reception to check out the Deaths column in the local rag.

'Any news yet?' I grab his arm and drag him through to Number One chapel. 'About the inquest?'

He whacks me on the bum with the rolled-up newspaper. 'Fuck all. Oops, no offence, mate,' he says to the old gadge in the coffin.

I rattle his shoulder. 'Look, let me know the second you hear anything, right? Wherever I am, find me.'

'Yus, ma'am,' goes Dean, doing that stupid saluting thing. He twitches his nostrils. 'A bit of air freshener wouldn't go amiss in here. Nothing personal, like,' he says to the deceased.

I bundle him out of the door. He's right, we have a whiffy-stiff situation on our hands. Me, I'm used to the pong of death, but the bereaved prefer to snort synthetic pot pourri or forest glade up their nostrils. I shake the can of Haze but it's nearly empty, only a pathetic little *phhttt* comes out. Typical! There's no refills in the cupboard either, only some old cheapo shite that should have been hoyed out centuries ago. We're supposed to use the dry air freshener, see, as the wet type dribbles and stains the furniture. Oh well, it can't hurt just this once. The can's so ancient it's rusting round the rim but I shake it like a maniac to swirl the ingredients up, then aim it at the ceiling and press the squirt button. A jet of foul-smelling liquid shoots out. It stinks rancid, worse than stale sweat, and I dodge out of the way of the falling droplets. Now I'll have to use *twice* as much proper stuff to get rid of the vile pongo. More haste, less speed, as Nana Vincent used to say.

When I get back from the supplies cupboard with the Haze, the stench in the chapel nearly knocks me flat. It stinks like wet goats tethered to a radiator. Pinching my nose, I spray nearly a whole can of the good stuff around the room. My throat's on fire, and sore from retching. That's when I notice the deceased. His face looks as if it's melting. Trickles of brown liquid run down the cheeks, settling like mud in the creases round the mouth. Oh, triffic, the gone-off air freshener must have drifted down on him like acid rain and reacted with something in the Permaglow. His face is covered in two-tone patches, like a disastrous Michael Jackson job. *Just* what I need, not!

It takes a couple of scrubbings with antibacterial Fairy Liquid to get him anywhere near human. Mr Scudamore's very particular about setting the features in an expression of peaceful repose, but this poor bloke looks as if he's stared into the jaws of hell. I squeeze and pinch and mould, but short of an instant collagen injection, there's not much I can do. The old boy's doomed to meet his maker with a face like a smacked arse. The sound of shuffling feet and hushed conversation outside warns me that the family's arrived, so I hide behind the door and scuttle out when they enter without anyone spotting me.

It's only when I'm safely in the staff room that I notice two of my nail extensions are missing. Oh, fuck.

The door swings open. 'You're here,' says Dean. 'I've been looking all over.'

'Any news?' Please God, make something go right.

'Yeah. All's cool, inquest opened and adjourned, no dodgy circumstances. We're collecting him tomorrow, funeral's on Wednesday.'

'Wicked!' I hug him in a non-sexual manner. 'That means I can get on and organise things now. Should we go for an eight o'clock kick-off?'

Dean screws up his face in an expression of mental anguish. 'Don't go through with this, Rowena. Please. I've got a real bad feeling about it.'

'Scaredy-cat.' I peck him on the cheek. 'Eight o'clock it is. I'll tell the crew.'

'When's the big day then, you pair of lovebirds?' Ray saunters up and slaps Dean on the back. 'And before you ask, of course I'll be your best man, mate.'

Dean stares at Ray over the top of his specs. 'What the fuck are you on about?' he says.

'There's no secrets in this place,' says Ray, tapping the side of his nose. 'Big box just arrived at reception, addressed to Ms Vincent here. From Perfect Day.'

The wedding gown!

I push past him and run round to the front office. Mrs Marr glowers at me. She's got a face on her like a bag of spanners. Mr Crowther's showing some people out of the door.

'In my office, Rowena,' he snaps, without looking at me. 'Now, please.' Uh-oh.

'If it's about the water . . .' I begin.

Mr Crowther pulls out the chair and sits me down, then closes the office door.

'Place your hands on the desk. Palms down.' He examines the eight false nails and two chewed stumps, then looks me in the eyeballs. 'Would you say this is *appropriate* wear for work?' The words come spitting out like shotgun pellets.

I shrug. 'Suppose not. Only once they're on, it's hard to get them off.'

Mr Crowther reaches into his pocket. 'But not *impossible*.' He deposits two nail extensions on to the blotter. They glitter purply, like an accusation. 'Exhibit A,' he says grimly.

The word according to Mr Crowther is that the grieving family, once they'd recovered from choking on air freshener, got very distressed about the deceased's facial expression. Apparently it reminded them of a soul in torment. They also demanded to know about the unsightly brown stains around the mouth. While Mrs Marr tried to pacify them in reception with glasses of water – yikes! – Mr Scudamore went in to rearrange the features. His first thought was that the bloke had some terrible undiagnosed illness that only showed post-mortem. It wasn't until he found a nail extension in the bloke's hair, and another one on the pillow, that the trail led to yours truly.

'This is an official verbal warning,' Mr Crowther's saying. 'It will be recorded on your personnel file.'

I pick at my two raggy finger ends, rolling the dried adhesive into tiny snotlike balls which I wipe on the underside of the chair.

'I hope you realise the seriousness of this, Rowena,' Mr Crowther goes on. 'You should consider yourself fortunate to work in an old-established family firm. In today's funeral services market, all multinational conglomerates and cowboys, wicker caskets and plastic headstones, we small independent businesses have to try that much harder. It's imperative that we maintain the highest professional standards. Do you understand?'

I nod dumbly.

Mr Crowther stares at me and sighs. 'Good. Let's hope you do,' he says. 'I'm placing you under enhanced supervision for the next four weeks, which means that Mrs Marr will be monitoring your output and identifying possible training needs. We'll agree a set of measurable targets and review progress in a month. Understood?'

'Yeah.' Could you just run that by me in English? 'I guess.'

'And I expect to see your fingernails as nature intended from now on.'

I shrug. 'Whatever.'

He shows me into the front office, shaking his head.

The petty cash tin's open on the reception desk. Mrs Marr's tapping like fury on a calculator and scratching her perm with a red biro.

'I can't get it to balance,' she flusters. 'Are you sure you settled up with me for that water?'

'Course I did,' I lie. 'Tried looking in your purse? Or the wastepaper bin? You'll probably remember when you're not thinking so hard. Hormonal imbalance plays funny tricks with the mind.'

'Hmm. Perhaps you're right, Rowena.' She locks the cashbox and puts it away. I can see red ink on her scalp where she's been scratching with the pen. 'Did Mr Crowther give you a dressing down?' she whispers.

'What?'

'Mr Crowther, has he had you on the carpet?'

'He never touched me. Just gave me a bit bollocking.'

'Hmm.' The old bat's miles away, probably fantasising about Crowther having *her* on the carpet. Gerr-oss!

I drum my fingers on the desk. 'Has anything arrived for me? A parcel?' I can't believe she hasn't mentioned it yet.

She smacks her forehead. 'Oh my goodness, my mind's gone completely! Yes, of course.' She heaves a box out from under the desk. 'I'm bursting to hear all about it.'

The box is white, with gold swirly writing. *Exquisite Bridalwear*, it says. *For Your Perfect Day*. No point pretending it's from Mandy Sweeney's catalogue, then.

Mrs Marr leans her bosoms on the desk, showing three inches of wrinkly cleavage. 'Aren't you going to open it? Oh, Rowena, this is so exciting. I never knew you and Dean were that serious.'

'Me and Dean?' I go. '*Me*? And *Dean*?'

'Well, it's addressed to Ms Rowena Vincent. And I'm not one to listen to office gossip, as you know, but I understood that you and Dean . . . So I thought . . .'

I glare at her. 'You thought wrong then. It's for Mum. She couldn't have it delivered to our house in case Fil— in case Bernard saw it. It's bad luck for the bridegroom to see the wedding dress before the day.' Like there's any worse luck than getting hitched to Filthy Luker.

'Oh. Of course.' Her face falls. 'She's getting married in white then, your mother?'

'Peach,' I say, as a picture of Ash's undies flashes into my mind.

'Peach, eh? Oh well,' she says, in a tone suggesting scarlet might have been a better choice.

Tucking the box under my arm, I march into the receiving room and stash it under the racks where the corpses are kept, covering it over with a body bag. Tomorrow I'll drape it on a coat hanger and leave it to smooth out. Don't want it creased to buggery like Princess Diana's wedding frock.

## 32

# Ash to Ashes

'Decided what you're wearing tomorrow night, Rowena?' Mum's hair's the colour of beetroot, a proper salon job by Sylvia of Kool Kutz.

'What?' My heart does a pogo inside my chest.

'For our Country and Western party at the Labour Club.'

Whew! I'd totally forgotten about that. It's such a painful prospect, Big G must have erased it from my mind.

'Promise me it won't be that leather porno get-up,' she says, meaning the Warrior Princess kit. 'I don't want you showing me and Bernard up in front of everybody.'

As if. 'I've hired something from the fancy-dress shop,' I lie. 'A cowperson outfit. Leather, denim, fringed shirt, all that. Don't fret, it'll be cool.'

'Are you bringing a friend?' What is this, *Fifteen-to-One*?

'Yeah. I asked Gemma Probert,' I fib.

'Let me show you some line dancing steps.' Mum rolls off her Marigold gloves and stands in front of the telly, thumbs tucked in her front jeans pockets. 'This is a grapevine. It's easy, look.' She shuffles her feet around in twisty knots and I pretend to watch, though really my brain's full-on thinking about Ash's Big Event.

'It's OK, we've been practising,' I tell her. 'Gemma rented that video, *Line Dancin' USA*. We can do all the moves.'

Mum plants a kiss on my forehead. 'Oh, Rowena, I'm so touched,' she says. 'You've made such a big effort lately. I'm really looking forward to tomorrow night. You should see Bernard's ten-gallon hat.'

'Can't wait.' Shame about the seven-pint brain. 'I'm turning in,

Mum, want to stay fresh for the party.'

'See you at the club then,' she says. 'Around eight?'

You'd have to rope me like a rogue steer to get me anywhere near that dump, and I'd rather pull my own intestines out than celebrate Mum's engagement to Filthy Luker.

'Count on it.' I give a thumbs-up sign. 'See you later, Mum.'

I sneak the phone up to my room, wedge the door shut with a chair, and dial Gemma Probert's number. It rings for ages. Come on, come on, why doesn't she answer? She's got no social life so she can't have gone out.

'Eh-oh.' About time too.

'Gem, is that you? You sound like Tinky Friggin' Winky.'

'Soh-ee.' Frantic chewing noises followed by a gulp. 'That's better. I was just having a Battenburg cake while the chips are frying.'

'Listen, it's all on for tomorrow night. Be there for eight o'clock. Will you let the others know?'

Gemma belches the word 'bol-locks'. 'Yeah, sure.'

'Phone me at work if there's any problem, right?'

'Right. Gotta go, Rowena, the chip fat's boiling over. See ya.'

Sometimes you just have to trust people.

I reread the plan for Ash's Big Event, ticking items off the checklist. Nothing more I can do, except pack my kit for tomorrow night as there won't be time for me to come home first. I've decided to wear the Warrior Princess outfit. Even though Ash never got to see it, I know he'd approve. (Probably want to try it on himself.) All the accessories are chosen carefully, right down to the shade of lippy, Red for Danger kissproof lipstain.

Once everything's sorted, I slip into the purple teddy, spread out flat under the duvet and play Ash's tape on my Walkman, gazing at the fluorescent stick-on stars on the ceiling until my eyes get heavy and I feel myself drifting away.

*

'Is he here yet?' I arrive at work just after the men, fifty minutes before my usual start-time.

'Ray and Gerry are just off to collect him,' says Dean. There's an edge to his voice. I guess he's twitchy about tonight. 'You can't hang about here, Rowena, they'll suss there's something going on, especially with you coming in early. Stay in the front office, stick to the normal routine. If anybody gets a whiff of this, the gig's off, I'm telling you straight.'

My pet lip juts out. 'Fuck's sake, stop whingeing, Dean, you sound like my mum. Just let me know when Ash gets here.'

Already I can feel a bit tension headache coming on so I nip it in the bud with a couple of Solpadeines swilled down with medicinal brandy from the first aid chest. When Mr Scudamore bobs outside for a swift tab, I sneak into the receiving room and exhume the Perfect Day box from underneath the bunks, praying the mice haven't got at it. In the women's loo, I unpack the dress and drape it on a coat hanger which I hook over a tall bendy pipe behind the bog as the gown's too long to hang on the door. The Thai silk feels like angels' kisses against my cheek but I have to resist touching it in case it gets smeared with blusher. The dress is a hundred times more beautiful than I remember. My eyes fill up with hottish tears that spill over and run salty into my mouth as I slide a body bag over the gown. It feels like a desecration but I can't think of any other way to keep it clean.

On the way out, I pin a note on the door.

*Danger, Blocked Bog, V. Smelly. Plummer Sent For. Use Men's.*

'What's that about?' asks Dean.

'It's to stop Mrs Marr poking her nose in. The men's lav will have to be bisexual, just for today.'

'Oh, great.' He wrinkles his nose in disgust. 'He's here, by the way. Your mate. Just wheeled him into the receiving room.'

My bodily fluids turn to ice. 'Can I see him?'

'Not just yet. Mr Scudamore's doing the honours. I'll tip you the wink when he's finished.'

I clutch his sleeve. 'Dean, I'm scared. What if he looks . . . you know.' Swingers, as they're known in the trade, sometimes turn grey and have a pop-eyed chokey look that's hard to disguise.

'It's cool, Mr Scudamore's giving it large, the full VIP treatment. You know what he's like when it's for one of Crowther's mates.' He gives me a bit squeeze. My eyes cloud up and tears roll like raindrops down my cheeks. 'Let's go outside,' he says. 'This calls for Uncle Dean's Red Leb special.'

I'm still buzzing from the spliff an hour later when Dean gives me the nod.

'Number four,' he whispers. 'And don't hang about, the family's coming to view any minute. Want me to come in with you?'

I shake my cotton-wool head and float zombie-like to the chapel to see my beloved.

Too late! Mrs Marr's showing a man and woman into the room. She's doing what Ray calls her Uriah Heep act (they were an ancient rock band, or was that Judas Priest?), fussing and fannying around, practically licking the ground beneath their feet.

'This way, Mr Mallison, Mrs Mallison,' she squeaks, in her cut-glass soprano that makes her sound like the Queen on helium. Spotting me in the corridor, she jerks her head and rolls her eyes manically, meaning *Vamoose, pleb*, then treats the Mallisons to one of her pathetic half-smiles straight from the Grief Management manual. It's supposed to mean, *I Can't Begin to Imagine What You're Going Through But I Share Your Pain*, but it comes out as *I Dozed Off Under the Sunbed and I'm Suffering from Prickly Heat*. There's some murmuring and the sound of the coffin lid being slid open, then she scuttles out, closing the door quietly behind her.

'You're supposed to be covering reception,' she hisses, shooing me through to the front office. 'Stay put while I nip to the loo.'

'Use the men's,' I tell her. 'The women's bog's blocked, it stinks like a plague pit. I've called the plumber.'

She glares at me. Her mascara's smudged to buggery under one eye, she must have blinked while it was still wet. There'll be a major apeshit explosion when she realises she's been sucking up to Ash's parents looking like a droog. Shame there's no mirror in the bisexual bog.

'Sit! Stay!' she snaps, as if she's training an unruly puppy. 'And if Mr and Mrs Mallison come out, remember to be polite and respectful. No yawning, chewing, sighing or rolling your eyes to heaven. Got that?'

'Hang on, I'll write it down. What came after chewing?'

'You're incorrigible, Rowena!' She sighs and rolls her eyes to heaven, then teeters off to the bog. Mrs do-as-I-say-not-as-I-do Marr.

I'm flicking through Craddock's monumental stonemason's catalogue when Ash's folks come back into reception. Mr Mallison's tall, with a look of Richard Gere only seriouser. The wife's like her out of *Dead Man Walking* and *Thelma and Louise*, wossname, Susan Sarandon. She's wearing a cost-a-bomb brown suit, and she looks the type who's used to ordering servants about. I just manage to stop myself clicking my heels. Her eyes are a bit shiny but there's no way *her* mascara would run, it'll be Estée Lauder or Lâncome, one of those poshgit brands.

'I'd like a word with Mr Crowther.' She talks in a don't-fuck-with-me voice like that woman reporter off the telly who's always in war-torn Kosovo with bombs exploding behind her.

I try for a smile. 'He's been delayed up the hospital. May I be of assistance?'

She looks right through me, like I'm invisible. I don't know what she's got to be so high and mighty about. I want to give her a good shake and say, *I loved Ash and he loved me. You threw him out on to the streets. It's your fault he's dead, so don't come the grieving mother act with me.* She glances impatiently at her watch. 'Is Mr Crowther's deputy available?'

'Yes, that's I. Me. How may I help?'

Just then Mrs Marr toddles through, a hot flush mottling her turkeyneck.

'Mrs Mallison,' she coos in her insincere voice, elbowing me out of the way. 'I'll take over now, Rowena.' I stand there dumbly like a sack of spuds. '*Thank* you, Rowena,' she says through clenched teeth. 'Now, Mrs Mallison, how may I be of assistance?'

Mrs Mallison arches one eyebrow. 'Isn't there somewhere we can conduct business in private?'

Mrs Marr bows, scrapes and practically prostrates herself like a welcome mat in front of the Mallison gods as she shows them into Mr Crowther's office. She shoots me a poisonous glance though fuck knows what I'm supposed to have done wrong.

I can't earwig outside the door because at that moment the O'Hara clan and their snivelling brats bowl in mob-handed and park their backsides in the soft meeting area. Hefty O'Hara, local hardman, protection racketeer and smack baron, has come to view his kid brother Danny, who got offed in a drive-by shooting. Obviously the rellies have decided to start the wake early. The blokes are swigging Guinness out of bottles, the wifies are chainsmoking like beagles (Crowther would have a seizure!), and the sprogs are scoffing crisps and exploding the bags. They can get on with it. There's no way I'm interfering, I'd only get the blame for sparking off a gangland war, so I flick through Mrs Marr's *Take A Break* magazine and pretend to do a crossword.

The men have just started singing 'Danny Boy' in dodgy three-part harmony when Mrs Marr shows the Mallisons out of Mr Crowther's office. She looks horrified at the clump of bodies, like she's witnessing a mass murder scene (which she will be, if she interrupts the O'Haras' Farewell Gig Live In Newcastle).

'. . . *The pipes, the pipes are ca-a-lling . . .*'

'Leave it with me, Mrs Mallison,' she shouts into Ash's mum's shell-like. 'I'll arrange everything.'

Mr Mallison heads for the door, stepping nimbly over the O'Haras and trying to pretend he hasn't noticed them. I guess he's used to delicate operations, him being a surgeon and that.

'. . . *Then come ye ba-a-a-ack . . .*'

Triffic, the women have joined in now, all missing the high note by a mile on account of their gravelly smokers' voices.

The door clicks shut behind Mrs Mallison, releasing a vapour trail of Poème.

'. . . *Oh Danny boy, oh Danny boy, I lo-o-ve yo-o-u so-o-o-o-o.*'

'Clap,' I mutter to Mrs Marr out the side of my mouth. 'If you want to keep your kneecaps.'

She smiles through gritted dentures and pitty-pats her hands nervously.

'Why, the lady wants an encore so,' slurs Hefty O'Hara, dabbing his eyes with a hanky. 'Two, three, four . . .' Hefty counts them in and they launch into a tearful rendition of 'Galway Bay'.

'*If you ever go across the sea to Oireland . . .*'

I grab Mrs Marr's wrist. 'Jesus, is that the time? The men'll be gagging for a brew.' She glares murderously at me. 'Oh, by the way,' I say pleasantly, heading towards the back. 'I dig the one-eyed panda look.'

'. . . *and watch the sun go down on Galway Baaaaaay.*'

At last. Now I can spend some quiet time with Ash. I feel geet scared as owt when I open the door to number four chapel. Darling, darling Ash, my first and only lover. I'm here for you. *True Luv 4 Evva*. Inching towards the casket, not daring to breathe, I close my eyes and caress the sweet face of my beloved, the smooth golden skin I adore. My fingertips brush softly against – a nose ring!

I leap back, startled. Omigawd, it's Danny O'Hara! He of the tongue stud and shamrocked neck. The late Wildman of the West End went for tattoos and body piercing in a big way according to

Ray, who was scared to touch the villain, even *in extremis*, and had to peek through his fingers from a safe distance.

The sound of synchronised belching heralds the arrival of the O'Hara posse so I scurry out of the chapel into the receiving room. Dean's pumping the arm of an old biddy to ease the stiffness and help the embalming fluid circulate. I tug his sleeve frantically.

'Where's Ash? Dean, what's happened to Ash?'

Dean stops jiggling the woman's arm. 'Moved him to number one,' he says. 'But you can't go in.'

'Why not?' I say a bit hysterically.

'Some bloke's in there. Mrs Mallison's hairdresser. She ordered a shampoo and trim, apparently.'

'No!' My voice comes out as a scream. 'I wanted to do his hair! Now it'll never back-comb into a bouffant, and the veil won't sit right.'

'Divven't cop a strop,' warns Dean. 'Otherwise the whole thing's off.' I can tell by his eyes that he means it.

I take a deep breath through my nose. 'OK, the haircut's cool,' I say calmly. 'Nilo problemo. But hey, Dean, give me a nudge next time you skin up.' At this rate I'll be a friggin' dope-head before the day's out.

Ash has been here for hours, and I'm so desperate to see him it's driving me mental. To top it all, Mrs Bloody Marr says I'm to work on the front desk all afternoon.

'Why can't I work in the back? We're not exactly overrun with customers. Why can't I? *Why*?' Jesus, I sound like a five year old.

Mrs Marr taps out some numbers on the calculator. 'It's just a temporary lull, Rowena. Take your feet off the desk and get on with some filing while I try to figure out the petty-cash discrepancy.'

'I'll do the filing tomorrow, honest. Please let me work in the back, please.' Go on, Rowena, humiliate yourself. '*Please*.'

'In case you'd forgotten,' says Mrs Marr, her face set in a concrete pinch, 'you're under enhanced supervision. That means you'll do what I tell you to do, and I'm telling you to do the filing. Now.'

I lean my elbows on the desk and gaze up into Mrs Marr's nostrils. 'Please. I'm begging you. Let me go and work in the back, just for half an hour.'

'You'll do that filing,' she barks. 'The subject's not up for discussion.'

*Ping!* Something snaps inside my head.

'You vindictive old cow!' I shriek. 'You bloody bitch! Just because I never said your mascara had run.'

'Rowena! For God's sake . . .!'

I seize the nearest thing, which happens to be the petty-cash box, and hurl it across the room. It crashes into the yucca plant, keys, coins, notes and receipts flying all over.

'You dried-up old witch!' I scream. 'You look about a hundred. I'd rather eat my own liver than turn out like you.' I grab the metal hole-punch, brandishing it above her head in a threatening manner. Mrs Marr crouches under the desk, cowering and shaking, shielding her panda eyes with her hands. Next thing, I'm bashing the hole-punch against the framed public-liability certificate on the far wall, showering shattered glass on to the banquette.

'You're insane!' shrieks Mrs Marr. 'You're mentally deranged!'

I'm kicking the shit out of the magazine rack when Mr Scudamore bursts through, all in a lather. The old bat must have pressed the panic button under the desk.

'*You!*' I yell, pointing at her with the sign of Satan and flashing the evil eye. 'Yes, *you*, bitch! You're dead!'

'Holy Mary Mother of God,' she babbles, crossing herself. '*Do* something, Edgar – she's possessed!'

'Blow it out your snatch!' I holler.

Just then, the door opens, and in walks Mr Crowther, followed by Mr and Mrs Mallison.

Oh, fuck.

So here I am, out of a job, out of my tree, wide awake on the bed, trying to block the disastrous day out of my mind. Trust me to lose it just when I most needed to keep a grip. I don't even blame Mrs Power-Crazed Bloody Marr, though she didn't help matters, obviously.

No, it's all down to Rowena M. Vincent. M as in Mad. As in Madder Than Logs. What's eating me? Why can't I act normal, stay in control? My head feels constantly about to burst – I'm a walking pressure cooker, a time bomb, an exploding microwave oven.

I wish I was dead.

My Swatch says six o'clock. Dean should be home now. I tap out his number on the phone.

'Kate Fairley speaking.' It's the same voice as the one on the answering machine. Maybe they've changed the announcement. 'Hello,' it says. 'Hello.'

This throws me. 'Are you a human person?' I don't give my name in case it's a CIA trick.

'Who is this?' the voice says sharply.

'Is Dean there? Tell him it's Row— Tell him it's Gemma.' There's some muffled noises while she puts her hand over the phone and calls Dean.

'Yeah? Rowena, is that you?'

'How did you know? I told your mum I was Gemma.'

He sniffs. 'She said it was someone with an identity crisis, so I took a lucky guess. How are you?'

'Cool. I'm cool. Look, Dean, we need to fix up about tonight. I'll meet you at the receiving-room door just before eight, right? Don't be late, best not keep the Madolescents waiting.'

There's a long silence.

'Dean? Still there, Dean?'

He does this exasperated sigh thing. 'What is this, *Death Wish III*? There's no way, spacemonkey. It was a mad idea in the first place, but after the way you kicked off today . . . Anyway, you're barred from the premises.'

Oh, triffic. 'Who's to know?' I say. 'It'll just be a simple, quiet ceremony, Ash's friends paying their last respects. We'll be in and out in an hour, no one will ever know we've been.'

'Can't be done, babes. End of story.'

My words come out in a mad babble. 'But, Dean, that wedding dress cost me the best part of a grand. We can't just leave it to rot in the women's bog. And I never even got to see Ash. Please, Dean, I have to say a proper goodbye to him. Otherwise—'

'Otherwise what?'

I sniffle and snuffle in a choked fashion.

'Otherwise *what*, Rowena?' He's on the hook, I need to reel him in dead careful.

I let out a long painful sigh. 'Don't ask me to spell it out, Dean. Just say goodbye and hang up now, if that's what you want.'

'Fuck's sake, Rowena, this is blackmail.'

'No, Dean. This is goodbye.' I do a couple of dramatic gulps for effect. 'You've been a good mate. Promise you won't grieve for me. Oh, and you're not to feel guilty, right?'

'Hang on, hang on. Christ, I could be locked up just for thinking about this.' My life ticks away as Dean's braincogs chug in silence.

'OK, you win,' he says at last. 'I'll meet you there in an hour.'

*Plop.* He lands flapping in my net.

'Cool, man. See ya.'

*Yessss!*

There's a rap on my bedroom door.

'Rowena, are you in there?' Mum pokes her head round. 'Why aren't you getting ready for the party?' It's only when I see her kit that I remember about the line dancing/engagement shindig at the club. She's a nightmare vision in blue denim and, Omigawd, it's that stonewashed shite! A shirt, full skirt with an inch of white petticoat showing, white cowboy boots, and a Stetson. Can this be the woman from whose loins I sprang?

'I'm getting dressed round Gemma's.'

'Well?' Mum twirls round. 'How do I look?'

Like a reject from a Klondike cathouse. 'You look fab, Mum, you really do.'

'Whaah, thank y'all,' she goes, pushing the brim of her Stetson back with two fingers. 'So long then, pardner. Oh, by the way, we've invited a few people round here afterwards so make sure you flush the toilet.'

'Puh-leeze!'

In a few hours, the world will know that Mum and her vile boyfriend are officially engaged to be married. In a month's time she'll sign her own living death warrant and become Mrs Filthy Puker-Luker. Then there'll be no turning back. They'll be moving on to a Barratt's estate, living in a poncey shoebox with swag curtains and Austrian blinds. Filthy will invite the neighbours round for barbies, pretending to be Chef from *South Park*. He'll have Celine Dion blasting out of the speakers till all hours, deafening the place out. They'll be pointed out in the street as 'those Lottery winners', filthy rich but common.

Jesus, it's too painful to think about. Fortunately I'll be long gone by that time.

I pull the jigsaw puzzle box from under the bed and take out the Mother's Day card from Dad. *Much love, Lonnie.* Dad wrote that. There might be some of his DNA in the ink. Maybe scientists could clone a new Dad – no, that wouldn't work, he'd come out as a baby. I want my real grown-up dad, the one I hardly remember.

As I put the card back, I discover something else in the big pink envelope. It's a photo. A picture of three men holding pint glasses up to the camera. On the back, in Dad's writing, it says '*Toasting Joyce. Bloomsday, Cork Street, Dublin.*' It's dated two years ago, just before Nana Vincent died.

A burning sensation shoots up my body. My head starts to fizz. I can't control my hands, they're trembling like bastards.

Dad! My dad's alive! And he's in Ireland. Maybe.

I try to study the faces but the outlines go all fuzzy and silver shapes float like giant snowflakes in front of my eyes.

Which one is Dad?

Who's Joyce? Why isn't she in the photo?

I check the clock radio. 19.02. Jesus, must get my skates on, daren't keep the Madolescents waiting. I stuff the photo in my rucksack and head off to Crowther's for Ash's Big Event.

Laid out in his coffin, Ash looks peaceful, and *so*, so beautiful, even before I apply his make-up. Mr Scudamore's done a fabbo job, you have to look really hard for the faint bruising on the neck. Ash's eyes have been gummed shut, the lids fringed by thick black lashes. I'm still pissed off about the haircut, it'll need all my creative styling flair to shush it up, but Mrs Marr's hotbrush should do the trick.

Dean's so anxious that nothing goes pear-shaped, he's appointed himself operations manager in charge of logistics (whatever they are). He's in the receiving room supervising the Madolescents while I'm prepping Ash in number one chapel. It needs to be organised like a military operation, so obviously I can't afford to be sidetracked by mundane details, disco lighting and suchlike.

My task is to prepare the bride for his big day.

Ash's skin is so soft and flawless, there's no need for foundation, but I pat on translucent powder so his T-zone won't shine on the video, followed by a light shimmering of bronze under the cheekbones. This is one bride who *won't* be blushing naturally. I pluck out a few stragglers to tidy up his eyebrows – he doesn't even wince or get watery eyes – then highlight just below the browbone with Silver Pearl. Poking about in the make-up tray, I find the Terracotta Crème which I apply to his eyelids, blending outwards from the corners, and draw a soft crease line above the eye socket in African Violet pencil, smudging it artistically with a cotton bud. A touch of browny-black eyeliner next, not that he needs it in real life, but it shows out better on camera. To finish off the eyes, I brush on two coats of ebony mascara with lash-thickening fibres.

I lean close and kiss his cold mouth, trying to slip my tongue between his lips, but they've been sewn up from the inside. It's a trick of the trade, a procedure to stop the deceased from gaping, involving a needle inserted through the nostrils. Mr Scudamore did it for the best, I'm sure, but the downside is I can't French kiss my lover one last time. I try licking his sexy lips but it leaves a bitter chemical taste on my tongue. Remembering the way Ash showed me, I outline his mouth with a tawny pencil and colour it in with two coats of Warm Apricot.

'You look gorgeous, Ash,' I tell him. 'If only you could see yourself.'

After squirting on some spray gel and scrunch-drying his hair, I give it as much body as I can with Mrs Marr's hotbrush. Finally I backcomb it and tease it into place with my fingers, setting it with a light mist of shine booster.

Dean pops his head round the door. He looks majorly harassed.

'How much longer? It's like a friggin' madhouse back there.'

'Give me a hand with the dress, then we're ready to rock.'

It takes some manoeuvring to slide the wedding gown on, but Ash looks totally breathtaking. Seed pearls and bugle beads glitter like tiny stars on the bodice, and the sweetheart neckline is really flattering considering the lack of bosoms. The tapering sleeves make his hands seem elegant and feminine. But the crowning glory is the gossamer-fine veil, wispy and delicate as a butterfly's wings.

'How does he look?' I ask Dean.

Dean does a low whistle. 'Fantastic. I'm gobsmacked, Rowena. I thought he'd be grotesque, a Bride of Frankenstein thing, but he looks almost like . . .'

'A real bride?' I offer.

'Yeah. It's bizarre.' Dean goggles at Ash in pure amazement, as if he can't tear his eyes away, until the raucous noises from the receiving room snap him back to reality. 'What the fuck are they up to now? Go and tart yourself up, let's get this fiasco over before my nerves are shot to pieces.'

A cheer goes up as I make my entrance into the receiving room, dressed as *Rowena: Warrior Princess*. Mickey leers at my boobs, doing a rumpy-pumpy action with his fists and waggling his tongue snakily, like he's in with a chance. At least he's washed his hair, which is something, and his Megadeth vest looks cleanish, but his jeans are so ripped to shreds, I dread to think what's holding them together. The Madolescents have all made an effort, I realise. Gemma's wearing a Marilyn Manson T-shirt and fringed hippy skirt, Coralie's in a black halter top and silver Spandex kecks, and Reuben – what a transformation! He's gone for the total NY Club Kid look, a spider's web sloppy top, latex pedal-pushers and stilettos, plus he's Gothed out on make-up and purple-moussed hair. I feel suddenly overcome.

Mickey hands me a Red Stripe from a mountain of cans. 'You look the mutt's nuts,' he slurs, swilling down a couple of yellow pills with Special Brew. 'Sup up, we're celebrating.'

A frown digs itself into my forehead. 'Celebrating? Is that what you call it?'

'No point getting doomy, we might as well make the most of it. We're celebrating Ash's life – and afterlife.' Mickey scratches his curls. 'And it's a bit special for me too. I've decided to get out of this godforsaken shithole. Me and Zed, that bloke in the Transit, we're off to Manchester, start a new life where nobody knows about our scummy past.'

'Mickey, that's brilliant! Ee, I'm made up for you.' Without thinking, I slap a kiss on his mouth.

He wriggles away, embarrassed. I knew he was all talk. 'Here, take your pick, top gear, this.' He offers me a polythene bag rattling with pills and capsules of every colour.

I hesitate. 'Maybe later, Mickey.' Maybe not. I intend to keep my head together, at least until it's all over.

Gemma waddles over bearing a paper plate stacked with brown stuff. 'Hope you don't mind, I declared the buffet open, something to soak the beer up.'

I decide to pass on the vile veggie scran, don't want to risk an attack of flatulence.

'Thanks, Gem. You've really made a good job of the room, all the balloons and streamers.'

'Yeah,' she says between munches. 'And the disco lights take the edge off the spookiness. There aren't any corpses in here, are there?'

'Hell, no,' I lie, as Dolly Parton's 'Jolene' blares from the speakers. Gemma and I stick our tongues out and mug daft faces as Coralie points her dad's camcorder at us.

'Hey, what about that Reuben?' squeals Coralie. 'Doesn't he look a total babe? He's got me all of a wag, narmean?'

We turn to look at Reuben at the tape decks, dancing jerkily and lip-synching to 'Jolene'. He's got that spacey expression I know so well. Come to think of it, so has everyone else. Uh-oh. Mickey's been doing the rounds with his bag of tricks. Just then, I feel a sharp tug on my hair. It's Dean, doing that furious eyebrow thing.

'Tell spaceboy to turn the volume down. I can't get through to him, fuck knows what he's on. Ask me, they're all off their tits.' He surveys the room anxiously.

I thump his arm. 'Party pooper, don't you like Dolly Parton?'

'That's not the point. He's got it cranked up so loud, they'll hear it in Gateshead.'

'Good, they could use a bit of culture. Come on, Dean, chill. Have some lentils.' I shove a wodge of brown gloop into his mouth. He's not amused.

'Rowena, don't fuck about. My job's on the line here, so do whatever mad shit you came to do and get these psychos out.'

'All right, don't have a cow, man,' I say in my Bart Simpson voice.

'Everyone's clued up about what's happening, there won't be any aggro. Find Mickey, he'll help you to bring Ash in, then we can start.'

Dean opens his mouth to protest but I silence him with a kiss, a smoochy deep-tongue job. It never fails.

'Trust me,' I say, popping another can of Red Stripe.

Somehow, without saying a word, everyone knows the gig's about to kick off. The air's fizzing with electric anticipation. Reuben puts on a tape of moody Gregorian chants, and the disco lights slow right down. Gemma sparks up the joss sticks and a load of candles she's borrowed from the Hill o' Beans. Behind me, Coralie whirrs the camcorder. Then, from out of the darkness, Dean and Mickey wheel in the coffin. As the lights flash to reveal Ash lying in his wedding finery, there's an intake of breath from Gemma, followed by a religious-type hush. Even Dean seems awed by the atmosphere, clasping his hands and bowing his head. Mickey walks towards me, hands outstretched, and leads me to the casket. Over his Megadeth vest he's wearing a white collar turned back to front, like a vicar. The monks' chanting stops. We stand like statues in the velvety silence.

'Dearly beloved,' intones Mickey. 'We are gathered here today for two reasons. Firstly, to say goodbye to our friend Ash Mallison. We knew Ash was troubled – well, we're all pretty disturbed, that's why we're in therapy, otherwise we wouldn't have met each other in the first place.'

'Get on with it,' snaps Gemma.

'We knew he was troubled,' Mickey picks up, 'and although he was too far gone mentally to be saved, we can comfort ourselves with the thought that he's found peace at last.' He pauses to take a swig of Special Brew, then stifles a belch out of respect for the departed.

'Disgusting pig,' snorts Gemma.

'The second reason we're here today,' Mickey continues, 'is to celebrate the fact that before he topped— Before he was taken at such an untimely, er, time, Ash found happiness, albeit shortlived, with our sister, Rowena.' *Sister?* He squeezes my hand and grins beerily at my chest. 'So let us join together and bless their union.'

Gemma claps her hands excitedly, then stops in embarrassment. 'Shit, sorry,' she mutters.

'Normal marriages are kaput when death does them part,' explains Mickey. 'But for Ash and Rowena, love transcends mere mortality.'

From the corner of my eye, I see Dean checking his watch.

'Step forward, Rowena.' Mickey takes both my hands in his sweaty ones. 'Who giveth this woman away, like?'

'Forget that bit,' I hiss. We hadn't rehearsed it and this is no time for ad-libs.

'No-no-no-no-no,' splutters Mickey. You've got to be give . . . guv . . . goven—'

'Me.' Dean strides up impatiently. 'I'll give her away.' I can tell from his voice he's ready to blow.

'Cheers, mate.' Mickey swallows another throatful of lager. He takes my hand and lays it on Ash's cold one. 'Do you, Rowena, take Ash to be your loving partner for life, even beyond death? Will you cherish his thingummy, memory, keeping yourself only unto him so help you God?'

A frog lodges in my throat. 'I will.' I can sense Dean squirming.

'And do you, Ash, take Rowena's love with you into the afterlife, via Limbo if aclipp . . . ablicc . . .'

'Applicable,' Dean chips in tersely.

'Yeah, that thing. Where was I? Oh, Limbo, right. Fuckit, Ash, you know what I'm trying to say. So, do you?'

An awkward silence descends, saved only by the drone of the camcorder.

'Well, do you, mate, or what?' Mickey's further gone than I thought.

'I do-do-do-do.' A voice echoes spookily through the room, followed by howls of feedback. I glance up to see Reuben swinging the DJ's mic.

'Thank *you*,' says Mickey. 'I now pronounce you, erm, corpse and wife. You may kiss the bride.'

I cup Ash's face in my hands and gently kiss his lips.

'OK, you bunch of loonies,' yells Mickey, 'let's partaaaaaaay!'

It's all a bit of a blur after that. I'm sure Mickey spiked my lager, I'd only drunk about six cans so it couldn't have been the booze. Memories come and go in waves. I definitely remember Reuben and Coralie getting it on in the bisexual bog because my feet got tangled in her Spandex kecks and I fell headlong into the cubicle where Gemma was puking lentils into the toilet. I sort of recall bumping into Mickey coming out of the chapel where Danny O'Hara was resting in peace, and maybe my mind's playing tricks, but I had the impression Mickey was zipping up his flies. I vaguely recollect Dean slamming me against the wall and yelling hysterically that the mad bastards had better get the fuck out, now!

What I *don't* remember is how the fire started.

It might have been the candles. Or the disco lights, the tape rig – anything. When everyone's buzzing on farmer's cuticles, accidents happen.

Watch a movie like *Backdraft* and you think, yeah, it's all special effects, computerised balls of fire rolling like buggery along the ceiling, great blazing gusts of flame in hi-tech 3-D animation. It couldn't happen like that in real life, right?

Wrong.

See, Dean and me, we're having a bit of a domestic in the corridor. He doesn't exactly strike me, but he's so mad it could be next on the agenda.

'They're going berserk through there, running a-fuckin'-mok, screaming their heads off. Get them out!' he yells, his eyes flashing with fury.

'It's a wake,' I explain. 'It's supposed to be noisy – to wake the deceased.'

'I'm deadly serious, Rowena,' he hollers, shaking me like a rag doll. 'Go and round the fuckwits up and tell them to get the fuck out, now!'

That's when the fire alarm sounds. Whew, I'm thinking, saved by the bell. Then the sprinklers go off. For some reason I start to giggle, a chemical reaction from the spiked drink, probably. My legs turn to jelly and I collapse in a heap, clutching my stomach, roaring with inappropriate laughter. Dean, wild-eyed and furious, grabs me by the armpits and drags me through to the receiving room. Jesus, it's total mayhem!

The empty coffins stacked against the back wall are well ablaze, sheets of flame roaring and licking up to the ceiling, as hot as a crematorium furnace. Clouds of acrid black smoke spiral upwards, dense and choking. Omigawd, where are the Madolescents!

I spot Reuben first. He's majorly out of his head, dancing beneath a sprinkler, his face stained bilberry from the dribbling purple hair-mousse. Ignoring the inferno, Coralie skips round him with the camcorder, her mascara smudged into clown's tears, capturing his bizarre performance art on video.

'Ash? Where's Ash?' I scream, as Dean hauls me kicking across the floor.

Tongues of flame shoot across the ceiling. Suddenly there's a deafening roar and the room's illuminated by the fires of Hades. Then I see where Ash is. Or was. The Thai silk wedding gown has turned into a fireball, the coffin a blazing funeral pyre.

Ash to ashes.

'Christ, there's Gemma!' I shriek. 'Dean, help her!' Gemma, her face as black as the devil's arse, her bare breasts bobbing, is furiously trying to beat out the flames with her Marilyn Manson T-shirt. Then I realise why she's so frantic. Mickey, his acid perm scorched to stubble, is rolling around under the table, screaming in agony, his Megadeth vest ablaze.

'Get out!' Dean bellows. 'Get out quick, before the whole friggin' lot goes up!'

'But Gemma! Mickey!' I scream dementedly.

Dean shoves me towards the door. 'I'll see to them. Just go!'

Two fire engines, sirens wailing, blue lights flashing, brake to a halt just as I get outside. I hobble across the road through the crowd of rubberneckers and crouch trembling in the florist's doorway.

'Let me through, I'm the keyholder.' It's Mr Crowther, done up in a dinner jacket and bow tie. He stares at the smoke and flames pouring out of the shattered window. 'Oh, dear God, no.' He holds his head, sobbing. His shoulders are shaking. I can't bear to look.

A wailing ambulance arrives, followed by another, then another. Paramedics leap out, leg it down the side alley. I huddle into a miserable foetal ball.

It starts to rain. Pitter-patter at first, then splats, then stair-rods, bouncing off the pavement and gurgling down the gulleys. It's what I deserve – to get drenched, to drown in God's tears, to die of hypothermia right here, in the gutter, where I belong.

## 33

## Not Drowning but Raving

My brain feels numb and hollow, like a lobotomised zombie's. Stars float in and out of my consciousness. Stars In Their Eyes. Stars of stage, screen and funeral parlours. Stick-on fluorescent stars. As the layers of numbness peel away it slowly dawns that I'm lying on my bed, gazing at the stick-on stars on the ceiling. Not remembering how I got here. Shivering in clingy wet leather. Not drowning but raving.

The first memory returns coated in whispery skin, delicate and protective, like tissue paper. Its colour is white. A wedding gown, glittering with rhinestones and bugle beads. A gossamer veil, light as a butterfly's wings. My mouth curves in a smile.

The next memory is tinged with brown, a rose petal displaying the first hint of decay. *You may kiss the bride.* Ash's beautiful lips, tawny lined, tinted in Warm Apricot, but cold and tasting of bitter chemicals. His lashes, thick and glossy, fringing the glued eyes that will never open. The smile is hesitant now, confused.

Darker memories struggle towards the surface. Reuben. His ravaged Goth make-up, purple-streaked face, glistening unfocused eyes. Coralie's smudged mascara transformed into the tears of a clown. The smile freezes.

A dense haze, grey and dark and ominous, unfolds to reveal Dean, his eyes blazing in panic as he struggles to rescue me from the inferno. And, sweet Jesus, a black-faced bare-breasted Gemma, flailing at the scorched figure of Mickey in a burning Megadeth vest. The mouth skin stretches back from my teeth in a grotesque rictus smile.

Then, *Whoosh!* A blinding flash of light illuminates the lifeless figure of Ash, his coffin ablaze, his wedding finery consumed by a raging fireball.

And all that's left is blackness, the deep scorching blackness of Hades. I want to die, to surrender myself to the unspeakable horrors of the dark netherworld. May my ears explode with the shrieks of unquiet souls, may I suffocate in the sulphurous stench. Let me surrender my twisted brain to Satan, let him pulp it, fry it, smear it in foul black slurry and toss it to the ravening hounds of hell. Food for the demons.

I'm a hundred per cent pure. Pure evil. I place a jinx – a hex – on other people. Everyone who enters my dark aura ends up suffering, drawn in like iron filings to a magnet, tainted, touched with my blackness, my madness, my *badness*. Cursed by my voodoo. Damned by my hexagony.

My negative vibes have destroyed the Madolescents, as if they didn't have enough problems to be getting on with. My good mate Dean, solid, reliable Dean, is in deep, deep shite because he tried to do me a favour. Look at Mum; her life became one big fat disaster the day she met Filthy Luker, although she may not realise it yet. How unlucky is that? And Nana Vincent's fatal stroke – I bet that was down to me too.

It's all my fault. Rowena: Warrior Princess of Darkness heaps doom on those who befriend her, yea even unto death. The rottenness inside me seeps out through my pores, spreading deadly contamination. Weed-killer runs through my veins. The Lord's Prayer is written backwards on my black heart, *I ♥ LUCIFER* tattooed on my soul. Deep in the fiery bowels of hell, that's where I belong – there, at Satan's right hand.

My jaw locks as a silent scream rips through me. *Ash!* Ash, my one and only lover. Asphyxiated by his own hand (and stockings), transformed into a human torch, and I'm entirely to blame. Me. Rowena M. Vincent. M as in Mass Murderer. Hot tears sting my eyes and roll down my face. I taste their saltiness.

Suddenly, as real as anything, I feel Ash's soft lips brush against mine. The tip of his tongue darts playfully around my mouth, teasing me, turning me majorly on. Then the whole beautiful length of it enters me, exploring, licking, lapping, sucking, thrilling me with slurping, smacking sounds, the taste of his saliva driving me wild as it mingles with mine. And I'm so gone, it's almost like he's inside me down there, where I'm slippery with wetness. Now I can feel his warm breath, his tongue playing inside my ear, his teeth nibbling my lobe.

'It wasn't your fault,' he whispers. 'It was too late. I'd made up my mind.' As my body gives itself up to him, he murmurs, 'I love you, Rowena.'

'I love you, Ash,' I say dreamily. His goldy finger strokes my cheek, then I watch in wonder as a silvery haze materialises above me. It hovers for a while, then floats to the ceiling, obscuring the stick-on stars. Or maybe it's just my eyes misting up. Whatever, I sense Ash drifting away from me, but strangely, I don't feel sad. Why would I? He came back to me, just like he did through the TV, with a message.

He came to tell me it wasn't my fault.

A foggy calm settles over me like a swansdown duvet. So much weird shit has happened recently, it's starting to seem normal. I must be crackling with psychic energy, wide open to visitations from the world beyond.

First Nana Vincent and baby Nathan, and then Ash.

And now Dad's back in the picture, or at least Dad's picture has turned up, just when I need him most. It has to be a sign. It must be *meant*.

Suddenly I'm wide awake, buzzing with possibilities. The sound of intoxicated jollity drifts upstairs, someone belting out a karaoke disaster. Omigawd, I'd forgotten about the engagement party! Mum and Filthy Luker, my vile stepfather-to-be. Never a father to me. Where would I rather be? Nearer my dad to thee.

Something clicks in my brain.

*If you ever go across the sea to Oireland . . .*

Toasting Joyce. Bloomsday, Cork Street, Dublin.

Stripping off the damp Warrior Princess outfit, I scramble into an Elastica T-shirt and a pair of Toastie socks. Travel swift, travel light, that's the trick. Rucksack, change of kit, bank passbook, notepad with funeral music (in event of plane crash), make-up, three pairs of knickies. And, v. important, the photograph of Dad. There, sorted.

I daren't risk falling asleep so I jack up my Discman and slap in a stray CD off the floor. It turns out to be Catatonia – *Equally Cursed and Blessed*. Another sign! See, it's telling me I'm not *all* bad! Cranking up the decibels full blast, I play it over and over for inspiration. When I unplug the earphones after the zillionth play, all's silent in the house apart from Filthy's piggy snoring. As the digital clock flicks to 06.57 I tune to the local saddo station, Radio My Arse, for the news headlines.

*Five people were rescued from a fire at a building in Newcastle last night. Twenty firefighters tackled the blaze at the premises of Crowther and Son, Funeral Directors, and three paramedic units were called to the scene. Four people were taken to the General Hospital suffering from the effects of smoke inhalation but were later discharged. A fifth person has been detained in hospital suffering from burns. His condition is said to be comfortable. An investigation is underway into the cause of the fire.*

Alive! The Madolescents are alive! All of them! Thank you, thank you, Big G. I owe you for this.

I slip into my rockin' black denim ensemble, purple T-shirt and biker boots. Heaving my rucksack on to my shoulders, I sneak down the stairs, remembering to avoid the creaky step, although the Last Trump couldn't rouse Pukey-Luker from his booze-induced coma.

I take a last skeg round my so-called home. As a parting shot, I dip Filthy's pockets. Two hundred quid and a mobile phone.

Result! I scrawl a few words on a Post-it note and slap it on the worktop.

> *Mum,*
> *Gone 2 toast Joyce.*
>   *Later,*
>   *R*
>   *xxx*

Just as I'm legging it up the path, a dark shape darts in front of me. It's Bundy, looking like the ship's mog off the *Titanic*, his fur sopping wet from the downpour, a rodent hanging limply from his jaws. Bundy, my Trusty Sidekick, my Familiar Spirit, my Guardian Angel. A lucky black cat, crossing my path! It's a sign!

I hitch up my rucksack and click the gate behind me. What's to lose?